The PENDRAGON™ fiction line presents the best of modern Arthurian literature, from reprints of long-unavailable classics of the early twentieth century to new works by today's most exciting and inventive fantasists. The titles in the series are selected for their value to both the casual reader and the devoted scholar of the rich, varied story cycle known as the Matter of Britain.

PENDRAGON™ Fiction

Legends
of the
Pendragon

Edited by JAMES LOWDER

GREEN KNIGHT PUBLISHING

Legends of the Pendragon is published by Green Knight Publishing.

Please address questions and comments concerning this book, as well as requests for notices of new publications, by mail to Green Knight Publishing, 900 Murmansk Street, Suite 5, Oakland, CA 94607.

Green Knight Publishing
Publisher: Peter Corless
Executive Editor: James Lowder
Consulting Editor: Raymond H. Thompson

Visit our web page at: http://www.greenknight.com

FIRST PAPERBACK EDITION

10 9 8 7 6 5 4 3 2 1

Green Knight publication GK6211, June 2002.

ISBN 1-928999-19-0

Printed in the United States.

ACKNOWLEDGMENTS

All works are original to this anthology, and are printed by permission of the authors.

"Introduction," by James Lowder. © 2002 by James Lowder.

"Keystones," by Shannon Appelcline. © 2002 by Shannon Appelcline.

"Hel's Daughter," by Nancy Varian Berberick. © 2002 by Nancy Varian Berberick.

"Dragons of the Mind," by Peter T. Garratt. © 2002 by Peter T. Garratt.

"Nimue's Song," by Marcie Lynn Tentchoff. © 2002 by Marcie Lynn Tentchoff.

"Forethought," by Alex Kolker. © 2002 by Alex Kolker.

"The Time in Between," by Beth Anderson. © 2002 by Beth Anderson.

"Tea and Company," by Valerie Frankel. © 2002 by Valerie Frankel.

"A Spear in the Night," by Keith Taylor. © 2002 by Keith Taylor.

"The Likeness of Her Lord," by C. A. Gardner. © 2002 by C. A. Gardner.

"The Lesson of the Other," by Steen Jensen. © 2002 by Steen Jensen.

"Squire Kay in Love," by Phyllis Ann Karr. © 2002 by Phyllis Ann Karr.

"The King Who Is to Come," by Cherith Baldry. © 2002 by Cherith Baldry.

"Six for the Sword," by Aaron Rosenberg. © 2002 by Aaron Rosenberg.

"Jester's Luck," by Gene Stewart. © 2002 by Gene Stewart.

"A Time of Blood and Steel," by John H. Steele. © 2002 by John H. Steele.

"The Enthronement of Arthur," by Andrew H. W. Smith. © 2002 by Andrew H. W. Smith.

"The Last of the Giants of Albion," by Darrell Schweitzer. © 2002 by Darrell Schweitzer.

"The Scream of the Gulls," by Joe Murphy. © 2002 by Joe Murphy.

"Follow," by Clarissa Aykroyd. © 2002 by Clarissa Aykroyd.

"The Questing Girl," by Cory Rushton. © 2002 by Cory Rushton.

TABLE OF CONTENTS

Introduction

In my beginning is my end.
—T. S. Eliot, "East Coker"

Stories about Camelot's founding often reveal something vital about its collapse. They lay the groundwork for the dream's demise even as they chronicle its birth. We cannot help but see a foreshadowing of Mordred's lust-tainted begetting in Arthur's own, the sins that doom the Round Table in the reckless actions of Vortigern and Uther. The familiar nature of the Matter of Britain's narrative provides readers—and writers—with this privileged vantage, from which they view the epic of Camelot's rise and fall as a whole. Individual stories can surprise and entertain, offer up wondrous feats and valorous deeds aplenty. However, our knowledge of the kingdom's fate lurks in our consciousness, reminding us that peace in Arthur's Britain is fleeting, victory often illusory.

Within the Arthurian cycle itself, this unusual relationship between the story and the audience is embodied in the character of Merlin. The backward-living mage knows what will come to pass and yet remains powerless to avert the tragedy. Why, then, should he bother to participate at all, if the outcome is both inevitable and grim? Why should the reader seek out new tales about Camelot when their endings are pre-ordained?

Of course the conclusion is only a small part of any story. Even when considering plot elements alone, isolated from such literary aspects as theme and such aesthetic qualities as style, the tale's ending is no more important than the path the characters take to reach that terminus or how they react to the destinies they meet there.

Little surprise, then, that Merlin, in many Arthurian tales, uses his special knowledge to guide the Matter's main actors and aid them in the journey to meet their fate. In that, the mage is an apt stand-in for the writer intent on creating original Arthurian fiction. Given the Matter's iron framework, which must be acknowledged for an Arthurian tale to ring true with readers, it is the author's daunting task to make the trek to the predestined catastrophe enlightening, or startling, or at least diverting.

To achieve this end, some modern writers offer a glimpse of unchronicled events, which allow the reader to perceive established characters and incidents in a new way—Merlin's futile struggle to confound Fate in Beth Anderson's "The Time in Between," or Tor's role in thwarting an attempted assassination of the infant Arthur in Keith Taylor's "A Spear in the Night." Other authors create entirely new characters—Gene Stewart's Cafex the jester or Aaron Rosenberg's rivals for the Sword in the Stone; by their very newness, these characters present original perspectives on familiar places and events. Still others craft detailed renderings of characters glossed over in other works, an approach exemplified in the present collection by the portrait of Vortigern painted by Peter T. Garratt, the compelling version of Rowenna created by Nancy Varian Berberick, and the contrasting takes on Pellinore and his pursuit of the Questing Beast found in anthology's final two tales.

In the end, though, such creative recastings still must take the reader to the same grim finale. Camelot cannot succeed as the perfect kingdom, the City of God on earth, because it is created by humankind. The struggle to build that ideal realm must prove as futile as Pellinore's search for the Questing Beast. And while we honor Arthur's efforts to push back the wilderness and celebrate his struggles to make a realm and rule through these new stories, we must admit that those efforts are doomed to fail.

Camelot cannot be.

It is in our acceptance of Camelot's failure that we can finally come to understand how the dream's demise, while unavoidable, is incomplete. For, just as the kingdom's destruction is to be found in its creation, its true beginning can be found in its conclusion. With each ending, the ever-renewed story cycle begins again.

Camelot cannot be, and yet it continues to be.

The comfort to be found in that revelation is another reason why readers—and writers—continue to come to the

Matter, a tradition whose tales can be both familiar and endlessly surprising, often at the same time. And if even the most seemingly carefree Arthurian story is tinged with sadness by our knowledge of the strife to come, that's the price we pay for our special vantage, gained through our interaction with the Matter in all its varied forms. We know that tragedy is the outcome of even the brightest beginning, but we also understand that this is merely the prelude to the triumph of Arthur's dream—its perpetuation as the story cycle in which this volume proudly takes a small part.

The tales you will encounter here tell of Camelot's founding, the events that set the stage for the realm's creation, the characters who inspire the dream and those who seek its destruction. They are organized in a roughly chronological order, beginning with the Enchantment of Britain and the reign of Vortigern, and ending with Arthur's earliest days as king, before he was joined at Camelot by his Round Table knights or his queen. The time frame encompassed within some of the stories, particularly those in the book's final third, foil any attempt at a strictly chronological ordering (even if we were to accept one timeline of events as inviolate). In cases where works are best juxtaposed because of theme or subject matter, such aesthetic possibilities trump the more rigid ordering by date. It is intended for the stories to be read in the order presented.

—James Lowder
March 2002

James Lowder has worked extensively in fantasy and horror publishing on both sides of the editorial blotter. He's authored several bestselling fantasy and dark fantasy novels, including *Prince of Lies*, *Knight of the Black Rose*, and *The Ring of Winter*; short fiction for such diverse anthologies as *Historical Hauntings*, *Truth Until Paradox*, and *Realms of Mystery*; and a large number of film and book reviews, feature articles, roleplaying game adventures, and even the occasional comic book script. His credits as anthologist include *Realms of Valor*, *The Doom of Camelot*, and *The Book of All Flesh*. He also serves as executive editor for Green Knight Publishing's fiction line.

KEYSTONES
Shannon Appelcline

Merlin stands among the shadows of stones not yet born. The shadows tower above him, reaching to twice his height, more. They surround him in circles and semicircles like broken ripples in a pond. Merlin crouches down at the exact center of the circles, feels the hard earth and damp grass under him. And he waits.

In future days they will call this place Merlin's Observatory or The Monument or Giant's Dance. Or Stonehenge. Today it has no name, for the stones are only shadows, and only Merlin can see them.

The shadows begin to murmur, as Merlin knew they would. Their whispered demands echo across Salisbury Plain.

Give us substance, the shadows say. *Give us life.*

Merlin shivers at their requests and remembers two other days still to come when their demands will be louder, more insistent. He remembers a Samhain eve when the spirits will whip through his hair like the wind, and he remembers that last day, at the very end. He tries to ignore the shadows' words, but cannot ignore what they say next. He can never ignore these words, the words that put him on his path.

We will bring back the legends, the shadows say. *We will bring back the heroes.*

Merlin sighs, shaking his head. His chin is still beardless. He is still tall and wiry, full of youth. But his time has come.

"Soon," he says.

The shadows quiet.

Merlin stands, and he begins to walk northeast, leaving the circle of shadows by an avenue that is not yet built.

He walks toward Vortigern, toward Ambrosius, toward Uther. Toward the future.

When Merlin strokes his chin and feels the first prickly black whisker, he knows that the time has come when the gray men will arrive. He remembers that he will soon meet the first of his four kings: Vortigern.

When Merlin thinks of Vortigern at the end he will remember little. Vortigern is a king, but not one of the Dynasty. He slew Uther's brother Constans and will be slain by Uther's brother Ambrosius. Today he will take his one important action. He will move Merlin along the path.

Merlin straightens his plain brown shirt and readies his rucksack—though he knows these gestures will be for nothing. Then he waits for the soldiers.

There are two of them, dressed in ragged leather. Roman *spathas* hang at their sides, the swords' scabbards as worn and scuffed as the Empire. The men stand at the entrance to Merlin's hut, framed by the dark wood of the doorway. They are silhouetted against a background of trees whose leaves have been dipped into the sun and come out scarlet red, vibrant orange, and livid yellow. Covered by grit and slime from the stone Roman roads, wearing worn leather, bearing pitted scabbards, the soldiers look gray against the vivid landscape.

"Myrddin Gwyllt," the first soldier says, the name alien to his tongue. "We have been sent—"

But Merlin has grown impatient. He has played this scene out too many times. He interrupts the broken Welsh of Vortigern's beast.

"You have been sent by King Vortigern," Merlin says. "The slayer of Constans. The Usurper. You have been sent to seek the fatherless son, to cement the stones of a round tower with his blood."

Merlin spreads his hands out and says, "I am, of course, not he."

It changes nothing; it never does. They descend upon him with their fists and feet and knees and elbows, and Merlin is battered and bloodied and broken till he falls to the ground, unconscious and unaware.

His rucksack lies nearby, ignored.

⚜

As Merlin's mind drifts through darkness, as his wounded body is carried to King Vortigern, he remembers a time still to come. He remembers a time when he reveals to the next king, Ambrosius, the secret of the fatherless son.

"I was born of stone," he will say to Uther's brother. "Belched up from the Underworld."

But he will not speak of the other stone, at the end.

"My life is spread out before me like your map," he will say, and he will point to the map that Ambrosius has been examining. He will point at the map depicting the east coast of Ireland and a mountain in its interior, a map that depicts Merlin's future just as well as the one in his own mind's eye. He will point at the map and at Mount Killare.

"I remember this expedition," Merlin will say. "Give me Uther and his men, and it will succeed."

And Ambrosius will.

When Merlin awakes he has been brought to a different mountain—Mount Snowden—to meet Vortigern. Merlin knows that his life is in danger, that the king intends to slay him in order to baptize the keystones of an impregnable tower at Snowden, but he shows no fear. Merlin knows he will perform only three true acts of magic in his life, and that he will waste none upon the usurper Vortigern.

Vortigern is small, and this always surprises Merlin the first time he sees the man. His dirty brown hair is graying. He huddles forward in his throne as if he were shouldering a great burden, and perhaps he is. He bears the burden of guilt from two kings betrayed; he bears the burden of hatred from two brothers bereaved; and he bears the burden of fear from his own too-human heart.

Though bruised and battered, Merlin stands strong before Vortigern, his own heart unflinching stone. Even if Merlin did not remember how this conversation would end—how Vortigern's life would end—he would look at this bent, broken king and know that he had already won.

"You do not need to hide in an impregnable tower," Merlin says, still full of youthful optimism. "You could be a hero. A ruler whose name will be remembered for ten thousand years. A legend."

Because he remembers what is to come, Merlin knows that Vortigern will not be a hero. He knows that if the king is remembered at all, it will be as a traitor. But still, Merlin does not try to change his words, does not try to change the unending circle of his life. It is too early in Merlin's life for doubts.

Vortigern simply shakes his head, looks about the tiny, cramped chamber that he calls his throne room. On the east wall—opposite a view of the barren mountainside—is a banner that is old and threadbare. It depicts a golden eagle, the symbol of the Roman legions, but the eagle has lost its luster over the years. It is colored tired brown now, as if it had been pitched to the dirt and forgotten.

Vortigern's eyes linger on the eagle for long minutes before he replies. "The time of heroes is gone," he says. He speaks slowly, pausing often, as if conversation were a trial. "There are no more legends in Britain."

Merlin realizes that Vortigern speaks the truth. He knows that the Romans have scoured the landscape and bound it with their stone roads. They have sacrificed the old gods and eaten whole the old cultures, leaving behind something that is cold and gray.

"The legends *are* gone," Merlin says, remembering the promise of the shadows.

Vortigern only nods, and Merlin sees that the king's eyes are as barren as the mountain.

"If you must build your tower," Merlin says, "know that your prophets are false." It is the truth, too, fair exchange for what Vortigern has given. Merlin knows that there are no actual prophets but he, and perhaps one other. Of all the people Merlin has known and will know, only he is unsurprised by the future.

"Their tales of a fatherless son are meaningless," Merlin continues. "No sacrifice is needed to complete your circle of stone. Your tower collapses because you build atop an underground lake." This is the second truth that Merlin offers Vortigern. He has already seen the lake, remembers that Vortigern will unearth it in the days to come.

In the days to come, when Vortigern tests Merlin's first two prophecies, their truth will be revealed. With the aid of Merlin, the king's True Prophet, Vortigern's round tower will rise up to the sky, unbending.

"No man will ever break these walls," Merlin will say, years later, and this will be the third and final truth that he offers to the doomed king. He will not tell Vortigern the other truth, that the king will burn to death in his tower, sent up to the skies on a pyre lit by Ambrosius Aurelius, brother of the betrayed King Constans, brother of Uther.

"All things must have at least two purposes," Merlin tells King Ambrosius on the day that they plot the expedition to Mount Killare.

He will tell Arthur the same thing, nearly thirty years later. He wonders if his advice will be remembered and, not for the last time, curses the fact that he cannot see beyond that last day.

"One purpose is enough for me," Ambrosius says, chuckling. "Bring back your Irish circle of stones. It'll make a fine monument, a worthy memorial to those slain by Vortigern and his Saxons. I don't care about the rest."

Merlin simply nods. Ambrosius is a good king, not craven like Vortigern, not haughty like Uther, and not stubborn like Arthur. But he has no imagination. With his carefully analyzed battles and calculated decisions, Ambrosius' reign will in its own way be as sterile as Vortigern's.

He is a king but not a hero.

"It will be a fine monument then," Merlin says, rubbing his full, black beard. "No more."

But Merlin knows there *is* a second purpose. He sees the reason in Ambrosius' demeanor and remembers it in the months to come as he trudges alongside Uther's army, down to the sea. He remembers his second purpose as his worn leather boots come down on the hard Roman roads, as he looks out over a Britain growing cold and gray.

Uther angrily agrees when Merlin insists upon stopping at Salisbury Plain. "Damned empty place," Uther snarls at one of his warriors.

Merlin hears the curse, ignores it, and strides toward the looming shadows.

"I remember your promise," he says. "We must bring back the heroes. We need the legends."

Atop Mount Killare the corpses of the dead are scattered around like so much debris. Irish and British bodies mingle together like old friends, united in death. At the center of the field the stones of Giant's Dance stand tall, towering above Uther's army, aloof.

King Gilloman of the Irish has fled. The day is won.

Merlin leans toward Uther and says, "The story is not in the battle, but what comes after."

Uther snorts, then laughs at Merlin. Merlin knows the war leader does not understand.

This is the last chance for things to end differently, before the journey back to Britain and the loss of a single stone. It is the last chance, and Merlin lets it slip by. He holds on to Nimue's future words, which will be spoken on that last day, and tries to forget what will come in between, in the land of Pellam, the Fisher King.

Uther's warriors stare up at Giant's Dance, at the circles and semicircles enclosing each other, at the monument they have fought for and won. They are awed, Merlin knows, though they cannot see what he sees.

Merlin looks into the circle and sees a green and verdant plain where glass towers rise up to the sky. He sees a prince with a silver arm battling against inhuman hordes. He sees bands of warriors, iron swords in hand, marching across the nine waves.

He sees a place of legend.

While Uther waits and fumes, Merlin begins to pace around the stones, to very carefully sketch them upon his vellum, though he remembers the effort will be wasted. He does not step inside, not in this place.

Inside the circle, flowers never seen upon the mundane isle bloom, releasing fragrances as intoxicating as the finest wine.

Merlin sketches the outer circle last, appreciates its perfection. The strong menhirs jut up from the Irish soil, forming an outline, a map. Atop those stones rest the flat lintels, joined together into an unbroken circle, like Merlin's life. Each lintel joins two menhirs; atop each menhir two lintels meet. It is perfect, and never will be again—except, perhaps, after that last day, in a time Merlin will never see.

Finally he signals to Uther, tells him to begin his assault upon the Giant's Dance. The monument will not move, Merlin knows, for the stones are held together by forces stronger than the muscles of Uther's warriors, stronger even than the war leader's will. But Merlin knows that Uther must be given his opportunity.

In the end Merlin will step forward and enact his first magic. He will speak to the stones and they will collapse to the ground; only then will Uther's men haul them atop their giant sledges to their boats.

Only Merlin will be able to bring down the stones, for he is Merlin the Prophet, born of the stone, returned to the stone. They are his brethren.

Merlin rarely dreams and when he does his dreams are only memories of the future or the past. Merlin dreams on the ship back to Britain, and this will be a dream that he always remembers.

The dream itself is of little consequence. He dreams of a future time when he will be content for a short while. He dreams of his house in Wales, where he will rest when Ambrosius is king. He dreams of a kingdom grown newly vibrant, where the people have hope, where they speak of the mighty monument at Salisbury and what it might fore-tell of the future.

He dreams of a place that he might call home.

But even in his dream Merlin knows that his content-ment will be short lived. He knows that ultimately his home will prove false, that he will only ever know two true homes: Stonehenge and Mount Killare, tomb and womb.

Merlin remembers his dream born upon the Irish Sea not because of the content, but because of what happens afterward. Merlin will always assume that the missing menhir somehow slipped overboard while he lay dreaming, while Uther's flagship fought the waves during a storm on the first night out of Ireland.

Much later, when he is writing twin inscriptions upon the twin graves of twin knights, when he is looking out over the wasted kingdom of the Fisher King, Merlin will trace everything that went wrong to this day when he dreamed.

But in the end, because of what Nimue will say on that final day, he will not be sure whether his dreaming was for good or for ill.

The shadows still lie on Salisbury Plain. They are quiet now, silent and somber. They are waiting. For substance. For life.

Merlin watches as Uther's men reconstruct the circle on the plain. They could not break the circle at Killare, but here they cannot help but rebuild it.

Merlin's drawing is unnecessary. The warriors need no guidance as they strain to heft the massive stones into place. They work as if entranced, rebuilding the old circles without error. The stones fill the shadows completely, and one by one the shadows disappear.

Merlin knows he should feel elation, but he feels none. His heart is rocky and hard.

When Uther begins to walk toward Merlin, his face a mask of rage, Merlin feigns concern. He already knows the problem, though. He has always known the problem.

A menhir—one of the robust support stones—is somehow missing. The two lintels that would meet atop it lie unused. In Ireland, the circle was complete, but here, he knows, it is broken.

As Uther approaches, anger sparking in his eyes, Merlin listens to the voices of the last three shadows. They whisper of their disappointment and regret. They have not grown loud yet, and so when Uther approaches Merlin, when he bellows out his news, the voices of the shadows are lost.

"There's a stone gone—" Uther begins, his voice raised, but Merlin cuts him off. He is impatient once more.

This is the second-worst day, eclipsed only by the night still to come when the spirits will whip through Merlin's hair like the wind, and his sister will beg for her son's life.

Merlin turns from Uther and pushes his way through the British warriors. He steps up to the circle and sees the two sandstone lintels lying on the earth, abandoned. They remind Merlin of the Irish corpses scattered atop Mount Killare.

A hole gapes in the circle like a wound.

Merlin whispers to the rocks and reminds them of their brotherhood. Then he conducts his second act of magic.

The lintels rise up and balance on the shadow of a stone that is not there, and so the circle of stones is closed.

For a moment there is nothing, and then the legends of Britain swell and rise up, filling the circle. Merlin feels the chains of the Romans breaking, feels their roads cracking apart.

He looks into the circle and sees four swans that settle upon the river Avon for three hundred years. He sees a man who can kill a dozen Saxon warriors with but one glance of his single, misshapen eye. He sees a golden-haired youth who is not yet born, wielding a blinding sword.

Somewhere far away the Roman Empire gasps its last breath, but in Britain the time of legends is reborn.

Years of tranquility have passed by the time Ambrosius dies, poisoned by Saxons. It is Uther who suggests that his brother should be buried at Stonehenge. Merlin knows that this will be the first of Britain's new legends—the story of the king who was buried in the circle of stones. If he could feel pride in his accomplishments, he would. Instead he simply nods his head, agrees to Uther's request.

He travels alongside Uther's army for a second time, heading down to the sea. It reminds him of the third time, still to come, when he will accompany Uther to Cornwall, where the fourth king will be conceived. Merlin ponders his beard, long and unruly, streaked with gray, and realizes that he is now closer to the final stone than to the first.

They are still a day out from Stonehenge when Merlin is accosted by a farmer—a tired old man, worn down by the years. Merlin waves away Uther's men, not even looking to see their approach, and allows the man to have his say.

"You're the king's prophet," the farmer says, and Merlin simply nods. He is tired too. He knows what the man will say, but he does not interrupt. His impatience is gone with his youth.

"There's something out in the woods," the farmer says and tells his story of a legend come to life. It is merely one of many stories that Merlin will hear in the years to come: of courtly faeries dancing in the glades under the full moon; of creatures made up of the parts of many beasts, sewn together like patchwork dolls; of serpentine wyrms, more unfeeling than the coldest Roman landlord, ruling over wretched lands; of everything found in the most wonderful dreams and the most dreadful nightmares.

When Merlin arrives at Stonehenge, he looks at the circle, now complete. It has been years since Uther's men excavated a sandstone block from the nearby downs and dragged it back to the monument, to replace the menhir that was lost. The shadow has not been filled, however, and it has begun to scream.

Looking closely, Merlin sees that the replacement stone is cracked and crumbling. It strains outward, as if holding back a flood. When Merlin blinks he sees the flood rushing past the stone, washing over it as if it were not there.

He sees the imps, dark and dangerous, that creep past the stone. He sees the dwarves, hunchbacked and clubfooted, who hobble by. He sees the wyrms who slither around the flawed block; they are still small, the wyrms, but growing even as he watches.

He sees all matter of legend and myth escaping from his broken circle, infesting the countryside like a plague, and finally he realizes what he has done.

It is Samhain eve when Merlin next returns to Stonehenge. It is Samhain eve when spirits whip through his hair like the wind.

The infant that Merlin holds in his arms is small and serious, his face set in a frown. His thin hair is dark like a shadow. He is a boy child, a fatherless son, born of a virginal mother. Merlin understands the sacrifice he must make to complete his circle of stone.

"Don't do it," Gwynddedd shouts. She is a shadow, too, garbed in rough brown cloth, her own dark hair falling down her back. She is gaunt like a skeleton, and Merlin knows that the boy child is all she has in this life.

Gwynddedd names herself Merlin's sister, claims that she, too, is a prophet, that she sees the future in the stars. But Merlin has never known another true prophet—except perhaps one other, at the end.

The child should be mewling, but is as silent as the stones. It is the last shadow that shouts. *Life*, it says. *Give me life.* And the spirits of British heroes dance through the air like leaves.

The other stones rise up around them, circle around semicircle, and the man, the woman, and the child are dwarfed at the center.

Merlin holds up the dark, somber baby by his right arm and pulls his short sword from its scabbard. Gwynddedd is still screaming, but wordlessly now. The spirits play in her long hair as it jumps in the wind. Merlin knows that she can see no future that does not end in her child's death.

Merlin is unmoved. His heart is stone.

As Merlin positions his sword above the boy child's chest, he looks down into his face. The infant's eyes are unblinking, but the right side of his mouth quirks up into a smile, and Merlin sees his own face there. The fatherless son.

And so he conducts his third and last act of magic. He whispers to his rocky heart, and it begins to throb and beat, coming to life at last.

After that, there can be no sacrifice. Merlin drops the child into his would-be sister's arms and departs.

There are no words, only the rustling of the spirits, the soft sobbing of a woman, and the scream of a shadow.

Merlin dreams of the future that night. He remembers his whole life like a circle, from stone to stone, a circle that he relives forever, a circle that he never changes because of what comes in the end. He remembers what will come and he wonders—as he can only wonder in these days after his last act of magic—about what might have been.

Merlin will watch Uther assume the reins of kingship and lose them. He will watch the third king battle the Saxons, then die, and finally—at last—he will watch Uther's son rise up after him.

Arthur.

Merlin's beard will fade into white as the winter of his life approaches, as the final stone draws ever nearer. Nearly two decades will pass by him, like water around a river rock.

Merlin will see the Enchantment of Britain grow from that single flaw in his circle of stone, and, for a time, he will think that perhaps he has done well despite the error. He will see Arthur become a hero—a legend of his age.

In his newly human heart, Merlin will know the truth, however, or perhaps two truths: Pellam's and Nimue's.

The Dolorous Stroke, the bards will call it, when Balin destroys Pellam's land with one blow. They will sing the Tragedy of the Fisher King. It will be a marvelous story, too, an epic, the story of the guardian of the Grail, forever wounded, forever waiting for his savior, the perfect knight.

When Merlin buries the brothers Balan and Balin, when he writes their inscriptions upon their tombs, he will look over Pellam's land and see the burned and ruined fields and the diseased livestock, all cut down by that single blow. He will look upon what he has done and he will know that the time of legends has truly returned to Britain, and that the land may not survive it.

Nimue smiles at Merlin on that last day in the circle of stones. The stones tower over them, twice their height, and Merlin feels smaller than ever, with his spine curved like a snake, drawing him nearer to the earth. Only Nimue holds the stones back, keeps their ancient weight from collapsing down upon him. She is still young and vibrant, her hair of gold reflecting the sun, and she seems to fill the circle entirely. She is Merlin's apprentice, his companion, his friend.

"It is the only way," Nimue says, and Merlin knows that she is right.

The single shadow still screams, louder than ever.

"The sacrifice of the fatherless son," Merlin says. The words sigh out of his mouth like Vortigern's did long ago.

Merlin's heart beats fast. He is afraid.

Nimue takes his hand in hers, holds it as they stand at the center of the circle, and Merlin sees tears in her eyes.

"He will be fine," Nimue says. "I'll watch over him." She speaks of the golden-haired boy, Arthur, High King of Britain now, his battles of unification gone with the winter snow.

Merlin tightens his grip on Nimue's hand, as if it is his

only remaining connection to life, and perhaps it is. He wonders upon the vagaries of Fate that brought her—his Lady of the Lake—into his life. It was surely the Enchantment of Britain that brought her to him, that brought her to Arthur's wedding feast, riding upon a white horse, following sixty black hounds, a single white hound, and a single white hart. The Enchantment of Britain brought her into his life, and now she will help end it.

Merlin barely remembers the day when she revealed that she knew the secret of the fatherless son. All he can remember is her face, so serious, and the way that his heart leapt up into his throat. All he remembers is his thought that perhaps she, a child of water as he is a child of stone, might actually see the future as he does, might actually see past this day. Merlin squeezes Nimue's hand one last time and lets go.

When Merlin reaches the mismatched stone he feels the shadow's need. *Complete me*, it says. *Give me life.*

Past the stone all manner of creatures still stomp and fly and slither. A giant steps over the stone, holding his head under his arm. A knight in black armor rides past, his steed burning hoofprints into the earth. A single garter snake slithers by, looking back at Merlin one time before it disappears into the grass.

"Will you do it?" Nimue asks, and Merlin can feel the concern in her voice.

Then uncertainty clenches at Merlin's heart.

He turns to her and says, "Don't you know I will? Haven't you seen it?"

Nimue shakes her head, says, "Of course." She takes a step toward Merlin, but the old man motions her back.

"I could do it differently," Merlin says, "next time, after I return to the rock."

He pauses, lets his doubt pour out for the only time in his life. "Did I do things right, Nimue?" he asks. "How will it all end?"

He feels blind this day. He always does, for he can see no further, cannot see past the end.

Nimue approaches Merlin, ignoring his gestures this time. She takes his hand one last time and places it on her heart.

"All will be well in the end," she says. "I have seen it."

Merlin nods. He recognizes the hope that Nimue offers, lets his heart grasp hold of it. There is almost a smile on his face, the right half of his mouth quirking up, when he turns from Nimue and looks upon the final stone.

Then he steps into the shadow and is consumed, completing the circle at last.

The circle is complete now, the legends contained. Nimue knows that the Enchantment of Britain will fade, but that the stories will remain.

She sits for hours and watches the images that fill the monument, the images that only she can see. Her back is against the final stone, now strong and firm. She leans against it like an old friend, which it is.

Looking into the circle Nimue sees a golden-haired youth wielding a blinding sword as he charges into battle. She sees twin dragons, red and white, warring across a scorched land. She sees a young, dark-haired man, still beardless, standing among the shadows of stones not yet born.

She sees a place of legend.

HEL'S DAUGHTER

Nancy Varian Berberick

On the night she was to be wed, Rowenna Hengist-
daughter went straight-backed along the way to the hall of
Vortigern the Thin. They called it his castle, a stone-
wrought hall gaping with arches and bristling with towers.
She went upon a narrow road that wound through moonlight and darkness, round and round a high caer soaring
above the midnight sea. Moonlight glistening on the stone
walls changed them to the whiteness of ice, and out from
the walls yearned creatures of stone, wing-spread, stretching for the sky. Rowenna thought they fought to tear out
from the rock and fly.

Who had caught them there? Who had cursed them?

Wind moaned high around the towers, it groaned in the
throat of the way up. Sea mist kissed Rowenna's face, chill
on the small vee of exposed skin at her throat, where her
cloak did not close. Mist glistened on the hair of those
around her, close-cropped dark hair, thickly braided yellow hair. Ah, golden hair, her father's and that of his men,
but bleached white in the moonlight.

"Angels," said the young man beside her, the thin
king's son. Vortimer he was called, and he pointed to the
winged and the stone-caught.

Rowenna looked around to be sure her father was near,
and Horsa her uncle, and the men who were proud to
name themselves the maiden's wardens. The sight of them,
the tall men dressed in blue wool and cloaked in wolf-skin
heartened her.

The prince did not like her, or even the idea of her.

He remembers his mother, she thought. Then she looked
at him and had another, keener thought. No memory of his
mother lay on Vortimer. The truth was that he did not welcome the woman who came to be queen of this misty land.
Power would be shared, between king and queen. Where
would the son be then?

Outside the bedroom door, no doubt, waiting to see if a new son would come to take his place, the pride of an old man got on a young wife.

"Angels are guardians," said the prince. "You have not heard of them in your winter land."

Guardians. The word thrilled. Would they leap free of the stone should danger threaten Vortigern's high castle?

"Warriors of your god?"

From behind came a voice made thin by wind. Pride, though, and a kind of scorn for her ignorance still held. "An angel guards the gates of God's garden with a fiery sword. Another will blow the horn to signal the world's ending."

These angels sounded like fierce creatures, and Rowenna heard warning in the voice of this second Wealas. Perhaps, like his prince, he disliked his king's foreign marriage. Perhaps he feared her. He would not had he known the prophecy Rowenna brought with her, the promise whispered over her in her father's high hall by the *sacerd*, his own brother Horsa, whose eyes sometimes were like stone, sometimes tender as a child's.

She was the pure hope of peace. In every bone of her body, every chamber of her heart, she knew the truth of this. Rowenna had heard her uncle's prophecy beyond her own birth wails. She had understood them in her soul and, later, when she was old enough to have words, she remembered what *sacerd* Horsa had said. At times in her life, she spoke those words over to herself, and she said, "This is who I am."

The road wound and it turned. They marched on, the dark Wealas and her shining Saxon kin until, at last, it opened upon a broad space of stone and Rowenna looked up at the castle, the rising walls, the broad arches and soaring towers of Vortigern the Thin. At the great oaken doors, upon tall columns, angels strained to leap out from stone. *Angels.* She thought of the word, in her mind pronouncing it as though aloud.

One, it seemed, looked right at her from stony, pupilless eyes. Blind eyes. Another, hair flowing over her shoulders and rippling on her breast, raised her sword high and stretched her lips as though in battle-cry. That one looked right at Rowenna Hengist-daughter and stole away her breath, the very next beat of her heart.

That is not an angel, she thought, catching back her breath. *That is a valkyrie, weaponed warrior woman. There is a fierce fighter ready to soar over a battleground, a dutiful daughter ready to reap souls for Woden!*

Shivering as the cold, misty wind had not made her do, Rowenna entered the hall of the king who would soon become her husband. Hengist her father, Horsa her uncle, kept close behind.

Vortigern's hand lay like the corpse of a bird upon Rowenna's, bony, dry, and light. He leaned close to kiss her, and he smelled of sweat and thick layers of unwashed clothing. His lips touched her cheek; his breath stank of rotting teeth.

All around, the hall roared with the voices of men and women come to a feast. Saxons and Wealas, most drunk, some already leaning across the tables, fists on the planks, chin to chin in beer-soaked argument. Noses would be broken tonight, eyes blackened, but it was likely no one would die of a sword cut. A custom old among both folk prevailed—no man sat at table with anything more dangerous than his fist or the knife he used for eating.

Hounds ran in the rushes, chasing flung bones. In the rafters hawks shifted restlessly from foot to foot; a bold one swung low to make a foray into the realm of hungry dogs. Between the floor and the ceiling, earth and sky, stone angels stood, and these in the hall stood with their hands upraised, for they held up the roof of the place and between them the rafters ran dark. Upon the walls banners hung, thick tapestries whose colors might once have been bright but now lurked behind soot. Hengist, like a drunken man, let his head fall back to see one of these, a stitching of a red dragon curled round the base of a tall tower.

"In Hel's name, what's that?" he shouted, leaning past his daughter to the man who would become, in the law of two kingdoms, his son. He bellowed to be heard above the drunken hall, but he did only himself seem to be drunk.

Just as Hengist did, Vortigern flung his own head back. Laughing, he let his son Vortimer answer.

"That," said the prince, "is the dragon who is the standard of my family. He wards the tower, and that means the

kingdom, the people. That . . ." He paused, looking for
some word to describe the kinship the law would forge
between them. Who was Hengist to him? The father of his
own father's wife, a man younger than he. "That, *kinsman*,
is the peace of the kingdom, of the Cymru. So our family
has been for countless generations."

Cymru, they called themselves; *the People. Wealas*, the
Saxons named them; *the Foreigners*. But only among
themselves did the Saxons say that.

Hengist belched loudly and laughed about it, as
drunks do. Rowenna dropped her glance. She knew her
father wasn't drunk, and she knew things about the man
who would be her husband.

Vortigern's kingship had not been the peace of the
Wealas, not in all the long years of his reign. After the
death of the great king Constantine, Vortigern had raised
up the old king's brother, the witling Constans. He had
ruled from behind that throne until the witling's death and
had not bothered to hold it for the brothers of Constans,
the child Ambrosius and the infant Uther. Rather, he sent
assassins to kill the young princes. He succeeded only in
driving them from the kingdom.

From his stolen throne, Vortigern had ruled badly,
never engendering a moment's peace for his people.
Prosperity, not a frequent guest in the halls of the Wealas
since the death of Constantine, forgot about the crumbling
kingdom. While the true king and his brother hid in exile
across a far sea, savage tribes from the island's northern
reaches stormed the old king's battlements. Vortigern had
no good defense, for the younger sons of his barons ran
rough over the countryside, wild boys whose fathers could
not afford them a cot and herd, certainly not lands enough
to support themselves and a kinship. These would not fight
for Vortigern the Thin, these barons' sons who ran wild
and waited to pick his bones.

A plague of younger sons beset Vortigern's kingdom.
They came from all quarters, for across the East Sea sailed
long boats filled with lusty Saxons whose own fathers could
give them nothing but a dragon ship, a good sword, and a
commendation to the gods for their fortunes. These adven-
turers soon learned that the land of the Wealas had green
hills and forests filled with fat deer, meads for plowing and

women not so well protected by their men. They harried Vortigern's coasts with all fierce joy.

And now, after years of Vortigern's ruinous reign, the brothers of the witling Constans were well grown in their refuge across the far sea. The elder, Ambrosius, was true heir to the stolen throne, Uther his strong right arm. They now looked homeward with fierce and hungry eyes.

Rowenna looked at her father, only a little beneath lowered lashes. He was a canny one, that father of hers. All this about Vortigern he had learned before ever he set sail from Juteland, for report of the worthless king had come to him like crows calling. Upon dark waters, under bright moons, he had woven the weft of his own plans with the warp of Vortigern's weakness.

Hengist wanted a kingdom for himself, a good and fruitful land with allies at his back and enemies kept well beyond his borders. Long-headed, he and his brother had made a plan. They came to Vortigern with a host of strong young men as offering to this thin foreign king, and a golden daughter who had been named Peace-weaver even as the women cleaned her of the blood of her birth. With these he bargained, and these the old king wanted—the warriors and the maiden.

Now, in the hall of the thin king, Hengist jerked his chin at his brother. Horsa left the high table, long-legged and loping down the hall in search of a jug of beer. No one had come to refill the one at the table, and no one offered food to the revelers. Though there were women in the hall, none had come to present a guest-cup to the one who would be their queen or to her kin. Vortigern did not seem to notice the lack, but his son did. Sitting at the high table, close at his father's left hand, Vortimer did not seem ashamed of this poor hospitality. The look of him, the thin-lipped look, said plainly that he did not consider these Saxons worth a better board.

Far down the hall, the broad oaken door opened. A man shining in mail came to speak a word to the prince. He had the look of Vortimer and his father, the hawkish nose, the icy eye. He was Catigern, a brother of the prince through some web of his father's wives or women. Of wives, Vortigern had had two; this much Rowenna knew. Of women . . . well, he was an old man who had not always been old. She was her practical father's child; she did not look for love where she had come to embody a treaty. Her father had led his people here landless. After tonight, they would go about the work of earning a kingdom. She would make that possible: Rowenna Peace-weaver.

A thin current of air, cool and damp, followed Catigern like a pale dog. Rowenna lifted her head to hear what he said to Vortimer.

"Child," interrupted the old thin king, drunken and not seeming to care what was said to his son. He patted Rowenna's hand, then his fingers moved higher, to her elbow, to her shoulder. Along the way, they touched her through the bodice of her woolen gown. "This feast is best left to others."

His breath sour on her cheek, she pulled a little away. "I agree," she murmured. She looked around the hall, as though searching. "But where are your priests?"

She wore her golden hair in two braids thick as her forearm. Winding through she had plaited slender chains of beaten gold. He lifted one of these braids, picking at the gold with a long fingernail.

"Is it not," said the king, "a custom in your country for a man to receive a woman from her father and try her to see if she will make him a good fit?"

Rowenna lifted her head, ignoring the slander. Though secretly angry, she didn't look to her father for help, or to her uncle walking by with a frothing jug.

Horsa saw, though, and he heard. He leaned down, bright Horsa who had pronounced her fate at her birth. His lips so close to the thin king's ear, only Vortigern and Rowenna heard him repeat his niece's question. "Where are your priests, old man? It is time to talk to the gods."

He laid his own hand upon the wrist of the Wealas king, the palm horny with callus, the knuckles scarred. Only a little pressure caused Vortigern to loose Rowenna's hair, to let go the gold. Horsa laughed, the harsh bark startling a thieving hawk back to the rafters.

Past the old man who would be her husband, past her uncle, Rowenna saw Vortimer rise, his brother fade into the shadows.

"Father," said the prince, all proper respect in his voice and ice in his eyes. "Father, the bishop waits in the chapel."

Vortigern heaved himself forward, and lost his balance to all he'd drunk. Vortimer put his hands under his father's elbows and lifted him easily to his feet, held him still while he got his legs under him, and guided him from the table.

Horsa leaned closed to Rowenna, his beery breath warm on her cheek. "Now, come along, girl," he said, taking her hand. It seemed a simple gesture, an uncle's grace. Rowenna felt the pressure of his gripping fingers. Did he fear she'd refuse? Did Horsa think she would run from Vortigern the Thin?

"Uncle," she said, "you of all men know better than to doubt."

His long blue stare measured her, heart and bone. What he saw, he liked. "Go, then, Rowenna Hengist-daughter. Hel herself will defend."

Rowenna rose. She smoothed her berry-brown gown with long, careful strokes. Head high, she left the hall between her father and her uncle. Golden Saxons followed, hall-guests falling into ranks behind their lord. The Wealas left the boards one and two, but only the men among them. Wives and wenches, these stayed behind. This marriage was not a thing for women; it was the work of warriors.

Vortigern stumbled in the doorway, then gained his legs again. He went out from his hall supported on either arm by a son.

Rowenna felt them, as though they were breathing; she felt the angels brooding in the chapel, the stone hold built into the heart of Vortigern's castle for the god of the Wealas. She felt them, watchers and wardens above an altar where the small flames of candles and the pennons of torches flared in the drafts. They looked down from stone blind eyes, and they had not captured only the heights. They held the corners of the chapel, they lurked in the shadows between rising marble columns, arms of stone holding up the roof. When the Wealas had shuffled to their seats upon the hard wooden benches they'd give these angels not a glance. Neither Rowenna nor any of her father's warriors failed to mark them. Standing now before an elder she knew to be a *sacerd*, a priest of the Wealas,

Rowenna knew the place of each of those angels and she felt them as though they were foes lurking.

"Who gives the woman?"

The elder's quavering voice scraped the silence in the chapel. He stood in heavy robes lined with fur. In his hand he clutched a staff whose head curved. Rowenna thought of him as a *sacerd*, but she knew his own kind called him "bishop." She listened to how people spoke of him so she knew this wasn't his name. It was a title, supposedly one of respect—despite the fact that people said he was a shepherd of his god's followers.

Rowenna stood alone at the left of the raised altar, tall as her father, her hair spilling as far as to her knees, shining golden in the a heavy haze of smoke from torches and pungent incense. Vortigern the Thin stood at the right, and he rested his hand upon the shoulder of his son Vortimer. When the elder called his question, the king turned to look over his shoulder, reeled a little, and caught himself steady to face the bishop again.

Hengist's voice thundered from stone walls. "I give the woman!"

Shuffling of feet, the rattle of shivering, and a few secret coughs fell silent. Hengist came head-high, his hand upon the sword he would not lay off here. He'd been asked to, and he had braced and refused. "Perhaps in the hall of a foreign king," he'd muttered, narrow-eyed. "Not in the hold of a stranger-god."

No one had argued the matter and the warriors of Hengist and of Vortigern stood in the chapel matched sword for sword. Hengist went to stand between his daughter and the king; he put himself before the bishop and he said, "Hear me! I am Hengist Whitgils-son, and here is my daughter Rowenna. She has the blood of a goddess in her, and at her birth my own brother, who hears gods speak, said this: 'She is the pure hope of peace, prayer of the people!'"

The bishop sputtered, his place usurped. Hammering the foot of his staff against the stone floor, he cried, "Silence! You will not speak of demons before the altar of God!"

The murmuring of the Wealas grew stronger.

Again the bishop shouted, "Silence!"

Hengist waited for the silence as though he had himself demanded it. That had, he turned and spoke as a king to Vortigern. Rowenna's heart rose with pride, for her father spoke boldly to this graybeard ruler of the Wealas.

"Vortigern Vorteneu, here is my daughter. To you I will be both a father and an adviser. Put your sons and their armies into my hands. Let them fight at my direction, beside my own men. Despise not my counsels, and you shall have no reason to fear any man or any nation."

Hengist took his daughter's hand and he took Vortigern's. His glance never touched his daughter; it never left the old king.

"She is sprung from the loins of a goddess, Vortigern. And that goddess is Hel, who receives the most of all who die and quickens them again to life. She is greater than all gods before her, even mighty Woden, and she is greater than any god you might lift up. Remember it."

In the chapel no one breathed. It was as though Hel's name, she whom their shepherd cried a demon, had stolen the air from their lungs. But in the high shadows above the altar wind did breathe; it stirred the torches. Fire's voice sounded like wings rustling. Hengist put their hands together, Rowenna's atop Vortigern's, and he did not disguise scorn when he said to the bishop, "Shepherd, you may make whatever rites please you. It is done."

Hengist turned from the altar and the bishop and the foreign god whose followers were sheep. He left his daughter there, her hand upon that of her husband, but not before he growled his wedding-night advice in her ear: "Get a son from him, girl. Quickly!"

She followed his sudden glance and saw Vortimer slip along the back wall of the chapel to join his brother Catigern. Two dark heads moved together, in the air between them a bright spark as from clashing steel.

In the shadows, angels rustled, their wings sounding like fire. Rowenna looked up. She looked up, and she knew as she had not known before that she was far, far from home.

⚜

"He's old," said Horsa, his voice rough in the shadows. When Rowenna glanced over her shoulder at her uncle, he shrugged and winked. "Old and full of drink. Don't worry about it going on long tonight, girl."

Rowenna didn't worry about that. She knew she had no lover waiting for her, only duty, and that gets done in the long or the short. To this duty she had agreed on the day her father and uncle told her she'd be sailing west to become a queen. No one had sought the agreement; still, she had given it. She'd thought it was important and though her father had turned away in the middle of her agreeing, Horsa had stood and listened. After he'd heard, he said, "You do a good thing, Rowenna. You, your father, and I—we are a kindred without a home, let loose to find our fate. With this treaty, by your marriage, you will help us make a kingdom, child."

She had always understood it so. This is who she was.

Now, gruff in his kindness, unsteady himself in drink, Horsa was Rowenna's only escort to Vortigern's chamber, for no women of her husband's hall attended her and she had no women of her own. At the top of the stairs, Horsa paused to find a way. Head up, a warrior on uncertain ground, he squinted hard into yawning darkness. Far down the corridor a door stood ajar, a wedge of light gleaming beneath. He did not follow, now he led, and when they came to that wedge of orange light, he thrust the torch into a bracket outside the door. The flame wavered, plucked by thin breezes and pale drafts. His eyes went soft, his glance tender as he put his two hands upon her shoulders. He kissed her once, a fierce brand upon her forehead. Perhaps he had kissed her so on that distant night when he heard gods whisper her fate.

"Remember who you are," said Horsa, then turned and walked away.

Rowenna watched him, and she smelled again the salt sea as it had smelled on the carrying breeze adrift through the hall door on the day he'd stood to hear her agree to be wed to an old king in a faraway land. When the darkness swallowed him, she turned and put her hand to the door, her palm flat on the wood, and swung it inward on groaning hinges.

Two stood within, Vortigern and a near-grown girl whose red hair in that moment fell unbound, flew like fire around her face and shoulders. She had worn a brown scarf to bind up the fiery masses, that now hung from the old king's thin fingers as though he'd bent to pick it up, carelessly fallen. Dressed in the rough gear of a servant, in her hand she held a filled goblet. The girl startled when the door opened. Blood-red wine lapped over the golden rim and ran on her white hand.

"Lady," she said, breathless. She offered the goblet, jewels gleaming in the firelight. "I have prepared your cup. All health."

Rowenna took the wine. She sipped, and offered it to Vortigern, who said only, "Dismiss the girl."

"Go," said Rowenna, her word flatly spoken.

The girl made a small bow with her head. Rowenna closed the door behind her. When she turned back to the room she saw that her husband stood ready for her, and he greeted her with a sudden word quickly snapped.

The child of a goddess, Rowenna believed in prophecy. The child of her father, fierce warrior's daughter, she believed in the rightness of the way things always were and always must be. Sons are warriors, daughters are peace-weavers.

And so she untied her gown and let it fall into the rushes. She shivered in the drafty chamber, and Vortigern rubbed his hands together like a cold man yearning toward fire. He pointed to the bed, and she wanted to run for the warmth of the bear-skins, to slip quickly under the furs and hide from the cold fingers of wind sliding in under ill-fitting shutters, through poorly chinked stone walls. She did not. She was no fond lover and she was no haystack slut, eager for the bed.

She was Rowenna Hengist-daughter. She went to Vortigern's bed with her head high, disdaining to shiver in the cold or even under her husband's greedy glance.

She thought, *It cannot be a long thing, this night. He is an old man.*

It was a long thing, the night of her first bedding, for though he was drunken and though he was old, Vortigern was determined. Long and long, and her husband's hands did never seem to become warm, though he had them often on her, moving. When he was finished, he left her and she was glad. She lay in the breathing darkness, listening to the wind and watching the white fingers of the bony moon creep beneath the shutters. She heard his voice in the hall. She heard a woman's whisper, then her high, excited laughter.

It was a long thing, the cold moment of understanding that her husband had gone from their wedding bed to another woman. A long moment, and then out from her bed went the daughter of a warrior. She thrust on her gown, in her mind thoughts of the serving girl whose hair had been lately loosed. Her father's blood rising in her, Rowenna went into the hall where Horsa's torch yet burned. Outside the light, in shadows dark, something moved. Heart leaping, Rowenna startled as the serving girl came into the light.

Squealing in sudden surprise, the girl scurried, running in white under-gown, red hair following like fire. In that light, in those shadows. Rowenna thought the girl had the look of the king's kin. Some bastard of Vortigern's, of one of his sons unrecognized, perhaps unknown? Far along the corridor, a door closed. Again the shrill laughter, and an old man's eager growling.

Rowenna's stomach wrenched in sudden disgust. What den of wolves had she come into?

Below, in the castle hall, the mood of the feasters had turned to belligerence. Challenges and curses flew in two languages while hawks screamed in the rafters, sounding like ravens.

After five nights much like the first, Rowenna left her husband's bed. She found herself a room in a high tower, one whose windows faced north to the sea.

In the hall Vortigern's folk began to name her *sais putain*, the Saxon Whore, for they decided that she'd bedded their king a time or two to seal the treaty and then would have no more of him while her father was out collecting his pander's fee.

II

"Sail!" cried the watch on the wall, the Wealas below Rowenna's window. She heard him stop his pacing, his armor creaking, and she heard him walk again. They went in mail from shoulder to toe, these Wealas, in iron grieves

and shin guards and beaten metal breastplates. They
clanked, walking, and Rowenna had heard them for three
years of nights and three of days, there below her window.

"One ship only!" the watch bellowed to answer a question Rowenna hadn't heard. "Blue sail, white dragon!"

Horsa's sail!

Rowenna put aside her needle and rose to see. She
threw wide the shutters and leaned far out. Beyond the
walls below, there where the watch walked and fierce
angels yearned out from stone, on the distant water she
spotted the ship, the one square sail, and yes, it was blue.
Sea blue, as was Hengist's. Upon her father's sails were
painted high-headed white horses from a pattern Rowenna
had herself made. Upon the sails of Horsa's fleet, wide-
winged white dragons.

Rowenna knew who sailed that dragon ship, a tall warrior of Horsa's known among the Saxons as Gar Speaker,
for he carried news between his two lords during battles,
and each year he returned to Vortigern after the war season
to let the Wealas king know how well his wife's kinsmen
fought for him. This he did, at Hengist's command, and
swiftly. Before ever Vortigern's own sons sent word, Gar
came first with the news.

One ship sailing. Surely this was Gar Speaker coming
in.

Soft, Rowenna sighed, and she closed the shutters
tight. Gar came with news, and he would leave with news.
"Tell me, Gar," her father would say, "is my daughter with
child?"

This year, as all others, Gar would answer the same
way.

"No, she is not. Her husband is an old, thin man. He is
a stingy king."

And somewhere, upon a heath before his campfire,
sheltering in the lee of old broken buildings glorious in the
days before the famous king Constantine, Hengist would
scowl, and he would send missives to his daughter,
secretly carried, secretly read, urging her to do all in her
power to get a son from the old man.

He did not know, and Rowenna would never say, that
she would bear no child into this kindred, no son and never
a daughter to an old man who did not know his own get

from the kitchen sluts. She knew what care to take, and soon Vortigern condemned her as barren and he did not come to her high tower, for he said he did not see the point of that.

In other ways, too, Vortigern was not satisfied in his wife. His people muttered and grumbled that though the Saxons banished the Picts to the cold lands at the top of the island, though the younger sons of his barons had begun to fill up the armies of Vortimer and Catigern to do battle on Thin Vortigern's behalf, though news of banished princes came less often and from farther off, the Wealas did not like this brightness of Saxons among them.

"They wed our sisters and daughters."

"They worship demons!"

"Who can tell if the children they get on our women are Christian or pagan?"

These were priest-inspired complaints. Practical men muttered that Hengist and Horsa had come very close now to fulfilling their bargain. Good and fair lands of their own choosing were due them, perhaps payable even this year. It was said widely, among Saxons and Wealas alike, that the lands Hengist favored were those down in the south of Britain, hard on the East Sea. They wanted Ceint.

Through the cold corridors of Vortigern's castle the rumor ran that the king was thinking about putting aside his wife and with her, her kin.

The long ago words her uncle had whispered harshly outside the door of Vortigern's chamber on the first night of her marriage came back to Rowenna, haunting:

Remember who you are!

She had been Rowenna Peace-weaver then, that night. Who was she now? Whore for her father, wife to an old man who now contemplated breaking the treaty he had once desired and putting aside the wife he'd once sworn to keep as his queen?

Who was she? She did not know. Would Horsa the *sacerd* know now, even if he looked upon her with gods whispering? Would he know and tell her?

For sight of her uncle's ship, Rowenna opened the shutters again. The sea burned with light; the light dazzled her eyes. She saw no ship, hardly the sea or the sky. Breathless, in a sudden moment between one beat of her heart and the next, Rowenna saw an angel yearning from the stone wall opposite. An angel, her hair undone, flying back, her stone sword uplifted. Day and day, night and night, Rowenna had seen this one, but she had been three years walking among angels, warriors of a foreign god. She'd long forgotten what first she'd thought about this one, weaponed warrior-woman.

"Valkyrie," she whispered, speaking from the ancient blood in her, Hel's blood.

Chill crept up her spine with spider feet. Swiftly, with force to startle the watch on the wall, she slammed the shutters closed. Her sight still leapt with light; she closed her eyes. In dazzled darkness, yet she saw the valkyrie.

Gar Speaker strode the length of the hall. Straight and tall, his golden hair hung upon his neck, shining in the light of the hall-torches. Gleaming in a good mail shirt whose polished links ran red with the firelight, Gar entered the hall with his sword belted on, and this was a thing for remark.

"Woman," said Vortigern, leaning close to his wife, "what insult is this?"

Insult, or warning. Rowenna, who knew Gar a little and her father and uncle well, would not have wagered on insult. Perhaps, in that moment, Vortigern thought again and took the same meaning from the bold sword as she. His fingers closed round her wrist.

Head high, Gar Speaker went along the aisle between the broad plank tables. Though people turned on the benches to see him, though silence followed in his wake, wondering, he looked not right or left. All the while he walked, his eyes were upon the dais where the king and queen of this hall sat. He went and stood before them. Once only, he glanced at Vortigern the Thin. After, his eye fastened upon Rowenna Hengist-daughter and never left.

He inclined his head, for like his Saxon brethren, he had never acquired the Wealas habit of bending the knee, that homage demanded first by their god, soon by their kings.

"Rowenna Hengist-daughter," Gar said, his voice strong enough to be heard far back to the great oaken doors. "I have come from your father, and I have news."

Vortigern's grip tightened. He leaned forward, and his grizzled thin beard lay upon the table, soaking spilled wine. He quivered, and Rowenna thought that was eagerness playing him.

"Warrior," he said, "you will speak to me!"

Gar Speaker did not glance away or ever acknowledge the command.

"Rowenna Hengist-daughter," he said, "your father has sent me to tell you that he and your uncle have scoured the kingdom of all your husband's foes. For this your husband should be grateful."

He tied them all to her. With his words, Gar Speaker knotted the well-being of father, uncle, and husband to her. He tied, and then he cut the ties, as though with a sword.

"But, hear me, Rowenna!" Gar's voice boomed in the hall, startling hawks in the rafters, causing hounds in the rushes to growl or cringe. On the benches, no one moved or even whispered one to another. "Hear me, lady! Hengist and Horsa have kept the vows made at your marriage. The sons of Whitgils have made your husband's foemen their foes. They have soaked the earth with the blood of your husband's enemies. And when they paused to rest from their war-work, they found one more enemy close by!"

Vortigern's breath hissed through his teeth. Rowenna turned and saw his face drain of color, his skin tighten over his bones to show the shape of his skull behind. His eyes glittered. Secret, hidden in his beard so only she saw, a smile twitched.

Like thunder, Gar shouted: "Betrayer!" Like lightning's own sword, his arm thrust, finger pointed to the thin king. "Your sons are shadow-goers! Cowards! They fell upon my lords even as our warriors rested from their battles!"

Cold to her bones, Rowenna looked from Gar Speaker to her husband, and she saw that Vortigern had heard no news. All this was an old tale to him.

Sly, he said, "How fared my sons, Gar Speaker?"

Gar lifted his head, his smile like a sword's smile, thin and bright. Rowenna was a warrior's daughter; she had seen that smile on the lips of men about to die well.

"As well as you wish, King, at Thanet. As well as you wish by the River Darent. Not so well at Epsford, that place you call Set. There your bastard died, King. Horsa gutted him on his own sword." Gar's eyes darkened, and Rowenna heard the words before he spoke them. "There did our brave Horsa die as well, but he lived long enough to hear Catigern's death rattle."

He blazed, golden Gar Speaker!

"And then—! Then, his brother dead, himself outnumbered and betrayed, our Hengist takes two armies, his own and murdered Horsa's, away from the field of fighting. He fills up his ships with them and he delivers them safe to another harbor.

"This deed your father did, Rowenna Hengist-daughter," said Gar. "And this I tell you now: You are not safe. You live among liars and traitors. Lady, come away with me."

How would she have answered? What would she have said? Rowenna did not know, though later she often tried to guess. In that moment, she felt her husband's hand leave hers. She saw him lift it. Then the thin bony hand gestured.

Out from the shadows at the side of the hall, out from among the stone angels that held up the roof of this hall, an arrow flew, whistling high.

Rowenna screamed, "Traitor!"

She knew even as she cried out that the shaming of the traitor king was the last thing Gar Speaker heard, dying.

Remember who you are!

He walked in her high northern chamber at night, Horsa Whitgils-son. Rowenna saw him pacing in all his war-gear, as perhaps he might have done on the headland the night of his last battle. A *sacerd*, one who listens to gods, his eyes had been known to her as sometimes tender as a child's, sometimes hard. The eyes of the ghost were like that now, hard. When he turned, she saw his mail shirt rent by the blade that had killed him. Rent from behind! He walked with his bright hair, gold mixed with silver, flowing from beneath his helm, and she heard the blood from his death-wound dripping on the stone floor though, hearing, never did she see mark or stain.

Remember who you are!

She felt the fiery imprint of his kiss upon her forehead,

a kiss made on her wedding night. She thought, *That
wasn't the first time he kissed me like that.* She put her finger to her forehead, the smooth white skin, and she felt
that he had kissed her there before, a long time ago, after
he'd spoken her fate.

The pure hope of peace.

"How now, Uncle?" she asked, speaking to Horsa's
shade. She trembled, speaking, not with fear but with
anger, for when she did not see the ghost of Horsa in her
chamber, in her dreams she saw Gar Speaker murdered,
the smile on the lips of the man who had known as he
walked into her husband's hall that he was walking to his
death. "How peaceful now?"

Horsa's ghost did not speak to her question. It followed
her round the castle, stood right behind her chair upon the
high dais when she sat at feast with Vortigern the Thin.
The shade whispered to her that she was a hostage, for her
father had killed Vortigern's last son in a battle terrible
and bloody. None stood between Hengist and Vortigern
now but his wife—whom he kept ever near, with whom he
even slept again, the old man making long nights of it.

On those nights, the ghost stood beside the bed, bleeding on the stone floor, the blood leaving no mark.

Remember who you are!

Hostage, she was hostage. She, the child of northern
fathers, the daughter of a proud line born of a goddess
whose breasts shone white as the moon, whose loins were
black as good dark earth. She was Vortigern's hostage,
who had been his wife.

And Horsa's ghost paced, while Rowenna dreamed of
murdered Gar and thought of that bold distant father of
hers, that one who had lain with Hel. Sometimes, staring
into darkness, Rowenna would wonder what it had been to
lie with the goddess who took the dead to her shining
breast and suckled them to sleep; who woke them again
when she bore forth their souls into new bodies, the man
changed into the babe, changed into the man, always to
come back to die in her arms. He must have been a bold
one, that long ago father of hers.

Remember. . . .

That ancient ancestor's courage lived on in her own
soul. This Rowenna recognized one night when, knowing

that Hengist's fleet of dragonships had been seen sailing down from the dark seas round the Orkneys, Vortigern the Thin commanded a soothsayer to come into his hall and tell him what fate awaited him.

"Your towers will fall!" cried the truth-speaker, a beardless boy with the kind of eyes that look sometimes hard, sometimes tender as a babe's. This is how their eyes look who are all the time seeing what others cannot. But this Merlin did not keep what he saw secret. He did a magic before the king and his queen. He called dragons into the hall, a white and a red, and they grappled with each other, the two terrible beasts. Men and women screamed, some fled the hall, others prayed to their god and shouted for angels to deliver them.

Upon his walls, trapped in his stone, the angels of Vortigern's castle did not move.

"Woe unto the Red Dragon, for his extermination draweth nigh; and his caverns shall be occupied of the White Dragon !"

Vortigern groaned, and his men cried out. Rowenna sat still, and she calmed her husband to hear more.

Cried the soothsayer: "Two deaths await thee, nor is it clear which one thou mayst escape. On one side, the White Dragon, upon the other the brethren you drove forth from their kingdom—!"

Remember who you are, said the ghost at Rowenna's shoulder, Horsa the White Dragon.

"Uncle," she said, soft, "I remember."

She said so, and the boy Merlin looked up from the magic, his strange eyes bright, seeing the ghost walk away.

Hel's daughter smiled at the soothsayer, a *sacerd* who saw one like himself. Queen and boy, their glances met, not to clash, but to spark in recognition. She had seen a prophecy, and she had seen her place in it.

Wife of a traitor, traitor's hostage, and still, in a way, a weaver of peace, in the morning Rowenna saw her father's longboats put in at the shore. She saw them not from her window, but from the watch walk behind a high battlement, and she stood with angels on each side of her, stone warriors of a stranger-god with swords high and blind eyes. What the angels could not see, she did, and seeing, she smiled, while beside her the ghost of Horsa Whitgilsson sighed, content.

The prows of Hengist's ships shone newly painted, each dragon white in the grim light of the new day.

In Vortigern's hall the folk were greatly afraid and the king quailed, for he had no such number of warriors as now appeared upon his shore. He thought to take his hostage to the walls and threaten, but Rowenna laughed at that.

"How hard do you think your death will be, husband, if my father sees that? How long do you think you will be at dying? His brother is dead; your sons have paid for that. What more do you think he wants now than what was promised? Give him the lands in Ceint, and he will stand against Ambrosius and his strong brother. He will fight for you again."

Vortigern reached, and he clutched her hand. Beset by the dragon and the twain he had cast out from their homes, he chose the dragon. And so it was Rowenna went down to the sea the same way she had, three years gone, come up from it. She took the winding way, watched by stony angels, round and round. No one challenged her. No one stopped her. All watched, though, and some cheered when she greeted her father in the name of her husband.

"Come in, Father," she said, her voice loud and clear and not torn even by the whipping wind. "Come in, for I offer you the hospitality of this hall, in my name and my husband's."

"Girl," he said, and then he stopped. He had not seen his daughter in long years, and now when he looked into her eyes he saw they were sometimes hard and sometimes tender as a babe's. Truth-teller's eyes, the eyes of a *sacerd*. "What do you advise," he asked, "to help me to my vengeance against this thin king?"

She looked at him long, took in all she saw—his shining mail shirt, his stiff leather helm, and the long knife sheathed at his belt. The grip was cunningly worked, inlaid with gold and with silver twining the length like two serpents in deadly dance. Longer than a dagger, shorter than a sword, this was the deadly *seaxe* for which her people were named.

"That is a fine blade, Father."

"It was your uncle's, and he got it off the corpse of an enemy he killed. Ah," he said, mistaking the look on her for sadness. "Daughter, he was the *sacerd* who named your fate. He was fond of you, child." He withdrew the *seaxe* and presented it to her, hilt first. "In his name, take it."

Smiling, she did, and then Rowenna Hengist-daughter reminded her father that he had asked her advice. "I will give it to you, Father, but you must promise me you will follow to the word and do nothing but what I say."

He hesitated, for he was not used to taking orders from his daughter. Then he saw her eyes, and it was like looking into the eyes of Horsa his brother. That one, Hengist had been long used to heeding. "Say," he told her.

In lean words Rowenna gave her advice, and her father thought it was good.

Rowenna kept her accustomed place beside her husband, and she looked out upon the hall at the feasters. Hel's daughter looked upon her handiwork and she thought it was good. Uneasily the Wealas and Saxons had come together, neither side certain of what to expect from the other. Treaties had bound them, treaties had been broken, and now the two sides were come together again by the will of king and lord in the hall of Vortigern the Thin to see how the feud between them could be mended. At Rowenna's asking, they did not separate themselves from each other, Saxon on one side of the hall, her husband's folk on the other.

"Come together!" she'd cried, her voice heard above those of the milling hundreds. "Let a man of my father's sit beside a man of my husband's, one and one upon the benches."

That had been a while happening until Hengist led the way, taking a seat beside Vortigern, his ancient son-in-law. "Sit!" he'd bellowed heartily. "All you Saxons! Sit in company with the Cymru!"

He chose his word well, for it pleased the Wealas and they made room on the benches for their erstwhile enemies. And so they sat, and so they drank, but Vortigern's folk did the most of the drinking.

In her seat beside her husband, Rowenna looked out,

down the long length of the hall. She knew hardly any of the Saxons, for these were men who had come to her father in the last year, youngsters fresh from the shores of home. They, as those who had come before, sailed the dark sea in search of a home, wide lands and women to wed. She looked for one among them, a ghost, and though she expected to see him there at the feast, she did not find him.

In her husband's hall, they feasted full on fishes and deer from the hills and, because it was the falling season, bowls filled with tender nutmeats. At her behest, Vortigern tapped the deepest kegs in his cellars, and his guests were urged to drink deeply. From time to time, Rowenna went herself among the guests and refilled their cups, always generous. She saw who was drunken, and who was not, and she admired the will of her father's folk, for they had listened to him in every way, though that must have been hard.

After her third pass through the hall, Rowenna returned to her father and her husband. She resumed her seat, and there she touched Vortigern's arm.

"Husband," she said, "I have heard you and my father talking, and it pleases me to think there will be peace between you again."

He turned to her, his eyes bright as though with fever. "Wife, you have done well. You do me honor to treat my guests so well."

"Indeed," she said, casting down her eyes and blushing modestly. "It is you, husband, who is generous. You have taken up an old treaty and made it new. You have welcomed my father and his people into your hall and fed them full." She looked up, her glance passing him, passing her father, looking for the ghost. Her uncle was not there. "They called me Peace-weaver," she said to Vortigern, "on the day we were married. I think peace will soon be woven here again, do you not, husband?"

He said that he did, and he said so eagerly, looking from his wife to her father, down the hall to his men and Hengist's at feast. Then he made many promises, and Hengist leaned forward to hear them as though he wished to remember every word. He made promises of his own, that he would support his wife's husband, that he would ever be a strong ally at Vortigern's back.

"Wars have been hard on us both, Vortigern. Be as a brother to me. I will be as a father to you."

Vortigern did not smile, but Rowenna saw his lips twitch a little in his beard.

"Father," she said, her hand upon the *seaxe* at her belt. "I have here a gift for my husband, one I wish him to have as a sign that, at last, peace is woven between our people."

Vortigern leaned forward, eager for the sign, eager for the peace.

From out the sheathe came the silver and gold *seaxe*. In the light of torches the blade ran red as with the ghost of blood. Vortigern cried out for the beauty of it, and upon the hall fell sudden hush, for half the throng fell still.

Up from the silence, like a hard bird flown, one of Hengist's men cried: "*Nimeth eure seaxes!*"

As one, blades lifted from Saxon sheathes, and blades fell, and all that steel flashing lit the hall brighter. Like rivers running, the blood of the slaughter flowed as each Saxon slew the Wealas beside him.

Through it all, she sat as still as a stone angel, Rowenna Peace-weaver, Hel's daughter. While her father watched, her husband flung to his feet and fled the hall. No one touched him, no one harmed. They let him go, for Rowenna said his blood would foul the steel that drew it; it was the will of the *sacerd* that he be allowed to flee.

And when it was done, the slaughter, and silence again fallen so that Rowenna knew no one of her husband's warriors was left alive, she rose and she stood before them all, red-handed Saxons and her own father.

"Now," said the *sacerd*, Hel's daughter. "Now, hear me. I have seen prophecy done in this place. I have seen in this very hall a battle between a red dragon and a white. This night, I have seen the prophecy fulfilled."

Men began to murmur, some in fear, some as though they would raise up their voices to cheer her, to acclaim. She held up her hand, and silence fell again.

"Listen," she said.

Heads cocked, but no one seemed to hear what she did. They heard only the rustle of floor rushes beneath their own feet. They heard the whisper of torchlight, the flames in the braziers. Rowenna smiled, and men looked away from it, for it was not a lovely smile. She turned to her father, and she said, "I have given you a kingdom, Hengist Whitgils-son. You wanted that, and I tried to get it with my body, but my husband was faithless. You have it now, but listen—"

In the shadows, wings rustled, stone angels breathed.

"Hear me, Father. You have this kingdom, this land you desired, and I say you will fight the fight against the brothers who come, and you will be a long time strong."

Then did a cheer fly up, a full-throated roar from men standing in the gore of killing. Her name flew to the rafters. Hengist's followed. Rowenna looked around the hall again, and at last she saw him, there among the dead, ghost-Horsa walking. He looked at her, his eyes gone tender and soft.

Do you hear?

She did, the rustle of wings, the whisper of angels, the warriors of a foreign god. Because she was *sacerd*, no longer peace-weaver, she knew this: Like Valkyries, they would come in time.

DRAGONS OF THE MIND
Peter T. Garratt

Once there was a war in this country, which lasted longer than the life of a man, or at least longer than the life of any child whose misfortune it was to be born in the year it started. From the beginning people went to the churches and deafened the Lord with their prayers that the war might end, and the cruel curse of the barbarians be lifted from the land: But the Lord was indeed deaf in those days.

Even Vortigern, the High King, prayed. Sometimes he took his retinue to the bishop's church, in the center of Verulamium, where the cobblers and blacksmiths and market gardeners who wore leather armor and called themselves legionaries could see him follow the approved religion, as if he were still a Roman official. More often he went out of the city to the small chapel of St. Alban, built on the spot where the martyr had been killed by the Romans. He took only a few bodyguards, men from his estate in the West; no hired men.

The boy had always lived in the convent. It was a pleasant place with white paint and icons on the walls. In certain light he could see the outlines of older paintings beneath the whitewash, but he had no idea what they could be. It was a house of women, but there were children also, orphans or the offspring of penitent women who worked when the nuns were at prayer. There were few boys and no men.

Aurelia, the boy's mother, was not a nun, but neither was she a penitent. The boy knew little of the world outside the narrow valley. It ran between high hills to a wider valley, into which the boy was forbidden to venture. He knew nothing at all of his own place in the world.

Vortigern walked more as he got older. He could hope for another ten years, if he did not allow himself to become lazy or decrepit like the old men who had been so common in his youth. And as a British High King, he could not be carried in a litter like Nero. He did not ride either, but that was because his joints, which could still cope with a walk, did not allow him to sit easily in a saddle.

On the day of his last visit to the chapel of St. Alban, he had just left the city when the road ahead filled with horsemen riding toward him. There were twenty or thirty, followed by servants on mules. Most had hunting hounds running beside their mounts. He wondered how much respect they would show their High King. Someone had abandoned a cart with a broken axle beside the road. Vortigern's shoulders were still strong, and he managed to scramble onto it without too much strain on his decrepit hips or his even more arthritic knees. He could still be an imposing figure, wearing the purple toga which had once belonged to Magnus Maximus. The horsemen were the bulk of the cavalry arm of the Legion of Verulamium. They came from local landed families, and unlike the much more numerous infantry, wore metal as well as leather armor. They seemed in a good mood, and he saw no empty saddles, though some of the mules had prisoners tied to them, or in one case, thrown across like a sack. The prisoners were all young women, Anglish from the style of their torn dresses. Some of the armored riders gave him a salute, others a less respectful wave, and he at once raised his arm stiffly in return.

After the cavalry had passed, Vortigern noticed a further, solitary rider approaching from a different direction. This man rode an oddly colored horse, roan on one side, white on the other. The High King recognized at once the horse, and therefore its rider, a man he needed to speak to: But not till he had prayed.

Prayer still mattered to him, though he did not trust the Lord to answer. As a child, he had only heard the psalms and the parables. Later, when he studied in Londinium, he rejected the harsh doctrine of the Roman priests that the Lord pre-ordained everything, not only men's vices, but their inability to cope virtuously with natural disasters, such as the floods that afflicted Christian and pagan alike. Inspired by his friend Ambrosius, he had joined the movement to expel the Roman tax-gatherers, only to find that the priests still taxed the people's souls, with their iron bargain of Salvation in exchange for unquestioning Faith.

The walk to the chapel did not tire him, but he was almost past kneeling. His knee joints were as stiff as scale armor that has been allowed to rust, especially when the weather was damp. Tiles had fallen off the chapel roof and not been replaced, so it was scarcely dryer inside than out. There were puddles in the worn parts of the mosaic, especially where worshippers stopped to admire the central image, of Alban being received into Heaven.

Vortigern had his own pew, with a cushion arranged to ease his kneeling. Kneel he did, though it gave him a foretaste of Purgatory. He did not ask for forgiveness: He felt his sins were mostly misjudgments. He sought guidance. All his life he had wondered if it were really possible to siphon knowledge from the Other World into this one. Few could have a better grasp of the way of this world than he did, but the world was vast and its inhabitants devious.

Trying to pray sincerely, Vortigern reviewed his life, wondering where he had been guided. Two decades earlier, when Emperor Honorius died and word came of chaos in Rome, he had prayed and that once had been given an answer. He was a rising man on the Council, famed for his good luck and physical strength. He had friends among pagans as well as Christians, and they called him Hercules. His policy was no truck with Rome, not even trade. The Romans sought to exchange the true wealth of Britain—foodstuffs, metals, even freeborn Britons stolen into slavery—for pieces of silver graven with the image of Caesar. He had swept the land with his promise of "No more rendering unto Caesar," and the people had loved him for it. Some had urged him to declare himself Emperor in Britain. Others had told him he could become Emperor of Gaul, Spain, even Rome itself, but those were not true friends. It was a plan that many had tried: None, save Constantine, had succeeded.

He had prayed and been rewarded with a vision, albeit

a strange, unchristian one. He had dreamed that fateful night that he was Hercules, fighting the Hydra, the golden many-headed dragon: But instead of snake heads the monster had sprouted the bronze helmets of Roman officers. The vision was more vivid than a dream: He could smell the monster's breath, not fiery or fetid, but perfumed, like a senator whose bathhouse is out of commission. Vortigern saw he must trust his own judgment. Even Magnus Maximus had found out too late that if one killed one Roman emperor, two more would spring up to take his place. He needed nothing from Rome, not even the glory of its name. He was hailed Vortigern, High King of Britain only. To the new Caesar he would be a distant enemy, not a close rival.

This had upset naive fools like Ambrosius, who wanted independent Britain run like the Roman Republic, but it pleased the people.

The choir sang a chant in praise of the Lord. Vortigern wondered if the Lord truly deserved to be praised. Priests sometimes took the Word to the barbarians, but never reached the ones who most needed it—Attila the Hun, or his own father-in-law, Hengist the Jute. In the meantime, everything seemed to deteriorate. Even the music was confined to a lyre. The organ, which he so much preferred, was broken.

The psalm ended. That was some relief; he would be able to sit back and spare his knees while he listened to the sermon. On the other hand, though he enjoyed the psalms and chants, he never found any guidance from the words of priests. Either they dwelt on the likely punishment of sins, with particular reference to those he was known to practice, or they ignored his presence completely. Vortigern doubted very much that sinners were punished more severely, let alone more justly, by Divine than by human law. Indeed he knew of a number of prize sinners who had never, to his certain knowledge, been punished by anyone.

He felt slighted but also relieved when the day's preacher chose to ignore him. Vortigern feared the passions such men could stir up. In that very city, just as he was starting to feel secure, there had been a great debate between the Roman predestiners and his native British preachers, who spoke for free will and the value of good works. To his educated mind, the British argument was clearly better, yet the perverse mob had taken the Roman side, and bishops had been appointed who preached for Rome. Some even called for a Holy War against the pagans, to be led by priests.

After that meeting, he had ridden with a heavy heart to Londinium, to assess its strength. The walls were high, but also long. He doubted he could spare enough soldiers to hold the empty town, marooned on the bank of the great river like the skeleton of a whale. If the Holy War took place, it would leave the Southeast unprotected. Of course, the Gallic coast opposite had been cleared of barbarians, but that was because Rome again ruled Gaul. The successor of Honorius was a child, but the mother, Galla Placidia, ran the remains of the Empire better than her brothers had. She was a woman who had captured the hearts of a Gothic warlord and a great Roman general. Both of these were now dead, and in an unaccountable moment of passion, Vortigern had written a few months earlier to Galla Placidia offering to marry her himself. She had not replied, and he had wondered if the Holy War was a ploy to allow Galla's general Aetius to invade Britain and win it for her without the inconvenience of conquest or marriage.

Most of the other worshippers were novice monks, and the sermon concerned new instructions from Rome about the rules of monastic life. It seemed it was important that the monks shave their heads in a way different to that fashionable in Britain. Not that monks followed fashion as such: They had Rules. Rules devised in Rome.

The children in the village called the boy Emrys. They had no Latin, and his real name defied them. He wasn't supposed to leave the small valley of the convent, but there was too little to do there . . . no boys apart from a couple of toddlers, and the girls were young and dull. He did, however, obey his mother's strictest rule—that he must never tell a living soul the name of his father. Then he began to elaborate and informed the village boys that he had never had any father at all. They decided he must have been sired by a visitor from the Other World . . . a king, of course, for only kings could travel between the worlds. Probably it was then they started to fear him, but that did not mean they turned against the strange visitor. In those days, love and fear went out and about and often played games together.

The service ended and left Vortigern with no inspiration. He fell back on the memory that he had hardly prayed at all on the day before his second, and last, important vision. It was soon after the humiliating debate with the Roman bishop. That spring had been a crossroads. The people had coped as well with the lack of Roman traders as they had earlier with the expulsion of officials and tax-gatherers, but the Irish pirates and the Picts had reverted to their old habits. The Council had demanded from the High King a replacement for the Roman garrison, but they had refused to agree to taxes. Taxes, they said, required coinage, and no one was bringing coins into the country. That was true, and Vortigern had always mistrusted Roman traders. Too many were spies. What he was never able to prevent was the entry of priests, men who denounced the native British preachers as deviants from the Church of Rome. To Vortigern's horror, his people seemed to be drifting back to the harsh certainty of Rome like sheep preferring a brutal shepherd and his dogs to the perils posed by wolves. Then that day in Londinium word had come of three long-keeled ships in the river. They were full of warriors, and their stemposts were carved into the heads of dragons, but on their masts they flew the olive-branch flag of peace.

On the first good morning of a late spring, with a breeze blowing from the east and only a hint of rain, he had walked down to the abandoned quay to meet Hengist the Jute. The barbarian spoke passable Latin and wore a Roman tunic over his cross-gartered leggings. He had looked young and fresh for the veteran warrior he claimed to be, with only one scar on his face. He did not have the wild eyes of the Pict, or the rank smell of the Goth. Hengist had explained that they came to do business, and Vortigern felt that he could do business with them.

The boy they called Emrys did not neglect his lessons, though he preferred reading by himself to listening to the nuns. There were a lot of books in the library: Holy Books that were read often and constantly renewed with fair copies, and old Roman books that were looked after but read seldom. His mother Aurelia had introduced him to those books: She had initially read them to him, then later enjoyed hearing him read to her. The books were very old, and as the nuns would not replace them, she was looking forward to the day when his penmanship would be good enough for him to start making copies. She did not do this herself, though she did write letters, which she gave to the traveling confessor. Emrys was bored by the prospect of so much writing, though he enjoyed the books themselves. His favorites were Livy's history of Rome and Julius Caesar's account of his wars. When he had read these twice, he made an effort to read the ones on architecture and engineering. As he came to understand them even these seemed more interesting.

What he did not understand was the gaps. Even the convent's collection of Holy Books was not complete: His mother lamented the absence of a Book of Ruth and one called The Song of Solomon. And none of the histories explained the dangerous world outside the valley, which he had been warned against rather than told about. He had read that the Romans oppressed the Christians and the Druids, but now the Romans were themselves Christians and the Druids persecuted them. Indeed, it wasn't clear how a barbarian island invaded by Romans had become a Roman island invaded by barbarians.

Above all, no one, not even his mother, would tell him anything useful about the evil King Vortigern, the person he most needed to hide from.

It was not raining, and there was even some blue in the sky. The High King was glad to be out of the chapel. He set out in the careful stride that pained him least, glad to get away from the novices, who looked at him like some demon they would soon cast out. A few years earlier, men like them had driven him into the arms of Hengist . . . not to mention Hengist's daughter, Rowann. The Jute had explained that his own country was afflicted by coastal floods, far more severely than Britain was at the time. As the land was also overrun with refugees from the activities of Attila farther east, he and his people were seeking better land, to hold in exchange for military service.

This had seemed a commendable exercise of free will, in response to the disagreeable destiny offered by whatever god determined the sea level in Juteland. Nevertheless, Vortigern did not agree at once. He should not take a decision like recruiting pagan mercenaries without the Council's approval. He was a British king, not a Roman dictator. He spent the rest of the day studying the map and consulting men he trusted, British patriots all. But he had not prayed; there were no churches open in Londinium. Despite this neglect, he was given a vision-dream that night of two great dragons: the red dragon from his own banner, and the white from Hengist's figurehead. They had flown together to the West and terrified the Irish, then round the bounds of the kingdom, holding back the Picts and even the Romans. He had felt the cool wind of Britain in his face as they flew.

He had been woken early by bright sunlight, the first that year, though it was almost Pentecost. He was in mid-dream, and had lost the end. Still, there had really been no doubt. A powerful military force loyal only to him would quiet the barbarians, the Romans, and his own enemies, like the republican fool Ambrosius.

Walking back to the city, he pondered on the missing end to the dream. As sure as Hell was beneath the earth, the red and white dragons no longer flew together. Yet what alternative had he had, but to employ the Jutes? Without firm leadership, his people would start quarreling among themselves and fall victim to the Picts and Irish, and the leadership of Rome offered nothing but priests and taxes.

A market was being held in the forum as he crossed it. It pleased him that it was almost as busy as the markets of his boyhood, when coin-rich Roman traders would have been swarming round with exotic, unnecessary imports. There was quite a healthy trade in all kinds of local produce, usually conducted without money, the root of evil. At the far end, the rostrum was being used to display the wares in a temporary slave market; it was rare for captives to be available for sale, and there was no regular arrangement. It seemed bidding was to be in coins, now kept entirely for emergencies and large purchases. Vortigern was too aware of the number of British girls who had been callously sold in that way in the past to feel entirely comfortable: On the other hand, the Anglish had joined the Jute's revolt with vicious gusto, and could scarcely be treated leniently.

The first lot was one of the girls he'd seen earlier, tied to a mule. Her coarse woolen dress was torn right down the front, but she made no effort to hold it together. She stared brazenly at the prospective purchasers, though Vortigern could tell from her tremor that she was afraid. Doubtless she hoped for a buyer who would use her for other things than drudgery, and not too roughly. For a moment he thought of bidding for her himself. It was a while since he'd had a relatively willing slave girl, and he could certainly afford her, having prudently kept a supply of worn coins for his own use. On the other hand, if he outbid the locals for a prized lot, he would get even less popular in his enforced capital.

Verulamium looked as shabby as any other city, but things could usually be repaired there. Clean water was still piped in, and Vortigern preferred its taste since wooden pipes had replaced lead. The sewers and toilets were fairly reliable, and there were even a few hypocausts working, most notably the ones that heated his small private bathhouse, and the larger one he had donated to the city when the public baths gave up the ghost.

On the other hand, he trusted the city folk no more than they trusted him. Behind the rostrum stood the standard of the Legion of Verulamium. The crude winged creature at the top was red; it was not the dragon of Vortigern, but the eagle of Galla Placidia. The city's most prized possession was not the bloodstained tunic of Alban in the church, but the letter from the late Emperor Honorius instructing them to look after their own defense. Folk said

Honorius had been a poor ruler, but Vortigern privately felt that a man who held his throne through thirty years of invasions and died in his bed could not have been that foolish. Certainly he had left a legacy of Romanised Britons who wanted to be legionaries, even if they had no intention of paying taxes.

The High King led his bodyguards closer to the rostrum, and caught the eye of the Anglish girl. She noticed him and started, then straightened her shoulders so her dress opened further, guessing the man's position if not its precariousness. Again he was tempted. This one would not need to be forced, as his ancestors had been. Then he realized the veiled woman standing beside the rostrum was speaking to the girl in Anglish, or rather Jutish. The girl replied sullenly and the veiled woman looked away, looked directly at Vortigern. He realized only then that it was his wife Rowann beneath the concealing veil. He felt relieved to have made no bid.

The first girl was sold to the man who had captured her. He would get back half the price he paid, the rest going to the legion's weapon fund. Next onto the rostrum was a girl Vortigern had not seen before. He guessed she was the one who had been thrown like a sack across a mule. She looked far more frightened than the first, her tattered dress pulled shut. He felt sorry for her, certain she would be sold to some peasant as a work-drudge. However, Rowann started to ask her questions in Jutish, and translated some of her replies into fluent Latin, with hints both of her own accent and the local one. She said the girl was unmarried and apprenticed to a wise woman. Then she bid two gold coins, more than anyone else was likely to.

As the High King moved away from the sad scene around the rostrum, someone shouted: "Hey, Vortigern! Aren't you bidding?"

Another, rougher, voice followed it: "Do you need the first barbara to pander for you?"

He froze, reluctant to turn back. Once he would have handled such a situation easily, but lately . . . Luckily, Rowann intervened: "Now, now! I've bought a slave to find herbs for medicines! There's *no need* for anything else!"

They all laughed, and Vortigern glanced back and smiled. The men weren't exactly hostile, but many seemed puzzled that he had made no bid. He solemnly saluted them, and their eagle, then walked off with as much dignity as he could muster. Most saluted back, but sloppily. His long years in Roman schools had left a mark that distanced him from the very Britons whose spirit he sought to free. He had imagined a liberator must be as democratic as the Gracchae, and that an aging ruler would be a wise and just figure in the spirit of Nerva or Antoninus Pius, men who could never be imagined bidding for bedmates in the market. What his Britons wanted was a Sun King, who would rut away cheerfully at his zenith, and be of little interest by evening. Their idea of an old ruler was the mad King Leir.

In the courtyard of the palace, he noticed the roan and white horse drinking from a trough. The Dung-Falcon would have arrived, the man who had the vision to soar above the land and see patterns and movements others missed; but was also able to look into the foul, sordid places where vital secrets could be unearthed. Vortigern suspected every ruler relied on such men. He was sure Galla Placidia employed several.

The Dung-Falcon was in the atrium. The map of Britain was unrolled, and he was putting out colored tokens that represented armies and warbands. He saluted and said: "I have something for you. I'm afraid you won't like it."

Vortigern was already not liking the distribution of tokens on the map. "Are you saying my sons have been forced back to Londinium?"

"South of the river, everything east of the city is in Jutish hands. They've also sailed round the coast and taken a foothold on the Isle of Vectis. There've been Saxon ships seen in the channel, and farther north the Angli are active."

The Angli had had been in Britain for years, a quiet part of the coastal defense system in the east, but they had joined the revolt eagerly. They were even more destructive than the Jutes, if less feared as fighters.

"We're holding them here, but . . ."

"You say there's worse news?" Vortigern sighed.

"Yes. I managed to intercept this letter. I doubt it was the only copy."

The letter was addressed to Aetius, Galla Placidia's general in Gaul. It was titled "The Groans of the Britons," and outlined, or rather dramatized, their grievances: *The sea drives us to the barbarians*—which presumably referred to the recent floods in many areas—*The barbarians drive us to the sea!* Further down, there was a list of usable harbors, passable roads, areas with supplies.

The worst was at the end. The seals approving the letter included not only the consuls of nearly all the cities where anyone could still melt wax, but two of the usually anti-Roman tribal leaders from the North, and worst of all, three of his four sons. He said feebly: "Don't they understand? If Aetius does come, he won't bring old-time Roman soldiers! He'll bring his own hired men, Goths, maybe even Huns!"

"They understand that you brought them Jutes!"

He stared at the unfriendly map. In the richest areas, nearly all the blue "loyal" tokens were now offered to Aetius. The far southeast was dominated by red Jutish tokens; of course he himself had placed them there, where the Romans could most easily cross the sea. On his northern flank, orange Anglish tokens were spreading into the heart of the country. The only clear place was the distant west: the pure-spirited but damp and uncomfortable region where people lived in valleys and the slopes of mountains, under which they still believed that dragons and mighty warriors lay sleeping. The Dung-Falcon followed his gaze and said: "You need to rally support where you have the most."

"Yes." Unfortunately, there were few cities in the loyal West, and those had never recovered from earlier Irish raids. Vortigern felt faint. He wanted the warmth of his bathhouse and the relieving medicine only his wife could make. He had become dependent on comfort. Literally, physically, dependent. "It's a decision I have to make soon."

"One other thing." The Dung-Falcon picked up the letter and looked significantly at the row of seals. "You've sometimes hinted that in this situation you would need to give me . . . drastic orders. Are you ready for that?"

The High King said tiredly: "Not yet."

Emrys had nothing to do but pray and copy the books. He was making a copy of the codex of Livy, and had reached page four. That summer, he offered through boredom to help the tanned, sweating penitent women with their work in the kitchen garden, and found them better company than he had expected. This upset the nuns, who complained to his mother. After that he went more often to the village, where he found himself suggesting games the older girls could play. He wasn't sure why.

Only two people traveled up and down the valley. The confessor called often. He seemed to expect Emrys to have new sins to confess, but all the boy could think of was to ask him to bring more books. The confessor could only come up with a volume of his own confessions, mostly to very obscure sins.

The other traveler was the black-dung merchant. No one would travel any distance to buy or sell dung: What he traded was trinkets and exotic foods, in exchange for black dung, the rock the locals cut from their hillside quarry and used as fuel. It was forbidden in the convent as devil's fuel, as it came from beneath the earth.

One morning Emrys was in the village, inviting the girls to join a new game, a swimming race, when the black-dung merchant rode up. He rode a mule, and led a train of donkeys loaded with black dung. He greeted Emrys cheerfully: "You're a big lad to be playing with the girlies. Soon you'll be ready to train for the High King's army."

Emrys knew the High King was bad and to be avoided, but he wasn't used to dealing with men. He said feebly: "I live in the convent, so I don't know much about fighting." He did know Caesar's tactics, but not how spears were actually thrown.

"Then it's time they had you trained! Tell your family, a convent's no place for a lad your age! Write to your father."

"No . . . I can't! I just have my mother."

"He doesn't have a father!" one girl piped up. Another said: "He doesn't have one at all! He's born of the faer—"

Someone shushed her, but the traveling merchant was taking an interest. Emrys felt very afraid. He couldn't think of a grown-up way of dealing with this so he muttered: "It's true. I don't have any father!" and then turned and ran back to the convent.

As a child, Vortigern had often dreamed of having a fortified tower to retreat to. That day, as he lay in the dry heat room of his bathhouse, he dozed off and the dream returned. He would build a tower with all the Roman comforts, but on a hilltop, as the old kings of the Britons had built, and in the West, where people would believe that ancient warriors and lost heroes rested beneath it, waiting.

Suddenly he was awake. He started, then realized Rowann had entered the hot room. He sat up, aware he was naked, then remembered she was his wife. She had an odd barbarian prudery, and though barefoot, wore a full-length dress, white with purple cuffs and hem. She wore exquisite jewelry, gold for her hair, sapphire for her eyes. She looked every inch a great Roman lady, except that Roman ladies had a habit—whatever finery they wore in public, it was thrown off as soon as an opportunity arose. A woman who lived in the revived British style he favored would do the same in the bathhouse, though for hygiene, not wantonness.

"I have your medicine." She carried a steaming goblet. It smelled, and tasted, like a mixture of apple cider and vinegar, but he had come to enjoy the drink. He always began to feel better as soon as he inhaled the fumes. Nor was it only a pain-duller: It enabled him to walk better and swim easily in the large bath. He said:

"What would I do without you?"

"Probably make yourself worse by going west to live in a damp hovel with your friends among the Welsh!"

He started. She had used a word he found obscene, a barbarian's word for barbarian, and applied it to his own people! Still, he did not remonstrate as she sat down on the next bench and slowly began to take off her rings and loosen her dress, as though she had remembered she was meant to be clean and wanton.

He wondered at her power over him. She was the most beautiful woman he had ever seen, as well as the most intelligent, but she did her marital duty without passion, and never really pretended to be his woman more than her father's. His first wife, Maxima, had been different. She had been a princess in the West, her mother a descendant of the half-forgotten British kings. Maxima had claimed her father had been the great Magnus Maximus: "He was a Roman, but the night he married my mother, he married the land, taking her in the open on the bare, damp British soil. That night I was conceived." And when he married Maxima, he too had married the land. Indeed, the ceremony had been repeated every time she conceived one of the four sons who had grown up to ignore him. She had a love of love in the open and the feel of grass and dew under her back, an experience Vortigern suspected had been the start of his arthritis. Eventually they had drifted apart. Her hatred of Rome extended to things as well as people, and she had gone to live in a hill-fort in the far west where there was no hypocaust and the toilet was a trench.

Now he had this Jutish medicine woman, who collected physicians and wise women like herbs, drying and storing their knowledge, giving the people cheap remedies at the palace gate. He feared the people would have turned against him sooner if not for her remedies, but the time was coming. He said: "I may have to go to the West." He remembered the interrupted dream and added: "I'll build you a stone palace like a tower, with all the Roman comforts."

"Till then, I'll hold things together here. I'll try to send your medicine."

"Will you? Or will you poison me?"

"Not if I can avoid it." She finished removing her jewelry, slipped off her dress, and turned to face him, at last completely naked. "I understand, as you should, that we are in essence enemies, though over the years we have also become friends. That we make love without passion, but we do in our own way love each other."

"So why? Please, why should we be enemies?"

"Because your sons make war on my father."

"Your father has driven all the people of the Cantii from their lands!"

"They wouldn't give the supplies you promised. And when your sons advanced on Canti Bury, the peasants helped them! My father has to bring our own people to grow food and fight to hold the land you gave him for defeating your enemies!"

She was sitting with her legs just apart, like a human box of Pandora that he had opened. He said: "Tell me, do you and your father mean to bring over the whole population of Juteland? Every one?"

"I hope so. The Gods have made Juteland a swamp, and it gets worse. Why should we defy Them when They offer us Britain? We know the Gods are not gentle or merciful, however much you wear out your knees praying to yours. But now Saxons and more Angles are following, and this war between our families has to stop!" She reached for something in the sleeve of her discarded dress. He froze, thinking she had a dagger, and meant to kill him there and then, for her father and his people, but it was only a roll of parchment. "Here is the letter your spy brought in. All you need to do is add your seal to the others. Write to Aetius yourself. Tell him your loyal Jutes are ready to join him in his war against the Angles."

It was a better plan than nothing, but a hard letter for a High King to write. He said: "I sometimes think dreams have reached me from the Other World that are more than dreams. The night I met your father, I dreamed correctly that the red and white dragons would fly together against my enemies. But I awoke from that dream without its end, and ever since I have wondered what it was. Do you have any herb or potion which can induce forecasting dreams?"

"How do you know dreams are windows to the other world? Do not men dream of things they desire?"

Vortigern did not answer. He had told her he dreamed of her when they were apart, as he once had of Maxima. Sometimes he had dreamed of women he did not know in the Bible sense, or even of phantom women he did not know at all. But he did not smell the dream women as he had the breath of the dragons.

Emrys felt foolish when he got back to the convent. He knew the High King was a bad person to fight for, indeed one to avoid at all costs, but he didn't know why. The black-dung merchant knew more about the world than he did, and if he was almost grown up, he should have stayed and tried to learn from him.

Someone soon told his mother about the incident. She

was furious, and ordered him to stop going to the village altogether.

"Why? What have I done?"

"You've . . . it's dangerous out there. King Vortigern . . . I don't want to talk about him. He's evil. He has spies everywhere. This merchant who trades in Devil's Fuel—he could be a spy, probably is! You just have to keep well clear of all of them; don't go anywhere near them!"

The hill in the valley was the perfect place. It was steep, but there was one track up it. It had a spring, so water would never be a problem. The valley below was fertile, and there were sheep on the high hills all around. The hills were silent save for the sound of sheep: There were usable old tracks, but no Roman road ran near them. An enemy who didn't know the area would probably never find it. There was a plentiful supply of stone. Best of all, the local people said two great dragons slept beneath the hill.

Unfortunately, the High King was still sleeping in a tent. He hoped to dream of the dragons, but they kept to their own dreams. The work was taking longer than expected, and even the outer walls weren't finished. In fact, every time they got anywhere near the required height, cracks started to appear, though the ground seemed solid enough. It didn't help that the mortar was of appalling quality, so poor that, once, the whole edifice simply collapsed. Sometimes Vortigern traveled the ten miles to the nearest Roman fort, the one that looked over the straits to the Isle of Mona, but impatience to see his project rise in stone kept bringing him back.

He was caught at the fort for a while by snow. There was no hypocaust, but the roof was sound and the furnace heated the rooms near it. As soon as the weather cleared, he hurried back, driving his chariot himself; he still couldn't ride, and wouldn't stoop to a litter yet. He found the walls had collapsed again, an even greater humiliation as he had two visitors.

One, he hadn't expected. His first wife Maxima was five years younger than he, but looked in worse shape and did use a litter. Probably the wild life of the damp hills suited her less than she had hoped; but most of their hopes had come to fallen stones and bad bones. She greeted him coolly: "So where is your young barbarian wife?"

"She did not come. She has the body of a barbarian, but the soul of a Roman."

"Ah!" She turned to the tower, ruined with the mortar scarcely dry. "What happened here?"

He shrugged. "It's hard to find a real architect in the whole country. I've written to the scholars, and they suggest nothing but prayer and fasting. One suggested a pilgrimage to St. Alban, which I'm starting to think about." A shudder ran through him. He wanted his hypocaust and his second wife's potions, but the news from the South wasn't good. Verulamium held out, but other towns were lost.

Maxima said: "Of course, the Druids say that in the old days, it took a lot more than prayer to sanctify a fort. It took sacrifice. I'll see if I can find out what kind."

Emrys knew when the longer offices were held, so he could still sneak to the village. He didn't play by this time, but sought out the elders. They told him about High King Vortigern.

The other visitor was the Dung-Falcon. He had a list of disasters: burned cities, permanent-looking Saxon camps. Another list was of traitors who wanted the Council of Consuls to depose Vortigern and appoint a new leader. Typically, they wanted a first Consul rather than a new High King. Vortigern was in agony from his knees and hips. He said: "Do they mean to make war on me here?"

"Not yet. They're so worried about Angles and Saxons in the east, I think they'll try to make peace with Hengist."

"Him! Will they succeed?"

"Let's put it like this: If Hengist agrees to a peace conference, whatever you do, don't attend. Or if you do, wear armor under your toga."

The elders explained to Emrys that when they were children the land had been menaced by the Irish, terrible barbarians from across the sea. Everyone had lost someone to their slave raids. The Romans were supposed to stop this, but they never tried very hard. King Vortigern drove the Romans out, and then took care of the Irish. He gave them such a thrashing that they fled across the sea and never came back. It was true there were other barbarians in other parts of the country, but they never came to the valley. Besides, Vortigern had married the barbarian's queen, who was a great wise woman, and they would sort everything out.

The Dung-Falcon promised to send a good supply of Rowann's medicine. Without being asked, he offered to send the lady herself. "She's a powerful piece on the board, and she's probably less dangerous when she's with you."

Vortigern wasn't sure, but he didn't disagree. His sons had written accusing her of being a witch, and he wondered if that could be true, if her medicine contained a spell that made him crave for it, made him crave for anything but this cold ruin-peaked hillside in the middle of nowhere.

For the first time in his life Emrys stood up to his mother. "The people say King Vortigern is a great hero! So why have I spent my whole life hiding from him?"

"He isn't a hero, he isn't anything I want to talk about! You're not ready—"

"The nuns say I'm ready to leave! They say I'm too big, I'm a temptation to the penitent women—though to do what, I don't know. . . . What am I to do? Where am I to go, if I don't know who to trust, or anything at all?"

"Very well." She composed herself. "Vortigern is a sinner whose sin is ambition. Out of lust he married a pagan Druidess, and then married a witch. He'll stop at nothing. When the Romans left, good people wanted to govern the land by the rules of the Roman Republic, with no emperor, no king. Your father was the best of men, and Vortigern was desperate to be king. So he killed your father, and that's why you must hide. If he finds you, he'll kill you. Oh, I'm sorry you have to know such things. I'll find a new place, maybe in Gaul. I'll write . . . arrange something."

Before he left, the Dung-Falcon spoke with Maxima about her Druid plans to sanctify the tower. "What do you have in mind?"

"A sacrifice. It's the only way. The spirits of the hills don't like to be crowned with stone. A sacrifice of a head to be placed under the gate and bear its weight."

"Any old head?"

"Only if it's any old gate. The hill-spirit wants a person of importance, though it could be an outsider."

"A Roman, perhaps?"

"Good idea. Someone unusual. A black-skinned man was favored."

"Not many of those about. How about an unusual ancestry?"

"That could be suitable."

"How about a boy with no father? I think I could find you one of those."

They came to the convent at dawn: the black-dung merchant, a party of armed men, and one who seemed to be in charge, who rode an oddly beautiful horse, half white and half roan. The nuns were at prayer and the penitent women preparing breakfast. Emrys was in bed. They told him he was needed: The convent was a center for scholarship and the High King needed scholars to help him build a great fortress. Emrys said he had a book on architecture, or rather the convent did. No one objected to him taking it, least of all the nuns, none of whom had read it.

He felt badly for his mother. She did not show the dignity of a Roman matron, but screamed and begged them not to take her son, not to harm him. He feared she was right to fear, but tried to calm her, and appear to leave willingly. He was riding with men at last, and must try to appear like a Roman man.

Vortigern prayed night after night for a vision to tell him if he and his first wife were taking the best course of action: But visions would not come, nor even sleep. He did not dare send for a priest, of any Christian persuasion, for fear he would be denounced as a sinner, and confess and repent.

In this mood Rowann found him. She had learned she was to be sent for under escort, and had come at once escorted by a bodyguard loyal to her. She had brought a good supply of his medicine, her two assistants—including the Anglish girl from the market—and a chest of dried herbs and fungi.

The medicine improved Vortigern's mood at once. He explained what was to happen as if seeking her approval, but she soon realized his heart was filled with one of his great obsessions, which he would not be talked out of. She said: "I know nothing of this Druid magic. My skill is in herbs, not spells. But I will observe, and see if anything is achieved."

The meeting of the two queens was not as icy as Vortigern had feared. One had loved him with great passion that had burned itself out slowly; the other had never loved him with passion at all.

Emrys was brought to the valley in the high hills on the morning of the feast of Beltane . . . the first of May, by Roman reckoning. He tried to be brave, though the men in his escort were uneasy. He had spoken to them on the journey, asking questions about the recent past of Britain, talking about architecture and telling tales of Julius Caesar. The black-dung merchant was warming to him. He said: "I hear the folk round here tell of two dragons sleeping under that hill. They're waiting there till Britain needs them. That's why the tower falls down."

At dawn his escort led him up the hill of the ruined tower. Red light shone over the great rim of hills, though the sun had not risen. There was a crowd: builders, Druids, Vortigern's escort and Rowann's, local folk from miles around. Some way off, a group of priests and monks had gathered and were chanting round a stone cross. A line of armed men stood between them and the crowd.

On top of the hill, by the remains of the ruined gate, stood a group of three. In the middle was an aging man leaning on a great sword. He wore a garment Emrys realized must be the purple toga of a ruler. This would be the evil king who had killed his father. He was flanked by two women, presumably the witches he had married. One was also old and leaned on a carved staff. The other was young with golden hair, but her blue eyes were cold as the North Sea.

The escort halted and the sinister man called the Dung-Falcon said: "I bring you a boy with no father." There was a gasp from the crowd, and he added: "Though he may have had one once, one who makes him a distinguished person."

There was a mutter of sympathy, and Emrys realized he might have a chance, if he seized the initiative as Julius Caesar would have done. He stepped forward and said: "My name is Ambrosius, and my father was one of the consuls of the Romans. I do not have him now because you killed him!"

He stopped, expecting to be ordered to instant death for that alone, but instead the old king tried to defend himself. "No. I didn't kill him. Not really."

"Not really?" the older witch exclaimed. "Either you did or you didn't. Either the boy has a father or he doesn't."

"Listen!" the king said, more firmly. "For years this land was ruled by a council of men like your father, who were happy to debate and discuss while the armies weren't being led and no taxes were collected. Then there was a great meeting and disputation, and I was voted the powers of a king for ten years. At the end of that time your father demanded that I step down and the kingship be abolished. But the people supported me. There was a small riot . . . people call it a battle, but it wasn't that. Your father wasn't a bad man, but he lost the disputation and the riot, and at the end of the day, he killed himself. In the Roman tradition."

Silence fell over the whole gathering. In the distance, the chanting of the monks could just be heard. The older witch was about to speak when the black-dung merchant said: "This boy has a Roman book of architecture. I never saw one before. Maybe he can really tell you why this tower fell down."

The older witch said: "This isn't a Roman tower. It needs a head. . . ."

People hissed, and the young witch snapped: "If you want a head, bury your own! Aren't you going to let him try with his book?"

"Very well." The old king started to explain about the whole project. When he came to the water supply, the boy exclaimed:

"That's it! I've read about springs! They can hollow out caves in the hill. You must never build over a cave!"

Someone shouted: "How can we find out?"

Another voice said: "It's the cave of the dragons!"

"Yes!" the old king said, suddenly looking younger. "Men, dig down to the cave of the dragons! I knew there was something sacred about this place."

Men brought shovels and got to work. Emrys was allowed to sit. Women took cups of water to the men, then, even before the sun was over the hill, cups of mead. The woman Emrys thought of as the white witch, the young, bright-haired one who had spoken for him, brought him such a cup. He looked at her with a mixture of gratitude and suspicion. "Thank you. But people say you are a witch. Is that true?"

"Not exactly. But no one knows more than me of herbs and medicines."

"So you could poison someone?"

"Not my friend. And I very much want you and I to be friends. But I ought to warn you: There is a war in this country, and some people fight with swords, and some with other weapons. I'd like everyone in the country to be friends, under my husband, and perhaps Empress Galla. But I doubt that's possible. So make very sure you and I stay—what's happening?"

The white witch hurried to where the men were digging, but he paused to take a long sip of the mead. It was warm and tasted of a strange spice. He liked it, so he drank some more, and only then walked up to see what had been found.

It was a fine morning. Over most of the land, the sun would already be up, but here, it was still just behind the hills. The light blue of the sky, the oddly shadowed colors in the valley, all seemed to be clearer, more intense. In the distance, Emrys could still hear the monks chanting. They sang without music, but suddenly it seemed as though the colors themselves were a kind of music.

Other strange things were happening. The black-dung merchant was shouting: "Look! The boy's right! There is a cave here, and a pool that feeds the spring. And—Oh *God*! What's that?"

The boy saw something fly up out of the excavation. He thought it was a dragonfly at first; but it grew till it resembled a flying lizard, scaled with red jewels, rubies. It circled the excavation as people fell back gasping in wonder, some of them praying. Then it turned in anger, growing as it did, as another flying creature came out of the hole. This one was white, and the red one growled at it. They circled each other, hissing like flying cats, still growing, growing, till they cast shadows over the whole hilltop, and spat fire.

That much, everyone agreed. Some said the battle of the dragons continued for ages with no resolution; others that the red dragon drove the white away easily; yet others that the white dragon never really went away, so the shadow of its wings was always over the hilltop. Over the group of people who stood there:

The old High King and his old wife, who would be remembered for destroying a nation they tried too hard to save.

The young wife, who would be remembered for giving herself to an enemy for her people's sake.

The boy whose future was allowed that day. The boy who would be remembered as the last of all the Romans in Britain.

NIMUE'S SONG

Marcie Lynn Tentchoff

Dinas, my father, raised me alone,
Not far from the waters that lapped from the lake,
Away from the troubles and intrigues of war,
Protected by ramparts of magic and stone,
From all who might harm me . . .
And all I might harm.

> Nimue growing by the lakeside,
> Running, barefoot, through the keep,
> Paddling, swimming, in the water,
> Tossing, dream-wracked, in her sleep.

> Nimue dreams about her mother,
> Water streaming round her head,
> Wakes in shallows at the lake's edge
> Stumbles, weeping, to her bed.

Mother had left us when I was small,
My father spoke seldom her name or her deeds.
He brooded and muttered and stared at the lake
Whenever I mentioned her absence at all,
Whenever I missed her,
Or wept for her lack.

> Nimue feels her mother's presence
> Drifting, mist-wrapped, on the breeze,
> Always strongest near the water,
> Fading, failing, near the trees.

> Nimue hears her mother singing,
> Warning words, a bitter tune:
> "Caring, careful, care not too much,
> Mortals, mortal, mort too soon."

Within the castle I wore fine gowns,
My maidens sat with me at loom or at lute,
And praised me for stitchery, melody, charm,
And yet, through the years, I grew chilled by the frowns
They tried to hide from me
When I sought the lake.

    Nimue swims far from the lakeshore,
    Tasks left waiting at the keep,
    Wide eyes open, underwater,
    Awed by glories in the deep.

    Nimue sees a group of women,
    Smiling, captivating maids,
    Swimming, dragging down some burden. . . .
    Nimue swims back home, afraid.

Father was prideful of my fair face,
He boasted to many of my skills and charms
And sought out alliances, titles and lands,
In trade for the beauty, accomplishments, grace,
His daughter had grown to,
For which she was bred.

    Nimue dances near the water,
    Shift-clad, suitors left behind,
    Stoops to catch at her reflection,
    Fingers, wavelets, intertwined.

    Nimue hears a noise behind her,
    Whirls, feral, hands like claws,
    Searching, angry, for a voyeur,
    Sees a face that makes her pause.

Glein was his name, though all now forget
The fact that he lived and he loved and was mine.
The son of a suitor, no suitor himself,
And although in retrospect I may regret
My feelings and actions,
I needed him then.

    Nimue smiling in her bedroom,
    Maidens giggling at her side,

Crying, sighing o'er her weaving,
Joy and longing now allied.

Nimue silent at the banquets,
Head held high and eyes alight,
Stealing glances at a squire,
Turns her back on all the knights.

Father had faith that my virtue would hold,
He'd raised me too prideful to sell myself short.
My heart was my own to bestow as I wished,
My hand, though, was his to be bartered for gold,
Or all of the other
Things daughters could buy.

Nimue stealing through the moonlight,
Dancing, naked, by the lake,
Arms about her youthful lover,
Dreamy, praying not to wake.

Nimue feels a rush of longing,
Instinct wakens deep within,
Drags him down below the water,
Mouth to mouth and skin to skin.

Suitors departed, gold in their hands,
Their silences paid for as best as could be.
My father, grim-hearted, gazed at the water,
Mourning lost power and allies and lands,
Or maybe my mother,
Lost long years ago.

Nimue, locked within her tower,
Watched and guarded day and night,
Weeping, singing, mad confusion,
Maidens huddled just in sight.

Nimue hears her maidens whisper
Fearfully, their voices low.
Hears her mother named a faerie
In the water down below.

Slowly, I learned it, my mother's fate,
Gathered from rumors and whispers and taunting,
Held in this tower, as captive and lover,
Until, with my birthing, his needs she did sate,
And bought herself freedom,
At her child's expense.

Nimue dreams of lake maids singing,
Dreams of luring men to drown,
Wakes, and weeping, vows to study
Till some answer she has found.

Nimue dreams again that evening,
Of fae love, and of its price,
Dreams of trapping men, still living,
In a cave of glass . . . or ice.

Nimue sneaks out of the castle,
Warders wreathed in dreams and spray,
Slips, all mist-clad, through the tree line,
Gains the lake and swims away.

FORETHOUGHT

Alex Kolker

PROMETHEUS: So let Zeus hurl his blazing bolts,
And with the white wings of the snow,
With thunder and with earthquake,
Confound the reeling world.
None of this will bend my will.
—Aeschylus, *Prometheus Bound*

"Merlin," I asked, as we settled down by the campfire for our evening meal, "if you follow the Old Gods, why is it that you allow me to worship the Christ?"

"Because I know the difference between the singer and the song," the old man replied gruffly. He said nothing more for the rest of the evening.

It had become an unspoken tradition between the two of us, in all the months we had spent in the wilderness together as teacher and pupil. When the day's lesson was over, I was allowed to ask a single question. If the question was a good one, Merlin could take all evening, or sometimes even several days, to answer it. But if he considered the question to be a bad one, the old wizard would rebuff me with a single curt sentence, as he had that night, and then refuse to say anything more.

I couldn't even remember how the tradition got started, but it had become, in my mind, just another part of my instruction. Whenever the question I asked was a bad one, Merlin spent the rest of the evening brooding, and seemed displeased with me well into the next day. When I posed what he deemed to be a good question, however, his eyes would take on a kind of glow, and he would hunker down on the forest floor beside me and talk well into the night. It was the only time he ever treated me as anything more than just his pupil.

Because of this, I had begun picking my questions and wording them quite carefully, sometimes mulling one over for a whole week before I felt comfortable posing it. The question I'd put to him that night had been one of these, and I had been quite proud of it in the end. And so, as we ate our evening meal in silence, I repeated it over and over to myself in my head, trying to figure out why Merlin had rejected it.

There was a storm late that night, and when I awoke in the dawn, drenched and shivering, Merlin was nowhere to be seen. With his knowledge of the future, he usually knew when bad weather was on its way, and how to avoid it.

Sure enough, he showed up—well-rested and bone-dry—just as the first fish I was cooking for breakfast was done roasting over the campfire. I knew better than to ask him where he'd been.

"Eat quickly," he told me, taking the fish from me. "Nature herself has conjured up a lesson for you today, Wart. And you mustn't ever keep Nature waiting."

I roasted and wolfed down the second fish, sucking the grease from my fingers. Then I put out the fire and followed the wizard deeper into the forest.

He led me to an oxbow in a small brook, where the water flowed slowly between mossy banks. Everything was emerald—including the sunlight filtering through the tree-tops above.

"It's beautiful," I said.

"Look there."

I looked to where he was pointing, downstream. In the night, in the storm, a tree had fallen across the shallow water, making a natural dam. The water already pooled behind the log. The land was flat and firm enough that there would soon be a wide reservoir on the spot where we were now standing.

I glanced over at Merlin, still confused about what he wanted.

"Look there," he said again, this time pointing down at the ground between us.

Grass. Moss. Rocks.

"I see nothing."

"Look closer."

I dropped to my knees to study the ground. I knew all

the species of grass and moss, of course. But somehow this didn't seem like one of Merlin's botany lessons.

And then I saw them: ants. Hundreds of tiny black ants swarmed around a small hole beside a half-buried stone. And hundreds more ranged across the whole bank, wandering through their jungle of grass and moss, on their daily search for food.

"These?" I asked, staring up at Merlin.

He gave a slow nod. "There are five entrances to their colony. Can you find them all?"

I found the first four easily enough, but couldn't find the fifth.

"The last one's by your left foot," Merlin told me finally. "You probably have several of them crawling on you now."

I stood up, brushing imaginary ants off of my legs and shins. Then I looked over at Merlin, but the face he showed me back was once again blank. I knew that expression well and understood what it meant: The lesson for today had begun.

I let my gaze wander, all the while trying to figure out what the significance of the ant colony was. Finally my eyes fell upon the fallen log.

"The water . . ." I murmured.

Merlin said nothing.

"The water—when it rises, it's going to flood the colony."

Still Merlin said nothing.

This was the test, then—to save the ants. It was a silly way to spend an afternoon, I knew. But I had long since learned that the tasks that Merlin set me to always had a deeper, symbolic meaning. I had to take this mission as seriously as if it were a village of men and women that I was trying to save.

The easiest solution was to move the log itself. I tried to lift it, but it was much too heavy. I tried to roll the log forward, but it was stuck fast in the mud. It wouldn't budge.

My second thought was to chop the dam to bits, but I didn't have an ax. I didn't even have a sword or dagger.

If I can't move the log, I thought, *maybe I can move the colony.* But I discarded the notion almost immediately as impractical.

That left me with only two other options: to build a wall

around the colony that would protect it from the rising water, or to dig a channel around the fallen tree that would redirect the flow and keep the reservoir from getting too big. Neither possibility seemed too promising. Even if I could surround the ant colony with a watertight wall, water would still seep in underground. And the fallen tree was so long, and the ground around it so mossy and firm, that I knew I would never be able to dig a deep enough canal in time. I didn't even have a shovel.

Still, I had to do something, even if it were a futile gesture: Merlin hated it when I gave up far more than when I failed. So I spent the rest of the afternoon digging a channel—first with my hands, and then, finally, with a long branch I tore from the offending tree.

I found myself wondering about the extent to which Merlin had engineered all of this himself. Had he, not the storm, toppled the tree? Had he used his magic to make the tree heavier? Called the mud forth to hold the log fast to the ground? Moved the ant colony to just the right location? It seemed like too much of a coincidence that he had just stumbled upon the perfect conditions for this test. I decided that this would be the question I'd pose to him that evening.

By midday, I had managed to add a small bay to the growing pond, but the water level was still rising.

"This is pointless," I told Merlin, throwing the branch to one side.

He nodded.

I was dumbstruck. It was so rare that he acknowledged anything I said while one of his lessons was underway.

"So we can leave, then?"

He shook his head. I studied his face, but it, as always, revealed nothing.

I went back to my digging, but gave up again after a few minutes. If Merlin himself agreed that it was pointless, why should I be wasting my time?

Merlin was sitting now, with his back against an oak tree—high up on the river bank, right above the colony. I sat down beside him, my mind racing.

Perhaps this is a lesson in futility, I thought. *He wants to see if I know when to give up. Or maybe he wants to see if I'll keep fighting even if the odds are against me.*

It was always impossible to tell what Merlin was expecting me to do.

Maybe there was some solution I hadn't reasoned out yet. I thought and thought. As the afternoon wore on, and the waterline crept higher, my ideas grew stranger and stranger. I could drop another tree upstream from the river to create a second dam higher up. Or I could set the log on fire, hoping it might burn a gap in the dam before the water put out the flames. Or maybe I should trample the ant hills utterly, putting them out of their misery.

Finally, the growing pond reached the lowest of the colony entrances. The hole filled quickly, and then vanished under the water. After several seconds, ants began pouring out of the other four entrances, rushing in all directions—many of them directly toward the water itself. By the time the fifth entrance was submerged, all but a few of the ants had drowned.

Merlin stood up and signaled for me to do the same. He led me back through the forest to our campsite, radiating disappointment all the way.

"That wasn't a fair test, you know," I told Merlin later that night, by the campfire. He ignored me, as he always did when I started complaining. "There was no way to save the ants," I protested. "I tried my best. I don't see as you have any reason just to sit there scowling at me."

I had been the old wizard's student long enough to know that nothing I said would faze him. He treated everything—even my tantrums—as just another way to test and examine and analyze me. Sometimes, I think my anger even amused him. I was still careful: For all I knew, he could turn me into a toad with just a wiggle of his little finger. But that night I was angry enough not to care. And so I found myself shouting at a man I could scarcely have looked at straight in the eye only a year before.

"They were only ants!" I ranted. "I know you've taught me to have respect for all living things—plants and animals, and even insects. But there was nothing I could do to save them. And you knew it, too. You knew it before you even brought me to the riverbank."

And then something else struck me. "Wait a moment.

You *knew* that I was going to fail! You told me before that you can see the future. You knew everything I would do to try to save the ants, and you knew that none of my plans would work."

Merlin lifted his chin a little, but his face was still blank.

"So why do you act so disappointed when I fail, if you know I'm going to fail before I even begin?" I shouted.

A small smile broke across Merlin's face. And I knew that the question I had posed was a good one.

"There's a land a long way away," he told me, an odd tonelessness in his voice, "across the sea and far to the south. The land is called Hellas. And in ancient times the people of Hellas worshipped gods known as Titans.

"One of these Titans was named Prometheus, which, in the language of Hellas, meant *forethought*. For Prometheus had one special gift: He could see the entire span of his life. He knew what was coming before it ever happened."

"So this Prometheus was king of the Titans?" I asked.

Merlin gave a slight smile. "No."

"I just meant—if he knew the future, surely he could have used that knowledge to his advantage." Merlin just stared back at me. "To—to the advantage of all the Titans," I stammered on. "I mean, he would be able to know what was coming, what danger lay in their path. Surely the others would follow his lead."

Merlin nodded. "It is a powerful gift. Imagine what his birth must have been like for him: to come dripping and wailing from out of his mother's womb, his head already crowded with the memories of his entire life. To know, at the instant of his birth, what would be the circumstances of his death. And all the long, long span in between. For you see, the Titans were immortals."

I leaned back onto my elbows, listening, entranced.

"The Titans ruled Hellas for a thousand years. Theirs was a Golden Age. The humans who lived under them were worshipful and happy. The Titans were loving and just. They had only one Law: to love. Love all things. Love all the world. For if the whole world is the object of your love, you cannot help but treat everything in it with devotion and respect. And no one believed in this more than Prometheus himself."

Merlin sighed. "But this came to an end, as all things come to an end. The Titans had children, who called themselves Olympians. And one day the Olympians revolted and overthrew their Titan fathers. Zeus, the leader of the Olympians, declared himself King of the World. He destroyed all the great works of the Titans, laying waste to all the wonders and achievements that they had spent a millennium building. Then he rewrote the myths of the world, so that everyone in Hellas came to believe that the Titans were monsters, rather than gods."

"But what about Prometheus?" I asked. "How could he have allowed this? Didn't he warn the Titans that this was coming?"

"No." Merlin stood up, pulled a mug from his pack, and bent down to dip it into the nearby stream. "Prometheus didn't warn his brother Titans about the revolt. And when the revolt came, he helped the Olympians to win."

"He turned traitor?" I gasped. "But you said that he, more than all the others, loved the world!"

Merlin's eyes glared out from under his shaggy eyebrows. "Think deeper, Wart," he said, sitting back down beside me.

I did, my mind running through what Merlin had told me so far. "The gift!" I realized. "He knew. He knew in advance that the Olympians were destined to win. That's why he helped them."

Merlin's face confirmed nothing.

"Or," I ventured, "he knew that should the Olympians win, in the end it would lead to a greater good."

Merlin shook his head. "That wasn't the case. As peaceful and loving as the Titans were, the Olympians were haughty and cruel. They fought among themselves, using their human subjects as pawns in their petty squabbles. Because of one simple disagreement—a debate over which Olympian goddess was the most beautiful—a ten-year war broke out on Earth. Hundreds of thousands died."

"And Prometheus knew that this would happen?"

"Yes."

"And yet he still helped the Olympians overthrow the Titans?"

"Yes."

"Then I was right the first time," I declared. "He was a traitor."

Merlin considered this. "I suppose he was." He drained his mug and set it down on the ground between us. "But remember what I told you: All things come to an end. And Prometheus knew, even on the day he took sides against his brother Titans, that one day the Olympians themselves would be overthrown, and someone else would take their place."

"The Titans again?"

Merlin shook his head. "No. Their time had come and gone. But Zeus had one failing: He had a taste for human women. Every hundred years or so he would come down from his mountaintop and take a human for his own. The children of these unions had Olympian blood flowing through them, which made them greater than the humans they grew up among."

"Demigods."

"Yes. They became great heroes and great thinkers. The leaders of Hellas. Under their guidance, Hellas became a great empire, spanning the entire coast of the southern sea.

"You see, Prometheus knew that, one day, Zeus would plant his seed in a human woman, and that the demigod born of that seed would lead the people of Hellas away from worship of the Olympians. He would teach them the One Law of the Golden Age of the Titans: to love. And thus he would bring about a new Golden Age.

"But Prometheus wasn't the only one who foresaw this. The Olympians' downfall and the new golden age were also foretold in prophecies. Zeus knew about these prophesies, and he knew about Prometheus' gift of foresight. And so he asked the Titan to name the woman who would give birth to this demigod. He believed that if he could kill this woman before he ravished her—or, worse yet, just afterward—he could stave off his overthrow, and rule the world forever.

"Prometheus refused to reveal the woman's name. He refused even to reveal when the ravishment would take place. And so Zeus imprisoned Prometheus, threatened him, tortured him. Finally, in a fit of anger, he ordered Prometheus chained to the top of a mountain, exposed to the elements. Every morning, an eagle—Zeus' own pet—would come to Prometheus and peck out his liver. But the Titan was immortal, and so by evening his liver had grown back again. Then the morning would come and the eagle would return. This went on, day after day, for over a thousand years."

The description of these tortures sparked an old memory in my mind. "I've heard this story before," I said. "A long time ago. I think it was my old nursemaid who told it to me." I paused, trying to gather up what scraps of the tale I could remember. "Her story was different, though. In her version, Prometheus was being punished for disobeying the gods—"

"For teaching humans how to make fire," Merlin said with a nod. "Yes, there are many different versions of this story. That sort of thing happens, you know, when people become legends." The old man stroked his beard, and a small smile crossed his lips. "It's something you'll learn yourself, soon enough." He paused to study my face for a moment. Then he went on. "My version of the story, set down by a myth-weaver named Aeschylus a millennium ago, is older than the one your nursemaid told you. It is also the correct one."

"Did Prometheus ever reveal the name of the woman to Zeus?"

"No, he did not."

"And did Zeus ever—" I couldn't bring myself to complete the sentence. "Was the demigod ever born?"

Merlin grinned. "Oh yes. You see, Zeus was a fool. He could have avoided his own downfall easily enough by keeping his hands off of all human women. If he'd shown a little self-control, the demigod would never have been born to overthrow him. But Prometheus knew that Zeus would not be able to control himself.

"No, the woman was ravished, and the demigod was born, and the humans turned away from Zeus and the other Olympians, and the land of Hellas was free."

I sat waiting for Merlin to finish the story, but he didn't speak for a long, long time.

"So, young Wart," he said finally, "what do you think of my story?"

"That's all there is?"

"Oh, there are other stories about Prometheus—about what happened after. But what do you think of this one?"

"I'm confused," I admitted. "At first, Prometheus let his brothers die, let the Golden Age come to an end. I thought he was a traitor, a villain. But then he survived a thousand years of torture in the name of the second Golden Age. Then I thought him a hero."

"Both labels are true," Merlin said.

"Did he let himself be chained to the mountaintop as penance for his earlier crimes?"

"No. It was not penance."

"So why play the villain at first, and then play the hero?"

"Because, young Wart, he was *playing* neither. Remember Prometheus' gift: From birth he could remember the whole of his life. He had known, since infancy, that when the Olympians rebelled he would be at their side. He had known for centuries that Zeus would demand the name of the demigod's mother from him, and he knew that he would refuse. And so, when the proper time came, this is what he did."

"What?" I jumped to my feet. "You're saying he didn't side with the Olympians because he believed in them or agreed with them, but just because that is what he foresaw?"

"Yes. In fact, it saddened him greatly to betray the other Titans."

"Then why did he do it?"

"Because he knew that he would."

"It never had to come to that," I protested. "He could have warned the others about the revolt that was coming. He could have stopped it from ever taking place."

"But he knew that he wouldn't stop it," Merlin said. "He knew that he wouldn't even *try* to stop it. And so he didn't even try."

"There was no way for him to change the future he saw?"

"There was no point in trying to change it, because the future he saw was the future."

I started pacing the camp, my mind racing.

"There's another story they tell about Prometheus," Merlin said. "One day, he decided to change something that he knew was going to happen. He did try to change it, but the event still took place just as he had foreseen it. And when his brother Titans praised him for at least making the attempt, he told them, 'I deserve no praise. I tried to change the future because I had foreseen that this was the moment when I would try. I knew, too, that I would fail. And so everything has happened exactly as it was meant to happen.'"

"But—but—but," I sputtered, "if you can't change anything, what's the point of knowing it all in advance?"

"Ah," Merlin said, that little smile playing about his lips again. "That is a question I've asked myself many times."

"So you have no effect on the future that you see either?"

"None."

"So what *is* the point, then?"

"You learn to trust, Arthur," Merlin said, stroking his beard. It was rare that he used my real name, and I sat down on the ground before him, transfixed. "You have to trust that the world is turning in the way that it should, and that you have been set in your proper place in it. I have that trust now, because now is the time when I am supposed to have that trust. Someday, that trust will waver again. But today is not that day.

"The secret is not to stop caring about what is going on around you, even if you know the outcome in advance. This is the lesson of the ants, Arthur. There was no way that you could have saved them. But that didn't mean that you shouldn't have felt sorry for them, understood their pain, stayed with them until the disaster—the one you'd known was coming all along—overtook them."

We were silent again for a long time, and then he reached out and clasped my shoulder. "There will come a time, young Arthur, many years in the future, when you will think the worst of me. When that time comes, I want you to remember this lesson—the lesson of the ants."

"Yes, Merlin," I told him, locking eyes with him. "I promise I will."

The wizard smiled, patting my arm. "I'm tired, Wart. Let us sleep. We have another long day tomorrow."

❖

That would have been the end of my story—this part of it, anyway—if it hadn't been for another conversation, a conversation that took place years later. This was after my days of glory—the unification of Britain, the construction of Camelot, the founding of the Knights of the Round Table—but before I was betrayed and abandoned by everyone dear to me, including Merlin himself.

The Archbishop of Canterbury came to Camelot one summer to pay his respects, on his way to visit the monasteries in the Northlands. He stayed for several days, for the most part keeping the company of Merlin. The two were old friends, which was a remarkable thing, because most of the clergy—even the priests and cardinals who served at Camelot—gave Merlin, as a priest of the Old Gods, a wide berth. It had been whispered that even the pope himself feared Merlin, and so it was odd that so holy a man as the Archbishop of Canterbury held the old wizard in such esteem.

On the first night of the archbishop's visit, we held a celebratory feast. Our guest of honor sat at my right hand, and Merlin sat beside him. The two talked long into the night. I passed the evening chatting with Guinevere and Lancelot, sitting to my left. But at one moment, during a lull in our conversation, I happened to hear a bit of theirs.

"All I know is what I've heard," the archbishop was saying. "The more powerful Arthur becomes, the more the Holy Father sees you as a threat."

"And do you know why?"

"I'm not sure," the archbishop answered. "My friends in Rome seem to think it has little to do with your influence in Camelot, or even with your worship of the Old Gods. It has more to do with something you *know*. Perhaps something you've foreseen?"

"No," Merlin said, "nothing I've foreseen."

"Well, whatever it is, His Holiness says that it makes you the single greatest threat to all of Christendom."

I froze in my spot, my back still to the two men, shocked by what I had heard.

"Can you get a message to His Holiness for me?" Merlin asked the archbishop.

"Of course."

"Tell him this: The secret I carry—the secret that he

fears—comes in two halves. I once endured a thousand years of torment refusing to divulge the first half of this secret. Can His Holiness think I would reveal the second half so easily—especially since it would surely throw all of Britain, all of Europe, into chaos, nullifying all the hard work I've put into founding this age of peace?"

The two men were silent for a time, as the archbishop committed the words to memory. But then his curiosity got the better of him, and he leaned forward, asking hungrily, "What is it, old friend? Surely it couldn't hurt to tell just me. What is this terrible double secret that you carry?"

When Merlin answered, his voice was calm and steady. "If I told you, then my message to the pope would be a lie." The old wizard leaned back in his chair. "Trust me, my friend, you're better off not knowing."

But *I* knew. And the knowledge chilled me—and filled me with wonder.

THE TIME IN BETWEEN

Beth Anderson

One by one they arrived. Three days in a row. Each day, one child. And because the earthen path on which they traveled led only to Glastonbury Abbey, their destination was a deliberate one. Upon her arrival, each of the three girls, looking tousled as children do when they first awaken, told the novices the same story: Her father had carried her all the way from her village and, where the road finally curved toward the abbey, handed her over to an impatient man garbed in a long robe.

The tales differed only in what the father uttered as he passed his child to this imposing old man:

"Take her. She is too willful and will not obey," claimed one man.

"She is too young to be so flirtatious. Curb her passionate nature or she will never make a good marriage," begged another.

"We love her, but she is too clever with her herbs and roots. There are rumors of witchcraft surrounding her. We are afraid for her life. Please take care of our Elthea," pleaded the last.

Over time, the girls adapted as well as abandoned children could be expected to adapt to a predictable life among the Glastonbury hills. They were treated kindly, as long as they did their chores and obeyed. The only one of the three who regularly invoked the nuns' hostility was the child who had arrived first—the self-possessed little girl with the black eyes and raven tresses. On her very first night at the abbey, the dark-haired girl had disappeared from midnight until dawn, when she was found asleep halfway up the winding path that led to the Tor. Several rough jostlings finally roused her, and when asked what she thought she was doing, the child, in her small voice, claimed that the strange man from the day before had called her there. His name was Merlin, she said, and he shimmered like the tapers did when she scrunched her eyes really tight. He had a gaze that frightened her and a voice that she didn't dare disobey.

All attempts to prohibit the child's wandering on the Tor, already a place rumored to be enchanted, produced only a baffled smile and a careless shrug of her shoulders. The abbess faced the same frustration when she attempted to elicit the girl's name. It was when the nuns were at their wits' end that the waif finally announced that she would allow everyone to call her Morrighan. "Even if," she murmured to no one in particular, "that is just my pretend name."

From the beginning, Morrighan's obedience was subject to her daydreaming. Reprimands neither frightened her, made her repentant, nor brought about any change in her behavior. Like the plucked leaves that could be made to float lazily down the river that ran by this sacred place, she drifted on her own current, oblivious to her surroundings. Too many times during her first year at the abbey, Morrighan disappeared as she had on her first night. One minute she would be stirring porridge or washing clothes, and the next she would be gone, leaving the porridge to burn on the stove or the clothes, unrinsed, to entangle themselves in the reeds at the river's edge.

The last time the nuns searched for Morrighan was a day, not long after her thirteenth birthday, when she had been missing from dawn until dusk. Several very out-of-breath women eventually found her on the Tor's summit, standing stock-still in the swirling mist and waning daylight, listening to someone or something they could not hear. Their interruption caused Morrighan to turn in their direction, her eyes violent and furious. The malice the nuns saw there prompted a retreat made more slowly than any of them wished, simply because they didn't dare turn their backs on her. From that time on, no one acknowledged her disappearances and she was, for the most part, ignored—although it must be noted that many of the novices made the sign of the Cross when the dark-haired girl crossed their path.

Elthea, although she shook her head and smiled at the nuns' well-meaning, but ineffective gesture, understood their response to Morrighan. If pressed, Elthea would admit that her fellow orphan *was* a little daunting, and even *she* watched Morrighan's comings and goings from afar.

Then again, Elthea herself was rather used to being looked at askance. By the time she was thirteen, her skill with herbs and roots had made her the healer for this hamwich. Her talent for selecting the right medicine for even the most stubborn illness unsettled the more superstitious of the convent, but Elthea knew that her skills had nothing to do with witchery or magic. She simply gazed into her patients' eyes where she could easily discern that too much wine had been consumed, or that some unspoken sorrow or fear was the cause of a pounding heartbeat.

Elthea would not have dared meet Morrighan's eyes head on; they could pull a person into a maelstrom. The look Morrighan gave people proved that she knew exactly what she was doing, and that it would be to their detriment to cross her. Once, a visiting nobleman, smitten by what he called her mystical nature, demanded the raven-tressed girl as his personal servant for the length of his stay. Morrighan glared at him with such womanly disdain that he mumbled an apology before he realized he had done so.

Helen was the exact opposite of Morrighan. In fact, within a month of the three small girls being pressed by their fathers into the waiting arms of Merlin, Elthea was able to recognize Helen's thoughts by even the quickest of glances at her eyes. She was flirtatious, but naive. Her gaze revealed a lack of understanding that one's actions had consequences. From the beginning, Helen decided which rules she would obey and which rules were silly. And she always appeared surprised when she was punished for failing to do what she had been told to do. She always apologized for her offenses, but neither apologies not punishments altered her behavior.

The ever-practical Elthea often wondered at that, for if Helen would stop defying the sisters and surrounding herself with such disapproval, surely she would better enjoy the sun-dappled afternoons of Glastonbury. Neither could Elthea understand how a few moments of flirting with the stable boys could be worth the price of penance in the chapel's damp and dark confines. . . .

If Helen remained fixed in her ways, so did Morrighan and even Elthea, in her own fashion, as one gentle season after another marked time in their world. The perfumed spring ushered in the rose-scented summer, which departed at the tangy command of an apple-flavored fall. The girls grew older and taller: Morrighan became more haughty, Helen, although lazy, grew exceedingly beautiful, and Elthea became more curious, forsaking people for her fascination with the curative strength of the plants that flourished in this strange and mystical land.

The years were unremarkable years, the days and weeks patterned, until one late fall day in the eighteenth year of the girls' lives. It was then that everything changed. Before the season had passed away, and the residents of this coastal abbey were forced to wrap themselves in coarse wool cloaks to guard against winter's cold, Elthea would understand who she, Morrighan, and Helen really were, and why they had been brought to Glastonbury.

Elthea's search for herbs, mushrooms, and other healing plants frequently led her deep into the countryside. Plants grew tall in the small valley that surrounded the chalk well, but the rarest and most valuable of medicines were sometimes found tucked among large and scattered pieces of limestone on the crest of the Tor. A day whose chill foreshadowed the end of fall sent Elthea there. Though she usually avoided the Tor, she knew that guilt would hound her through the winter days of sickness if she left precious herbs there unpicked.

Hardly had she begun her search when she started at the sound of voices. She knew that politeness should turn her away, but her curiosity held her in place. Without warning, a male voice at her side startled Elthea so much that she shrieked and dropped her basket of herbs. Head down and hands covering her face, she steeled herself for whatever punishment was bestowed on eavesdroppers. But the expected blow never fell. Instead, a hand touched her arm rather gently and a second, familiar voice spoke her name.

Elthea raised her head to find Morrighan's face inches from her own. "Leave right now," Morrighan mouthed in a whisper that lost all its kindness as her hand tightened painfully on Elthea's elbow. "Go back to the abbey. You have no business here. Go back to sorting your plants."

"Hush, Morrighan," the male voice admonished. "I want her here. You are welcome, my dear."

A different pressure at her elbow directed Elthea toward a nearby stone; she folded herself onto it and looked up for the first time at this man who had the courage to contradict Morrighan.

He was clad in a simple, full-length gray robe, lightweight enough to billow in the slight breeze that also stirred the hair draping over his shoulders and blending with his short, manicured beard. The whiteness of his hair and beard, and the wrinkled face that defined his age, stirred only the vaguest of recollections in Elthea. But the lightning that flashed within the large oval ring on the man's left index finger matched an unforgotten image from that long-ago day when she and her father had met this stranger as they approached the abbey.

"Why are *you* here?" whispered Elthea.

"By my faith," replied the old man, "that's an easy question to answer. I am here—and want you here, as well—because you need to hear what I have to say."

Morrighan started to object, but the stranger raised a restraining hand. To Elthea's amazement, the raven-tressed girl closed her mouth. Then the old man turned back to Elthea, smiling at her visible anxiety. "You need not worry, my dear. My intent is not to harm you. Quite the opposite. My name is Merlin, and when you were but five years old, I brought you to this place. How quickly thirteen years has passed. How lovely you are."

Comforted by both his tone and his words, Elthea relaxed and gathered her wits. As always, her duty pressed itself to the fore of her thoughts.

"I am the healer hereabouts," she said, pointing to her spilled basket. "I am most interested in what you have to tell, but may I please have just a little time to finish my work? I was collecting the last blooms of the season and they are important. We will need them this winter to guard against coughs and agues." Elthea's speech was overly long for her, and she turned red at her own presumption.

Merlin chuckled, and in his eyes Elthea saw warmth and caring. "Yes, my dear Elthea, with your herbs and roots you *will* be able to help everyone at the abbey. I know very well how valuable these things are."

"Well," Elthea began, sensing a kindred spirit, "I can't help *everyone* because I do not have all the skills I need.

But if you have craft in the healing arts, perhaps you can teach me some of what I cannot learn by myself."

"I could," Merlin sighed, "but that is not why I am here. We need to discuss a different sort of healing."

Before Merlin could continue, eldritch screeches shattered the air. An electric jolt coursed through Elthea's body, a shock of fear at the sight of the things now swirling around Merlin. Three ghostly female forms surrounded him, hovering a foot above the ground. The bright afternoon sun highlighted the beauty of their faces, but their bodies trailed away into mist. That roiling fog flowed from them toward Elthea, lapping against the rock upon which she sat and hiding the sandaled feet of Morrighan, who now stood beside her. A curious smile twisted Morrighan's lips, a sharp contrast to the terrified look on Elthea's face.

"Merlin," one of the spirits cried, "how many times have you been told that you cannot change human beings? And still you keep at it!"

Another leaned close to Merlin. As she did so, she leveled an insubstantial finger at Morrighan. "See how her eyes narrow as she takes in all we say. Once again you underestimate her. Her appetite for knowledge and power is as voracious as it ever was."

The third spirit continued: "How can you not realize that by telling Elthea you could add to her healing skills, you have already failed? She will hear nothing else you say, so anxious will she be for the healing knowledge you might impart."

The weird women paused, awaiting Merlin's response. In the heavy silence that followed, Morrighan said boldly, "I know who you are."

"Yes," one of them answered, "you do."

Elthea's small voice pushed through the awe smothering her. "Please," she said meekly, "who are you?"

"You would be better to ask who *you* are," announced the second spirit. "Each of you girls—you, Morrighan, and Helen—carry within you the essential qualities of all women. How you behave, how you change, and how you influence the men you love—those actions determine the fate of all women. And thus we are you . . . and you are us."

"You may call us the Three Sisters," the first spectre continued. "We three and you three came into being when time began. We will be you for eternity, and we change as you change. Your progress alters the world until it reaches perfection. Then, we will no longer be needed. We are here now because Merlin is causing an imbalance. He is trying to make you change before you are ready."

"I—I don't understand," Elthea admitted.

"Simpleton," Morrighan spat, her eyes filled with loathing.

The Third Sister turned on Morrighan. "Do not assume you have advanced enough yet to see the world as it truly is, dark one. Even Merlin cannot recognize the true warp and weave of all things."

Before the mage could fashion a reply, the Three Sisters once again focused their attention on him. "Your magical powers were intended to allow the sword to be pulled from the stone, to pull humans from the Bronze Age to the Iron Age. And that was *all* you were to use them for," they chorused.

"When you unseated Time," the Third Sister continued, "and transported these three into a time between lives, you—"

"Enough!" bellowed Merlin. "Leave me, all of you."

"Even a mage as clever as you must obey the Old Faith," the First Sister persisted. "Why do you even pretend to challenge it?"

"I do not pretend," protested Merlin. "I know the strengths of the Old Faith—and its weaknesses."

Three female voices became one: "You know far less than you suspect, Merlin, because you see only what you wish to see. Even now, if you would look carefully at your prisoners, you would know that what they are here is what they will be in their next lives."

"Merlin," the Second Sister interjected, kindness clear in her voice. "You are weakening. You cannot travel backward through time without exhausting yourself. If you pit yourself against Morrighan here—even here, in your orchestrated world—you will lose. She will imprison you, as she always does. The future is beyond even you to change." She ran a ghostly hand across the mage's cheek. "It doesn't belong to you alone. Neither do its people."

Their words spent, the Three Sisters simply, silently evaporated. Merlin, too, broke apart and dissolved, as if he had never been there at all. Despite Elthea's stammered questions, Morrighan turned away without a word and headed down one of the spiral paths that led to the abbey.

Atop the Tor, the sun's last rays painted the stones red. Somehow, hours had passed since Elthea started up the hill for her herb gathering, and now she stood in the growing and silent twilight, pondering all that she had witnessed. She still understood little of what had been said. All she could acknowledge was that her orderly, calm life was gone. Merlin and the Sisters were arguing like children over her future as if it were a toy, and Elthea had seen what happened to toys when children fought over them.

On shaky legs, Elthea tiptoed from the Tor and went straight to her pallet, where, expecting a sleepless night, she instead slept heavily and dreamlessly.

The clear, sun-bright sky that greeted Elthea when she awoke the next morning made the strangeness on the Tor seem something she had imagined. *Perhaps I fell asleep after I breathed too deeply of a mushroom I was cutting*, she thought as she went about her chores. *That's happened before to careless healers. . . .*

Her attempt to apply a possible explanation to the impossible events of the previous day fell apart when she saw Morrighan in the kitchen. The raven-haired girl sat atop a stool in the room's center, ignoring the annoyed novices who were bustling around her, completing Morrighan's tasks as well as their own. She seemed not to feel the deliberate bumps of her stool or the elbows that grazed the side of her head. Though her body remained still, even statuelike, her face was a storm of emotions. A furrowed brow was banished by a calculating smile, which in turn was driven off by a scowl or a sigh.

When she spotted Elthea, Morrighan turned her awful gaze full upon her. Elthea knew right away that Morrighan was searching her face for some understanding of the previous day's events. When she was met by Elthea's usual fear and avoidance, Morrighan leapt to her feet.

"Don't you ever dare follow me again! The truth is for me alone!" the raven-haired girl screeched, in a voice that sounded frighteningly like that of the Sisters. She continued to shout threats until the novices all fled, leaving Elthea alone with the raving girl. By then, Morrighan had turned her attention to the empty air. Elthea followed Morrighan's eyes into the smoke-darkened rafters and cobwebbed corners, terrified of finding Merlin, perhaps, or the Three Sisters, lurking there.

Soon, the words Morrighan shouted made no sense to Elthea. She could not even recognize the language the girl spoke. Elthea found it all but impossible to identify this wild, irrational thing with the cold, calculating girl who had inhabited the abbey all these years. It was as if everything that had been seething beneath Morrighan's icy exterior had erupted.

Although Morrighan's behavior frightened Elthea, she refused to run away. *There must be some way to calm her down*, the healer told herself, *to soothe her rage.* But soon the old fear overwhelmed her, and Elthea found herself tongue-tied, a frightened little rabbit in the glare of Morrighan's eyes.

She fled the kitchen before she really knew what she was doing.

As she made her way across the yard to nowhere in particular, so long as it way away from Morrighan, Elthea kept her eyes on the ground. It was a habit with her, born of years of searching out healing roots and growing things. Now, though, it struck her as pathetic, yet another sign of her cowardice.

"How many strange and wonderful things have I missed? How much of what is really important in the world is found somewhere other than on the ground?" she wondered aloud, and forced herself to look up.

The abbey's chapel stood before her.

Unsteadily, she moved close to the simple little building and leaned against the door frame, allowing the cool stone to calm her trembling body. Her respite was short-lived, though. Loud whispers from the chapel's interior told of a discussion on the verge of becoming an argument.

"These creatures know nothing," a male voice said harshly. "Their advice will damn you."

"No," whimpered a girl, her sweet voice plaintive, yet full of petulance. "The women on the Tor told me to be true to myself. They told me not to obey anyone if I didn't believe that I should. They said that no one could force me to change." A sudden burst of tears turned her last words, almost spoken with real defiance, into whimpering.

Elthea recognized the voices of both speakers even before she slipped inside the chapel and hid herself within the benches.

The male voice belonged to Brother Marcus of Caerwent. He had appeared at the abbey three days past, unheralded and unconcerned at the lapse in protocol caused by his unannounced visit. Except to waddle out for meals, the bulky little cleric had rarely emerged from the chapel since his arrival. No one seemed to know the true meaning of his visit, but what Elthea had overheard convinced her that she had discovered that purpose.

"Those three . . . *things* are but devils in disguise," Brother Marcus announced sternly. "Ask God's forgiveness for listening to them."

The young woman standing before him would have been lovely in any circumstance, but seemed especially beautiful now with the emotions that flushed her cheeks and the candlelight that danced around the golden crown of her hair. This was Helen.

"I can't ask for forgiveness," she sobbed, "because I wouldn't mean it if I did." She awaited Brother Marcus' reply, but he remained stonily silent. Finally Helen stamped her foot and balled her white hands into fists. "Why must I always listen to *you*? Why won't *you* listen to *me*? Why won't you listen to what *I* want?"

The cleric's voice lowered once more, and his words took on an air of unshakeable reason. "My dear child, these women dissemble. They do not know you, nor do they oversee your soul. Only God can do that. To listen to these creatures—well, you are allowing yourself to be seduced by evil." He patted Helen's head, as if she were a small and wayward child. "And by refusing to submit to my wisdom, you are succumbing to the sin of pride, a sin that is worse when it is found in a woman."

To Elthea's surprise, Helen did not acquiesce. She did not refute any of what Brother Marcus had said, but neither did she tell the cleric what he wanted to hear, as she had done with the abbess all those times she had been caught and punished.

Brother Marcus did not take her silence well, and his voice was harsh when he spoke again. He was finished with kindness and gentleness. Full of the power of his beliefs, he bellowed, "It behooves you to mend your ways, young lady, if you care at all for your immortal soul! If you want your freedom, obey God. Then you will be free. Then you can express all of your passion, but only in doing God's work. Remember this, Helen: Beauty is as beauty does. Your name may bind you to that Helen of old, but your soul does not. It must perform its duty, no matter how small, if you are to help yourself and this fallen world fulfill God's plan."

Helen drew a sharp intake of breath. "All my life," she shrilled, "I have been told that if I want to be free all I need to do is follow God. I know God wants me to be humble and obedient, but I can't be, no matter how hard I try. Why did God make me the way I am if He doesn't like me this way?"

Elthea knew enough about poor Helen to understand. Even if it weren't obvious to anyone else, it was obvious to a healer: Helen truly believed that God didn't like her at all, and neither did anyone else. Morrighan seemed intent on proving those suspicions correct, too, always glaring at Helen and having something mean to say. Once, quite by accident, Elthea saw Morrighan corner Helen in the gardens, saunter in front of her, and then, hands on hips, say ever so scornfully, "For the life of me, I can't figure out what anyone sees in you, or why anyone would waste time on you. And for the life of me, I can't figure out why you disturb me so."

Helen's voice brought Elthea back to the chapel. "What upsets *me* the most," the beauty continued, "is that Morrighan spends so much of her time daydreaming, and nobody lectures *her*. In my opinion, daydreaming is much worse than what I've done. At least when you have a little passion, you get things done."

In the time it took Helen to voice these thoughts, Brother Marcus had turned from her and left the chapel. At the altar, Helen genuflected and then turned to follow the priest. "Now see, Helen," she sighed to herself as she hurried after Brother Marcus, "there you go again. You must stop letting your emotions guide your tongue."

The light that streamed in through the chapel's half-closed door lit the aisle and altar. The dust motes in the sunlit path stretching over Elthea, still crouched in her hiding place amongst the benches, reminded the healer of how many other things in the world she couldn't see unless the sun illuminated them. That, she decided, must be the way God works, too. It is the light of God that lets people see the hidden universe.

Fearful suddenly that God would demand more of her than she would be able to give, Elthea knelt to pray. But her devotions were cut short by a screeching voice that cut through the chapel.

"Ah, Helen," cried one of the Three Sisters. "She is, as always, such a perfect little fool. She will do exactly what she has done so many times before, will again be the creator of her own misery."

"How empty her desires," chuckled the Second Sister.

"How useless her passion," the Third Sister answered.

The three spirits gathered near the altar, but were more ghostly than they had been upon the Tor, as if their presence here were weaker somehow. Still, their voices rang with enough power to send a shiver up Elthea's spine when they shrieked in unison for Merlin.

"The good friar seems to have failed you," the first apparition mocked when the mage stepped from a concealing shadow behind the altar.

"And if *he* cannot sway Helen from her path," the second added, "what power do you think *you* have to prevent her from surrendering to her passions when she takes her place in her next life?"

"Ah, you witches," the mage uttered scornfully. "Helen may still fool you. She wants to obey, and I may yet teach her a better way to earn the approval she seeks."

"Yes," the Third Sister purred. "You have succeeded so admirably all the other times you've tried to teach her to follow her reason rather than her heart."

Merlin swept a hand through the spectral forms. They parted like mist, but quickly reformed. "Have you never been wrong, you harpies?" he hissed. "Have you never misjudged?"

The raucous laughter of the weird women echoed in the chapel. "Temper, temper, our dear Merlin," they scolded. "How can you expect to instruct poor Helen when you cannot even master yourself?"

One of the sisters, darker and more sinister than the rest, moved before the mage. "Human passions must run their course. You cannot use your powers to quell them. Uther Pendragon should have taught you that." She came closer still, her face a hairsbreadth from Merlin's. "Or can it be that *your* passions are the ones that need to be checked? Is it fury at some old and unconquered enemy that unsettles your judgment?"

Merlin turned away and stalked back into the shadows, where he vanished once more. The voices of the Three Sisters followed him into the darkness and lingered in the chapel even after the women, too, had disappeared.

"The three are as they should be and must be. You will fail, Merlin, as you always fail."

Those words haunted Elthea. She turned them over and over in her mind, trying to unlock their full significance, until the awful inevitability of it all pressed down upon her and she could barely breathe.

Even in this hour of awe and despair, when she fought to raise herself from the chapel floor, Elthea found her thoughts and her sympathies going out to Helen and to Morrighan. How they, too, must be suffering!

Elthea knew that she was the one who might ease that suffering. Whether or not it was her destiny to care so much for others mattered little. Elthea only knew that it was the right thing to do.

She stood and made her way toward the chapel door, even as the nuns began to file in for Vespers. She knew that Helen would need her most, so she set off in search of the beautiful, selfish girl, determined to find her, even if it took all night.

Dawn brought a moist wind to Glastonbury, and a sky strangely silvered. Clouds scudded over the Tor and mist flowed down the hill into the valley of the well. Tree limbs creaked ominously; animals were reluctant to be their usual morning-loud selves.

The first sliver of light woke Elthea and she was instantly alert. Her search for Helen had been fruitless and she had finally stationed herself atop the Tor on what she now considered *her* stone seat. But exhaustion soon overwhelmed her, and she'd drifted off to sleep certain that whatever was going to happen next would happen on the Tor. Now, as she looked about her on that most magical of hillsides, she saw that she had been correct.

Merlin and the Three Sisters were arrayed in a silent semicircle, the weird women floating, Merlin seated atop a large piece of limestone. The mage had his head bowed. Before them, as if she were granting them an audience, stood Morrighan, regal and poised. No one looked at Elthea, or reacted when she sat up and stretched her cold-numbed limbs.

"I have decided," Morrighan announced as she turned toward the Three Sisters. "Now is the time for you to tell me everything. I *will* know all. No, Merlin," she ordered even as he opened his mouth to interrupt, "I do not want to hear from you. I do not trust you."

Morrighan paused, prepared for objections. When they didn't come, she went on. "I will tell you what *I* know. I have seen you watching me in this sacred place since I was a child, and I have had dreams of other times and places. I have had visions and gloried in what I witnessed: the clashing of swords, heartfelt oaths of allegiance, a bright kingdom built and ruined. I heard the names *Arthur* and *Lancelot* echoing throughout a land filled with enchantment. Merlin appeared to me and offered an explanation of these dreams, but it was incomplete, an effort to control, not educate me. Never once did he help me to understand what everything meant. *That* I figured out by myself."

Morrighan's hands were fists held tightly against her thighs. Her cheeks burned with color, and her eyes flamed defiance. Chin thrust high, she challenged Merlin and the sisters with a look that dared them to tell her she was wrong. The spectral women merely smiled. When Merlin finally met her gaze, his eyes were sorrowful and far away.

Elthea understood that for many people like Merlin and Morrighan, submission meant weakness. She was glad that she wasn't like those two, but Merlin's sadness tugged at her all the same.

If Morrighan felt any sympathy for Merlin, she did not show it. Her smile was cruel as she continued to reveal all that she had pieced together.

"I will have a place in the history of this bright kingdom," she said. "I will be beautiful and magical. I will be powerful and seductive." Morrighan glanced at Elthea and sneered, "She will have her role, as will that simpering Helen. And I know now that we will all be true to those roles, true to our-selves. . . ."

Merlin groaned as if that last were a sword stroke. At his pain, Morrighan smiled all the more broadly.

"Oh, mage, you have no reason to groan!" the Three Sisters criticized. "Do you not see that Arthur and his Round Table did not build the most glorious, lasting aspects of Camelot by themselves? Did not Elaine help her son to achieve the most holy of quests? Did not Guinevere stir men to glory and honor, and take it upon herself to spend her life in prayer for the sad part she played with Lancelot in the kingdom's undoing?"

"And if one other of Camelot's women took a darker path," Morrighan said coldly, "it was the passions of the men that set her upon it—their broken vows and over-whelming pride. If you wonder at my hatred of Arthur's kingdom, look to his begetting, to your own part in foster-ing and concealing his father's lust for my mother."

Merlin nodded grimly. "I will not deny the truth of your observations. Human passions—and not just those of women alone—toppled Camelot and killed King Arthur. Lust, greed, and pride. Yours, to be sure, and perhaps my own. Would Camelot have failed even had I succeeded in turning you three from your fates?" He sighed. "Perhaps."

Finally the mage stood and extended a hand to Morrighan. "You will always be clever and intelligent. Once, more clever than I," Merlin said gently. "You have lived before and will live again. The Lady of the Lake and the sword Excaliber tell us that people need to cleanse and renew until they become paragons of virtue and chivalry. Only then will they deserve a world that is eternal." When the dark-haired girl slapped at his outstretched hand, Merlin turned away and said sadly, "I fear that we have a long way to go."

"Perhaps not as long as we had a mere moment ago," the First Sister whispered, not unkindly, coming close to the mage, "now that you understand the truth of what we have tried to tell you all these lifetimes."

For Elthea, time had stopped with the uttering of two

names: *Elaine* and *Lancelot*. Their familiarity thrilled her and wounded her. She was paralyzed by a torrent of memories that belonged somehow both to her and to someone else—tenderness and betrayal, triumph and defeat, glory and infamy—until a trembling hand clutched her shoulder and shook her.

Helen looked tousled in the early morning light, but still beautiful. "Brother Marcus tried to lock me in the chapel, but I escaped," she said. Though frightened, the girl fairly glowed with an inner strength that up until now had been directed only toward her whims and fancies. "I escaped because I wanted to be here," she concluded as she took a seat next to Elthea. "Did I do right?"

"For once," Morrighan said.

"You did right," Merlin noted, as if Morrighan had not spoken. "For this place out of time must come to an end, and you must be allowed to become the women you will be when next you are born into the world."

The mage paused for a moment. "Sisters, you have not interrupted me. Am I telling true? Am I fair?"

"Yes, Merlin," they replied. Their bodies had grown faint, seemed wispy and far away, but their words were sharp and clear. "But you must tell them the cost. Tell them the price they will pay until they overcome their weaknesses and correct their misdeeds."

And so Merlin did. He gave them the last words they would hear before they were hurled into the vortex to start again. He went on as shadows began to darken all of Glastonbury, a village already in mourning for the three women whose disappearance that autumn day would become the stuff of legends.

"Time is a continuum," the old sorcerer began. "It has no beginning and no end. Some of us can travel the continuum and witness the weaving of the pattern of life. Others are a more integral part of that pattern. Our place grants us power. Some can read men's destinies, see into the future, and cast powerful spells. But that power has a price."

With a sweep of his hand, Merlin took in all three of the weird women, even now the merest of shadows on the hilltop. "For the Three Sisters and me, the price of our vantage and the knowledge gained there is to watch the birth and death of you and countless others, time and time again. Ours is an eternity of loss.

"For you three," Merlin concluded, "it's different. For the power of your passion and your humanity, the price is always death."

At the word *death* the sky split open and pressed down on Merlin and the three girls, whose startled eyes reflected glimpses of the lives they had already lived and those they were yet to live. Overhead, suns rose and set with a speed that was blinding. The castle that would be Camelot came together brick by brick and then fell into ruins. Avalon's lake filled and evaporated into marshland. A silver chalice appeared, sparkled in a momentary sunbeam, and vanished. As a bloody, armored hand flung a sword end over end toward a lake, the hand transfigured into a slender ivory one that rose from the water to receive it. The faces of two knights spiraled around the three women, catching them for a moment in a macabre and seductive dance. Male voices caressed with mouths that did not open.

"Lancelot," breathed Elthea and Helen as one.

"Arthur, my darling brother," hissed Morrighan.

Elthea and Helen had to cling to each other in the face of the tempest or they would never have remained upright; Morrighan raised her arms to embrace the sky and the chaos. Thunder and lightening erupted, engulfing the figures on the Tor. Sounds, like those made when the earth awoke for the first time, roared as the continuum slipped another notch and fought for purchase in a new time. The light lost its dominion in a world that slid from color to black and white and then, finally, to utter darkness.

Slowly, a portal opened in the blackness, and in it appeared the promontory of a far off and barren expanse: the land of King Pelles. As the scene came into focus, a figure was seen moving into it. The figure was Elthea—or, rather, Elthea as she would be in her new lifetime. She halted, her eyes captured by the sea, until a voice interrupted her reverie.

"Elaine, my dear, come please. Your father awaits you. He is once again in pain and needs your attention."

"Of course, Nurse. I will come right away. It's just that I feel so . . . strange, as if something or someone is coming for me. The wind touching my face brings with it names that I both know and do not know. Nurse," Elaine asked, "do you know the name *Galahad*? I like that name very much, but it makes me sad."

"Elaine, my dear, I don't know what to make of you sometimes. Last week you made your father attest three times to the presence of the Grail. Who did you think could find it, so carefully hidden as it is? Come now. If I listen to you any longer, I will be afraid to sleep tonight."

As the first portal closed, another opened, bringing with it the petulant sound of a young girl's haughty whine. Replacing the barren promontory of King Pelles' land was a lush garden of flowers and apple trees. Seated on a stone bench was the girl who had been Helen, again a defiant child with a beauty that would last her through her long, tumultuous life.

"I will stay here as long as I wish," she stated imperiously.

"Your father demands your presence, Guinevere, and you will come *now*," Leodegrance's seneschal commanded. "You do not wish to incur his wrath."

"He can never stay angry at me. I'm too pretty," she sighed, secure in her knowledge, even at the age of ten, of where her strength lay.

"I don't see pretty," retorted Lionel. "I see only a most unpleasant and spoiled girl."

"You don't mean that. I know you will do anything I ask you to do. Anyway, I was just teasing you. And practicing."

When Lionel did not reply, she stamped her foot. "Well," she demanded, "aren't you going to ask me what I'm practicing for?"

"No," the seneschal flung back. "I am *not* going to ask you. You've been practicing for weeks now on everything from me to these apple trees! I am well aware what you're up to. You need to learn that not every man in your father's realm will be enchanted enough by your beauty to obey your every command. Your first proof will be me. Go to your father. Now!"

As the roaring began anew, this portal closed, and the warm breeze of a gentle spring became the biting wind of a cold winter. Time re-calibrated itself; the familiar world returned. The earth had shaken off Merlin's shackles and returned once more to its endless odyssey.

In a dank and dark room lay a raven-tressed child. She was bleary-eyed and shivering on the cold hearth, but refused to submit to sleep or even accept a blanket from the strange man who stood by her mother's bed. "He frightens me, Mother," she repeated in her small, child's voice.

"Go to sleep," the man snapped, but the girl ignored him, tugged again at her mother's hand and began to cry hot, calculating tears.

"Morgana," Igraine soothed. "Can you not see that this is your father, Gorloise, come from battle, come from defeating Uther Pendragon? The sounds of the wounded in the courtyard and the cries of widows and fatherless children have given you a nightmare. That is all. You are safe here with me and your father."

The little girl still did not believe her mother. The gore-stained man looming over her mother was not her father. But that was not the only source of her fear. From the shadowy corners of the room she heard voices, little more than a susurrus, and they said things that confused and terrified her.

"Merlin," the shadows whispered, "we see your work before us and feel you hovering in the cold mist of the night air. Time has begun to unwind again. You may play the part assigned to you, but no more than that. This time, let it be. Let *them* be."

Morgana blinked away her tears, reminding herself to be strong. It was then that she saw him—a robed figure standing at the shoulder of the man masquerading as her father. He must be invisible to her mother somehow. Magic, Morgana decided. That would explain why he shimmered like the tapers did when she scrunched her eyes really tight.

She listened carefully as the robed man turned to the shadowy corner from which the voices had spoken. "Ah, sisters," he countered. "Even you do not comprehend how right you are. It has begun again . . . all of it."

TEA AND COMPANY

Valerie Frankel

"Niniane!"

Niniane stirred on her seat beside the kitchen fire's hot embers. She had few visitors. Actually, that was an over-statement. She had one visitor, and he'd only journeyed here once before. Now was the second time.

"I'll be right there," she said, and hurried about, plug-ging gaps in the floor and walls where the water had seeped through again. Living in a mysterious grotto had some serious disadvantages, the main one being flooding. The small cave was normally neat and tidy, all the simple yet cozy furniture scrubbed as clean as the stone floor. Yet when Niniane went into her trances, the water struggled against her spells, flooding the land above and her under-water chambers below. Normally she didn't mind, but hav-ing a guest changed everything. Niniane grimaced at the mildewed shelf and puddles on the floor. What would he think?

Where did the time go, after all? One moment she was gazing into her fire (enchanted to keep from going out whenever it flooded) and the next, it looked as if no one had mopped for weeks. Or bailed. Whatever. She put the kettle on for tea, then hurried into the next chamber and scram-bled to build up the fire. The waterlogged living room mostly under control, Niniane opened the door for her guest.

He looked so thin! His beard was still dark but it had grown scraggly in the past few years. The shadows of his robe bore tears and snags from the long journey, and he limped slightly as he came in.

"This is an expected honor," she said as he slumped into her company armchair. The poor man looked as though he'd been trying to manage the entire kingdom singlehandedly. Of course, he had been.

Niniane pushed her usual wicker chair back from the fire. She didn't care for its heat as he did. The woven seat had grown soft with mildew and would need replacing in a few months. That was the biggest problem with living so far from civilization—no one to help keep the place tidy. Not to mention the dratted floods. No one had mentioned this part when she'd become Lady of the Lake.

He settled into his chair with a sigh, staring into the fire as if her incense for trancing, long dissipated now, still perfumed the room. "It's good to see you again, Niniane. Strange to say I've missed you when we've only met the one time, but . . ."

"I know. You see me often in your dreams, just as I see you. We're each other's futures, Merlin, and that binds us together, even if we're not aware of it yet." She rested her hand on one of the greenish doilies that graced her chair arms. They were not mildewed, but she had colored them that way so they wouldn't show deterioration as strongly. It seemed to work. Niniane decorated her rooms mainly in shades of green, as the cool colors helped her relax. She knew Merlin preferred purple and red, colors of the world above. Well, if he could change his lifestyle, so could she.

"So you know why I've come." It wasn't a question.

"Of course I do. And you know what I'll say," Niniane replied.

"Then I make the counteroffer."

"Which I decline."

"You won't change your mind?" Merlin's voice was resigned rather than pleading. He clearly knew what she'd say, his own arguments, and everything she could reply. And Niniane knew as well; that was the entire point.

"I'm sorry, Merlin, but you know my price. I can't spend my entire life alone in this swamp, making love philters for Druids and weaving pretty embroidery for your heroes. I've made you a masterpiece, and you owe me for that."

"It's finished?" For the first time, Merlin sounded surprised.

"Of course. I knew you'd want it. And as soon as possible. Tea?"

"Yes, yes, of course you understood. You probably even know I'd like tea."

"I suppose so." Hot water bubbled at the back of the kitchen fire. She added the leaves slowly. The poor man needed a few minutes away from the problems of the world.

At last, Niniane poured two cups of tea, dosing Merlin's with plenty of honey before carrying them back. She had never asked him his tea preferences before, but images of drinking tea with him thousands of times in the future crowded into her head.

He took it without comment and drank a long draught. For a few moments, he just stared into the fire. Then, low and soft: "He needs me."

"He'll manage. You know everyone has to make their own mistakes someday."

"But he's already met her. Gwinevere, I mean. Whenever I look at her, I see all that'll take place. The wars, the deaths, the misunderstandings. . . ."

"It's hard seeing the future and being helpless to change it," Niniane said. "That's why I fled here. The Druids still come, sometimes, but at least I don't have people asking me daily to dream up visions for them. Although, the nuns asking for charity still find me somehow."

"Yes. He's very good about that, you know. Doesn't want prophecies of the future at all. Can't say I blame him, come to that. And he tries to take my advice. But I know it'll all happen, just the same."

"It's so hard. We both have ultimate power, and yet we're powerless."

"Exactly." Merlin drained his cup and held it out hopefully for more.

Niniane filled it up and handed it back. "Vanilla cookies? They're freshly baked." Vanilla wouldn't exist in Britain for close to a thousand years, but since she could see the future, there was no need to stint herself.

She went to fetch them, arranging the cookies on her last clean plate. Goodness, she would have to keep an eye on her prophetic trances or one day she would wake up to find her home a bog. If only her over-cleanly mother could see her now. It would certainly help to have a live companion, instead of just the dreams.

His quiet voice greeted her as she returned. "Could I see it now?"

"The scabbard?"

He nodded, and she hurried off. The scabbard lay in a locked chest, the only truly watertight one she owned.

Niniane kept it hidden in the back of the house, under protective wards and spells. She opened the chest, pushing aside her stores of elixir of life and vanilla beans to reach the bottom, where the scabbard lay hidden. Kings would beg for that sort of gift, and give their entire fortunes to possess it, but that wasn't why she valued the scabbard, or why she'd labored for so many months to make it perfect. It was her key to companionship.

Niniane returned and offered the scabbard to Merlin. She'd woven it from pure gold thread, enchanted to be light as several feathers. (Niniane couldn't quite push it down to one feather; magic always had limits.) Crystals and rubies were scattered up and down its length, sparkling in the room's shadowed light. The actual magic sprang from the runes in eleven magical languages, commanding enemy weapons not to touch the bearer's flesh. There were other runes, for luck, for strength and skill. Niniane had a flair for such things, although she rarely had such fine materials to work with. Lead could be turned to gold, but it was a long, time-intensive project.

"It's beautiful," Merlin said. "As I knew it would be. You'll come to him, later?"

"Yes. And after that, you will return here. Forever."

"I need time. To teach him and guide him."

"And I need—" Niniane stopped herself. There was an easier way to argue. "Don't we agree on a year?"

"I suppose." Merlin turned toward the door, then stopped himself and walked back to her. "Tell me, Niniane, if we both knew everything we would do, why did I come here at all?"

"To see the scabbard?"

"You would've brought it soon enough."

That was true; she wasn't about to let Merlin dodge his fate. "The tea?" she asked. "The companionship?"

"Perhaps." He smiled at her. "They were both quite good."

Niniane felt a ray of sunlight brush over her cool skin at his gaze. It was odd, she knew, that they had fallen in love in reverse, caring for each other because of their future actions, rather than their past. She had seen him so little, yet understood everything, had endless memories of their life together as it would unfold in the future.

"Yes," she said, dragging herself back to the moment. Merlin was waiting, after all. "Bring your pupil to me and I'll give him the gifts."

"I know you will." And he left.

That night, as Niniane slept, the scene played out behind her eyelids. Months from now, Merlin stood beside the lake, his protégé at his side. The young man held his sword up to catch the sunset's light, and swished it through the air. Niniane knew Excalibur drew with the smoothness of an arrow in flight, and had a balance not to be found in the future kingdom that Arthur would build.

"Which do you prefer?" Merlin's weary voice asked. The past year grew steadily harder for him, she knew, as he tried to put all his affairs in order. Soon he, like the sun, would slip below the lake. "The sword or the scabbard?"

"The sword, of course," Arthur responded. The boy couldn't know that it was a trick question, didn't realize its price or what sacrifices would be made. "A scabbard is useless without a sword, however pretty."

"Not this one," Merlin said. "Keep it with you always. For this scabbard is magical, and will protect you from injury while it's buckled to your sword belt. Guard it well." Merlin turned away and only Niniane heard his final words: "You little know what it has cost me."

This was true enough. Niniane had kept Excalibur until the young king could claim its powers, but the scabbard she had made herself, as a favor to Merlin. A gift and bargaining tool together. Soon Merlin would come to her, keep her company and care for the house while she tranced, as she would do for him. Niniane would make sure he took some time for himself, away from the problems of the world, until they would both be needed again.

That day would come soon enough.

A Spear in the Night
Keith Taylor

Myrddin, the first Archdruid of Britain in four hundred years, had imperative business in the Summer Country. There, around Camlodd hill-fort, King Erbin bred the big war-chargers that were the future of Britain. It was past time for Myrddin to visit them again and see with his eyes how they did. Besides, his prophetic powers had told him that he would meet a murderer at Camlodd.

He had also foreseen a meeting with a boy who had a gift for handling horses. This boy would help him find the murderer. Without him, the business would have few chances of success. Thus Myrddin kept a sharp eye out for such a boy throughout his journey.

He traveled with glamour for a disguise. Those he met saw a lean, dark, narrow-boned man who carried a harp and wore a patched tunic. The shadow he cast was still his own, and so he went by night or in cloudy weather as much as possible.

Near Camlodd, he found shelter and concealment in a small patch of oakwood. He watched the green meadows where King Erbin's horse-herds grazed. Conspicuous among them was one red stallion with a white mane and tail, master of all his rivals, a fierce fighter. He reminded Myrddin a good deal of Uther Pendragon, dead now by stealthy poison.

Britain had lapsed into chaos without him. The island needed a king again—a *true* sacred king, not a half-Roman who bore the title Pendragon only by common acclaim. Even though Uther's courage and prowess had saved much, in his day, there was more to achieve. Almost impossibly more. . . .

While Myrddin watched, a boy appeared. He wore a calfskin tunic that had seen better days. Tall and thin, with a shock of dirty brown hair and muck of the byre on his feet, he would have been eight or nine. He fixed his gaze on the red horse and drew nearer, one smooth step at a time.

Men were afraid to approach that brute. Greatly as his coloring appealed to a warrior's desire for show, and eager as many were to ride him, none had managed it. Four had been almost slain. Although he sired strong colts, the horse-breeders glumly spoke of having no recourse but gelding him.

Now, as the boy approached, the horse tossed his head high. Yet the boy stood talking softly, holding out his arm with something whitish in his hand—a piece of honeycomb, or an oatmeal cake. The stallion stamped, blew, and then trotted forward. Its lips pulled back from teeth that could have shorn the boy's arm like a flax-stalk. Its tongue, thrusting out, took the morsel. The boy gave its nose a pat and stroked the white mane.

The stallion accepted his caress.

Myrddin seldom felt astonished. Chosen for sacrifice while a boy no older than this one, spared that fate, now a lord of prophecy and intimate of Britain's last dragons, he had seen—perhaps not everything, but most things. Still, this sight raised his brows.

Yes, this boy was the one. Clearly it could not be the first time he had faced the stallion. Reaching into his budget, he produced a second treat. The horse took it neatly from his outstretched palm, again. Once more the boy reached up to stroke his mane.

Then, Myrddin saw him grip the mane for purchase and leap astride the red back. A good—no, an excellent standing leap for a boy his age, but one that courted death. Courted it? Kissed and bedded it!

One casual buck and the idiot was rolling across the grass. Myrddin rushed from the wood, whirling his short cloak around his head. The stallion charged him. Myrddin allowed it to come closer—closer to him, and thus farther from the gasping boy—before stopping it in its tracks. This he did simply enough. After casting his cloak so that it tangled around the horse's head, he ran to seize the youngster. Before the stallion could see again, they were back within the oakwood.

"Light of the Sun!" he swore, in his character as an itinerant bard. "You must have fed that red devil before, to do

it and live today! Do not tell me you were never warned
away from the king's horse-runs, boy."

"I've been commanded to keep off," the youngster said
defiantly. "Beaten for not listening, too."

"Then you need a sterner thrashing," Myrddin told him,
and after a moment added, "or to be made a horse-boy for
your persistence. D'you wish it? To attend the horses at
Camlodd, would you shovel their dung?"

The boy nodded vigorously. "Any amount!"

"Then come with me. I am on my way there. I'll speak
for you."

Wordlessly, the youngster fell into step with Myrddin,
glancing at him from time to time, sidelong. The Archdruid
knew what the boy saw: a shabby, nondescript bard from
one of the West Country's ancient tribes. A bard, nevertheless, and as such sure of a welcome anywhere. Hope
grew in the boy's face.

They went on toward the hill-fort. The boy continued to
glance at Myrddin, but as they walked, he happened to look
at the bard's shadow on the ground, and his gaze leapt
back to Myrddin's face, startled. The shadow was that of a
huge, burly man.

The more often he looked, the more discrepancies he
saw. The bard's shadow, besides being large, seemed to
have a great beard and shaggy mane of hair. The boy's
trepidation grew. His thoughts were so intense that the
Archdruid almost heard them, but he neither ran away nor
blurted out questions. Myrddin approved his sense and
nerve; yes, he had promise.

Camlodd drew nearer.

The hill-fort was old. Taken and destroyed long ago by
the legions, abandoned, occupied again, then abandoned
once more, its earthen ramparts remained, four of them,
ring within ring on the hilltop. Grass grew long and thick
over them. The precious horse-herds were driven up there
each night for safety from raiders. Every spirited prince in
Britain schemed to lift them, despite King Erbin's promise
that he would not regard it as a challenge in sport, but as
war in red earnest.

Two warriors rode down to question the pair. One was

bald, with a cheerful face and brawny arms, while the other owned black hair and striking good looks. Myrddin knew them both, though because of the glamour that disguised him they did not recognize him.

"A harper!" the handsome one enthused. "You are welcome, but where did you find this pestiferous boy? Among the horses again?"

"Indeed." Myrddin gave a spurious name and origin for himself. "I am seeking a place in King Erbin's household."

"The king doesn't dwell here," the bald man said bluntly. "His hall's to the south. Surely you didn't suppose he lodges in this forgotten circle of grass? D'you see anything but horse-yards and a barn?"

"I have the prophetic gift, Rheidwyn Longarm. I see the colts of these horses carrying men in helms and mail shirts against the Saxons. I see the banner of the Dragon in the wind. I see this 'forgotten circle of grass' topped with tall ramparts. And this will be before twenty years pass. As for today—King Erbin hunts yonder, today." Myrddin pointed eastward, at the Forest Savage's huge dark expanse. "His hunt will go well. When it is finished, he will pass this way. He will arrive before the sun sets."

The warriors did not reply at once, impressed by the ring of certainty in Myrddin's voice; but they did not know he was Myrddin, and every bard in Britain made big claims of prophetic power.

"You know more than we," the handsome one said, "if you know that."

"I know it, Casnar ap Gilvaith."

"You call us by name? Well, that doesn't mean prophetic sight. Our names and appearances are known to a good many. Our lineage, nurture, and deeds, too." Casnar indicated the cowherd's boy. "It might mean something if you knew *his* name."

"His name," Myrddin said calmly, "is Tor."

The boy's head jerked around. He said incredulously, "I never told him! Sirs!"

"Make him a horse-boy," Myrddin said. "Teach him to ride, and train him to arms. It's in my mind that he will repay the trouble. But perhaps I will read his future to discern more."

"I'd wash him first," Rheidwyn said, grinning. "Else you'll discern nothing through the dirt."

Finding a quiet corner of the enclosed hilltop was easy; it covered some eighteen acres. Myrddin shared his food with the boy and tuned his harp, speaking little. Tor kept quiet and watched him gravely. Myrddin approved the lack of babble, but observed that his companion chewed tensely. His gaze kept wandering to Myrddin's shadow. A pulse twitched fast at the base of his throat.

At last Tor said, "How did you know my name?"

"As I knew Rheidwyn's and Casnar's. You heard me tell them I am foresighted."

"Yes." Tor swallowed. "You said you would read my future."

"Do you wish to know it? The news may be bad."

"When the new king comes, will I ride in his band? That's what I would know! Tell me nothing else."

"Which new king?"

Tor shook his head. "Don't joke with me. The one you spoke of, sir. The new king of all Britain. He that'll carry the banner of the Dragon again! Uther Pendragon's son. Myrddin has taken him away for safety and is rearing him in secret. Everybody knows that."

"Do they, now?" Myrddin said. "Will you accept advice from me? Be wary of believing what everybody knows."

"But this *must* be true! Wasn't the great Uther poisoned? King Erbin was his trusty friend, and he's breeding the big war-horses that made the Pendragon's knights so strong in battle, so that his son will have a well-mounted band when he appears. They say that—"

"Yes. They say much." Myrddin wiped his birchwood bowl with earth and a handful of grass. "Well, then. I'll answer the question that means so much to you. Sit there. Hold the bowl in both hands, between your knees, so."

Myrddin filled the bowl with clear water. Tor not only sat still, he scarcely breathed. Myrddin stared into the water and beyond it for many long moments.

"You will become a horse-boy here," he said at length. "Do well, and King Erbin will have you taught to ride and use arms. Those warriors—Casnar and Rheidwyn—will be among your teachers. They are good men. Thereafter I see many paths you may take, branching widely. The way to becoming a knight remains marked and clear, always, more than any other. If you are determined, you will achieve it."

"If?" Tor seemed disappointed. "Isn't it certain?"

Myrddin said flatly, "Nothing is fated, and nothing is certain. I have seen you with a helm and shield, riding a horse of the same color as the red one today—a grandson of his, and fiery like him. You ride behind the red dragon banner, even as you desire. But neither idle wishing nor half a heart will take you there."

Tor's eyes glittered with longing, and then he looked crestfallen. "How can it be? I'm a cowherd's son."

Myrddin knew otherwise. He had seen Tor's certain past as well as his possible futures. The cowherd this boy called his father was not. He had been fathered, instead, by a king, taking a quick lusty tumble in a hayfield. King Pellinore, now dead in battle against the Saxons.

Yes, but it would not help the boy to know that, yet.

"Barbarians and cowherds' sons became generals of Rome," Myrddin said. "Even its emperors. You heard me predict that King Erbin will arrive by nightfall. Will you believe me if he does?"

Tor nodded eagerly.

He desired to believe. He would do whatever Myrddin asked, which was good, because the Archdruid needed him.

Somehow the boy was the key to finding a murderer at Camlodd. No common murderer, either, but the slayer, by poison, of Uther Pendragon.

"He was right!" Casnar exclaimed. "That down-at-heel bard foretold aright! It's a royal hunting party, Rheidwyn."

Even from the crest of Camlodd hill, there could be no mistake. A well-mounted group of sixty riders could be nothing but royal. Bright cloaks and blowing horns made their rank more certain still. Word passed around the hill-top like a fire in grass, and men stared at the stranger bard with new interest, not a few of them stark amazed.

Myrddin had not been looking eastward. Nor did he now. He continued gazing north, at the high, mysterious place known as the Island of Apples—Ynys Afallon—blue within the glassy meres of the marshland surrounding it.

Tor had grown up within sight of that place. He believed

without question that it led to the Otherworld, where King Gwyn ap Nudd and Queen Morgan reigned, always young in a realm where fruit and crops neither failed nor withered. If Tor's new acquaintance looked at it so fixedly, maybe it was because he belonged there.

Myrddin turned his gaze away from the island and considered the horse-herds being driven to Camlodd for the night. Many in Britain said, believing it, that these were otherworldly horses themselves, a faerie breed that carried their riders to certain triumph. Of course, they were not. Myrddin knew the difference from his own experience. Camlodd's horses were foreign chargers, large, strong, and enduring, the kind ridden by Visigothic heavy lancers. During Uther Pendragon's reign they had been brought up from Spain by his friend King Leodegrance, the famous shipman. Leodegrance and Erbin had been the only kings Uther trusted—except, at one time, Gorlois, and Gorlois had turned against him, a rival for the high kingship of Britain.

He had died for it.

The high kingship, ancient and holy as British earth itself, formed no part of Roman concepts. These were passing like cloud. Scarcely a Roman town supported anything but a shrunken, desolate populace. Many had long been wholly deserted. Chieftains from the west and north had come with their war-bands to make themselves kings of the fallen *civitates*, and when fighting was done against the Saxon invaders, they wielded the swords. Nobody dreamed of the legions returning to set Britain in order—not any longer. Those who dreamed and yearned, yearned for a Pendragon, a High King. The ancient magics stirred in response.

Uther had never truly understood. He'd been more Roman than anything else. The people had called him Pendragon for his fierce defense of their realm. When he married Ygerna, who was royal in her own right with the blood of the ancient goddess-queens, he might have become Pendragon in truth. But someone had killed him with a strange, enchanted poison.

Myrddin and Ygerna had conferred, and whisked her infant son into hiding, swiftly. The boy was now three years old. And, despite their caution, someone had discovered the child's place of safekeeping, and tried to destroy him with the same poison that had consumed Uther. Myrddin had forestalled the attempt. Someone had underestimated the old man, to hope the same method could be used with success to murder *two* of his protégés. Nevertheless, Myrddin recognized that the murderer must be subtle and cunning, to have discovered where young Arthur had been concealed.

And now, the time had come to stop him.

Britain must, *must* have a High King again, with confirmation and sacring by the Archdruid. Arthur, no other boy-child, carried the blood of Uther and Ygerna. There was certainly no other that Erbin and Leodegrance would support, and one of them had in his keeping the war-horses that meant victory, while the other possessed the great ancient Table of Kingship. Without these, no man could be Pendragon, and no lord but a Pendragon could unite Britain sufficiently to subdue the Saxons. Without a Pendragon, there soon would be no Britain.

Broodingly, Myrddin looked at the riders as they approached the hill. He intended to deal with Uther's assassin in a way that no man who witnessed it would forget. And none, with that lesson in mind, would make another attempt on Arthur's life.

King Erbin's hunting party rode over the earthen causeway, a stained, muddy, cheerful band. Their dogs ran footsore, and the gralloched bodies of stags were tied across two horses' withers. King Erbin led them, a small, dark, muscular man with a black beard and abrupt, assured movements.

Six trusted nobles rode with him, including his two brothers. Myrddin knew well that he needed their presence. Some deaths that occurred hunting did not come by mischance. Erbin's chief guests had kinsmen and close companions beside them also.

"This is more than a hunt," Myrddin told the boy. "King Erbin has all the greatest Midlands kings with him. Do you know them?"

"I know that one," Tor said, staring. "I mean, I know who he must be. With the flaming red hair and the tattoos on his arms and legs, he'd be King Erp of Hamo. His mother is Pictish, they say."

"They say the truth," Myrddin agreed. "Erp rules the southern coast and the Isle of Vectis. What of that one—in the red and green cloak that would suit a younger man?"

"Is he a king, too?"

Tor's tone was dubious. The man in question, powerfully built, with a grim, heavy, debauched face, looked like an unpleasant ruler. In fact he was not much worse than most. Although no woman, including nuns, was safe from him, and he dispensed stake and noose too freely, he kept his realm safe from outsiders.

Myrddin nodded. "That's Ulthin of Calleva. He rules the ancient lands of the Atrebates. Behind him on that swift black horse is King Llygad of Highcross."

Gray-eyed and watchful, his sandy hair thinning, Llygad still enjoyed finer looks than Ulthin, and had less that was brutal or scandalous known against him. In his boyhood, his own brothers had warred against him to seize the kingdom of Highcross. He had won. The experience had not left him a trusting man.

Tor said with interest, "The old man would be King Beroticus, wouldn't he? I've heard of him, too. They say that for all his white hair, he can ride and fight with any of the younger men."

"You keep your ears open and hear a good deal," Myddin said. "Your eyes, too. You said before that you've heard stories about the young son of Uther?"

Tor's eyes shone. "Yes, sir! It's said—oh, there are a hundred yarns. But everybody knows he is alive, and great Myrddin is raising him. They say he will be the Pendragon."

"As he will." Myrddin's voice deepened. "He will break the Saxon advance as no other could do. Women will gather driftwood on the beaches in safety. Crops will flourish in his reign. There will not have been a king like him since Lud. He will never be forgotten, nor the knights of his war-band. A thousand years from now, there will be songs and stories about them."

Tor was looking as though he had seen a god. "Did you mean it when you said I could be one?"

"I saw it plainly, and my sight does not err. Only—someone tried to poison that infant boy this past month, Tor."

"*Poison* him?" Tor's reactions hid nothing. The blackest blasphemy could not have appalled him as did that news.

"Truly. The plot failed, but the one who ordered it will try again if he is not caught. My prophetic sight tells me he is here at Camlodd now, and can only be a king with the desire to become Pendragon himself—or to see his son as Pendragon. It tells me no more."

Tor lowered his voice to a whisper. "One of those four?"

"One of those four." Myrddin looked into the boy's eyes. "Will you help me to find which one?"

"Yes! But how can I do that?"

"Help care for their horses. Watch, listen, hear all you can, but let nobody see that you are spying. Is that within your power?"

A grin flashed white on Tor's dirty face, a cocky, mischievous grin.

"Is it? Sir! I had to get away from my mother unseen each time I visited the king's horse-runs—and she sees everything! Then I had to dodge the king's riders to throw a leg over any horse's back! Of course I can do it."

Myrddin did not smile in return, but he answered, "So I rather thought. Remember, though, these men will lose their lives if found out. They will not treat you kindly if they guess what you are doing. Tread with care."

"I will. But then—why, here in Camlodd, should they be silly enough to say anything worth hearing?"

"Because I mean to disconcert them. Before the night is over, someone will not only say, but perhaps *do*, a thing that will betray him. Try to be there when he does."

"I will, sir." Tor swallowed, looking at the thin, dark bard with the huge shadow looming behind him. "I think that I might be able now to guess your name."

"You appear clever enough. But whatever name you are thinking, do not utter it. Now vanish away! I will make it right for you to help with the hunt-horses."

Men soon informed King Erbin of the strange bard's prediction. He became interested, and sent for him. Either the fellow had true prophetic powers, or knew too much about his movements by other means. And Erbin knew only one man in Britain with reliable powers of prophecy.

Speaking with Myrddin face to face, the king soon realized who he was, though he never betrayed it. When Myrddin mentioned in passing that Tor would make a good horse-boy, the king as casually confirmed it, knowing there was reason. Erbin knew that Myrddin's reasons were invariably both deep and excellent.

Tor found enough to do. He aided in rubbing down the royal horses. He listened with both ears to all the talk from the four kings' attendants, as Myrddin had bidden, and worked hard to remember what might be useful. Not much, as it turned out. He had rightly supposed that no one with guilty secrets would mention them in Camlodd.

Tor valued the opportunity to make friends with the kings' various horses, however. They were fine beasts, and he had a rare knack. By nightfall they were settled in the hill-fort's rough stables. The breeding herds of the Summer Country had also been penned and, in some cases, hobbled.

As meat roasted over cookfires, Tor helped carry ale around. He surreptitiously watched the kings. Ulthin was his own choice for villainy. Most of what he had heard about the man was bad, and his looks matched it. Beroticus . . . men said he was crafty, but they also said he was generous and good with horses, the latter a strong recommendation to Tor's mind. Llygad by repute honeyed his most lethal intentions with suave manners. Erp, half Pictish, was thereby half savage, and his witch-mother knew all about poisons. Tor placed Erp and Llygad as equal second choices.

They all looked like men with easy hearts in the firelight, though. Ulthin roared with laughter at some joke. Llygad, smiling, ate his meat with such admirable neatness that its juices hardly wet his sandy mustaches. Erp described some battle or other with bright eyes and expressive gestures. How could someone with murder on his soul behave like that? Tor was baffled.

His new mentor sat close to the kings, tuning his harp. At Erbin's command the apparent bard told stories, then sang love songs that seared the heart, and war songs that lifted it. Late in the firelit night he gave them the great "Lament for Uther." More than one fierce eye shed tears; more than one hand gripped sword or spear, hard. Yet still none of the kings showed a sign of unease or guilt.

Then Myrddin gave the kings and warriors a song they had not heard before:

"Sing a brilliant song
of boundless inspiration
Concerning the Man who is to come
To destroy the invaders.
His staff and his entrenchment,
And his swift devastations,
And his ruling leadership,
And his written number,
And his red purple robes,
And his assault against the rampart,
And his appropriate seat
Amid the great assembly.

"Has he not brought from Annwn
The horses of the pale burden-bearer,
The princely old man,
The cupbearing feeder?
The third deeply wise one,
Is the blessed Arthur.
Arthur the blessed,
Renowned in song,
In the front of the battle
Shall be mightily active.

"Who were the three chief ministers
Who guarded the land?
Who were the three skillful ones
Who preserved the token,
And came with eagerness
To receive their lord?
Great is the mystery of the circular course.
Conspicuous is the gaiety of the old.
Loud is the horn of the traveler,
Loud the cattle toward evening.
Conspicuous is truth when it appears,
And more so when spoken."

Conspicuous is truth when it appears, and more so when spoken. These were words of very dark meaning to a guilty man, Tor thought, listening in fascination. Why, the Archdruid might be hearing the thoughts of those kings as he sat so near them, or at least their strongest, most immediate ones.

Those thoughts must have been powerful indeed in the next moment. As the plangent harp notes ended, men exclaimed in awe, or felt their tongues stick immobile in their mouths. Where the lean dark bard had sat, they now saw a huge man in a blue robe, with a fan-shaped beard to his chest. The firelight accentuated the strands of roan red still left in his gray mane. His large-boned face appeared like a lid locked over a coffer containing mighty secrets.

"Myrddin!" the whisper flew around. "It's Myrddin the Prophet!" Less Christian or more knowledgeable, some said, "Myrddin the Archdruid!"

Myrddin rose hugely to his feet. "Let you all be sure," he said, "that what I have sung is so. Uther Pendragon's son is alive." He smiled through his beard. "Because you are horse-warriors here, it will matter to you, and so I will tell you he rode as soon as he toddled. He's his father's son. Yet more patient, less arbitrary, so far as one may tell with a boy not yet four; and my foresight affirms it. His battle-prowess will be great, his justice greater, and at seventeen he will be High King of Britain."

"Druid's sight is what he means," Rheidwyn said softly. "So! Young Arthur's alive."

"And Myrddin wishes it to be known," Casnar murmured. "Now cousin, *that's* of interest."

It interested the four kings, of a surety. Ulthin blustered that this was only talk, that the boy had yet to reach four years, as Myrddin said himself, and they died like flies at that tender age. Who could build hope on that? Erp pointed out that fifteen years was long to wait, and neither the Saxons nor a kingdom's needs would bide in patience. Beroticus, not unkindly but with bleak humor, remarked that he himself was sure to be dead by then, and could not bind his heir to a promise from within his burial mound.

"For my part," Llygad said, rising, "I plan to be living. And the prophecies of the lord Myrddin are not to be dismissed lightly, as we know. If a Pendragon comes who is as great as we are advised . . . I will follow him."

"We will talk of this at the council in my hall," Erbin

said. "I think we must. You will join us there, my lord Archdruid?"

"I will come," Myrddin answered. "For tonight, I will sleep on the rath and watch the stars. The sky looks clear."

In fact there was cloud, though not much. For Britain it was a clear sky.

As Myrddin departed like a great walking menhir through the throng of warriors and herdsmen, he passed close to Tor, sitting agog, his heart pounding. He never so much as glanced at the boy. Tor felt let down. Surely the Archdruid could have given him some sign, some command of what he wished, in a way that would never be noticed? Had he himself no notion of which king would most bear watching?

But since he'd lightly left Tor to his own devices, the boy made up his mind to act.

King Llygad stroked the neck of his black hunter. She whinnied softly. His henchman looked at him, impassive and ready for any mischief, but steeped in habits of caution.

"Lord, we should not speak of this. Not anywhere in Camlodd. There are too many ears."

"That is why we are speaking here. Lucrece will warn us if someone is about." He had so trained her. "We are secure if we do not talk long or loudly."

"The Archdruid—they say that if anybody speaks, the wind carries the sound straight to his ears."

"He's not so all-knowing as that. Besides, it will not signify for long. I am sure he lied about the boy's being alive yet. I'm going to ask that we all see him."

"None has seen him since he was a babe! The Archdruid could show any boy younger than five."

"He might, indeed. With his power to foresee the future, he could also pick an impostor who will grow into the image of Uther. It was ill-conceived to do away with Arthur while Myrddin lived. The Archdruid should have died first."

His henchman's voice dropped lower. "Then it must be done here, lord. Once he departs Camlodd, we will never know his whereabouts. No man does until he appears. Poison? There's one dose left."

"Ill-conceived again. I cannot be sure it would slay him

even if he swallowed it. The Church contends that he's a demon's offspring."

"And he might be! But he's mostly human, mostly mortal, that is sure."

"It's true that the best chance, perhaps our only chance to deal with him, is here. We will use it!" Llygad's voice rang with resolve. "He won't be proof against a spear's cast. I know no swifter hand or surer with a horse-javelin than yours. Steal one—from Ulthin's followers if you can do it expeditiously. It will be well if they take the blame."

Llygad's henchman gave a small, measured nod. It was the gesture of a man who did not quibble. His voice, when he spoke, matched it.

"He declared he'd be communing with stars on the rampart. Deep earth witness me! With those shoulders outlined against the sky, there'll be no missing him, even at midnight."

"Good," Llygad answered crisply. "Yet you are not to be caught in the act. Abandon, if you cannot do it neatly."

"Cannot? Lord, you yourself said it. You know no defter hand with a javelin than mine."

"I've seen you hurl one through a dangling ring no bigger than my palm, four times in five. And stalk a wary deer through wet bracken to hardly more than spitting distance. Go, then."

The second man's footsteps diminished, while Llygad remained a moment, stroking the black mare's neck again. He laughed quietly, and said, "You may carry a Pendragon before you are much older, Lucrece."

Llygad departed as well, and left silence behind. Nothing broke it for long moments except the mare, moving her feet and snorting a little. Then the pile of hay in her stall rustled and stirred. Tor's brown head rose out of it, dusty with chaff. He smothered a sneeze.

"Pendragon!" he muttered in disgust. "I'd rather herd cows all my life than follow his standard!"

Tor approached the mare, Lucrece. He had rubbed her down and cleaned mud from her legs only hours before. She welcomed him with a friendly nicker.

"He trusted too much that you'd warn him," he whispered. "His training cannot be as good as he reckons."

Tor half believed that a god had guided him there and

given him the chance to listen to Llygad, when he had been planning to spy on King Ulthin.

"I thought he was the one," he said softly. "He's still drinking back at the cookfires, though." Shaking his head at how wrong he'd been, he set off to find Myrddin at once.

The Archdruid paced slowly along the third earthwork of Camlodd. Guards had been posted, with spears and shields. They all walked wide of the huge man. He studied the stars, with rags of cloud passing across them, and felt the earth of Britain under his feet, which had seen and swallowed so much.

In the ditch below the rampart, a man squirmed stealthily closer. Grass and huge weeds gave him cover. He held a short javelin in his hands. Its narrow, sharp tip would drive straight through Myrddin's breast-bone, if it struck him there, let alone his ribs—and five terrible barbs behind the point would keep it stubbornly in the wound.

The great figure outlined against stars and cloud came within range. The waiting slayer's heart beat faster in bloodlust. His arm swept high and he threw, biting back the war-yell that rose naturally in his throat. He knew as the spear left his hand that he had thrown true.

He never understood what happened after that, and little enough time to comprehend was given to him. Myrddin's towering shape seemed to move *before* the javelin flew. The Archdruid reached out. The weapon's point and barbs showed a brief, dim glitter in the starlight as it halted dead in Myrddin's great hand.

Then the javelin came back. The slayer felt a savage blow in the stomach that knocked him into the grass again.

He stared incredulously at the shaft sticking from his body at an angle. He arched and kicked and uttered short, choked screams.

The sentries on the earthworks came running, but even before they reached the Archdruid, Tor had appeared, with King Erbin's two brothers beside him. Myrddin, half-sliding down the side of the earthen rampart, reached his would-be assassin where he lay groaning. The javelin barbs were sunk deep in his entrails. Even above his pain, astonishment stretched the man's eyes wide.

"How?" he whispered. "How did you do that?"

Myrddin did not answer the question. "Tell why you did this, and I will do all I can to cure you."

The slayer set his teeth and said nothing.

Tor and the two nobles stood above him. The boy swallowed as he looked at the dreadful wound, but he spoke steadily.

"He tried to kill the lord Myrddin, sirs! I heard him plan it with his master. They talked of using poison, decided no, and settled on a spear from ambush."

"Yes," Myrddin confirmed. "It's so, but speak of it before King Erbin, boy, and then you need not say it all more than once. Bring my attacker on a litter, my lords."

The slayer was failing fast when he finally came before Erbin. The other kings gathered around to hear, turning their eyes suspiciously on Llygad. He did not even lose his temper.

"The testimony of a cowherd's boy? Am I to answer it? He is a green youth dazzled by the lord Myrddin's fame. Better to ask this man—" He gestured at the figure on the bloodstained litter. "He will tell you I am innocent. And it is difficult to see why a dying man would lie."

"Because you have made your usual threats against his family, he will say nothing," Myrddin noted flatly. "He has done your work for years, and I dare say there are many here who know it."

Beroticus did not speak, but some noticed his eyes narrow in the torchlight, and his head seemed to move in a tiny, dour nod. As Llygad's immediate neighbor on the northeast, he knew most about the man's affairs.

"Is this a formal accusation?" Llygad asked. "For if it is—why, it seems I must answer after all." He waved a hand in the air, as if brushing Tor and his testimony away. "Would I be such a fool as to send my well-known hench-man to do murder here in Camlodd? More likely someone else coerced him, since his guilt seems clear. Besides, it now appears that even an Archdruid can lie, since your tale does not convince, Myrddin. You say he hurled a javelin at you from hiding, *and you caught it and flung it back with these fatal results*? In the dark? That's a feat the most skilled warrior here would be doubtful of performing. I ask you, Erbin. Myrddin is no warrior, but a Druid, as we're all knowing—and as the bishops decry. Who credits this claim of his?"

It was a shrewd hit. Men looked thoughtful, and gazed at Myrddin in doubt. The wounded man on the litter gave his death rattle and perished in that moment. Llygad curled his lip.

"And there, alas, dies the one who could truly tell us."

Myrddin answered thunderously, "Yea, there he dies! He, too, asked how the feat was done. It puzzled him greatly. You are right; it was not war-skill. Of that I have little. But as all here know, I can foresee the future as no others can. The deeper into the future, the vaguer the seeing. The nearer, the more vivid. I foresaw his javelin-cast a few heartbeats before he made it, more clearly than the darkest night could obscure. I knew where the spear would fly, where to reach out to snatch it. You doubt me, Llygad? You disbelieve? Then give me the lie! It's simple enough."

Myrddin took a dozen of his huge paces away from Llygad and turned his back.

"Take a javelin yourself and throw it," he said scornfully. "Let those standing in front of me see that I even close my eyes. If I lie, if I cannot do as I say, then I will have a nasty wound at the lightest. But if I *can* see the cast before it happens, and you throw—look well at your henchman, Llygad. That is how *you* will be, a count of five score from now. Why hesitate? Take a spear."

The count of five score went by. Llygad had not moved, and his hands remained empty. His fellow kings grew contemptuous of visage. Even his own hearth-companions moved away from him a little. Scheming and treachery any man there might have accepted, even condoned; murder some of them reckoned a trifle. Failure of courage, no.

"From sunrise, Camlodd is barred to you," King Erbin said harshly, "and we will not require you at our council in my hall. Who disagrees?"

None demurred, and Llygad slowly whitened.

"I might kill you here," Erbin went on, "for you tried to murder my guest while you too were my guest. But you are still a king. I will visit you soon with a war-host. I have small doubt that my cousin Leodegrance will join me."

"As will I," Ulthin growled.

In some respects a stupid man, King Ulthin was known

to be crafty in war, and anyone could see the outcome of a campaign advised by Myrddin.

Llygad realized it, too. His pallor increased. Without a word he walked away, holding his shoulders straight with manifest effort. By sunrise he was gone from Camlodd.

"You did well, Tor," Myrddin told him. "Llygad might have succeeded, except for you."

Tor said doubtfully, "I don't understand, lord. If you can foresee the future as well as *that*, why did you need a warning from me?"

"I was not even certain which king was guilty. All I had foreseen until then was that you would be important. When you came to me, though, and told me Llygad was plotting my death that very night, I knew which possible future to look for. It grew clearer by the minute. And so, this—the reward you asked for." Myrddin looked somewhat amused. "Does Arthur disappoint you?"

"No!" Tor said staunchly.

The little boy playing on the beach had not disappointed Tor, precisely. He was strong, healthy, and not unhandsome. Certainly he was one of those who rode as soon as he walked, and clamored to get on a horse's back whenever he saw one, a passion that Tor appreciated and wholly shared with the smaller boy. And yet . . . Arthur did not seem like Tor's idea of a mighty king-to-be.

Well, he had not turned four years old yet.

"Where will you take him?"

"To greater safety. You are the only one, since I took him under my protection, to have seen him at all, save his mother. Even the kings Erbin and Leodegrance have not visited him. But you earned it." He smiled warmly. "Do not forget my prophecy that you will ride among his knights in the future. And do not doubt it."

"I won't, lord."

"Good. The ship is ready to leave."

Tor said his farewell to young Arthur, and then watched Myrddin carry him aboard the green-sailed longship. Thinking about Myrddin's promise, he felt his heart swell like the longship's sail. He remained on the beach, watching it, until it had vanished beyond the skyline.

THE LIKENESS OF HER LORD

C. A. Gardner

They stood side by side before the mirror, he dark and slim, she with a grace and beauty that belied her age. His arms circled her waist and they danced slowly, their faces turned toward their doubles. "It's like dancing with a ghost," she said softly. His image rippled faintly in the mirror as he kissed her.

"Don't forget the living man in your arms."

She turned to face the mirror, hands resting on the massive dresser to brace herself from falling into the silvered dream. "But in the morning, you're so different. Sometimes . . ."

"What?" he asked gently, smoothing golden hair. Her eyes sought his in the mirror.

"It's as though *we* don't exist. This life. Our love. You look at me as though we haven't spoken for years . . . as though we're still sleeping in separate rooms."

He chuckled, swung her to face him so her hair went flying, held her tight. "That, my dear," he murmured, "is because love is like magic. To last, it must be guarded close as a secret."

She leaned back in his arms as they watched themselves again, wise Igraine and the man who looked exactly like the duke, her husband. The tenderness in his hands was that of a man who touches the mother of his child, and he looked at her with a kindness she'd not had from her true lord for decades, had she but known the truth.

Kissing her, he said, "You should rest, my love, for the journey tomorrow. You'll want to look your best for King Uther."

"That lecher," she muttered, and pulled away to stand staring into the small chest of items packed and folded for the trip—one never knew how long a stay the king might require. Hiding her face, she plucked at an azure robe, tucked it back around a worn-edged book of spells. The book's marker showed a cygnet that Morgan's father had made her, whose shape shifted magically to form a swan. They'd have to leave the girls behind. They wouldn't be safe in that court, her three daughters with their magical gifts, born of a long line of wise women into an age when magic was growing suspect. Morgan, the youngest, was by far the most eager pupil—ten years tender, for the memory her mother had of how Morgan's father had grown kind before the child's birth, becoming the love of which she'd always dreamed. They shared everything now, even the secret of his own talent with the arts—a trust she'd guard with her life. Sometimes, in the evenings, Igraine would slip her youngest child up to her bedchamber, where Morgan's father taught her many secrets of spellcraft under dark's protective veil, delighting in the enthusiasm of her strong young mind.

Now her love said to Igraine, "I'm sorry to leave you tonight. There are things I must attend to before we depart."

She hugged him impulsively about the waist as he slipped on the silver-stitched tunic, belted on the sky-blue surcoat with the duke's crest, and placed a slim silver circlet back above thick brows, nestling it firmly in dark brown curls. He looked every inch a duke, with a face famed for the strength of its mouth, the certainty of its nose, the decisiveness of the hard blue eyes that twinkled now as he kissed her hand, bringing a blush to her cheeks. As he closed the door and wound down the spiral steps in the old stone tower, he could hear the faint sound of her singing, bringing a smile to his lips, a joy pure as flame, for love of the strong soul of Igraine.

Quietly, he passed through the shadowed corridor that led to the postern way. Then he stepped out into the night, under the stars, and stretched until his spine cracked and his chest curved up toward the night. As he released a long, wavering breath, the light from Igraine's distant window slid off black silk and dyed leather, vanishing in hair as dark as the wrong side of the moon, save for a few pricks of silver. He searched behind the hedge, brought out a round brown pebble, and threw it to the ground. As it struck, it cracked open like a shell; a horse sprang forth, snorting and pawing.

They rode through the night, across fields speckled

with shadows, over water spangled with stars. The roan snorted when they crossed each bridge, as though he did not like the moving water, but the man chided him gently, and they moved on.

At the outskirts of Caerleon, the man dismounted, spoke softly to his horse, and stroked its neck. A piece of parchment in his hand, he crossed beneath the arch that led into the city. As he did, the shadows worked their magic, and he emerged an old man, stooped over a trailing beard, his blue eyes sharp beneath a knitted cap and deeply scored brow.

As the old man walked into the city, Sir Ulfius marked his passage from his post atop the wall. He noted well, but said nothing, for there was but one man who held many guises at his command, and that man had the king's ear.

The king had grown old, and had no heir. With his penchant for wars, the land was in constant turmoil, and his barons feared what might happen if the succession were not secured. King Uther remembered that Igraine, wife of his enemy Gorlois, was famed for her beauty and wisdom, and that her castles held a powerful vantage on the Cornish coast. So Uther ordained a great banquet, where he arranged for Igraine to sit on his left, his counselor Merlin on his right. Duke Gorlois glowered at the foot of the table, where he fumed and did not bother to take meat, his eyes filled with the sight of Igraine's golden head bending graciously toward the king, the white flash of her teeth as she laughed, the knowing curve of her smile when the king leaned forward to impart some secret humor. Across the table, the king's mage watched their sparring with a small, indulgent smile. Her cheeks flushed with triumph and conspiracy, Igraine lifted wide green eyes to Merlin in a look that laughed and pled for mercy.

But as the night waxed longer, the roses wilted in her cheeks and her laugh grew forced. The king leaned over her till he spilled a glass of wine down the bodice of her silken gown, then insisted on wiping the stain himself, so vigorously he bruised her. Merlin's only answer to her silent plea was a short, sharp shake of the head when the king pressed his face close to hers.

So Igraine retreated to her husband's side as soon as the feast was over, drawing him to the privacy of their room. But when she said, "My lord, we must leave now, lest the king dishonor me," Gorlois looked at her with hatred, as though it were her doing. He barked orders to the groom, and they rode off at breakneck speed. He cursed the horses and drove them on to Tintagel, till the animals' wheezing sounded loud as their hooves and their flanks shone dark with blood. When Igraine dismounted, her palfrey staggered and dropped to its knees. The lady cried out and reached to help, but Gorlois bellowed with a fury she'd not seen since the night he'd almost killed her, after Elaine was born—before they'd taken separate rooms, and his manner changed; before their newfound love had brought them Morgan. He raised his riding crop and she fled into the castle, bolted her bedroom door, and wept with terror and with rage, and for the thought of his lip curled against her the whole way home.

He didn't follow her, didn't pound on the door or even say farewell. She could hear him screaming orders to the servants, to the guards, closing up the castle by the sea as though the fiends of Hell were hard on their heels. At last day broke, a gray light spreading over the sea. His bellowing ceased, though the rattling of mail and weapons continued. When she woke after a fitful sleep, she found he'd done more than retire to a separate room. He'd warded her, then left for a separate fortress—Terrabil, Tintagel's twin.

Through the long mustering of men and supplies and the first days of the siege, Igraine didn't see her husband once. She found herself longing even for his hatred, the jealous rage that was so close to tears, anything so long as she could see him, and have a chance to explain. Sometimes, when she stood on the stairway with the sun slanting through the window slits, she would set one foot half in, half out of the sunlight, wondering if she were losing her mind, and she'd only dreamed of love.

One night, months into the siege, she lay awake, shivering at the distant screams beyond the walls. It had begun to seem she had always lived this way—cut off, alone, under threat of death.

Out of the violence of the night, she heard a soft rap on the door.

She rose, clad only in her shift, her bare feet cold on the stone. In a sudden pit of stillness, she stood staring at the closed door, watching the play of the moonlight through the branches, feeling helpless. Had he come to kill her, as he'd nearly done when his early violence led her to seek gentleness from another, and he'd discovered by the small dark features, the silky black hair, that Elaine was not his child? Had she even heard a knock, or was it only a dream, insubstantial as their love had been?

The sound came again, a light scratching, the faint whisper of her name. Slowly, she drew up the bar, pulled open the door. Gorlois stepped forward, his features gray in the moonlight, the shadows from the trees shifting on his face, banding his eyes, hiding the door that yawned now on a well of darkness. They stood in silence, staring at one another, until Gorlois murmured, "My love," and Igraine stretched out a careful hand to touch his cheek and assure herself that he was real.

He took her in his arms, careful and tender as he'd been on a day long ago, when he'd returned from the war that spared her from his wrath over Elaine. He'd gone to quell the uprising of a minor baron, whom she'd always thanked in her heart. News of the disaster had reached Gorlois while he was drawing the knife over her skin, leaving scars she'd worked long with her arts to erase from arms and belly. When he returned, she'd been prepared to die. Instead, her duke had soothed her, speaking gently, as to a frightened horse, holding her with a clumsiness softened by what seemed like genuine love for the first time.

Now he sat with her on the bed and she wept into his shoulder, clutching him hard enough to feel the muscle beneath all the layers of cloth. Such relief, he wasn't dead, his reality solid and firm beside her, his light hand brushing her hair and his endearments making her cry harder. At last she raised a face shining with her tears, her smile. And everything was right between them.

Afterward, they spoke of the siege and Uther's reign of violence. The only hope for relief was that the king had no heir. Lying with her head on his arm, snug in the hollow, Igraine listened to dreams through the happiness of her own. Her love was saying, "If I had it in my power, I would shape this kingdom to a land of peace, where fighting men protected the poor instead of preying on them, where a woman need not fear to meet her king. A place where rich and poor, young and old, women and men, magic and mundane were accorded equal respect. I'd unsettle folk by disguising myself as those they most despised, to make them think again. . . ."

Igraine turned in his arms to trace the lines about his mouth, the care upon his brow. Her hair brushed his cheek, his chin. "Easy to dream, hard to do," she teased. "You've not much influence with yon Uther, I'm afraid. Better to start at home."

His smile was gentle. "My lady, we already have. Methinks we've caught a star this night."

When his siege showed no signs of breaking through the defenses, the king took to his bed for pure rage. Though he had the right to take any woman he wanted, he would have none, but demanded that his men bring him Igraine, till his cries were mixed with fever and he could not rise.

Sir Ulfius, the king's right hand, came to see what he might do. The knight looked to be regent for Uther's child, should the happy event occur and Uther not live to see the boy become a man. By the dim lantern in Uther's tent, Ulfius' eyes gleamed as he said, "Merlin is the man for you. He has a certain talent with disguises."

Uther waved weakly in assent. Normally, it might take months to find Merlin, who could appear as a tree or a stone, young maid or beggar king. This time, it took Ulfius but an hour's ride to a sheltered grove just beyond the tower of Tintagel, from whence he focused a sharp eye on the postern gate.

Finally the door cracked into shadow, and a young man emerged, sharp-faced as a hawk, dark-clothed and easy to miss in the moon that slipped between the clouds. Not a sound marked where he'd been as he slipped from shrub to bush, visible only in the ghostly glimmering of hands and eyes. When he reached the wood, the young man straightened and sauntered down an invisible path.

Ulfius stepped forth to the crack of twigs, the rustling leaves. The other froze, face tense in the lantern that Ulfius unshuttered with a grin.

"Well, my lord. You know why I've come?"

"I haven't the faintest idea." The youth crossed his arms upon his chest.

"King Uther lies sick, and he calls for his mage. He thinks you can help him with the problem that has caused this siege. And so do I."

"Why come to me in the night? I have naught to do with war—nor ambush."

"Ah, but this is ambush of a different sort," Ulfius said with a smirk. "Who knows better than you how to breach the castle, and the defenses of the lady within? Don't worry—I'll claim no credit, if you swear to help."

"You mean, you won't tell Uther what you suspect," the man said bitterly.

"If you care to put it that way," Ulfius said jovially. "I care not what man's seed may take the lady. Should you support my bid for regency, I'll find it no trouble to hold my peace."

Under the lantern light, Merlin's blue eyes shone dark and shrewd. The light cast dancing shadows as Ulfius' glove slipped, ever so slightly. But the dark-haired man only bowed his head and passed on to Uther's camp. One look at Ulfius, and the guards let them through without question. At the king's tent, the slim young man pushed his way through the curtained entranceway, his black hair flying about his head like crows.

Uther rose up on one elbow from his sickbed. His aged face cracked in a smile as Merlin approached. From behind, Ulfius said, "Merlin knows how to resolve your dilemma, my liege."

"You know how I pine for fair Igraine? I must have her. If it takes ten thousand deaths—"

"Even if the lady does not want you?" Merlin asked quietly.

Uther snorted, fell back on the bed. "Especially then!"

Merlin held his peace, though his thoughts whirled like the lantern that turned faintly with the breeze, suspended from its pole at the center of the tent:

Calmly, quietly; the king must think nothing amiss. This is it—my deal with the devil, a choice between love and the hope for a better day. No way to stop once it is set in motion. Can I really trade the one I hold most dear to the very tyrant my actions have sought to forestall? Would she ever forgive me if I did. . . ?

The possibilities yawned before Merlin, cold and terrible, even as Uther's eyes transfixed him with all the force of his passion, a glittering desperation akin to the fear that the mage felt crystallizing inside.

"Ulfius is right," Merlin said at last. "I know what might be done."

With her face before his eyes, he added, "Get you ready, Majesty. Tomorrow night we ride down to Tintagel, where the lady will welcome you with open arms. In return, of course, I expect something of my own."

Ulfius stirred, reflected lantern flames shifting like water upon his bared sword. Mail clinked as he leaned closer, his eyes on Merlin ironic beneath peaked brows.

Uther growled, "Say on."

"You will give me your firstborn child, to be nourished as I choose. In turn, I'll make certain that he's raised to be a proper king, far from the dangers of the court."

Uther's silence was overridden by the distant shouts of fighting men, the clink of the shortened lantern chain against the pole. Merlin waited for the answer, his stomach tight with a bleeding pain, the pangs of birth.

Released at last by the king's "Yes," Merlin wandered out under the stars, pain bursting within him. His eyes watered as the wind cut at his face, till the stars streamed and streaked under his vision, and he could not tell anymore where his world ended, and theirs began.

Merlin marshaled them out that night, wry-grinning Ulfius and Uther, who had suddenly found the strength of ten. Merlin draped them all with seeming, till Ulfius, in the guise of Sir Brastias, might not have guessed which of them played Gorlois and which Sir Jordans.

They rode by Merlin's secret paths down to Tintagel by the sea. Merlin knocked on the gate, a code he'd used before. The old steward opened to them, eyes wide as he saw the two knights and the duke. He faltered in his speech, then settled on, "How goes the battle at the front, my lord?" Then he ushered them into the hall and gestured for hollow-eyed pages, boys gray for lack of food and sleep, to gather the reins and guide the horses to their stalls. "My lady is resting already for this evening, but if you would like for me to summon her—"

The boys busied themselves about the visitors, so sleepy they nodded visibly as they helped unbuckle swords and shields, helms and hauberks. Merlin made excuse to brush the old man's sleeve, to clasp his hand as if for balance, to squeeze in such a way that the seneschal cast a shrewd and startled glance into his face, then nodded once, almost imperceptibly. The false Sir Jordans led the way up to the lady's suite. Merlin found them a privy closet close to Igraine's rooms, where they might watch and warn the king.

And who shall know the torture that Merlin went through that night, sitting self-prisoned while he knew what his lady was suffering mere feet away? But he stirred not an inch, holding his breath, biting his tongue, diving deep into the center of himself to try to find some peace.

In the other room, Igraine stood before the mirror with Uther, as she had often stood with her love, each marveling at the other. The man before her looked different somehow—a shadow shifting over his face, behind his eyes. When he took her about the waist and threw her upon the bed, she lay looking up at the ceiling in wonder and sorrow. Here was the old Gorlois, the man whose hands were rough, thirsty, taking what they chose without regard for her. She bit her lip to hold back the cries as he tugged and tore and bruised her flesh, burrowing deeper and deeper despite the fact that she could no longer keep her face clear of her feelings, clenched now with silent pain.

In the morning, the seneschal, anguished and rushed, woke her. Her duke had disappeared during the night, it seemed; she was weary, but glad to struggle up out of an empty bed.

"My lady, he is dead!" the seneschal stammered when she had got to her feet. "The duke your husband is slain! They say he fell an hour after sunset!"

"Before he came to visit me?" she asked ironically. Yet she did not feel surprised. It seemed fitting, somehow, that he should die just before she was visited by the ghost of his former self. She had already drowned in silent grief last night, when he'd ground out the embers of their love. Now everything looked stark and clear, without emotion, as shock shielded her eyes.

Thirteen days later, King Uther proclaimed he'd marry her, and she didn't bother to protest. He wanted a mass ceremony, marrying her daughters as prizes to his allies, as well. Her half-hearted attempts to plead for them, and Merlin's surprising intercession, won reprieve for the youngest, Morgan, who was nonetheless cast adrift, into a nunnery, to learn her spellcraft there as best she could.

As for Igraine, she sank into dullness until the night when she could no longer conceal her growing child. Uther demanded to know, and she gave him a tale that she herself could scarce believe, of a man who was and was not her husband, like a vengeful ghost come to claim his due.

"It was I," Uther crowed, triumphant, and repeated the conquest of her body. But this time Igraine bore it with a heart that was far away and full of light. Uther did not know that she and Gorlois had already been expecting a child before that final night. She rejoiced that Uther—cursed, blessed Uther—had been the man that night, and not her lord at all. The last time she had seen him, Gorlois had loved her, and shared his heart and dreams.

As Uther rolled away from her on the bed, Igraine lay still, borne up by a strange, dark joy.

When the day came to fulfill Merlin's bargain, Igraine felt the walls of fate closing down around her. Ulfius threatened to kill the babe and give Merlin its corpse if she refused to part with the living child. With the mage gone much of the time, Uther relied on Ulfius more than ever. It was Ulfius who would bring the baby to the postern gate, unnamed and wrapped in cloth of gold, to be handed to the poor man waiting there. Still fresh from childbed, Igraine feigned sleep, then slipped out after Ulfius with a poisoned dagger.

The narrow hall was dim and cold; the shadows from Ulfius' lantern reminded her of the staircase at Tintagel. Shards of former happiness cut her like glass.

Ulfius waited before the gate, and Igraine crouched in the shadows, watching the babe in his arms. How could she surprise Ulfius, without her son falling to his death on the stone floor? As the silence stretched, her anxiety grew, terrible as the poisoned dagger. If Merlin took her son, what would become of him? If she managed to flee with the babe, would Uther hunt her down, and kill them both?

Her thoughts were shattered by the rap upon the door.

The old man looked worn, ragged with years, his beard streaked with time, his habit as brown and tattered as a hermit's. Yet his eyes were twinkling blue and kindly. . . .

Igraine instantly knew those eyes. Slowly, she stepped out of the shadows. As she passed, Ulfius cast a murderous look at her, but he could not draw his greatsword with the king's son in his arms.

"You would take my boy," she said to the old man.

"I would watch over him as a father watches his son. There is a good knight who will raise him, where he will learn the things he cannot here."

"As Uther's heir, the child will be in danger. . . ."

"The chief dangers lie here at court."

She looked at him. Something in the words, the manner of speech. . . . Slowly, she said, "Before you take my son, I would speak with you privily about his upbringing."

As Merlin searched the lady's face, Ulfius stepped forward and held out the babe. "Take him! Igraine, it's time you were in your bed! Uther will not like to hear that you've been exhausting yourself this way, so soon after the birth."

"Yes, lady," Merlin said, his tone quiet and deliberate with threat. "Take your child, and say goodbye."

Ulfius passed her the boy. The instant she'd taken him, the knight's hand was on the pommel of his sword; the next instant, his chin was on his chest, which rumbled with gentle snores. Merlin lowered his hands.

The light returned to Igraine's eyes. "Quickly," she said, "before they realize we're gone. There's a cave below Tintagel—" Igraine stepped to pass Merlin, but he caught her in his arms.

Protective and gentle, tender and strong—yes, a touch she knew in the dark, in her sleep. She looked at the mage in hurt and bewilderment. "You—"

She gasped as his features melted, shifted, rearranged to form a face she never thought to see again. He held her tight, as if afraid she'd faint. Instead, she struggled in his arms.

"How dare you mock me," she cried, her voice harsh and low. But Merlin stepped back, and only watched, and her heart misgave her. Only one man had ever looked at her that way.

"I'm so sorry, Igraine. My love. I've betrayed you."

"You gave your form to the king!"

"The duke's form. I loved you, but you were too frightened to have me any other way."

Her head spun as the world shifted. "Then you—you protected me from the duke." And bitterly she added, "But not the king."

"I loved you," he repeated.

"And now? You would take my child away. My last hope," she whispered.

"Our last hope, Igraine. Away from Uther's influence, the boy will have the chance to learn justice, honor—and compassion. Our child, Igraine. Born of perfect love, not lust. Born to set the kingdom right. He'll make a great leader, the like of which this land has never seen."

"Born of illusion," she whispered. "Of a man I loved, whose name I never knew." She raised her head, fear flashing like defiance in her eyes. "How will he know to separate the truth from lies? How will he know we loved him? Stay by me here, in whatever guise you wish, and help me teach him all those things!"

Merlin stepped close, traced the baby's soft features, an infant fist, a lock of hair. "And when he grows, and Uther sees no trace of his own likeness? What then, Igraine? They must believe he is the king's son. It's the only chance we have."

"Let me go with you!"

He looked away, but not before she'd seen the tightening of his jaw, the glistening in his eyes. "You know what would happen if I did. I couldn't go on, if you died, and we can't hide forever. I need you here, my love. Your son needs you—needs his mother to be queen, to acknowledge him, after I give the folk a sign to point the way."

"A true king, in the old fashion," she murmured. "Traced through the queen's blood, mother of the land." The baby turned his head and sighed, his breath soft upon her arm. Impossible to reconcile this tiny child with such a weighty prophecy. She could not bear to let him go.

She could not bear to lose her love again.

"At least let me see what his father truly looks like," she managed, though grief choked her.

Merlin bowed his head. When he looked at Igraine again, he was younger, slender as a boy, though there were faint traces of silver shining like stardust in the jet of his hair. The mouth was smaller, the nose more sharp, but the eyes—the eyes were the same.

"I'll look after him. I won't fail him, the way I have you," he pleaded.

Silently, she handed him the babe. Watched him arrange the boy closely in the crook of his arm. Tried a smile, rushed forward to embrace the mage before he could see what a crumpled thing it was. "Keep safe," she whispered into his rough habit, "keep well. Go to Tintagel, watch the gulls and the sea from my little cave. Remember me to the land I love."

"They'll call it Merlin's Cave for the time I spend there."

No more words. She kissed him, her life upon his lips, then turned her back so she would not see him go. There was no need to see; she could feel him moving away, a long line stretching taut between them, till her heart snapped and he melted into distance. She turned around.

Nothing but the rising mist, fog clinging to the trees in the moonlight. Nothing but Ulfius, yawning and stretching and sneaking guilty looks at her as she stood just beyond the gate, sucking in the sharpness of the cold night air.

And out there somewhere in the night, the promise of a love she had not dreamed.

THE LESSON OF THE OTHER
Steen Jensen

"It is not the Lord's way," stated Bors, looking out over the lake. His voice still cracked some from boyhood.

Lionel sighed. He was taller than his brother, and more rangy. "And I would not so scorn God," he answered, "had we not to this shore been so well led." He leaned from his saddle. "Do not think that we two shall part now. Together we have always been, even against the scorn of Claudas when we fought free of that wicked king."

"I fought not," answered Bors.

"You stayed at my side and warded my back all the same. We are one blood, and by that duty bound. I will not now go on alone."

"Not so alone, my beloved Lionel," said Seraide softly. "I shall be also at your side." She smiled. "Have faith, young Bors, in my lady Viviane's powers. The water of the lake will harm you no more than has your time in hound shape."

Bors blushed deeply. She had transformed them without warning, when Lionel and he had been brought to bay by the king's men. As dogs, they had run to safety and in that shape had reached the borders of the Lady's lands.

"Brighten you so?" Lionel laughed. "Do you forget the joy of the hunt?" He shook his head, looking from his brother to his love, then back. "But for sport, I would have it again, to so simply run side by side. Come, Bors; as then, together we two should ride into these waters."

Bors would still not have it. It was the fact that he had enjoyed the hound shape, its easy sensuality, that shamed him now before God.

The men at their back, restless at the delay, stirred. They had joined the three at the edge of the Lady's lands, even as the brothers had been restored to their human forms. Though King Claudas had not dared to pursue them farther, the three still had need of an escort against such outlaws and giants as haunted the waste. Even now, some among the guard paid careful attention to their back.

Bors looked into the empty, broken land.

"Brother," Lionel went on more gently, "know that I value your words and your good sight. True you have often been proved. But here—" he glanced around at the desolation "—I see no other choice than that we continue. From birth, we have been as one. As I will go, you must not stay. As elder, I command: attend and follow."

Bors bowed his head, but God neither answered his dread nor freed him from the duty of kinship. Praying for forgiveness, he nodded. Then, alongside his brother, he rode into the lake. The water splashed, reaching quickly the flanks of his mount, caressing the boy's leg—cold, then like no more than warm air. The horse, of the Lady's stable, ducked easily beneath the surface and drew the boy after. Bors crossed himself and heard Lionel swear as the lake closed over their heads.

The waters swirled, bubbled, and then grew calm as the glowing surface receded. Bors, who had not thought to hold his breath, swallowed in what seemed no more than warm, moist air. He looked at his brother. Lionel grinned and shoved Bors playfully, but unwittingly with a strength that nearly staggered the boy and his mount from the path. A great pike, the moment before oblivious to their descent, caught the boy's eye, then lost it again as the horse found its footing. Bors felt the water of the lake as a sheen of sweat on his face and arm.

"Have more care," whispered Seraide, from Lionel's other side. "We are safe with the Lady, but her great magics should not suffer so your buffets." She spoke most to the older brother, whose hand she still held, while Bors was left to wipe the dampness from his brow. Their escort, more used to this most strange of roads, followed as plainly as they might to market.

Bors saw only darkness below them. Above, sweeping to one side, the pike pursued a school of perch, while higher, as though through the roof of the world, the webbed feet of ducks wagged. Face to the light, the boy prayed that God might still see him, even in this dark and strange place.

Lionel swore again, and Bors looked down. Below, lights

had risen from the gloom, hazy at first, then more clear, resolving at last into pale blue fires burning atop four great towers. As the white light from above faded, the blue from below lit their way, from the watch-fires and then from the lamps and torches and other such shinings that revealed the descent of the four towers into a great castle. The people of the place moved within the fairy light as casually as they might through an earthly hold. Clashing of weapons, though muffled by water, told of knights at play. The moving shapes of warriors followed, then passed, as the company's descent unveiled then enfolded again their quick forms. The castle's outer walls, as the brothers swept down toward the gatehouse, at last closed to them all view of what lay within.

The lands that spread beyond the wall proved to be of mud and silt, with the wrack of the lake bottom rather than meadows for the play of knights. The beacon fires from above offered little light, and only the cool glow of the gateway lit the reaches. At the edge of sight, a long, monstrous shape flicked by, even as the men of the watch saluted the men of the escort. The guard opened the way for them, then bowed as the boys and the maid moved through the passage and into the main bailey.

A ring of blue torches lit the party that awaited their coming. Forward of all stood a tall woman whose blue drapings rippled down the flanks of her mount, and in whose pale hair tangled a crown of pond-leaves. She smiled as she said, "Welcome, children of Gaul—brave Lionel and good Bors. Your time approaches; your training must be completed; your blood must be joined."

Lionel straightened in his saddle. "In truth, lady, I stand already proved. By my hand was slain Claudas' son, when his father, hoping to delay us, dared lay hands upon my fair Seraide."

The maid touched the scar that marked her cheek.

"So was she avenged," concluded Lionel.

"Bold boy," answered the Lady of the Lake, "I require more than blood and violence."

"I transformed them to hounds," offered the soft-spoken Seraide, "to fool and flee those men of the king roused by the death of that prince."

The Lady looked piercingly upon the older boy. "And

thus led Claudas' men to the edges of my land—as consequence will always follow action."

"As it will," answered Lionel hotly, "and so must be met. But such must not slow a knightly deed. . . ."

Viviane's eyes shone. "Rashness! Your bloody hand must learn check. That is why you will have my lessons."

Lionel sought to speak, despite the soft hand that bade him to be still, but his youth's tongue had run its course.

"To rest then," said the Lady more gently. "You are weary from the strange way that you have come."

Certain of her attendants came forward. Glancing to the sweet-faced Seraide, Lionel suffered himself to dismount into their care. Bors likewise yielded to a gentleman and a groom, but hesitated even after Lionel and Seraide had begun their way to their rest.

"My lady," he said in that soft, clear voice that would mark him through his long life, "do you serve our Lord in Heaven?" His vision of the Lady shimmered, and he again felt the touch of the lake against his skin.

"We are not in enmity," she answered through the thickness of the water. "But we are not of His. With that you must make your peace, wise Bors."

Bathed in the castle's strange light, pressed by all the weight of the water above, Bors would yet have questioned more and so risked his host's displeasure—even to the expulsion from her realm, or worse. For he was ever ready, and glad, to go to God in a righteous cause. But Bors saw among the Lady's entourage a boy of his own age and of such a mien as did make him reconsider. This other, from beneath heavy brows, revealed so much a lost soul that Bors was reminded of his duty to those with whom he shared this earthly world. Lionel might thrive without him, but this sad-faced stranger had about him a need that Bors knew he must answer.

Looking to the Lady, Bors crossed himself and went with her people to his rest.

In the lands of Claudas, Lionel and Bors had lived as loathed fosters, sharing an adequate but unpleasant pallet in a single cell. Lionel, aware of the privilege of those in the king's favor, had chafed at the meanness of his own state, making him a poor and tossing bedmate. For his part, Bors had found in the simple setting both an antidote to the court's clutter and a clear window for his piety. He found neither in the room to which the Lady's servants led him.

Bors' quarters offered luxury worthy of a king's son: an unshared bed in a private room, with servants to attend his needs. It left him uncomfortable and unhappy. After testing with a hand the feather-filled bedding, the young man spent the night sleeping in peace on the floor.

He was awakened by the dawn, though one rising not from the liquid gloom beyond his window, but rather from the gradual brightening of the room's blue lamps. He lay cold, both from his hard bed and the pallor that the odd light gave to his flesh.

The chamber's door flew wide. "Brother," cried Lionel, then stopped when he saw where Bors lay. "What, have you fallen?" He grinned.

Bors rose quickly to avoid his brother's toe. Needing to pray, he wished Lionel gone.

Instead, the older boy laughed. "It's foolishness to seek such a grim bed when luxury surrounds you. Surely God will see you whether you rest upon feathers or stone." He slapped the coverlets. "And these . . ." He sighed and then laughed again. "Now I better understand how like dogs we were kept by that false king. Had I not been so prompt in cleaning my blade, I might treasure still his son's blood upon my sword. But come—" Lionel swung back to the door "—Seraide brings word from the Lady. We are to have our first lesson even before our first meal." He bounded from the room.

Bors looked to the nearer of the windows, but saw only the thickness of the water where he would have welcomed the sun.

A brazier at the center of the courtyard burned with such magics as lit the space with the light of the world above. Past the blaze a strong boy worked on a pell. Though the sword was only of whalebone, the post groaned and moved with each great blow until at last the weapon shattered. Without pause, the young man turned for another from those who watched.

"Your cousin is among the onlookers," Seraide whispered to Lionel and Bors, even as the lady Viviane came into the yard.

"I had bid you not speak," said the Lady of the Lake to her maid. "Your youth so does betray you."

Seraide bowed her head.

"Cousin indeed," Viviane said more gently to the two brothers, then called across the yard: "Lancelot, attend!"

From among those who watched the strong boy, one of lesser build separated himself and crossed to where the newcomers waited. He was a plain, honest-looking young man but newly passed from boyhood.

"We have no cousin Lancelot," said Lionel. "The last of that name was father to my father Bors."

"At christening," explained Lady Viviane, "he was your cousin Galahad, son of your uncle King Ban. But now and henceforth, as a mark of his time in my care, he is Lancelot of the Lake."

Lancelot, having reached them, smiled. "Until these last few days, Cousin—as I may now say, be you Bors or Lionel—I had no kin, nor none of blood known, but only my friend Servause." He looked back to where the strong boy had left off his practice and come some way toward them.

Bors saw now that this other was the boy from the previous evening, the stranger whose lost stare had kept him in the Lady's domain.

"You three," Lady Viviane went on, "of the blood of King Lancelot of old, have but of recent time come upon your manhood. Now you must gather and ready yourselves for the future. The fourth, your kinsman Ector de Maris, shall soon arrive. Worldly tutors will follow who shall remind you of the world's common ways—even as my own lessons prepare you for a most uncommon lord. So instructed and so joined, you four will most ably face the trials of your remarkable future."

Lionel frowned at such pronouncements, but Bors for kinship simply offered his embrace to his cousin.

"I am Bors; we had thought you dead."

Lancelot, with a natural grace, received him. "To the world I was." He nodded and grinned in a lopsided way. "In truth, I have but with your coming found myself. And you," he said to the other brother. "You are Lionel?"

"A cousin—lost, now found." Lionel clapped Lancelot on the shoulder. "Three we are then in kinship. With Ector, four." He looked to the Lady of the Lake. "So as one we shall stand, but for the right and duty of our blood—not from the design of others."

The Lady smiled. "So our lessons begin." She looked to Lancelot.

"To the rule of knighthood," said the boy simply, "we must as well accord."

"And to God," added Bors softly.

Lionel frowned at each. "In battle, I would more value your swords and loyalty than your fine words and faith. Let brother stand by brother, and cousin by cousin, and good will follow."

"The duty of a knight may confound kinship," answered Lancelot. "If a brother were to strike an innocent—what then?"

"I would stop his hand," said Lionel. "Or join, if his cause be good."

"A knight should always protect an innocent."

"And so it would be," Lionel insisted. "But blood must first be answered, together to act, and not by words drawn apart."

"God would guide," said Bors suddenly.

"Enough," said Lionel, waving a hand. "Better we should strengthen our sword arms, and train, than toss words so."

"Better you should understand your cousin and brother," said Lady Viviane.

"That I do full well." Lionel faced the Lady of the Lake. "I know beyond any the worth of my brother's words, and do respect the import of my new cousin's thoughts. But in the end, whatever we might puff, it does come to the sword and the will." He smiled. "To that exercise, before all, we must attend."

"By long custom, good lady," added Lancelot, "at this time we do practice." He looked to his cousins. "And in truth, I cannot long abide to be away from my sword."

Lionel laughed. "Then let us to it; I would well know my kinsman's strength."

"Then come," Lancelot said. "I would be glad to see your skill, as well, and learn what you might teach." He grinned again in that lopsided way. "And I would offer to you in turn what I might know." He took them both and led them toward the trainers, and to where the other boy waited. "Though I doubt any one of us will match the strength of my friend Servause."

"It is but the Lady's sorcery, and not truth," stated Lionel, stretched at length in a bath of warm, herbed water. Bruises marked his body.

Bors was dressed for a feast. The water within water, the too-luxurious warmth, had sped him through his own cleansing, but left him now waiting upon his more sensual brother.

Lionel groaned and stirred the scented water. "Seraide could see; she knew." He opened his drowsing eyes and smiled. "She is mine."

Bors looked away.

Lancelot, though younger, had handled them easily in their sparring. He had a great talent that had been honed by a training begun before his memory could report. Lionel, with Bors, had received no more than the training due to any foster of the king. Bors had learned best the skills of the lance and horse, while Lionel, driven more by dreams of vengeance, had preferred the brawling of foot combat. Lancelot, with an ease that drew from Bors an ever greater love and respect, surpassed them in both.

"That other, though, is a coward." Lionel rested his chin upon the water's surface.

"Servause chose not to fight," answered Bors. "He is well able." They had watched him, witnessed his strength, and when he rode against the quintain the steadiness of his lance matched or surpassed even that of Lancelot's.

"Twice, I asked him," said Lionel. "Twice, he refused. He said nothing; he but turned from me." The boy huffed. "He would not even take his eyes from the ground."

Bors had seen. The boy had borne even Lionel's hard and rude shove. "He has the respect of our cousin."

Lionel rose from the water. "Lancelot is but a boy, and Servause is his friend."

The feast hall was quieter than those they had before known. Lionel had often to lower his voice as he spoke, and twice drew the frowning attention of Lady Viviane from the nearby high table. The four boys were all still of an age to serve their elders, but in honor of the arrival of the two brothers, they were allowed this one evening's respite. Lionel sat to the left of Lancelot, with Seraide as his other companion, while Bors had their cousin's right, with Servause at the place farther along.

Lionel was again speaking a bit more loudly than he should when he said to Lancelot, "You but jest, or toy with my wit."

"I speak but truth, Cousin," Lancelot replied. "My skill is my own, and has no touch of the Lady's enchantment."

"Nay." Lionel, red in the face, leaned toward Seraide.

She touched lightly his shoulder. "My love—"

He covered her hand with his. "It is with provocation that I so lift my voice. It is beyond reason to accept that my good cousin, raised from swaddling in this swimming world of great magics, has not taken some part of those enchantments into his nature, nor bears them in his armament."

"It is as your cousin reports," answered the maid. "I am my lady's intimate, and can attest that he is untouched of her power."

"You, too, but tease." Lionel laughed too loudly, then glanced at the lady Viviane to see if his excesses had drawn her notice. But she remained engrossed in a conversation with some small group before her.

"I do not tease at all," Seraide replied. "And once again I do beg that you more properly heed my words. Not lightly are they spoken, but with good intent to your need. By our love, treat them not so recklessly."

He squeezed her hand. "I hear them," he said, "and understand your wish, but it would be unknightly of me to set aside my manhood at no more than your whispered word. Surely you would not wish me so small." He offered her a deep grin. "You must understand, sweet Seraide, that a man must see to these matters in his own way."

She blushed, then smiled, but before she could say more Lionel had looked away.

"Tell truth now," he continued to Lancelot. "Upon our shared blood, how can one so young and small stand so resolute against my tried and bloody hand, if not but by the protection of the Lady and her wiles? Training, I will grant you. Your form I will laud as flawless. But such force rides upon your blows and thrusts as cannot be credited to learning and strength alone."

Lancelot sighed and looked down to the fish on the trencher before him. "I will not so lightly swear upon our blood, Cousin, or offer any other such oath. Of all things, I am loath to be foresworn." Raising his gray eyes, he held the other young man with his gaze. "Upon courtesy I would rather depend, that my simple assurance would serve as sufficient answer to you. I say again: There is neither art nor false seeming in my skill. All that I achieve, I achieve by my own hand and will.

"If that assurance fails, then upon great compulsion I will swear upon our blood. But I would rather we have that simpler trust, the sort of one knight to another." Lancelot smiled. "Grant that trust, I beg, and let us more simply talk of such-and-such—the step-and-turn, for example, that took you from your feet this day in our practice."

Lionel worked his lips, but failed for words.

"He speaks true," said Bors. "That is plain."

Lionel glanced at his brother. Then someone farther along the table caught his eye. "What gape you at, clod-pole?" he snapped. "Look away from your betters."

Servause continued to stare.

"You are not of our blood," Lionel sneered.

At that, the boy turned away.

"I would have you not speak so to my friend," Lancelot said gently.

Lionel turned to him. "What cause have you, Cousin, to defend the lummox? He is not of us. That he even sits here is a puzzle—this coward, this . . . *thing* that will not fight when challenged."

Lancelot stood, so quickly and with such grace that he was on his feet before his intent was known.

"My young men will be seated," said the lady Viviane clearly. "I believe that your chattering has made you negligent of the business that has come before us."

For some time, petitioners had been presenting their woes. Beyond the lake, the lady Viviane held such sway that the peoples of those hard lands would come to her for aid. A small group of such, terrified by the weight of court and water and wonder, waited now before her. That they had not yet spoken only Bors knew, for alone among the boys he had attended to the duties of the time.

Lancelot still stood.

Lionel glanced at the hard eyes of the Lady. "Sit," he hissed. "I will honor henceforth your pet. Sit, please."

And Lancelot did.

"Thank you. Now—" the Lady turned to the petitioners "—speak."

In the smaller rooms of the castle a visitor might forget that all around him lay the waters of the lake, but here in the great hall those waters gave to sight a waviness, and to hearing a dullness. There was also the occasional dismaying passing of some large, dark fish. It was of little surprise that the headman spoke with a terror-tremor in his voice.

"Dread lady, we small folk have suffered greatly at the hands of a giant. We dare not sleep for fearing that our homes will be cracked open and our babes plucked away. Now—" he blinked and swallowed down his fear "—we well know that you have not abandoned us. You have sent us brave knights, and broken and dead have they been hurled back upon your waters. But so beaten are we by need and fear that we must come again here before you to plead that your own great power be turned on this infernal curse. Dread lady—" and they all knelt "—save us. We are past hope."

Bors looked to the Lady, but saw in her only the stillness of the lake's waters.

"Where are my knights?" she said then, her voice filling the hall. "Will none serve me in this?"

Bors looked to the older men, shocked to see the fear of those who had all lost strong friends. Servause moved, then Lancelot, but Lionel, pulling free of Seraide's hold, leapt first to his feet. "By the blood of King Claudas' son, I swear the death of this giant." He grinned and glanced at Lancelot, who settled again into his seat, and then to Seraide, whose horror-struck look drove away the young man's cheer.

Lady Viviane smiled as coldly as the waters. "The boy must then be your answer," she said to the quavering embassy. "But trust that I will prepare him for success."

Bowing, they retreated, weeping in confusion to have so green a boy as their savior, but glad in the end to be gone from the Lady's hall.

"Why did you stir?" asked Bors of Servause. "Would you have risen?"

The big youth looked so sharply to the younger, his eyes for that instant so bereft of confusion and seeking, that Bors thought another sat beside him. Then Servause was lost again and looked away.

Jugglers followed to lighten the mood, then finned people who danced high into the waters, and such other entertainments as idled away the evening. Such a show, so touched by the Lady's magic, was a wonder to Bors, a pleasure to Lancelot, and an irritant to Lionel, who spent the time whispering with the maid Seraide.

At last the Lady of the Lake turned to them. "Lionel, son of Bors, come before me."

Lionel rose boldly, but turned first right, then left, before he found his way around the tables to reach the space in front of Lady Viviane.

"Brave Lionel," said the Lady of the Lake, "to a thing unsuited you have come; but for your courage, and for the need, I shall fashion something for both your instruction and success. Young Seraide, come forward."

The girl gasped.

Bors rose, but Lancelot stood first to offer his hand in escort, and so guided the maid around the table. Seraide, face pale, crossed the open way alone and found her place beside Lionel.

Dark and menacing, Lady Viviane had much the look of the pike that had passed them on the previous day. "I am disappointed, young Seraide, that you have failed to ward this boy from this foolishness."

Lionel stepped forward. "My lady—"

"Speak not."

"I will," Lionel said, "for she is my—"

Lady Viviane moved a hand and the waters choked any further words from the young man. He could but gape as silently as a fish.

"Seraide."

The girl bowed her head.

"Great powers I entrusted to you for the purpose that

you have failed. Infatuation has censured your right counsel and rule. Your rebukes should have stopped Lionel
before he thought to rise; your hand alone can never hold
this one from his folly." She paused.

"It is . . . my folly, my lady," Seraide replied. "Too fond
I have grown of Lionel to be of good counsel."

"As I do see. And, as in foolishness you two are wed, so
shall it be in life, I now decree."

Seraide gasped, first for shock, and then as much for
joy at so welcome a punishment.

Lionel looked as though he had been struck.

"Lord and lady you must be," continued Lady Viviane,
"and as lady you shall continue as ward of your lord. To
you, I shall pass the power to keep Lionel proof from
death—but only once, and for a brief time. It will be your
task to choose that moment well." She turned from the girl.
"Young Bors."

The boy felt as though his heart had been seized. "My
lady," he murmured.

"Your words have been golden, and, by my faith, will
continue so. Come forward."

He rose.

"Will you hold your tongue?" asked the Lady of Lionel.

At his nod, the force holding him silent fell away. He
blinked, then parted his lips.

"Mind," the Lady said with a hint of a smile. "If that
tongue wags again, out I shall have it as an eel."

"Discourteous," he said only, then looked to Seraide.
"But not unkind. I will have you gladly."

"And you," said the Lady to Bors as the boy reached his
brother's side, "will you have them? So besotted are they
that I would place their rule in one wiser. Guide them,
speak true to them, but meddle not in what they finally
choose. Will you so accept my charge, wise Bors?"

"I am ever my brother's keeper," he answered. "But,
before God, I will hold them apart as husband and wife
until in God's way, and at their own will, they are more
holy joined." His heart felt light.

Lady Viviane considered the boy. "Your piety, young
man, will need check if you are to live in this world. The
power that binds these two lies beyond both mine and
yours."

"A man has but to obey the commandments of God."

Viviane smiled. "Such hard words can be but false prophecy. I fear that you have set the stumble in your own course. A lesson you must have, though your sight be true. Still, join these two in this adventure, and you are free to counsel them as your heart will have it."

"Gladly."

"Then we are done."

Lancelot stood.

Viviane looked to him.

He nearly spoke, then paused, then began again. "A boon, my good lady. . . ."

"You may not accompany them."

Lancelot drew a long breath, then continued. "To none do I owe more than you, my dear Lady of the Lake, and I speak with only the greatest respect. I have been long alone, save for my good Servause, until this arrival of my cousins. Now as a bloom opened am I, that cannot so fall again to a closed bud. Duty calls me that as the knight I would be I must rightly and strongly attend these affairs of my cousins. For mercy—"

"That I deny," Viviane said flatly.

He took another breath. "A knight cannot suffer his fellows harm through a want of strength not offered. I cannot be true if I but watch so unlikely a matching of strengths."

The Lady shook her head. "Your sword shall not answer their need."

Lancelot opened his pale eyes more widely. "By that God of Bors, then, by that Seat in Heaven, I beg you not to hold me from a knight's right duty. This giant—"

"The giant is mine," Servause interrupted, rising.

Lancelot turned to the other. "No, it is mine."

Servause, standing straight, shook his head.

Lancelot touched his sword. "My sweet friend, do not think to take this from me."

Lowering his eyes, Servause replied, "It is not yours."

"My young men," said the Lady gently. "Both of you now come closer."

Looking carefully from each other, the two came around the tables and joined the three already before Viviane.

"Speak now, Bors," she commanded.

Bors felt cool and wise. "God drives you not in this," he

said to Lancelot. "Know better His touch, and use the holy name more righteously."

Lancelot blushed and looked away.

"Servause," said Bors, near lost in the depths that again shone in the other's eyes. "Heed the Lady's words. She is your teacher; trust her judgment to match your will. So does she serve God."

Servause made no change, yet yielded to the words.

"And I," said Viviane, very softly, "see now that I must have a boon of you, my Lancelot. Will you freely grant it?"

"Without hesitation," he answered. "These quarrels cannot touch my loyalty and trust."

She looked then to the other. "Servause, foundling, come you so to your fate? Over this matter, would you so set your strength against one raised alongside you as a brother?"

"No," he answered.

"I had not thought it possible. Still, that one oath shall answer another, I would have of you that same boon. Will you so grant it?"

"Yes."

"Swear then to me," she said to both, "that never, in malice or sport, or through mistake of guise, shall you two ever meet at arms."

Lancelot looked surprised, then slowly smiled. "No oath would I more gladly swear, I that will not swear any oath lightly. Servause—" he faced his friend "—that I did come to see you as something other, when I found my true blood, I fear to be true, and do now repent. I would not so lose you. As brothers we were; as brothers I would have us continue. So I swear that neither by will nor ignorance nor sport shall I ever raise weapon against you. Will you like swear to me, for kinship, and for our lady's pleasure?"

"Gladly," said Servause, though his expression remained grim.

Lionel offered bright jests, and Seraide smiled to hear him, but the two rode with Bors always between them. They had passed well beyond the lake, leaving their escort upon the shore, and traveled now alone along a decayed road within the giant's realm.

Lionel was armed with helmet, hauberk, and shield, and wore his sword at his side. He handled his lance and mount well enough, but with less skill than would have pleased his more practiced brother. Bors went unarmed, save for his own sword, while the maid rode lightly upon her palfrey.

"A waste." Lionel looked out over the empty land. "I might well have left this task to Servause. He would have found no man here to cower from." He laughed, but stopped when none joined in. Then, frowning, he added, "Yet, upon my sword, I would not yield such honor as I shall have to such an oaf."

Lionel looked to Seraide, but she looked away. Shifting the point of his lance, he turned instead to Bors. "The Lady did say that the task would be accomplished; she promised as much to those poor folk." He looked around again, but in so wild a land the people were well hidden, leaving the open ways to outlaws and errant knights.

"Best trust to God," said Bors.

Lionel snorted. "He has not placed at my side a maid with the powers of my Seraide."

Pale, she looked up.

"You do poorly to mock our Lord," said Bors. "My faith is that all comes at His hand. Have more reverence."

Lionel looked away, then sighed. "I fear I bark words at this emptiness. They mean less than I say. Still, I am glad of a brother at my side, though I would that you had ridden fully armed."

"I am not to fight."

Lionel shook his head. "Fwew upon the Lady's words. Had she but allowed Lancelot—he is a likely boy. . . ."

"I would rather have had Servause," Bors noted.

Lionel leaned away. "The white-livered? We would have had more gain from him as a pack animal than we would from the use of his sword."

"In the hall he stood in offer to take up the task."

Lionel barked out a laugh. "More like to take himself to the jakes." But he had heard Servause's words, seen the other's desire for the quest. He looked away, out at the lands. In places, the old trees of the wood closed tightly about them, while bracken and boulders filled most clearings. What few farmsteads they saw were broken and hollow. "A waste land. . . ."

Seraide wept.

"Do not fear," Lionel said, looking to her. "You carry the Lady's powers. By her will, we are safe from harm, if you but choose the right moment."

She looked at him as though upon a baying hound.

"She weeps for the people," Bors explained. "For the suffering here."

Lionel reddened and turned away, but his gaze lingered on the next lost hovel they came upon—a half-fallen cottage down from the road to their right. He stared until he heard a great, long groan roll down from the slope to their left. He turned again, sharply, but tangled his lance in the branches overhead as he did. Cursing, he wrestled with the weapon until the wanderings of his mount forced him to drop it. "Damn." He shed his shield and slipped from the saddle. "Brother, draw and watch for trouble while I recover my spear."

But Bors was watching Seraide. Her frightened mare had retreated back down the road. White-faced and staring up the slope, she had little sense of what the animal did. And then the attack came.

Two went for Bors—rough, fearful-eyed men who sprang from ambush. The boy drew his sword and angled his mount into the one that bore the man-catcher, knocking the outlaw back before the hook could fall. Then, with his blade, he swept the pole from the man's hands. Swaying to avoid a cudgel blow from the one at his back, Bors twisted and brought his own weapon down. At the last instant, he turned his blade flat so to spare the man and not draw the blood of one so mean. The bandit, amazed to be still holding life and startled by the quick prowess he faced, promptly fled. The first had recovered the man-catcher, but dropped it and followed his friend in retreat as Bors turned back to him.

Seraide shrieked. Three bandits surrounded her. One had the reins of her mount, while a second struggled to pull her from the saddle.

Lionel roared. He had knocked one man senseless, then drawn his sword and cut down a second, but a half-dozen more were upon him. "Brother," he cried, "to me!"

Bors rode to Seraide even as Lionel called out a second time. He had the surprise of the one at the mare's reins and knocked him reeling with a flat-edged blow. Another outlaw, marked by Seraide's kick to his face, came brawling in, swinging an axe. Bors pulled back deftly from the blow, but the man, straw-haired and lean, with cruel eyes, set his weapon into the skull of the boy's horse. Pitching forward, Bors drove the pommel of his sword into the straw-haired man's brow. The axe man fell as heavily as the horse, cushioning the boy and allowing him to quickly rise. Seraide's attacker, his arms wrapped round her, had dragged her from the saddle. She had spat and scratched his mustached face, but swayed now from some blow Bors had not witnessed. Her clothes were torn.

"Bors!" shouted Lionel again from within a desperate storm of blows.

Bors leapt forward. Seraide's attacker, seeing that he could not fight the one while controlling the other, pushed the maid free and ran. Bors caught Seraide and saw blood on her lips. She clutched at him.

The great groaning cry that had begun the encounter came again, from closer by.

"To your horse," said Bors to Seraide and freed her. Turning, he saw that many of the bandits stood frozen, their faces ashen. The mustached man had scrambled to the edge of the wood.

"Hurry," cried their captain. "Be done before the beast arrives and steals our prizes!"

The outlaws closest to Bors rallied. The cudgel man had found his courage and circled in search of an advantage, while his fellow crept up to recover his discarded man-catcher. Beyond them, Lionel hung securely in the grip of two; he had been smashed about the face, but two bandits lay bloody on the ground at his feet. The final three, the outlaw captain among them, started toward Bors.

"Say the words, whatever they be," whispered Bors, backing to where Seraide had found her horse. "For his safety." He feinted toward the cudgel man, who retreated back to the company of the man-catcher. "Say them."

The words that passed Seraide's lips burned Bors' Christian soul, but he knew now that his brother would be safe. "Come," he hissed and leapt suddenly onto the horse, pulling the maid, who was already half-mounted, before him. "We must have help; you must be safe."

When they saw that Bors and Seraide were in flight, the outlaws cried out and Lionel roared. The mustached man, with drawn sword, ran to intercept them, then froze and stumbled back. A harsh, guttural chuckling echoed down to them from high on the slope. Bors glanced back as he rode and saw a great face, dumb and monstrous, vacant of any soul, peer over the hill's crest. Bowing his head and seeing only God before him, the boy drove the horse as strongly as he was able.

They had not far to ride; three curves of the road brought them to Lancelot and Servause. Scrupulous to the Lady's will, Lancelot had not accompanied the three, but as soon as he dared, he had followed. Both rode in full harness, lances held high, and seemed in every particular knights of full prowess.

Bors reined to a halt. "I left Lionel for the sake of the maid—she must to safety—but you two . . ."

Seraide turned in Bors' embrace. Tears stained her bruised face. "I have abandoned my lord, as well. Do not make me a cause to delay his rescue. I have means to summon the Lady, to bring aid." Trembling still in fright from the attack, she slipped free and dropped from the horse.

"What face we?" asked Lancelot.

"Outlaws," answered Bors, "all in terror. The giant is near, and they hurried to have us before it arrived."

Joy touched the mild face of Lancelot. "We shall free your brother, but not—" he looked down to Seraide "—at the cost of your fear and abandonment."

Bors was loathe to let others take up a task he knew should be his, but recognized himself the least of the three in arms and skill. "I will stay by her side."

Seraide shook her head. "I will be safe."

Servause caused his mount to step back. "I will not go."

Lancelot looked at his friend.

"Not for my brother?" asked Bors.

Servause shook his head.

Bors turned to Lancelot, expecting to see some censure in those pale eyes.

But Lancelot's face was calm. "My friend has not lust to battle men, Cousin; we two will ride."

They came quickly upon the outlaws. The band, having gathered both Lionel and his horse, had moved down the slope to the ruined cottage. They had raised spears, and had now some few bows, as well, but held them directed toward the hillside in guard against the coming of the giant, rather than toward the road against the return of the boy and the maid. Thus Lancelot and Bors had the advantage in angle and surprise, but still brought on themselves a volley of arrows. From his place in the lead, Lancelot took two in his shield and one as a glance off his helmet even as he drove into the line of spears.

Bors feared for his cousin, but that dread was replaced by amazement at how ably the boy avoided the points. Lancelot set his lance into the best armored man almost before the outlaw captain raised his own weapon. Terror took the rest as Bors barreled in among them, using the palfrey as a ram to batter the scattering men. The few who stood were quickly and stoutly dealt with by Lancelot, who had his sword out before the abandoned lance had touched the ground. The bandits attempted to rally, as Bors reached the ruined cottage and his brother, but Lancelot, baiting them first to draw their bow shots, hurled in to rout them again, then once more, until in a riot of fear they fled in every direction. Many were wounded, but few were dead, as Lancelot was near as loathe as Bors to shed the blood of even those villains.

Lionel had been thrown as a sack against the outside wall of the cottage. His hands were bound at his back. His lips were broken and swollen, and two of his teeth were gone. "You left me," he hissed.

"Only to see to the safety of your lady." Bors knelt to cut his brother's bonds.

"I am your brother." Lionel flexed his hands and glared at Bors. "Yet you left me."

Bors stood. "Would you rather that I had left Seraide?"

"Yes." Lionel rose to his feet. One finger on his left hand jutted brokenly. "Left her only so that, together, we would then have gone to her."

Bors thought of Seraide in the hands of her attacker. "She would have suffered more."

With his good hand, Lionel struck his brother's face. "And I did not?" He snatched the knife from Bors' hand and slashed the air with it, but the younger boy did not flinch. "Together, we would have killed them all!"

"You were in no peril of your life," Bors said. "Seraide warded you with the Lady's enchantment before we fled."

Lionel struck Bors again across the face. When his brother did not react, did not raise a hand in his own defense, a cold, murderous rage took hold of Lionel. He stared at the knife in his hand, then pointed it at Bors.

"As God wills." Bors knelt. "I will not fight, and will not fly from my blood."

Lionel raised the blade, but a cry stopped its descent. Seraide ran from where Viviane, well attended by her knights, had appeared from within a mist. The Lady of the Lake sat straight upon her mount, her robes trailing nearly to the earth.

"No," Seraide gasped. She fell to her knees before Lionel. "Not for my sake should you slay your dear brother. Would that I had rather died."

Lionel scowled at her. "No harm would have come to you; that I swear. Had brother stood with brother, naught would have kept us from you." He looked back at Bors. "So this treason I cannot endure."

Rising, Seraide grasped her lord's arm. "Upon my love—"

"It will not, in this matter, suffice," interrupted the Lady in a clear voice. "Bloody and hard must your husband be, sweet Seraide, attentive to, but not all bound, by your love. Now, perhaps, you know more full well the man into whose arms you rushed. Release him."

She did, somewhat surprised by her own action, but knowing also that, as had been the case at the feast in the Lady's hall, Lionel would have simply shaken her away had she persisted.

Lionel stared down at his brother, who prayed before him. With his bad hand, Lionel pushed back Bors' head to reveal the face and expose the throat. The younger boy's lips murmured, and the peace in his eyes revealed that he no longer saw this world alone.

"Hold," cried Lancelot, just arrived from a foray to the road in search of the giant. "What outrage is this?"

"My brother left me," Lionel said with broken lips, "as no knight should ever leave another."

Lancelot leapt from his horse. "Then I will have his place," he offered, "as champion for one who so holds himself, for brotherly love, from his own defense." He drew his sword and moved to block the knife's blade.

"Stay your hand, Lancelot," said the Lady. "From that God above your young cousin seeks his salvation, and not from the sword. That knight's weapon, though it be the best in the world, will not answer such a trial as this."

Lancelot looked at his patroness, then back at the two brothers. He set his jaw. "Blade on blade is what I know."

"If persuasion so fails," answered the Lady, "then I command you, by that right I still have over you. Hold your hand, my boy, and learn that your strength shall not always answer your need."

Lancelot quivered, then turned away not to see.

Lionel's expression grew hard. "Now you must die." He moved the knife toward Bors' throat, but found his hand stopped. He struggled to free himself, then pulled with a rage of frustration that would have toppled many a good knight, but Servause was unmoved. Unseen, on cat's feet, the other had come upon them all. In his right hand he held Lionel's wrist, while in his left he bore his drawn sword.

Lionel turned, but Servause's strength drove him to his knees. He wailed in outrage and looked to Viviane.

The Lady of the Lake smiled. "I cannot command Servause to hold; he is not of mine. Brave Lionel, yield now your unholy rage, and so learn that it can find check. And Bors, raise up from your holy prayers, and so find cause to hold you at hard need within this world."

Lionel glared up into Servause's eyes, but found there such clear might that a weakness spread through him, as it might befall a man raging into the face of a storm. All strength abandoned him then, leaving but grief for his deeds and a desperate gladness that the other's strength had overcome his anger. Yielding so to helplessness, he wept, finding around him Seraide's arms as she joined her own tears with his.

Turning to see, Lancelot found before him all that he had been denied, but so wildly done as did lie beyond his will. So free from both censure and praise stood Servause that Lancelot understood, finally, that for all his own strength he could never that way go, that ever he must be bound by the regard of his peers.

And when Bors looked from his God to see Servause, he saw the right hand that held in check his brother's wrath and the left that held the drawn sword. And so, in the eyes of the other, he found the duty that would now hold him to earth, while others went their way to Heaven.

"The lesson is done," concluded the lady Viviane. "Let us now return to our home."

Later, after Lionel had recovered enough to beg peace of his kin, the three together sought out Servause. They found him alone in the practice yard, working hard upon the pell. The boom of each blow, as the rhythm of a heart, echoed through the Lady's castle. Facing his back, they wondered if, so steady and untiring, he would ever stop. When he finally turned to greet them, his eyes, caught as ever between their dark clarity and their earth-bound confusion, revealed to them that Servause had known that they were watching, without ever having seen that they were there.

Lionel spoke first. "You slew the giant."

Servause did not look away.

"We saw the blood," added Lancelot more gently, "on your sword." It had not been red, but clear and ichorous. Few, other than the boys, had noticed it. The giant had not thereafter been seen.

Servause, his eyes showing as portals, nodded.

"Yet you will not fight men." Bors stepped forward. "Which is, before God, a knight's duty."

"Then no such knight shall I be," Servause answered, "for I know now that I may not so shed the blood of man."

And then, at long last, Servause smiled.

SQUIRE KAY IN LOVE

Phyllis Ann Karr

First, we must make it clear that Maid Iris of Southvale is not in any way the romantic interest of this story. The daughter of Sir Ector's favorite clerk, she eventually married another clerk, with whom she lived a long and happy life, raising several little clerks. Her only reason for being in the present tale is that she witnessed it, having grown up with its heroes as a playfellow whose gender was largely irrelevant to all their young lives.

In months—not years, but only months—Iris was older by twenty than Sir Ector's firstborn, and by twenty-five than his second son . . . though all the world thought it was by thirty, and Iris herself would not have known the difference between Kay's age and Arthur's was so awkwardly short, but that one day when she was about two years old, playing quietly on the cleanswept image of a man with goat's legs dancing amidst many small creatures, while wooden pillars supported a dark wooden canopy high above, she had heard her father come into the room with Sir Ector, talking all unaware of her presence.

"Thy wife still has milk, has she not?" Sir Ector asked. (At that time, Iris was but newly weaned, for they nursed babes longer at the breast in those days.)

"Aye," the clerk replied. "But, my lord, high though this honor is that you offer us, to put your own son to my wife's breast and this new babe to that of your own good lady, it will cause even more wagging of idle tongues than if my wife should nurse the new one."

"And for that reason, among others," said Sir Ector, "we leave this manor as soon as the child is delivered, and travel by easy stages to my Welsh holdings, where they have not seen their master for so long that they cannot know otherwise than that his wife has borne him a second son, a mere ten months after his first."

"But why all this secrecy, my lord?"

"That," said Sir Ector, "is a matter it behooves us not even to guess. Only that it seems there are those who must not know what has become of this child."

For many years, Iris had thought this stray memory a dream, the more so in that she had never again seen the goat-legged man frolicking amid the small, colorful creatures. But it was true that her mother wetnursed Master Kay, making Iris in some measure almost a stepsister to him. And at last, the night her mother told her privately how it was with women, she told her mother of the supposed dream, and learned it was true: The goat-legged man was on the mosaic floor of the clerk's office in Sir Ector's manor near London, which they had not visited since Arthur was delivered, and Iris must have been unseen beneath the scribing desk to underhear words not meant for her ears; for though Arthur might be Sir Ector's son, he was no child of Sir Ector's wife, and the difference in the lads' ages was only half what it was commonly believed to be.

"But then, who is Arthur's mother?" Iris had wondered.

"Some comely young serf nearabout London, most like," her own mother had answered. "And our fine, proud young Artus—" she spoke in love, using the sportive form of Arthur's name "—can surely be not even so wellborn on his mother's side as I am myself, and so the less said of her, the better, seeing as how our good lord will raise both boys on the same level, as trueborn sons—unlike certain other noble lords and even kings one might find in these evil times." For then, as now, folk considered themselves to be living in evil times.

Arthur must have been Sir Ector's single lapse, and his lady's nursing of the new babe bore witness that she forgave all. But from thenceforth Sir Ector had lived a life resembling that of some knightly hermit, retired from the world at large and limiting his personal attendance to his Welsh manors, while avoiding those of his lands that lay nearest to the late King Uther's favorite court city of London.

Yet even the most retired of knightly hermits must open his house for travelers, hospitality being incumbent in those days upon everyone, but most especially upon those who could best afford it. There came a day when no lesser folk than Uriens, king of Gore, together with his wife

Dame Morgan—who was daughter to the late King Uther's widow by an earlier husband—sought hospitality at Sir Ector's manor of Southvale, on their way to a great tournament at Bedegraine Castle.

Despite her husband's retinue of multiple barons, knights, and other attendants, Dame Morgan traveled with a single gentlewoman, stern-faced and elderly. It was the first sign that all was far from well between these royal spouses, though it was hardly the last that Maid Iris observed, as Sir Ector's wife bade her sit at the high table for a more courteous balance between lords and ladies.

Kay, having been weaned early from his true mother's milk to make way for Arthur, was moving with similar dispatch through his education, and stood already in his twelfth year a squire of some accomplishment. He was proud to serve such royal guests at table. Even while remaining lean and hawkish of face and frame, Kay had always delighted in the arts and courtesies of the banquet, making it one of their earliest childhood games to serve Artus a dinner of pilfered dainties carved up fine and called by fancier names, while directing Iris how to provide the minstrelsy—or sometimes, as the younger boy grew to pagehood, to reverse their roles and feed Iris while Arthur harped and sang.

Tonight Arthur insisted on helping serve the high table, too. He was not likely to be esquired for two or three more years yet, for in some ways he seemed a little dull of understanding even for his supposed age, though Kay, who thought Artus a full ten months younger than himself, fondly compared it to the slowness of an eagle that can scarcely deign to learn flying to the lure.

As Kay carved meat and Arthur poured wine for the visiting queen of Gore, she remarked, "These are two very fine sons you have, my lord and my lady."

Sir Ector replied at once, in a firm, hearty voice, "Madame, they are that indeed."

His wife added, in tones equally hearty, "We are both very proud of them."

"Indeed," Dame Morgan went on, "I could hope that my own son Ywen, who is as yet too young for this journey—"

"*Our* son, madame," growled King Uriens, "for all that you coddle him to your skirts, pretending that a lad of full four summers is still too tender to hear men's bones crack, even in tournament play."

"Our son, my lord, will do very well and manly, when the time comes. But until the day of his esquiring, I demand my mother's rights over his infancy and pagehood." Dame Morgan uttered these words with no further rebuke from her husband, since he was once again concentrating more fiercely upon his meal. Turning back to smile at her cup-bearer, the queen added, "And how fairly shines young Arthur's hair!"

"Madame," said Kay, "will it please you to try this sauce? It is seasoned with rare cardamom and pepper from the East."

Kay so seldom tried to seize attention from Arthur, that at first Iris could scarcely believe it was not mere happenstance this time.

Undeterred, the queen of Gore went on, "It is rare, I think, for so golden a head to spring from two dark-haired parents."

"Rare, madame, but not unknown," Maid Iris said quickly, speaking from her clerkly father's knowledge. "It is not so rare as for a dark head to spring from two fair parents."

"True," Dame Morgan agreed. "Both of my own parents were dark of hair—although my mother's eyes are blue—and yet my sister Elaine was crowned with gold from birth. Arthur, now—his hair is exactly the same hue as our late High King's. Uther . . . Arthur. You must have admired King Uther greatly, my lord Sir Ector, to make your younger son so near a namesake."

"Madame," Kay asked, "will it please you to permit me to salt your meat for you?"

She nodded absently, though without taking her gaze from Sir Ector, who replied,

"Madame, I did greatly admire King Uther Pendragon."

Dame Morgan cocked her head and half murmured, "Might one make so bold as to inquire why?"

"No, madame, 'one' may *not*!" King Uriens snarled, and immediately returned his somewhat sottish—saving his kingship—attention to his food and wine.

"Madame," Kay bid a third time for her glance, "will it please you to try a pinch of cinnamon in your wine?"

Now, at last, Dame Morgan looked at the elder brother, smiled, and granted him a gracious nod of her diademmed head. And Maid Iris saw, with strange misgiving, that for the first time in his life her old playfellow was completely besmitten.

Actually, as far as Maid Iris knew, Kay might have been smitten before, when Sir Ector was sojourning at one of his other manors, for some of them had good clerks of their own in residence, so that occasionally Iris stayed behind with her parents at Southvale. But she did not think that Kay could ever have wrestled with Cupid before now, or he would have confided something of it to her on his return, as he confided this present infatuation to her later that same night.

She had come, between dinner and bedtime, to sit awhile by herself in a favorite place on the bank of the small brook that gurgled just north of the manor. Here, as the sun set on one side and the full moon rose on the other, Kay came also, probably by happenstance. Yet he seemed as well content with her fellowship as he would have been with only his own.

"Rixith," he said, using an old pet name, "is not Her Grace of Gore the most beautiful, gracious, queenly woman thou hast ever seen?"

"She is very beautiful and queenly, surely. But she is dark as midnight!"

"So art thou, and I, and my father Sir Ector, and my own beautiful mother. But if Dame Morgan is dark as midnight, it is a midnight with starlight in its eyes and the moon in its smile!"

"Why, Kex, where didst thou learn poetry?"

Kay shrugged. "Probably from the minstrel who summered with us at Broadlea two years ago. Remember, I told thee about him."

"Yes, but we laughed—thou harder than I—at what thou rememberest of his songs."

"Well, I was still but a page. Now that I am esquired, is it not time to choose me a liege lady?"

"Ah! So this is a practical matter, a part of thy squirely education."

"That," he protested a little heatedly, "it is not! Even if fair ladies grew hereabout as thick as blackberries on bushes, Dame Morgan would still be the only one worth worshipping."

Iris did not remind him how few other ladies he had, as yet, seen. Nor did she point out that the queen of Gore was his elder by at least as many years as he himself had been alive: In that era, age made little difference. All in all, it seemed to Iris a safe enough arrangement that Kay should choose for his first liege lady one as far removed as Dame Morgan would be once the people of Gore had left South-vale. She said only, "Well, then, be a little prudent in thy worship while they are still here, for I think the king of Gore might be an old-fashioned sort of husband, who does not understand courtly love."

"He is worse than a beast to her! Only this morning, simply to settle a quarrel, he snatched her best ring from her finger and hurled it back to the far side of the stream they had just forded, and forbade anyone to go back for it."

"Who told thee this?"

"The lady herself!" he answered proudly. "I saw and seized my chance to speak with her after dinner, to pledge her my allegiance."

"Kex! What if you were seen?"

"We were not. I am sure we were not. Or, at least, not noticed. It was wonderful, Rixith, how she sat in the alcove, and I knelt before her, and no one who passed turned an eye toward us or paid us the slightest attention at all."

"Perhaps the lady knows some enchantment," Iris mused, with a tug of misgiving at her stomach. "Did she even go so far as to tell thee what their quarrel had been about?"

"Her own mother's last child, the one that disappeared so strangely, years ago. Uriens said that Queen Ygerne had probably strangled it at birth to keep any son of the Pendragon's from succeeding to the throne, because—he said—Ygerne must have hated Uther as Dame Morgan hates Uriens—again by the king of Gore's own account. But my good lady maintained that the child must have been another demon's whelp, like Merlin, for all that Uther might claim the fatherhood—perhaps himself misled—but that even had it come out with horns and a cloven hoof, she misdoubted that her tender mother could have slain or ordered it slain, and so it must have been snatched from her. That was when Uriens said, 'Like this, madame?' and snatched the ring from off her finger. Rixith, that ring was very dear to my lady, a gift from her sister Dame Margawse, King Lot's wife of Orkney. It has a ruby the size and shape of a robin's egg, set between the mouth and tail of a silver serpent, as if the serpent were about to swallow it."

"I wonder that she could lift her hand when wearing it," Iris remarked.

"She has granted me the task of getting it back for her," Kay went on, more proudly than ever. "To prove my devotion."

"Why, where is this ford where it was snatched and hurled?"

"About four hours' travel by horseback to the north of here, not along the main track, but on a path scarce wide enough for horses in single file. There is a great old lightning-blasted oak to one side of the stream, and three big rocks set up endwise in the middle of the water to mark the ford."

"I know the place!" said Iris. "I rode that way with my father when we went to copy a book they have at the nunnery of Whitethorn, two summers ago when thou and Artus were with your parents at Broadlea. But, Kex, how to deliver the lady back her ring? It will take most of the day to recover and return with it, if thou canst find it in the shrubs and dirt, and the people of Gore leave tomorrow morning after Mass."

"My lady does not. She will feign sickness. Whereupon her loving lord will prove his tender affection by riding on with most of his men, leaving her only enough for a meager escort to come after him whenever she feels herself recovered. Which will be when I have restored her ring to her."

His smile shone so happily in the moonlight that Iris lacked heart to tell him her misgivings . . . for which, after all, she could find little ground, save in her impression that Dame Morgan was well able to match her husband, and oddly willing to share intimate family details of a quarrel she seemed fully capable of having started herself. But then, the mystery of what had happened to Queen Ygerne's missing child, who should have been King Uther's heir, belonged to the politics and public gossip of all Britain; so all Iris said, before they parted for the night, was, "I will go with thee as guide, Kex, since I have traveled that path."

"Only the once, by thy words. And, armed with my good lady's directions, how can I miss finding the place? Moreover, it is past time that I should know every least trail and footpath of all my father's holdings. But come if it pleases thee, Rixith, for the company."

Of course, Arthur came too. Though still too young to understand romantic love, courtly or otherwise, he would never have abided being left behind in such a game as the recovery of Queen Morgan's ring.

In those days, the young were allowed precious little leisure for idle pastimes. Nevertheless, Kay and Arthur, and Iris when she was with them at the same manor, had all their lives been in the custom of seizing a holiday for themselves when they wished one badly enough. Not since Kay reached the age of seven had Sir Ector's people begun the hue and cry as soon as the children were discovered both, or all three, missing. They simply awaited the truants' return, and made them pay with homilies, missed meals, extra hours of work and study, and various other penances—all of which the trio regarded as not too onerous a price for their stolen sport. Nor did they ever truly go hungry, seeing that Kay always saw to it they had provisions both for the outing and in secret caches near the manor.

Once, and once only, had there ever been blows, and that was the time, two summers past at Broadlea, when Kay and Arthur spent the entire night in the forest. On that occasion, Sir Ector's people had begun the search at sunset, with lanterns and torches and great anxiety; and Kay told Iris—perhaps making light of it—that by the time they were found, Sir Ector's arm had been shaking too much to strike true, and so the thrashing had, after all, proved little to boast about. The younger son had got no more than two blows, and that only because Artus himself demanded them, refusing to let Kex take all the blame.

Of late, Iris had begun to wonder at their lord's extreme tenderness toward his sons. Her own parents had already warned her two years ago that she was fast approaching the age when there would be far less leniency for her, were she ever to indulge in such an adventure as hiding in the forest overnight. She judged, as she was now almost four-teen, that this would likely be the last summer she might allow herself the freedom of an occasional stolen day with the lord's sons. She must begin showing her maturity . . . come harvest time.

Of course, now that he was esquired, it behooved Kay to show some maturity as well. But for boys and men, it was somewhat different. To choose a sovereign lady in the Courts of Love, to make extravagant vows in her name and faithfully carry out every foolish errand she might set him, was part of being a grown knight; so in riding forth to recover his lady's ruby ring—which was, after all, not nearly as foolish an errand as some they had heard of—Kay was simply furthering his education for knighthood.

For that matter, in those days brave damsels rode questing about the countryside, too. Seen in that light, Iris was merely serving her old playfellow in the role of blame-less maiden guide, as Artus was serving him in the role of squire.

About halfway to their destination, Artus rode his hack close to her palfrey and asked, "Rixith, will I sound as silly as Kex, whenever I have to fall in love?"

"Not if thou learnest to be a better poet," she replied.

The first hour, Kay had talked on and on about Dame Morgan's perfections, heedless of the fact that he had to invent most of them himself, seeing that he was so briefly and superficially acquainted with her. Tiring of that, he proceeded to making up poems and songs in her honor, but still, after an hour, had got little farther than rhyming *June* with *moon.*

Artus called up to him, "I think thou ought to serve her up a fine banquet instead, Kex! I think she'd like that much better than one of thy poems."

"Thine opinion in this matter is worth half a bowl of cold porridge, Artus," Kay called back. "Didst not see how little she ate at yesterday's dinner?"

"Yes," Iris argued, "but that was in the presence of her husband, whom she obviously hates. And thou art a much better poet with the arranging and overseeing of a meal than thou art with words, Kex!"

"Speaking of which," said Artus, "how soon can we eat?"

"Munch some bread and cheese in the saddle," Kay replied. "Or a bunch of raisins. We shall make our dinner at the ford, after we find my lady's ring."

"Then I hope we find it right away!"

"No, thou dost not," Kay returned with a rare laugh. "For I have brought a skin of good wine to cool in the stream while we search, and toast our success after we have found the precious bauble."

"Wine?" Iris exclaimed. "Oh, Kex! It will be missed."

"So would a like amount of ale, from any stores properly inventoried and governed, but sometimes I think that I am the only one of my father's people who understands such work. Anyway, say it is missed—it should cost us only two or three meals with water for our sole beverage." Then he went back to seeking another rhyme for *moon* and *June*.

They came at last to the place. There was no mistaking it: There were the three stone pillars marking the ford, and the great old lightning-blasted oak on the far side. Kay dismounted long enough to suspend the wine carefully and securely where the water would cool it well. That done, they forded the stream, Kay leading, Iris in the middle, and Arthur bringing up the rear. Though the water came up to the horses' chests and chilled the riders' legs unpleasantly, the crossing proved quite safe.

Kay was already on the far side, and Iris rocking in the saddle as her palfrey swung its hindquarters onto the bank, when Arthur shouted, "Kex! Rixith! Here it is! How did you both miss seeing it?"

They turned to look. Sure enough, there atop the last stone marker—the gleam of a bright red ruby ablush with the kiss of the sun.

Iris reined her mount aside so that Kay could ride back into the stream. But before he reached the column, Arthur had already reached out and seized the ring.

When he lifted it from the stone, a huge sound filled the air, like the tolling of a vast bronze bell struck by a heavy iron clapper that was itself a smaller bell with a little silver bell for its clapper, and so on, to an innermost bell with a clapper too tiny to be seen—although why this image came into her brain, Iris could not have said.

As this monstrous tolling faded away, the marker stone increased in size and changed into an ogre. Not, perhaps, the largest of ogres, but surely one of the ugliest, even if he was the first ogre they had ever actually seen outside of tales. His eyes were yellow as egg yolks, his nose the shape and color and very nearly the size of a cooked ham, his chin hung down on his chest, his scraggly hair and beard looked like wilted leeks. His naked skin was like that of a shaved fowl with the quills of clipped feathers still sticking out, waiting to be plucked. His jagged nails might have been the scales of some monstrous fish, his elbows and the muscles of his arms bulged as if they were stuffed to bursting with uncracked walnuts, and Maid Iris could only be grateful that all his nether regions remained beneath the water. Over one shoulder he carried a club knobbly as his arms and heavy enough to stun an ox.

In a deep, growling voice he demanded: "Who rang that bell?"

"I did, sirrah!" Kay flung back at once, fumbling out his squire's sword. "What wilt do about it?"

The ogre looked back and forth from one boy to the other, and grinned a grin that showed off teeth very much like stained and broken grindstones. "Thou didst indeed, my fine jackanapes? Then what is my ring doing in the hand of that other young scoundrel?"

"Yes, Sir Ogre," Arthur said, making his words less confession than challenge, "I took the ring—"

"Artus!" Kay shouted, holding out his left hand.

"But this is my brother's quest, so I took it for him!" Arthur finished, throwing the ring to Kay.

It arced across the distance between their hands with a silver flash and ruby glow that, Iris thought, made it a sight to treasure in her memory . . . sufficient repayment, almost, for the ugliness of the ogre and the moment of fear lest the ring be lost in the water. But Kay caught it neatly and spiked it onto his thumb for safekeeping.

"And therefore, Grunchface," Kay went on, "if you want a fight, thou must fight us both!"

Or all three, for, though Iris strategically said nothing, she began looking about for a branch or other likely weapon.

But the ogre only roared an immense, guffawing laugh. Then he waded forth out of the water—somehow leaving the stone marker behind him, even though he had seemed to be that same rocky column transformed. Iris dared not take her eyes from an enemy they might soon have to fight, so she held her gaze resolutely fixed on his upper portions . . . and beheld them shrink, step by step, growing ever smoother, softer, and daintier, while coarse beard and hair turned into a fine gown, mantle, wimple, and veil of costly dark silk from which the water coursed down as from a duck's feathers, leaving it dry. Heavy club became a light wand or sceptre tied about with a crimson ribbon whose ends fluttered gracefully in the breeze. A coronet of gold appeared on the head, and soon it was the queen of Gore herself who stood on the bank, calmly regarding the boys, still on horseback in the river.

"Well, my brave young gallant," she said, quirking one of her dark brows at Kay, "will you hail me as fairer than sun, moon, and stars, swearing me thine eternal fealty and begging any task—however small, foolish, or perilous—to prove thy deathless devotion, and the very next day call me 'Grunchface' and offer to lead thy brother into battle with me, two against one?"

Kay looked at her once, then slowly urged his horse forward out of the water, Arthur following. When they had gained the bank, Kay dismounted. Again Arthur made to follow his example, but this time Kay motioned the younger boy to sit still on his hack.

Then, rather stiffly and grudgingly, Kay went down on one knee before Queen Morgan, looked straight up into her face, and said, "Madame, if you choose to wear such a disguise as that, I conceive you must accept the consequences, and I hold myself blameless in this matter."

"As do I, also," Arthur said imperiously.

"As would any fair and impartial judge," added Iris.

Queen Morgan looked at her briefly before turning a longer, harder stare upon Arthur. "Young Arthur," she said as if musing aloud. "Arthur, with the hair and nose, not to mention the lordly manner, of the late Uther Pendragon, thy near namesake. And the eyes and chin so like those of my own mother, the good Queen Ygerne. And the age. . . . What, exactly, is thine age, young Arthur?"

"His age, madame," Kay answered at once for Arthur, "is exactly ten months less than my own, and he is my own trueborn brother, both of us the sons of Sir Ector and his good lady our mother, for all that he is fair and the rest of us dark."

The queen of Gore plucked the crimson ribbon from her sceptre and twisted it as if idly through her long white fingers, meanwhile turning again to the older boy and saying, "Well, Master Kay, my good champion—question thy parents about this matter. Question them both, closely and shrewdly, and then turn the question to all of thy father's people whom thou canst, most particularly the older ones. And when thou hast done all this, send me the true report of whatever thou hast learned, and thou shalt have a favor from thy lady: this crimson ribbon which, when worn about a man's arm in battle, will prevent his blood from leaving his body, no matter how deeply he is wounded."

"Madame," said Kay, "keep thy ribbon, and I will keep my brother."

Iris stifled a gasp at hearing him use *thy* to Dame Morgan's face—from squire to queen, from any boy to any grown gentlewoman of two days' acquaintance, a monstrous familiarity had it been said in love, and a monstrous insult if said in any other spirit. And Kay had certainly not spoken it in love. He might as well have slapped her face.

But Queen Morgan only sighed, then laughed lightly as silver bells, tucked her crimson ribbon away in her purse, and held her hand out, palm up. "Wilt thou also keep my ring, Master Kay?"

"Nay, madame, take thine own back. I have no use for it." Still on one knee, he plucked the ring off his thumb and cast it up at her.

Catching it with one swoop of the wrist, she replaced it on her finger. "So," she observed, "love's young dream, alas, is over. Fare thee well, Master Squire Kay. Years will pass before we meet again."

"Madame, I could wish they were aeons." Getting at last to his feet, Kay told his companions, who had been sitting these past moments as though transfixed, "Come on, Rixith, Artus. Let's get our wine from the river and find some other spot to make our dinner."

They found a spot just out of sight of the path, leaving the queen ample opportunity to return to Southvale and be gone after her husband by the time the truants should come home. If, indeed, Dame Morgan traveled, when alone, as other folk traveled, which they now saw some cause to question.

Or, at least, Kay and Iris might question it. Before either of them again brought up the subject, Arthur asked suddenly, "But ought we to drink this wine? We have nothing to celebrate, the ring falling into the water like that, and being lost in the river."

Kay exchanged a glance with Iris. She nodded to show him that it had not all been wiped from her memory, as it had from Arthur's. "I think," she said softly, "that the lady has power enough to hold her own against any husband, however cruel or churlish."

Nodding back to Iris, Kay answered his brother's question. "Artus, we drink to comfort ourselves. And celebrate our return to things as they have always been."

THE KING WHO IS TO COME
Cherith Baldry

Kay mounted his horse and trotted briskly down the path from the stable yard. As he came in sight of the practice ground he drew to a halt. A second horseman was riding at the quintain. His lance point struck true in the shield's center and the straw figure swiveled round. The rider avoided the swinging sandbag, crouching low over his horse's neck as he galloped away.

Kay sighed, suppressing a moment's envy. The precision, the easy, fluid movement . . . pure skill. His younger brother, Arthur.

He urged his mount on again, more slowly now, and waited for Arthur, who wheeled his horse at the end of the practice ground and came trotting toward him. He was laughing.

"Where have you been? You said you would ride a course with me."

Kay shook his head.

"I can't, not today. I've been talking to Master Benet," he said. "This wet weather makes his joints ache, and he can't ride out to the sheep runs. I said I would go for him. Of course," he added thoughtfully, "he's too old to be steward, but Father can't replace him. It would break his heart."

"But you can't go now," Arthur objected. "Surely you haven't forgotten what tomorrow is?"

Kay shook his head. The hard lump of apprehension in his chest, that he had tried for days to ignore, seemed to weigh even heavier. Tomorrow, on the Feast of All Saints, he would be made knight.

"That's tomorrow," he said abruptly. "There's time enough to ride out and talk to the shepherds. The sheep must be down from the high fells before winter sets in."

Arthur grinned and leaned over to clap him on the shoulder. "Better today, then. We can't have it said that Sir Kay's first knightly deed was to go and look at sheep!"

"You've been listening to the harpers," Kay said. "But they've turned your head if you think that knighthood is all tournaments and battles with monsters and rescuing fair ladies. It isn't like that here—and not in the rest of Britain either, not since King Uther died. Just one petty war after another, until the whole land is sick of it."

His voice began to shake on the last few words, and he stopped himself, appalled, wondering if Arthur had noticed. But his brother gave no sign of it.

"We need a king." Arthur's eyes shone. "A High King, who would set all to rights. We—"

"We're wasting time," Kay interrupted. "And you shouldn't keep your horse standing."

"I'll ride with you, then," Arthur said good-humoredly. He drove his lance point into the ground. "Wait a few minutes while I go and beg some bread and cheese from the kitchen."

Without waiting for Kay's reply, he set off back to the house, his lithe figure straight in the saddle, his tawny hair tossed by the wind. Kay watched him go. Not for the first time, he wondered how it would be: to have his knighthood, and a squire who was taller, stronger, and more skilled in arms than he was himself. For a moment he imagined the mocking comments of true knights—nobles, kings' sons—if he should meet with them, and he burned with humiliation.

Then he steadied himself, took a breath. His life was not laid out along that road. Besides, if he should ride out on some knightly enterprise, it was impossible to imagine himself with anyone but Arthur at his side.

And that thought led him to what he did not wish to consider. He believed that he could be content, here in this remote valley, with the small duties of the estate that one day would be his own. But Arthur was a younger son, and Sir Ector had no inheritance to give him. When he was made knight in his turn, next Easter or perhaps Pentecost, Arthur would leave.

He would be the kind of knight the harpers sang of, Kay thought, if anyone could. He would win honor in the tournaments, with a lady's favor fluttering from his helmet. He would come home with tales of battles in distant lands, and all the dragons and ogres he had defeated. If he came home at all.

Kay sighed. He could tell no one—least of all Arthur himself—of the pain that pierced his heart when he thought of the future. Tomorrow, when he became knight, the easy, unquestioning world of his childhood would start to crumble.

Impatient with himself, he began to walk his horse slowly away from the practice ground in the direction of the sheep run. He had not reached the edge of the plowed land before he heard hoofbeats behind him and turned in the saddle to see Arthur. His brother had not only provided himself with a heavy bag of provisions, but a bow and a quiver of arrows slung over his shoulder, and two hunting dogs, his Cabal and Kay's own Luath, loping along beside his horse.

"I thought we might try for a hind," he called out as he came up to Kay. "Something to grace your feast tomorrow night."

Kay shrugged. "As you like."

As they set out along the track leading to the fells, Arthur began to talk again of his hopes for a king. Kay listened, said little, and tried to hide his impatience.

In this remote valley, battle had swirled around them and gone on. Their father, Sir Ector, had shown no wish to join any of the warring kings. For news they relied on wandering harpers, pedlars, gossip picked up at markets and horse fairs, and the occasional visit from their father's friend, the enigmatic Lord Merlin. Whatever their hopes might be, they had no power to turn them into something real.

"They say that Uriens is a good man," Arthur said. "Would he make a good High King, do you think?"

"Too old," Kay said. "He'd never hold the crown."

"Rience, then?"

"Rience? He's a lout," Kay said disdainfully. "You or I would make a better king."

Arthur laughed. "Rience is trimming a cloak with the beards of defeated kings. I met a horse trader who said he'd seen it with his own eyes!"

Kay made a small, derisive sound. "And did he see if Rience's goats still have their beards?"

Arthur laughed again, and urged his horse into a faster trot. Kay followed, casting an expert eye over the plowed fields and the grazing land, noticing a thin place in the hedge that would need a stake or two to keep the cattle from straying.

If he had been born a king, he thought, he could have made the whole of Britain into a well-kept estate, orderly and prosperous, instead of draining the land for pointless battles. He smiled wryly to himself. He would wait a long time for a sign that the crown of Britain belonged to him.

They reached the sheep run and the shepherds' hut after an hour's ride. While Kay talked to the shepherds—an old man and a boy, his grandson, who played sharp tunes on a straw pipe—Arthur rode down the hill with the dogs to draw the nearby woods for game.

By the time Kay and the old man had agreed on arrangements for driving the sheep down to their folds, the sun was beginning to go down. There would be little time for hunting, Kay thought, as he said his farewells. Unless Arthur had already killed. Soon they would need to go home, where Kay would prepare to keep vigil in the chapel ready for the ceremonies of the following day.

He rode under the outlying trees, drew rein, and listened. There was the sound of someone crashing through the undergrowth, not far away, and Arthur's voice calling, "Cabal! Cabal!"

"Arthur!" Kay shouted.

He heard the sound of barking, and his own dog, Luath, shot out of a hazel brake and pelted across to stand panting beside his horse. Arthur followed a few moments later. He was disheveled, and he looked distraught.

"What's the matter?" Kay asked.

"Kay, I've lost Cabal."

"What—how?"

"We started a hind, and chased it, but the trees were too thick and I couldn't get a shot." Arthur thrust a hand through his hair. "It looked . . . strange."

"Strange? How?"

"Pale . . . silvery. Like a Faerie creature. And then it vanished, and Cabal didn't come back when I called him."

Kay's first reaction was that Arthur had lost his wits, but his brother looked so upset that he only said, "The light's going already. That makes everything look silvery gray. And Cabal is probably sniffing after rabbits."

Arthur let out a crack of unsteady laughter. "I hope so."

Kay dismounted and led his horse farther into the wood. Arthur did the same, and caught up a long branch to poke into the thickets as they passed, all the while calling the dog's name. Luath bounded on ahead.

They followed the tracks back and forth through the forest as the sun sank further toward the west.

"It will be dark before long," Kay said.

"I'm not going home without him!"

Arthur began calling again. Just then, Kay thought that he heard something else. He put a hand on Arthur's arm. "Wait. Listen."

A dog—Luath—barked close by, and then came an answering bark, far in the distance.

"Cabal!" Arthur's face was flooded with relief. "But where is he?"

The barking came again. Following the sound, they arrived at a rocky bank. A spring of water trickled over the stones, and, above the place where it spilled out, a slab of stone, high as a doorway, was wedged into the hillside. It was rough granite. A ray of the dying sun touched it, and Kay saw markings on it that might have been the carved face of an old man, wreathed with leaves, but so worn away that it was hardly visible.

Luath nosed around the slab, whining, and from behind it, but still far distant, came the sound of Cabal's barking.

"He's there!" Arthur said. "And listen—there's an echo, as if he's in a cave."

The barking came again, and Kay could hear what his brother meant. For one fanciful moment, he imagined that this might be a hill of the Faerie, and Cabal a prisoner in their enchanted realm. Then he put the thought away, irritated with himself.

"There are caves under these hills," he said. "But how did he get down there?"

Arthur was already scrambling up the bank to examine the stone. Kay followed, until he could see, at the top of the slab, a place where the ground had fallen away. A narrow hole led downward into night.

"He's down there," Arthur said. "I'm going in after him."

Kay clutched his brother's arm. "Don't be stupid! What if you're trapped down there?" As Arthur pulled obstinately away from him, he added, "You wait here. I'll ride home and bring help—tools, and rope, and something to make a light."

"There isn't time," said Arthur. His face was white and set. "If there are caves down there, he might wander away, and we'd never find him. I'm going down there now. If I can't get out, then you can go and get help."

Kay measured glances with him for a moment. He could think of all kinds of arguments, or he could stand on his authority as the elder, so soon to be made knight, but he knew that it would be quite useless. Arthur would do what he thought best.

"All right," he said.

Arthur had not waited. He let himself down into the hole and dropped. His tawny hair disappeared in a shower of loose soil, as if the earth had swallowed him. Peering down after him, Kay could see nothing.

"Arthur?" he called.

Silence, for one moment when Kay thought his heart would stop. Then his brother's voice came again.

"Kay! There's a stair down here!"

"A stair? There can't be."

"There is." Arthur's head and shoulders reappeared at the bottom of the hole. His face was streaked with earth and his eyes were alive with excitement. "Come and see. It's quite safe."

Kay felt a pulse of pure terror, even while his mind told him there was no reason for it. The hole was not so deep that it would be impossible to scramble out. And as Arthur withdrew again, Kay could see that there was a tunnel leading away from the opening.

"Wait a minute," he said.

He tethered both horses, spoke a reassuring word to Luath, and then let himself down into the ground, following Arthur.

At first he had to crawl on a floor of loose earth and tree roots, but a few yards on the tunnel grew suddenly wider, and he could stand upright. A faint light reached down from above, showing him a downward slope, earth giving way to rock cut into a shallow stair. Arthur was standing there, barely restraining his eagerness to go on.

Kay brushed earth from his tunic. "Arthur, this is madness, without a light."

"We won't go far," Arthur promised. "Just until I find Cabal. We can come back later with torches."

He led the way down the stair. Kay followed, glancing back uneasily at the faint spillage of light that showed where the entrance was. Ahead, everything was dark.

He stumbled down the steps, not sure how deeply they were penetrating the hill, until he gradually realized that he could see Arthur as a dark silhouette ahead of him. A silvery light was diffusing up from below.

Kay halted. "Arthur!"

His brother turned. His eagerness had become harder, tenser, but Kay could see that he had no intention of going back. Without speaking, the younger boy drew his belt knife and went on.

For a moment, Kay stood still. Down here, with that pale light ahead, thoughts of the Faerie did not seem quite so absurd. Then he realized that Arthur was leaving him behind, and spurred himself into motion again. He hardly knew whether he was afraid to be alone, or wanted to stand beside Arthur to face whatever danger lay ahead.

As Kay hurried to catch up, Arthur stopped, half turned, and beckoned to him, making a sign for silence. Coming up to him, Kay saw that the stair had ended. Ahead of them was an arched opening. The silvery light poured through it, stronger now, so that at first Kay was nearly blinded, after the darkness of the tunnel.

Arthur put a hand on his arm, and drew him forward cautiously to the archway. As Kay's vision cleared, he saw that they were standing in the entrance of a vast cave. Pillars of stone soared upward to a distant roof. The walls curved in an almost perfect circle. No one was there, and all was silent save for a joyous barking from Cabal as he launched himself from the other side of the cave and flung himself on Arthur.

While Arthur calmed the excited dog, Kay took a few steps forward. Light filled the cave, but he could not see where it came from. The air was cold, moving gently against his face.

In the cave's center spread a circular mosaic, a work of the Empire, now gone from Britain. It showed two dragons, a red and a white, locked in combat. The white dragon looked larger and stronger, but the red dragon had beaten it down and, with one clawed foot, crushed its throat. Flames seemed to flicker from the red dragon's jaws as the glass tesserae caught the light.

In the very center of the mosaic, with the dragons coiling around it, stood a stone table, and on the table rested a sword. Light glinted from jewels on the scabbard, and smoldered in the rubies that encrusted the hilt. Kay's breath came short, and he raised a hand to his throat as he felt the power singing out of the ancient weapon.

Around the edges of the mosaic, like petals on a vast flower, were low slabs of granite, roughly carved as if they were meant to be couches, with the feet toward the center. All were empty.

Kay wondered what, or who, would occupy them. He found that he was shivering.

"This is magnificent!" Arthur's voice came from further round the circle. He was moving slowly around the outside of the couches, gazing up at the roof of the cave. "What is it? What does it mean?"

"I don't know, and I don't care!" Kay snapped. "Arthur, we shouldn't be here."

"Maybe we should." Arthur paused. "Maybe we would never have found this place if we weren't meant to be here."

"Your wits have gone wandering!" All Kay's suppressed fear was pouring out in irritability. "All this has nothing to do with us—how can it?"

Instead of replying, Arthur plunged forward suddenly, across the dragon mosaic. Kay cried out, half expecting one of the fierce creatures to raise its stone head and blast his brother with fire.

Reaching the table, Arthur rested his hands upon it and gazed down at the sword, his lips parted in wonder.

"Don't touch it!" Kay said hoarsely.

He started toward his brother, wanting to drag him away, but at the edge of the mosaic a chill fell upon him, as if he had been drenched with icy water. While he could still see the sword lying on the table, he felt as if it were raised, flaming, to bar his way. His terror was more for Arthur than for himself, but not even for his brother could he take another step forward.

Arthur laid a hand on the sword hilt, as if he would draw the blade from the scabbard. Kay tried to shout a warning, but now everything was dissolving into a whirling darkness, and he did not know if Arthur could hear him.

The next thing he felt was Arthur's hands firmly gripping his shoulders. The darkness scattered, and he was looking up into his brother's face.

"Kay?" Arthur was frowning, worried. "What's the matter? Are you ill?"

For a moment, Kay leaned against him, feeling his warmth and strength, and then, bitterly ashamed, thrust him away.

"Let's go back," he said abruptly. "Bring that damned dog, and let's hope the hole in the hill hasn't closed up."

He expected a protest from Arthur, but his brother scarcely hesitated, only glancing back at the sword on the table. Then he gave Kay a cheerful nod of assent, and whistled up Cabal. This time, Kay took the lead back through the archway and up the stair to the world outside.

He had a few bad moments, especially when there was no light ahead to guide them on their way back. His heart began to thump uncomfortably, and he was acutely conscious of the weight of earth and rock above their heads. Then he remembered that when they entered the cave the sun was going down. By now it would be dark outside.

Almost as soon as he remembered, he came to the head of the stair and the narrow tunnel, where he had to crawl to reach safety. Then he was pulling himself up to the surface again, where he crouched for a few moments on the turf, taking in great gasps of the cold night air. The forest surged around him.

The sun had gone, and the moon had not yet risen. The bare branches of the trees were hardly visible against the sky. But the darkness was not unbroken. Kay grew tense again as he saw a spark of firelight a few paces down the hill.

Behind him Cabal scrambled out, scattering earth; he and Luath danced crazily around each other and tore off into the undergrowth. Kay sighed. Little hope now of avoiding notice, if an enemy had made the fire.

Arthur was a dark shape standing over him. Kay rose to his feet and jerked his head toward the firelight. "Visitors?"

"Let's go and see."

Kay drew his belt knife. He gave his brother a fierce

look, knowing it was probably lost in the darkness. "*I* will go. Stay back. If there's trouble, ride for help."

No reply, but as Kay picked his way down the slope toward the fire, he could hear Arthur following a pace behind.

Another horse, a magnificent gray stallion, was tethered beside their own mounts. As Kay drew closer, he could see one man alone, bent over the fire, feeding it with branches. He was bundled up in a heavy cloak, the hood pulled down over his face. Something prickled along the length of Kay's spine.

He stepped forward, his knife at the ready, and drew breath for a challenge. It was never spoken.

The man said, "Put that away, Master Kay. You won't need it, unless you care to dress these rabbits for supper."

Well-kept hands rose to put back the hood. Kay found that he was staring at the silver hair and autocratic features of Lord Merlin.

"Merlin!" Arthur's tone was joyful. "What brings you here? Why didn't you ride on to the house?"

"I was waiting for you," Merlin said simply. "Sit down. We may as well share supper. Later the moon will rise, and then we can ride together."

Arthur sat down at once, asking for Merlin's news. For a moment, Kay held back. He had always felt that Merlin took more interest in Arthur than in anyone else in Sir Ector's household—certainly more interest than he took in Kay himself. Kay was not sure he liked it. Merlin, he knew, had been councillor to Uther, the last High King, but there were other stories about him—darker stories of enchantment and shape-shifting and a power that might have come from Hell.

In the light of day, Kay did not believe such tales. Here, in a wood at night, with that unearthly cave beneath their feet, he found that he was more credulous.

Beside Merlin were the two rabbits he had spoken of, efficiently snared. As Merlin and Arthur talked, Kay skinned and joined them, balanced them on pointed sticks over the fire, and threw the leavings to the dogs. Almost as if he were the squire, he thought ruefully, and Arthur was his knight.

Part of him felt ashamed. Through all that had happened, Arthur had taken the lead, while he himself had followed, reluctant and afraid. He should not have allowed it. He should have insisted on his own authority, and made Arthur obey him. This was all wrong.

But it had felt right.

When the job was done, Kay went to wash his hands at the spring. As the setting sun had lit the granite slab, now the firelight threw into relief the carving—if it was truly a carving—of the old man's head. Kay studied it, glanced back at Merlin, and his spine pricked again.

As he returned to the fire, he heard Arthur telling Merlin about the cave.

"Such a wonder!" he said eagerly. "Lord Merlin, did you know it was there? Do you know why?"

Merlin bowed his head. "It is for the king who is to come. Long will he reign, and when his reign is over, he will sleep there, with his knights, until the world shall change."

"The king who is to come?" Arthur repeated, as if the rest of what Merlin said had passed him by. "When—now? Soon? Is there to be a new king soon?"

Merlin began to speak of a great tournament to be held in London, at which the High King would be revealed. "I have come to invite your father," he said. "It seems good to me that all three of you should be there."

Arthur laughed delightedly. "Kay, you'll be able to fight in the tournament!"

Kay did not respond. He stood in the shadows at the edge of the circle of firelight. He was barely listening as Arthur went on eagerly questioning Merlin; what could it have to do with them, after all?

Instead, he looked at Arthur. He felt a pain he could not describe, to see the boy so familiar, so dear to him, and suddenly, for some reason, so far away. His brother's face shone in the flames, his amber eyes glowing with excitement. All his being was caught up in what Merlin was telling him. The firelight touched Arthur's tawny hair and turned it to pure gold, as though he wore a crown.

SIX FOR THE SWORD

Aaron Rosenberg

"Arise, Timone. Your time is at hand!"

"Wha—?" The man by the campfire whirled, sword already halfway out of its scabbard, then relaxed as the figure stepped close enough for flickering firelight to illuminate features.

"Ah, Merlin, it's you." Timone slid his blade back into its sheath while the old sorcerer unceremoniously curled up on the ground across from him. If the enchanter had anything particular to say, it was not urgent enough to stop him from being his usual cryptic self.

"You aren't wearing your mail," Merlin observed, and received a snort of laughter in reply.

"What, my heavy plate?" Timone shook his head. "There's no way to get into that contraption without at least one squire, and after the last jackass who served me I have no desire to tote around some whining boy just so he can help me dress in the morning. Besides—" he thumped a brawny arm across the ringed shirt he wore "—this fares well against most blades, and it weighs far less."

"A crossbow bolt would go right through those rings."

"A crossbow bolt would go right through most plate, as well, and I'd be just as dead." He leaned forward a bit, as if imparting a secret. "This mail is almost as effective, much easier to deal with, and with it I'm ten times faster than any oaf in a full suit. In battle, that will make all the difference."

Merlin nodded approvingly. "Very clever, Timone. You always were good at finding the advantages."

"I've got you to thank for that one, mage," the knight replied, hoisting a chunk of meat out of the fire and inspecting it. When he was convinced that it was done, he offered it to the wizard, then took a second piece for himself. "It was you who taught me that out-fighting someone wasn't enough. I had to be able to out-think them, as well."

"Yes, precisely—and that is why I chose you," Merlin replied between bites. He let that statement hang in the air while he finished eating, then set the empty stick down, wiped his mouth and beard on his sleeve, and focused on his host.

"The time has come to finally reveal why I have been training you. You see, there was a purpose to it all."

"I sort of figured that." The knight took a last swig from his waterskin and set it aside. "You did not select a fledgling squire and teach him for years on a whim. Some folk say you are crazed, but since I have never seen that in you, I must trust there was a reason for everything you did."

"You are quite correct," his mentor beamed happily. Then he sobered again. "Know, Timone, that you are not alone in my tutelage. There have been five others, and I have trained you all for the same purpose."

"And that is?" Timone was leaning forward now, intent on the old man's words. He had never even suspected that there might be others, and the revelation intrigued him.

"Look into the fire."

The blaze in question was still dancing merrily, and Timone obediently gazed into its center, letting his eyes lose focus until they only caught the glow and flicker before him. The enchanter had displayed information this way in the past and, just as before, an image now resolved itself out of the bright movement, taking on color and solidity until the knight felt that he were actually looking upon the scene from close by. It was a courtyard of some sort, with a large stone building behind. In the yard's center stood an iron anvil atop a waist-high block of red marble, a gleaming swordblade impaled through both.

"Behold, the Sword in the Stone—maker of kings and symbol of greatness," the wizard intoned.

"Aye, the stone in St. Paul's," Timone commented, mainly to head off the lengthy declamation he knew was coming. The interruption had precisely the effect he'd planned; the image vanished abruptly into a tongue of flame, and Merlin scowled at his student.

"I never taught you about that."

"The thing's only been sitting at St. Paul's these last fifteen years." Timone laughed. "How could I *not* know of it? Every lord, knight, and squire has tried his hand at that sword, and not a one ever budged it. Truth be told, I tried it once myself, ten years back—with no result, of course."

"Ah, but that was then. Now it is ready for the hand of its king." Merlin drew himself up once again, wrapped anew in power and mystery. "You could be that king."

"Me, a king?" If it hadn't been for the old man's intensity, Timone might have laughed. Instead he struggled to grasp the notion. "Why me?"

Suddenly Merlin's power fled, whisked away behind an invisible curtain, and he was just an old man who sat back and hunted in his robes for a battered clay pipe. "Who can say?" he replied, grunting with satisfaction as his hand settled upon the object of his search. "Even after all these years, I have no understanding of where the Sword comes from, why it appeared when it did, or how it chooses its contenders." The pipe and a small pouch appeared in his grasp, and his hands seemed to function without any attention from the mage himself. A quick tap shoved tobacco into the bowl, a flicker appeared at the end of a finger, and Merlin deftly lit his pipe, taking a long puff before continuing. "What I have been able to determine is that this New Year's Day is the time for it to be drawn, and that there are five men alive with the potential to draw the blade forth."

"And you've been training all five of us against this time—wait, earlier you said you were training six."

"There used to be six of you, actually. . . ." An expression of embarrassment mixed with regret crossed Merlin's features. "Jasper died in battle nearly five years ago, and I was not near enough to prevent it. He was a good man." He brushed the unhappy memories aside and continued. "Of the others, Micah is still in Syria, fighting to free his people from the Turks. He simply refuses to leave what he is doing. I cannot say that I blame him, but it is a shame; he is also a noble choice. A bit headstrong, perhaps, but worthy nonetheless. Pellinore—"

"*King* Pellinore?" Timone interrupted. "Him, I know. He's a good ruler, and a worthy warrior. Perhaps he'll draw the blade and simply expand his domain."

"Perhaps," the enchanter agreed. "And you are correct—he is already a good king. But there is no telling who will get to the sword first, and you must not assume that the winner will automatically be a worthy choice."

"Of the ones you've named thus far, only Pellinore is not incapable or disinterested." Timone paused for a moment, and Merlin was pleased to see the spark flickering behind his brown eyes. "So at least one of the remaining two is someone you do not consider fit to rule." A grin split his broad face. "I assume, of course, that I am not the candidate who's got you so concerned."

Merlin tried to suppress the fatherly pride he felt, and hid its telltale signs by blowing a prodigious puff of smoke from his pipe. Even then, a small chortle escaped him. "You are one of my first choices. Pellinore has more experience, and a good deal of majesty, but he has not your brains, nor your interest in innovation. If the two of you were one, you would be ideal. His wisdom could temper your enthusiasm for change, increase your chance at creating true and lasting improvements. His poise could soften your gruffness and warm you toward others. No, there is another who concerns me. . . ."

The air grew colder somehow, even close to the fire, and the shadows cast on the wizard's face made him appear far older and possessed of a sadness Timone had never seen in him before.

"It's my own fault, I'm afraid," Merlin continued. "Agnostes did not believe my offer of training when we first met, and so I foolishly revealed the reasons behind my efforts to better him. Then, of course, he was eager enough to learn." The enchanter's mouth twisted under his beard. "He learned everything he could about the Sword, and about the rest of you, then spurned me and took his own way. I fear that he may have been involved in Jasper's death and may even have spurred on the sudden renewal of Turkish aggression that has distracted Micah."

His eyes leapt across the fire and froze Timone with their sharp gaze. "He is dangerous and he is determined. Agnostes means to have the Sword, and will gladly eliminate the rest of you to get it. What is more, he's not simply a warrior. He's also a sorcerer, a master of the black arts. It was the spark of magic in him that led me to say too much—I have a dangerous weakness for students of magic—and by now he has surely fanned that spark into a blaze capable of consuming us all. It was because of him that I never revealed to the rest of you the true purpose of my training, or the fact that you were not alone. I had to be certain of your mettle first."

"Of course. But you haven't mentioned the sixth student," Timone pointed out. "Who is he?"

"Ah, yes, the sixth." A crafty look came over the old man's face. "I will tell you nothing about that one. After Agnostes' defection, I took pains that he should remain hidden and protected, and I have trained him only in secret, so that no word of it should escape. He is my trump card, if the rest of you fail." Merlin turned serious again. "But he is only a trump, Timone, and not to be relied upon. I want you to do everything in your power to reach the Sword first, and to claim that destiny as your own. The stars point to a fortnight from now, New Year's Day, as the time when the blade will accept a master. You must be at St. Paul's then, to support one of the others or to take the task upon yourself."

Timone considered that for a moment. "I have no skill for leading, old man."

"Nonsense. You're a born leader. You'd just prefer to avoid such responsibility." The wizard's eyes seemed to steal light from the campfire; they blazed brighter and brighter, forcing the words he spoke next into Timone's consciousness. "The Sword is a heavy burden, one you are worthy to bear. But do not take it up because of my prodding—only consider your own duty to the realm and your ability to rule."

"Well, I don't know that I believe you as to whether I am fit," Timone replied, "but this Agnostes clearly must be prevented from reaching the Sword. I'll do my best to get there in time."

The light in Merlin's eyes faded, and it was only his wise old friend who faced Timone across the fire. "I had no doubts. Remember, too, that I will be there to guide you should you earn the crown."

"That promise is one I'll hold you to," Timone said. "Try to duck out on it once I'm king, and I'll hunt you down and imprison *you* in that stone, so help me!"

The smile on the old man's face was smug. "Wizards are not easily imprisoned in simple stone. But fear not—I'll keep my word."

Suddenly the old man was standing, the flowing of his

robe the only indication that he had moved at all. "And now, to sleep with you. London is many miles away, and you had best be rested for your trip. I will bring news of the others when I can." Then he vanished into the night, a whisper of blue and black swallowed up by the forest's deeper darkness.

"Sleep well yourself, mage," Timone muttered. "I suspect you'll need it as much as I will."

He damped down the fire, propped his saddle upon a log, and tried to settle into sleep. His dreams were filled with images of a gleaming sword, of a six-way battle, and of a gaunt man with yellow eyes.

The next two days passed uneventfully, as Timone journeyed through the fields and valleys of upper Britain, in the direction of London. Alone, he was able to travel quickly, and he enjoyed the opportunity to ponder things without distraction. Nonetheless, when Merlin appeared again on the third night, Timone was pleased to see him.

"Sit down, old man, and have some fish." He pointed at the silvery forms basking in the heat of the fire. "They must have known you were coming, since they all but jumped into my arms."

"Hmph!" was all the wizard said as he seated himself on the ground, but the way he bit into the fish and carefully hunted down every scrap of meat showed that he did appreciate the food. Timone kept silent while they ate. It was unlikely that his mentor had sought him out just for company, but the knight knew that if he was patient, he would learn Merlin's purpose eventually.

Sure enough, after the fish were only bone and memory, and Merlin had lit his pipe again, the wizard explained why he had come. "Pellinore has disappeared."

"Disappeared? How could that happen?"

"He has been bewitched," Merlin replied shortly, the pipe smoke seeming to hiss from his temples instead of his pipe. "That whoreson Agnostes must have cast a geas on him."

"So he's on a quest, then?" Timone's voice betrayed his confusion. "Why would Agnostes send him on such a thing?"

"Because it's a fool's quest!" Merlin snapped, then bit down on his pipe to quell his temper. "Pellinore's after some mythical creature, apparently. His advisors said that he simply arose one morning and announced that he must capture the beast, then rode off alone, in full plate mail. No one's seen him since. And the worst part is, the beast isn't even real!"

"Well, can you not break the enchantment?"

"Probably—if I can find Pellinore, and get the time to study him. But the enchantment hides him from me, just as Agnostes wards his own presence. Ten days is not enough time to locate Pellinore and defeat the geas, so he's out of the running." Again Merlin's jaws locked down on the pipe, and he began muttering softly around it. "Damn that Agnostes. He's sharp, all right, curse his eyes!" Then his gaze came back up to Timone. "Watch your step, lad. He won't try the same trick twice, but I'm sure he's got others up his sleeve."

"Aye, I'll wager he does," the knight agreed. They didn't say anything more that night, and when Timone awoke the next morning, Merlin was gone. Left on his own again, he repacked his supplies, mounted up, and returned to the road, all the while scanning the horizon for trouble.

It was that same afternoon that Timone first ran into anyone else. The road continued over a wide river, spanned by a wooden bridge just wide enough for a wagon. After a few more bends and turns, it led across a shallow stream, where two sturdy planks proved sufficient to bridge the gap. An armored knight stood atop the planks, sword brandished.

"Hold, you!" the stranger cried. Timone reined in, coming to a stop just as his horse's front hoof tapped the near end of a plank.

"Step aside, sirrah. I am in a hurry, and must pass," Timone announced, but the other did not move.

"You may not pass, Sir Knight," came the reply, "until you have bested me in battle."

Typical, was Timone's thought. Why was it that every knight out to prove himself had to pick some bridge and station himself across it? Not that this was much of a bridge, but it was the obstacle that mattered. Such battles should be fought in town squares and the like, where it was more convenient.

Shaking his head, Timone dismounted, took up his shield, and drew his sword. "Do you fight everyone who wishes to pass?" he asked as he stepped cautiously onto first one plank then the other. "What about all the merchants and farmers who take this path to sell their wares—do you challenge them as well?"

"Only knights must face me," was the response.

From this closer vantage, Timone could tell that the armor hung loosely on his opponent, and the voice inside the helm belonged to someone not more more than twelve or thirteen. He took another step, to within striking distance, but did not raise his blade.

"And how many knights have you faced thus far, lad?"

The figure hesitated for a second, then attempted to stand taller as he replied, "You will be the first to fall before me."

"No, I don't think so."

Timone's blade flashed out, sweeping under the edge of his adversary's, then cut back up. The boy was unprepared for such a maneuver, and his own sword went flying, only to land with a slight splash in the water a little way off. Timone followed that move with a solid kick, which sent the boy toppling after the weapon. He landed with a cry and the dull *squish* of heavy armor striking mud.

"You'd best climb out before you rust," Timone advised as he sheathed his weapon and returned to his horse. Then he mounted and cantered across the makeshift bridge, past the figure that thrashed in the shallow water below.

"Take off the helmet first, you silly sod, or you'll drown before you can right yourself," Timone called as he passed. "And I'd advise you to practice before you try this again. The next knight you challenge probably won't be so kind."

Then Timone was back on dry land, and hurrying again to his destination.

"I was never that foolish," the knight muttered to himself as he kicked his horse into a gallop.

The next encounter was four days later, and a good deal more serious. A tree had been stretched across the road, and when Timone slowed to find a way around it, three figures slid out of the shadows. These men wore only leather armor, but they looked desperate. One of them carried a crossbow.

"All right, Sir Knight, hand over your money and your weapons," the one in front shouted.

Timone noted grudgingly that they were smart enough to stay out of sword range, and that the one with the crossbow was stationed behind the other two. Altogether too well planned for men such as these, who looked none too bright. It was this last bit of information that decided him on what to do.

"Oh, please, sirs, don't hurt me," Timone cried, wringing his hands and inching his horse a few paces closer. His apparent concern took them by surprise, and his advance was uncontested. "I am only a poor squire, carrying my master's arms and supplies. Do not kill me!"

"A bit old for a squire, aren't you?" the second ruffian asked, but he didn't sound very sure of himself.

"Oh, aye," Timone agreed, hanging his head in mock-shame and shuffling a few steps closer still. "It is to my eternal shame that I have never been able to win the spurs and armor of knighthood for myself, but am forced to wear only ring mail and ride in another's service."

The fact that their victim didn't wear plate mail finally seemed to strike the bandits. The first two men muttered curses. The third went so far as to lower his crossbow.

"So, where is your master, eh?" the leader inquired.

Timone took the question as an opportunity to walk his horse forward yet again. And when he replied, he spoke in hushed tones and leaned forward conspiratorially, even as his right hand crept back toward his dagger.

"He is right behind me, sirs. His name is Sir Timone, and he is powerful indeed." At the name, the thieves all glanced at one another.

Timone beckoned the leader closer, and lowered his voice still more to draw him in. "Truth to tell, sir, he is a harsh master. I would be better rid of him."

"Oh, you will be, friend, and right soon, too," the man cackled, which was all that Timone needed to hear.

With his left hand, the knight tugged on the reins, causing his mount to shift to the right and knock the closest man down. At the same time, Timone let fly the dagger in his other hand. It hit the crossbowman squarely in the chest, crumpling him to the ground. Then Timone's sword was in hand, and he cut down the final bandit with ease. When all was done, he dismounted to survey his work.

The fellow with the crossbow was dead already, the dagger sunk into his chest. The leader was only unconscious, and Timone slapped him awake. He questioned the man briefly, then, knowing he couldn't leave an informant behind, slit the man's throat. After that, he gathered up the bandit's supplies—food and water, a jug of cheap ale, a few coarse blankets, a coil of rope, and a surprisingly large bag of gold. He added the food, the ale, and the rope to his own packs, and took to the saddle again, picking his way around the log and back to the road. The gold he left behind.

"They were definitely after me," he told Merlin that night, after the wizard appeared at his campfire and helped him dispose of the ale. "They recognized my name, and the one I questioned after said they were paid by a tall fellow with funny eyes. I'm sure that anyone else would have been waylaid and robbed as well, but only as victims of opportunity. Obviously Agnostes knows who I am, and even where to find me."

"Aye, he must be tracking your movements somehow," Merlin responded tersely. "A scrying crystal, perhaps. . . ."

"No, he cannot see me," Timone replied with a certainty that startled Merlin. "That's the only advantage I had today—their lack of details about my appearance," he explained. "They had expected me to be in full plate, and so I was able to confuse them. Agnostes is either guessing at my rate of travel or tracking me through something other than sight."

"A sound point, but knowing how he isn't tracking you doesn't exactly solve our problem." The old enchanter took a last swig from the jug and stood to go. "In any case, I had best be off. Until I understand this more fully, it's best not to give him the chance to strike at us together."

"Fair enough." Timone stood and accepted the jug from the enchanter, then peered into it suspiciously. "Hold, now! You've drunk it all!"

"Of course," came the reply from the shadows. "I am a wizard. 'Tis my role to make things disappear!" And then the mage himself was gone, with only the echo of his voice lingering behind.

"Well, next time you can conjure up some more before you go," the knight muttered as he readied himself for bed. He expected little sleep, wary as he was of another attack, but since he also expected the next day to prove an exciting one, he did his best to accept what rest the night might grant him.

In fact, the next day passed uneventfully, but on the day following that, Timone came across a town—or what was left of one. Some of the buildings had been reduced to smoldering rubble, others stood as skeletal frames blackened by fire. Corpses littered the muddy street. The survivors were just as sad a sight. Many of them had been beaten or burned, and despair twisted their faces.

"What occurred here?" Timone asked an old man who lay by a shattered stone wall.

"Soldiers," the old man wheezed in reply. Smoke hung heavy in the air, and it hurt to draw breath. The old man shifted his body, but winced at the effort; Timone could see that his legs had been broken, possibly by a horse. "An army," the old man continued after a time. "They took what they wanted, beat anyone who resisted, and set fire to everything before they left."

"Where were they from?"

"Cameliard. Or maybe Lothian. They've been sighted nearby recently, too." The man looked up at him with tearing eyes. "Will you help us?"

"I cannot," Timone replied, though it pained him to say so. "My mission is urgent, and there is little I could do for you, even should I remain. But I will remember and, after my task is complete, I will do what I can."

The old man gave no response, and Timone—saddened by the pain and the destruction, yet eager to be away from that pathetic place—hurried on his way.

Two days later, as he rounded a bend, Timone heard the sound of a woman weeping. Reining in, he spotted a maiden by the side of the road, sitting upon a large rock and covering her face with a kerchief. Her gown was of fine silk, but dirty and torn, and her long golden hair was matted with dirt. She looked up as Timone approached, and he could see that her face, too, was lovely but ill-used—a large bruise covered one cheek, and blood dripped from a wound along her forehead.

"Aid me, Sir Knight. I beg you!" she cried in a voice hoarse from crying. "Brigands have stolen my dowry, and my honor. They have slain my father, who alone in the world would have avenged me!"

Timone's heart ached at the sight of such injustice, but he steeled himself.

"Alas, fair maiden, I may not tarry," he called out, kicking his horse into motion once more. "When I may once more command myself, I will return and lay my sword and my life at your disposal."

And he rode on. Behind him, the maiden cried out for him to stay, but soon her pleas faded, until at last he could no longer hear them. But in his head they echoed on.

That same afternoon, Timone found himself on the edge of a forest. The trees rose tall and broad, their branches hanging high above the road and casting a welcome shade across his path. But from the nearest tree an additional shadow fell, and as he drew closer Timone could see that it was in the shape of a man. Finally he came close enough to make out the details of a body hanging from a stout branch, a thick cord knotted around its neck. The corpse swayed, twisting on its rope, and finally turned toward Timone. The knight let out a low curse. It was Sir Cerwin.

Cerwin was of an age with Timone; the two had fought in several battles together. He'd been a sturdy fighter and an honest man, though given to drinking and wrestling and singing songs to pretty girls. Now he hung there, face bloated and blue. His armor was gone. On his chest was tacked a crude sign proclaiming *Death to All Knights*.

Timone cut down his old friend and buried him there beside the tree, saddened by the lack of arms to mark the grave. He burned the sign to ash, and scattered the remains with his boot. Afterward, he sat for several long minutes, debating with himself. In the end, he turned and rode away, swearing to return and avenge Cerwin's death. He could not bring himself to look back, though, and avoided the shade on the road for the rest of his trip.

The following morning another band of highwaymen attacked him, this time where the road turned and cut through a small cliff. Timone actually welcomed the ambush, although this time there were four of them, and one actually had ring mail on himself. But here, at least, was a threat he could deal with at once, in a definite and conclusive fashion.

The battle took a few moments. Fortunately Timone was able to maneuver the lone crossbowman so that a comrade blocked his aim, giving the knight enough time to kill him with a thrown dagger. The two swordsmen in leather fell readily enough, but not before the man in rings landed a sword stroke across Timone's back. The knight's own mail stopped the edge from penetrating, but the strike laid a welt like a whip lash across his spine. Still, he was used to bruises and injuries, as every true knight was, and the stiffness did not prevent him from stabbing his opponent through the neck, all but removing the man's head from his body.

That last blow proved to be a lucky one, and, after catching his breath, Timone took advantage of it. He severed the head with a final chop, then kicked it unceremoniously into a ravine and laid his own shield beside the headless form. With any luck, Agnostes might be fooled by that, at least long enough for him to complete his journey. Then, wincing slightly from the pain in his back, Timone climbed onto his horse and continued on his way.

"Something is bothering you, Merlin." Timone could tell; the wizard had been pleasant enough when he first appeared at the campfire that night, but as the knight recounted the events of the last few days, Merlin's mood grew darker and darker, until he sat glowering at the low flames, his teeth locked down on his pipe as if it were a mortal foe.

"If this is what's worrying you—" Timone pointed to the bandages on his back "—it's only an inconvenience."

"I know that, you idiot!" Merlin didn't even bother to take the pipe from his mouth; whether through wizardry or practice, he was perfectly understandable around its stem. "You're a knight. You fight people all day long; of course you'll get hurt!"

"What, then?"

"Never mind." Merlin continued to puff angrily for a moment, then changed the subject. "Have you heard anything about the tourney?"

"A tourney? I've heard nothing."

"You'd do well to know of this one," Merlin retorted. "Word has spread that New Year's Day is the time for the Sword. I'd blame Agnostes, but he wouldn't create obstacles for himself. Most likely some idiot astronomer read it in the stars and told his lord, who told others. Whatever the source, the news is out, and there's to be a grand tournament in London on New Year's. Many kings and nobles will attend. All will fight—with the crown as the final prize."

"Only one of the six may draw the Sword—so you said."

"Aye, but that won't stop others from trying, or from claiming the right. Even if the winner cannot draw the Sword, the assembled lords might still declare him king."

Timone thought about it. "Perhaps that's not such a bad thing. Armies are on the move even now, no doubt riding to support their lords' claims to the crown, if necessary. If all the lords agree to abide by the tourney's results, a great deal of bloodshed could be avoided."

Merlin snorted. "You argue it well, Timone, but not everything can be won by reasoning. Some things, no matter how sensible, are still not right."

They spoke little for a time, until, finally, Timone said, "This sixth student—" He held up a hand to ward off the protests already forming on Merlin's lips. "Hear me out, wizard. I won't ask who he is or where. I don't wish to know. But answer me this—is he a good man?"

"He is," the wizard replied. "He's bright, though not as

smart as you by half. He has a good heart, warm and kind and generous, and is trusting almost to a fault. And he loves people."

"Then he would make a good king?"

"In time, yes." The wizard's eyes narrowed. "Why?"

"No reason."

"That you care to share with me," Merlin concluded. "That is, of course, your right."

The enchanter rose and departed without a farewell. Timone watched him go, but couldn't decide if the look he'd seen in the old man's eyes was anger or something else, something more complex. He puzzled over that for a time, then drifted off to sleep, only to be plagued by images of burned-out towns and defiled maidens and knights wandering the earth as restless spirits.

The rest of Timone's journey passed without major incident—a man hobbled up and tried to make off with his pouch, his horse was spooked by a wild boar and almost pitched him into a river, a band of merchants begged him to settle a dispute, and three young women attempted to seduce him in the hopes that he would then take them away from their dreary lives. Timone ignored all these distractions as best he could. Even taking time out to run down the thief and spear the boar, he arrived at the outskirts of London almost a full day early.

The city was bedecked as if for a pageant, with streamers and ribbons hanging from every post and every frame, and people milled everywhere, singing and dancing and watching street performers and generally enjoying themselves. Knights rode through on chargers, some in shining mail and others in dented plate, and the sounds of a joust rang from the field to the south of the city, along the river. It all appeared jolly enough, if you ignored the various armies camped beyond the city walls, and the soldiers walking the streets and openly sizing up any they encountered wearing the badge of an opposing liege lord. Some of these soldiers had even taken it upon themselves to stop certain knights at the city gates, but Timone's travel-stained ring mail and lack of a shield helped him to avoid any unwelcome attention.

He rode a bit farther into the city, then pulled up alongside a tavern, reined his horse, and stepped inside.

"Good morrow, stranger! Come for the tourney?"

The man had hailed Timone while he was still blinking from the room's sudden darkness. The knight could only make out a blur. Then his eyes adjusted, and he saw the stout man behind the bar, already filling a flagon with ale.

As Timone quickly learned, the ale was not the best in the land, but neither was it the worst. He downed it in one long gulp, then set the flagon down for another. "Where might I enter my name for the lists?"

"South to the river, just past the jousting field."

Timone drained the flagon again, pulled out a coin, and tossed it behind him as he headed for the door. "That should cover my room for the night, too." Once outside, he ignored the barkeep's directions, turning instead toward St. Paul's.

Timone jostled his way through the crowds, earning several choice words and even more angry looks, but eventually he reached the churchyard. A stout rope run through thick, waist-high stakes kept the throng at the outskirts. Their attention was focused on the clearing, where a dull iron anvil rested atop a block of polished red marble. And through the center of both, a blade that seemed to be forged of sunlight. The Sword in the Stone, just as he remembered it.

Timone studied the crowd. All were intent on the Sword, or the long line of men waiting to try their hand at it. He didn't see anyone he recognized, or any sign of Merlin, and at last he turned away. Tomorrow would be the true test, and he had best be ready.

As the fates would have it, the next day dawned cold and gray, with a steady rain that turned the churchyard's hard-packed earth to mud. All but the most determined spectators had stayed indoors, awaiting a break in the weather, and the area around St. Paul's was empty when Timone arrived.

The knight was surprised to find no one there, and a moment of doubt assailed him. Timone wondered if he had somehow misjudged the situation. But, no. Even as he paused to consider his next move, a second man appeared out of the downpour.

He wore gleaming plate mail, highly polished but obviously functional, and an empty leather scabbard. Ornate rings and pendants covered the man's hands and neck, and even dangled from his ears, but his head was bare. His narrow face was dominated by eyes of yellow—not the pale yellowish cast of sickness, but a golden hue of power. Though Timone had never met the man, that face had haunted his unquiet dreams.

"Agnostes," the knight said simply.

"Timone."

For a time neither spoke again. They edged closer together, subtly maneuvering for some advantage in the confrontation to come. It was Timone who angled them sideways, so that they would meet a distance from the Sword itself.

At last Agnostes spoke. "You have not drawn the Sword yet."

"No, and I do not intend to. I renounce any claim I may have upon the crown." He watched his foe's eyes widen at that, then narrow again.

"This is a trick of some sort. You and the old sorcerer are plotting something."

"No trick. I've thought the matter over—I've come to realize that I am not meant to rule."

And he had. All along the journey, Timone had considered the possible outcomes of this day, the role he was best suited to play. He knew he was a good man, but was he really fit to be king? He was strong, certainly, and handy with a sword, and smart, but was that enough? In the end he decided it was not—and Merlin had unwittingly confirmed his decision.

"He loves people," the old man had said of his sixth student, and that was the difference. A king should love his people. And Timone, while he would protect them, could not love them. It just was not his way. The journey here had proven that. The ruined town, the despairing maiden, poor Sir Cerwin—they had all deserved his aid and his pity. And, as a knight and as a decent man, Timone should have given both gladly. But he had kept to his purpose; he had ridden on. Certainly that was the smart thing to do, but that did not make it the *right* thing to do. Merlin had not thought so, even if he would not say so openly, and Timone found himself agreeing. The people had to come first. Before anything else, even reason. That was the mark of a true king.

Not that he explained all this to Agnostes—those were private thoughts. Out loud he simply repeated, "I am not meant to rule."

His rival clearly did not believe him and saw this all as part of some elaborate ambush. And Agnostes had come prepared for just such a trap. While his scabbard hung empty at his hip—a seeming sign of good faith, and a convenient place to put the Sword once he'd taken it—he had a long dagger in his belt. The handle of another blade peeked from his boot-top.

With open hands before him, Agnostes took a step toward Timone. "You're clever, but I already knew that. As clever as I am, perhaps." Agnostes scowled. "But why play these games? We could work together, you know."

Movement behind Agnostes drew Timone's eye. A young man had entered the churchyard. The youth, scarcely more than a boy, wore squire's clothing, but something about him gave the lie to the mean costume. Timone had seen several kings in his life, but none had possessed this youth's aura of majesty.

Agnostes' scowl faded, and what was meant to be a friendly smile appeared, although it bore more resemblance to a wolf's hungry gape. His attention was still focused on Timone; he clearly hadn't noticed the youth.

"You don't want to rule—fair enough," Agnostes said reasonably. "All the more reason for us to pool our resources. Despite what Merlin has told you, I have no desire to enslave Britain, my friend, only to make her strong enough to expel the Saxons. But I need the Sword to achieve that noble goal."

"Why not just take it for yourself?" Timone replied. He was certain he already knew the answer, but the question gave him a chance to back up a few more steps from the Sword, drawing Agnostes with him. "You're already here. Take it!"

"I would, save for one minor problem." For the first time Timone saw hatred, and perhaps fear, dancing behind

Agnostes' eyes. "These damnable nobles. One man alone cannot stand against them, no matter how powerful. Merlin has already set them against me, the meddler." That hatred surged to fill his strange eyes, the raw malevolence made all the more frightening for the cunning Timone saw there, too.

"I can deal with the old man," Agnostes purred, matching the knight's subtle retreat from the Sword step for step. "But I cannot face both him and the nobles at the same time. The two of us, Timone, we could best them together. You could counter the poison Merlin has poured into their ears, while I take the poisoner himself to task. And when all is settled, you can advise me from beside the throne, be my conscience even. I'll admit I might need one." That wolfish smile was back. "Come, friend, what say you?"

Timone chose not to reply in words. Instead, he drew his dagger and lunged forward. Agnostes' own blade was in his hand in a heartbeat. As the two came together, the knight stabbed Agnostes under the arm, between the armor joints. Even as he struck, Timone felt a sharp pain in his own side, a narrow blade slipping between the chain links, and knew Agnostes' action had mirrored his own. Then they hit the rain-slicked ground and fell apart, each rolling to his hands and knees.

"Why?" Agnostes hair was plastered to his head, and his yellow eyes were already turning dark. "You could have had the world. . . ."

"It's not yours to give," Timone gasped back, feeling his legs go numb.

The knight stared past Agnostes, who had slumped to the ground, to the center of the churchyard. He saw the clouds part and a beam of sunlight illuminate the young man standing hesitantly before the block of marble.

"A gift, my liege," Timone whispered, tasting blood, "from an older, cruder time. Reign well, and with love."

And, as his sight faded and his limbs grew cold, Timone watched Arthur son of Uther draw the Sword from the stone, fulfilling the destinies of them all.

JESTER'S LUCK
Gene Stewart

King Leodogran's jester—Cafex, by name—dodged a brickbat, tumbled leftward off the stage, and rolled through a splash of mud. This both delighted the crowd of urchins and fishwives that had gathered to watch his impromptu performance and served to remove him from the Celtic brutes who had decided to express their objection to his performance by throwing things at him. Cafex, dripping mud and horse dung, stood for a moment and scanned the fairgrounds, then scowled and walked toward Leodogran's tents. He'd earned only a few extra coins; the fair was not going his way at all.

Indeed, the fair was itself a poor thing, more village festival than royal gathering. Several visitors had gone missing in the woods, too, which prompted rumors of yet another ravening beast. Cafex strolled through the fairgrounds feeling trapped by a world that wanted only to eat him.

The banners snapped in the breezes, pennants fluttered like a hennin's veil, and clouds scudded past the sun now and then, a curtain drawn on bright-lighted melodrama. Past horses carrying ragged knights, wagons laden with pelf and spoils from raids on the hill-country, and peasant farmers dragging children and wares to their year's only half-chance for fun and profit, Cafex trudged. He'd lost his jester's bounce. He felt as worn down and defeated as Leodogran's kingdom and wondered if he might have acquired a bad influence from one of the dark stars that hovered just beyond the bright dome of daylight sky.

"Jester, halt."

Cafex skidded to a stop, not daring to look around. Just his luck. He recognized the gruff voice; it raised hackles. At least he knew the expected formula: "Good sir Nial, I—"

"Silence, fool. Take this."

Cafex jumped as a gauntleted fist thrust a rolled, beribboned scroll into his hands. He clutched it to his chest and still did not look up. He trembled a bit, on purpose, to show he was properly cowed. No use inviting a beating.

"Take that to the king at once, and say it is from me."

With a nod that was half wince, Cafex trotted forward, expecting to be kicked, but relieved to have escaped the encounter without a blow to his shoulders or head. Nial, a boaster and bully, was a kitchen knave with pretensions of chivalry. He based them on an uncle's fortunes, which waxed and waned enough to keep Nial from being recognized, yet, as a true knight of the realm. With his lofty ambitions and not-so-secret promises of knightly honor, Nial rarely missed a chance to harass the likes of a jester, even one of the royal court. It seemed to soothe his own sense of lowly origins to knock on the heads and shoulders of those who would be stationed under him should his uncle's fortunes ever stabilize for the better.

Most knew enough to humor him and call him Sir, even though he did not—yet—deserve such an honorific, and would not unless his uncle's fortunes changed.

The things we do to survive, Cafex thought.

Bells on his hat jingled, bells on his curl-toed shoes jangled, and his teeth chattered with fear as he came to the first of the guards. Carrying a message to a king was serious business, and a proper show of fear could only help. He was waved past without interrogation, however, and so made his way on paths of fresh sawdust and sand to the grander tents, where he discovered his brother, Falltree, clanging his hammer on his anvil in a makeshift smithy as royals strutted by. "What ho, Brother?"

"Cafex, what ho." Falltree was bigger, darker, and calmer, a man's man with broad shoulders and a full curly beard. He smiled and struck the horseshoe he was making, then cursed, displeased by how the metal was shaping up. "The horses shod with this brittle Roman metal will surely stumble at the joust."

"I'm to give a message to the king himself."

"A message of mirth?"

"No, an actual one."

Falltree, one of the royal smiths and armorers, heated the horseshoe in the coals again, applying his left elbow to the bellows and sending up sparks and smoke that smelled of sulfur and metal. He glanced at his brother and smiled, but gave no indication of having heard or understood. He was distracted by this chore, which he, as armorer, no doubt found beneath him.

Seeing this, Cafex moved on and this time was forced by the guards to do a silly dance and some pratfalls before they would let him into the king's tent. As usual, it was crowded and hot, the smells of unwashed bodies, beer, sawdust; the fumes from smut-spewing torches; the droppings of the many exotic animals on display; and countless foods and wines mingling to form a miasma Cafex secretly called the Royal Stench.

Worming his way through knots of supplicants, visitors, and guests, he found his king, Leodogran, brooding on a Roman couch, a goblet of wine in one hand and a falconer's gauntlet in the other. A merchant stood before the king, talking fast and displaying two magnificent white hawks, each with gilded beaks and talons.

Cafex smirked and stepped up behind the merchant. He bumped the man and managed to startle both birds, which squawked and flapped and stirred up a moment of chaos.

As Leodogran blinked and tried to decide whether to bellow laughter or anger, Cafex stepped forward and, kneeling, lowered his head and extended the scroll. "Sire, I was bidden deliver this to your hand but a few moments ago, at the fair."

"Rise, Jester."

Cafex rose, the scroll snatched from him as he did so. He looked up and suddenly his breath caught in his throat, for beside Leodogran stood his daughter, Guinevere, the most beautiful woman anyone had ever known. A blush arose and, to cover his awkwardness, Cafex pulled a silly face and let his joints go loose. He tumbled to the ground like a puppet dropped, and thrashed in a spasm of nonsensical distress.

Out of the corner of his eye Cafex saw Guinevere smile and, heart lightened, he sprang to his feet and backed away from the royals. As he did so, he noticed that Leodogran looked even more worried than usual as he stared at the scroll.

And then the king crumpled the parchment and let his face fall into his hands with a sob of despair. "He offers a deed of honor. He promises to dispatch the beast." He moaned, shaking his head. "That I am come to this, my knights outdone by a kitchen knave."

Cafex, shocked, slipped out of the tent and went to find his brother, who often knew more of what was going on at court from hearing the guards talk.

"A beast, they say. That's why they want new shoes for the horses, to raise a hunt. Those rocks in the hills are hard on the mounts, and harder still on this metal." Falltree held up a horseshoe he'd made and, without even a grunt or grimace of effort, twisted it between his hands. It snapped and he dropped it. "Poorest quality metal I've seen." He sighed and scratched under his beard.

Cafex sipped ale and shrugged. "Beasts have taken from us before. Surely that alone would not cause a king to cry." He sat on a barrel of nails, feet up, back braced against a tree, as his brother attacked yet another chunk of red-hot metal.

"This Nial, he is of no account save for his uncle, a noble whose fortunes were lost in the last of the hill people's raids. It is whispered the uncle's estate is regained, and this would permit him to sponsor his nephew, this Nial, as a knight. And so Nial, eager and overreaching, promises to slay this foul beast as a deed to honor the kingdom."

Cafex nodded as it became clearer that the bully might have prospects after all, if but the desperate kind. "Those hills are full of caves."

"Aye, and each must be checked for this beast. Some say it be a dragon, as of yore."

Cafex snorted. "Hardly that, Brother. A bear, perhaps, hungry from a bad forage and eager to fatten up for winter."

Falltree nodded, hammering now. He swiped sweat from his brow with the back of his left wrist, then frowned and held up the misshapen chunk of metal. "Look at that. No matter what I add, it remains softer than a baker's behind and brittle as crusty bread when it cools."

They visited for a few more minutes, and then Cafex went out again in search of more coins. He performed his stunts and juggling tricks until thirst once again tortured him into buying a draft of ale. He quaffed it resting beside a currant bush someone had planted in an old water trough by the dirt road.

That's where Nial found him.

"You, jester, on your feet. My page has an ague and you shall serve in his stead on this hunt."

"But good Sir Knight, I have not trained—"

Nial grunted. He tossed down a bundle that weighed almost as much as Cafex, which buried the jester and spilled the dregs of his tankard of ale all over him. "Minerva blast your eyes. Now hurry."

Cafex stood, thinking that Nial certainly cursed like a noble, if nothing else. He shouldered the bundle and staggered off after the would-be knight's horse, which offered several opinions Cafex sidestepped only by sheer luck. He soon realized that he'd been chosen to serve as Nial's page because no one else would let themselves be bullied into it.

While the true knights rode forth to search the caves in the hills, the prospective knights were sent to scour the lowlands, a task they accepted with good grace, thinking it, perhaps, the less dangerous. Better, they reasoned, to be in the open than threading through dark, narrow caverns.

Nial, Cafex noted, was in rare form, even for him.

"There's talk of a new champion, a warlord Arthur." The name sparked a ripple of interest in the circle of beast hunters. Nial, having said the name so familiarly, said no more, though, and no one asked as he chomped at the joint of meat he held. He tore flesh from bone with the gusto of a hunting dog, then swallowed it without chewing.

His next words changed the subject. "I wonder if my uncle could prevail upon the king to grant me the boon of a greater deed to perform, a quest worthier than scurrying after a dire beast in this awful swampy wood." He drained his tankard, then thrust it back behind him to be filled, not noticing how the others gaped at him, his audacity, his sheer bravado. Or his idiocy.

Once again, Nial's ale-fueled dreams of grandeur provoked enough disgust to cut off scornful laughter. His boasts often took away the breath of any who knew better. Although they tolerated him for his uncle's sake, theirs was a thin tolerance, like dangerous ice at the start of winter.

Cafex kept a straight face. He jumped up, hefted the pitcher, and filled Nial's tankard, careful not to slosh. He had managed to nibble a few bites of an apple, and had sipped a few stale dregs of ale and one potent mouthful of mead, but the meat the knights were eating—pheasant, rabbit, and even some beef—seemed destined to be devoured long before he'd have a chance to grab any of it.

Just as well, he thought, as it wouldn't do to get a bellyache with all the work yet to be done.

By him, and the other pages.

While the would-be knights mimicked their betters and their betters mimicked drunken gods.

Cafex rolled his eyes.

He'd helped set up camp, and had even gathered dead-fall for firewood, wandering among the damp, dark trees cautiously but bravely enough. Or so he told himself, conveniently forgetting the chills he'd experienced. Molds grew on every surface in the dank wood, and mildew tickled his nose. Sounds echoed, coming from everywhere and nowhere. Water trickled, dropped, and splashed constantly, even though it had not rained in days. Any ravening beast that found such a place wholesome and homely was no doubt a terror unimaginable. Cafex stayed as near camp as possible, once he'd helped make it.

He slept that night in a small tent with two pages who laughed at his own attempts to take care of his master. "I'm a jester, and he's a kitchen knave," he kept saying, and they kept laughing and answering, "Oh, we thought those were page's bells and his fat that of royal sloth."

He wished Nial had thought to find him a page's garb as he drifted into a fitful sleep. He also wondered what lowly urchin he'd replaced; the poor fellow was better off anywhere but serving under Nial, it seemed.

Cafex awoke dreaming of a bath, something he'd experienced a few times by sneaking in after a royal had been bathed. Warmth drenched him and, for an instant, he luxuriated in it.

Remembering where he was, he sat bolt upright. Pitch darkness clasped him. He scrambled to his hands and knees, tangled in rough blankets. He shook the page to his left, who yelped and sat up, bashing their heads. Rubbing his forehead, Cafex shook the page to his right, but that one would not waken. And then Cafex realized where the warm wetness had come from.

He screamed.

"That a beast could sneak into camp and devour a page as we slept is the mark of the supernatural."

So said one of the knights and, despite Nial's sneer, no one gainsaid this opinion. Prayer was offered all around, what remained of the page's body was buried, and they broke camp in a nervous, irritable way, splitting into small groups.

The morning passed with growling stomachs, for their haste had permitted no breakfast. Nial complained loudly of this as he rode along, and the few other would-be knights riding with him in their small group answered in kind.

Carrying a torch, Cafex led the mounted Nial through dense woods, following as best he could the spoor of the beast: Red smears of blood on dark green leaves; deep three-toed prints in rusty loam; and a rut in the black, softer ground as if a huge tail had been dragged all marked the beast's way. Talk of dragons, griffins, and worse filled their hearts with dread.

Morning wore into afternoon in the dank darkness of the wood, a transition marked only by the shift of light above them, filtered as if strained through the highest leaves. Cafex wondered if the darkness clotted so thickly in these trees had not somehow infected King Leodogran's kingdom or his rule, causing things to be so run-down and chancy. He tried to shake off such superstitious thinking, not needing the extra goosebumps.

They followed the trail to a small river, where it vanished. Cafex, relieved, stood ankle-deep in the river and gazed up at his master, who scowled and flared his nostrils as if to scent out the beast like a tracking hound.

Nial dismounted. "We must camp here and await the beast's return."

This astonished the others, who argued and shouted until Nial's insistence won the day. In truth, it took little persuading to halt them.

It struck the pages that real knights would not squabble that way. Then again, none of the pages even had the gumption to try becoming a knight, so they ended up criticizing only softly and among themselves.

Cafex and the other pages wearily set up camp, pitching the tents far back from the river's edge and setting up a small picket of sharpened posts around the tents. The miniature palisade was flimsy, and came up only to Cafex's waist, but it was the best they could do, and this faint echo of the Legions made them feel better.

One page suggested a small moat, until reminded that the beast apparently liked to swim.

Another wanted to sleep in a tree and for a few moments this idea seemed good, until one of the knights tried and failed to climb an oak. Grounded, the knight declared the idea moot and the trees off limits, and so the pages resigned themselves to a sleepless, fearful night of waiting on the ground.

The prospective knights, for their part, roasted game and drank ale and kept themselves in merry spirits as the night came on. None showed guilt at consuming goods pilfered by Nial from the royal kitchens. They took them as simply their due, and never once wondered aloud how the true knights fared in their brave searches of the many caves. They seemed determined to remain awake and alert but, one by one, prompted by too much mead and ale and wine, they fell asleep. Their snores made some of the pages laugh, others shudder.

Cafex stayed awake, holding one of the sharpened sticks across his lap, his back to the fire. When he heard a slithery, scraping sound, every hair on his body stiffened and he stood and called out a warning. "Wake up. It's coming."

Pages roused soused knights. Sir Nial responded to Cafex's touch by lashing out with a fist, missing the jester's face by a finger's breadth. Lolling to one side, Nial snorted one last snore, then sat up. "Where?"

Cafex bade him listen.

Slithering, scraping, and now a ragged breathing came from the darkness beyond the fire.

"A torch, page." Sir Nial stood, grasped his sword, and strode to his mount, pausing in annoyance when Cafex did not at once leap in front of him to light his way.

Snatching a brand from the fire, Cafex lit a torch and held it high. He kept one hand on the steed's bridle, walking sideways, one eye on the darkness around him, the other on Sir Nial, who now led the way ahead of the other knights, most of whom were still fiddling with breastplates or weapons or horses. Some of the horses sensed danger and whinnied as they balked.

The creature's evil was upon them, Cafex thought.

It lurched at them just then, from under a laurel bush.

Cafex, shouting in surprise, fell back, dropping the torch upon the scaly thing. It was twice the size of a man, at least, with beady eyes, huge teeth, and a jaw fit to gobble a jester whole. It scuttled on its belly but moved fast.

Nial, crying out a battle prayer, thrust his blade forward and downward, as if parrying from on horseback a foe's slash of sword. His blade entirely missed the creature, which promptly chomped the front leg of Nial's horse. The mount fell, throwing the knight into bushes.

Startled, Cafex picked up the torch from the path. Now behind the beast, he was surprised to see Sir Nial's sword on the ground before him. It must have been flung when the knight was thrown. Picking it up, he stepped forward and, without thinking, brought it down as hard as he could onto the beast's back.

It bounced off.

He'd struck with the flat of the blade.

By now Sir Nial was on his feet again and fumbling for another weapon. The other knights, approaching warily, brandished spears. "Attack," Nial bellowed.

A stone flew past Cafex's ear.

Dropping the torch, Cafex raised the heavy sword again—this time with both hands—and struck point first, just behind the creature's beady eyes.

It squirmed and thrashed, its tail whipping sideways to sweep Cafex from his feet. He fell into bushes and tried to roll away from the creature.

By then other swords were being put to good use, skewering the writhing, rolling creature. Blades bit. Blood flowed. The beast hissed and roared. Its struggles slowed between frenzied spasms of effort, until it finally expired. A long, fetid breath fouled the air as the last of its blood gushed.

Stunned, head spinning, Cafex nearly fell to his knees when Nial's heavy arm came down across his shoulders.

"By Minerva's girdle, you struck a fine blow." Nial clapped the jester on the shoulder again, then strode to examine the dead beast—and to pose for his fellow would-be knights with his hand on the sword's hilt, one foot on the creature's head.

In day's light, back at the fair, the monster was identified as an African crocodile of the Nile variety, according to a legionnaire who had seen them on campaign under Theodosius. "They start small, and I'm thinking maybe some soldiers brought some little ones to Britannia for sport and one escaped. Or maybe more. I've heard tell of lake monsters in the north. . . ."

King Leodogran laughed in delight and had the carcass gutted and preserved. He called it his Great Salamander and displayed it hanging from the rafters of his tents when away from the castle, and hanging over his great hall's table when in court.

Nial was rewarded not with a knighthood—his uncle's estate had once again been pillaged and taken—but with an appointment to head the kitchen servants. This both gladdened and galled him, and it would not be long until he began ingratiating himself with the new center of the court's attention—Arthur, who had designs, it was said, on Guinevere herself. He certainly possessed the family name to win her, for he had been revealed as a true son of King Uther Pendragon.

And Cafex, Leodogran's jester, who had struck the first blow to kill the beast, was rewarded by a place in the king's retinue. This quickly devolved into leading a small troupe of comedic players for Guinevere's amusement. As her favorite jester, he remained with her throughout her fabled life, and always in later years considered himself, much to his surprise, lucky.

A Time of Blood and Steel

John H. Steele

At the base of the cliffs, far beneath the tower, white-caps broke against the rocky shore. Farther out, the fading sun bathed the swells crimson. Perhaps sun and sea contributed to Duke Gorlois' sanguinary mood, or perhaps he buckled under the weight of insult heaped upon him by his liege. The duke had endured injury greater than might be expected of any lord noble-born—than might be expected of any man. Now he could only throw off the yoke or break beneath it. His face, not so long ago youthful, was wrinkled by fatigue and black-blooded scars; his stern bearing had grown more majestic, tempered within the crucible of war wrongfully waged.

Brastias watched his lord Gorlois, the duke of Tintagel; the knight watched the neglected flagon of wine in the duke's hand. Brastias watched, too, the sun sinking farther and dragging all color with it beyond the sea. The spray from the waves, product of heedless, relentless violence, could not reach the two warriors here in the tower, but the wind did its duty. The room atop Castle Terrabyl was cold. The defenders were saving firewood to heat pitch, should the High King's army storm the walls, and so Gorlois, like all his men and women, was forced to await the morning and the re-emergent sun to warm his bones. The duke, his back turned upon the blood-red sea, gazed southward along the coast, toward the sister tower Tintagel, not ten miles distant.

"Surely the barons will not long stand this," Brastias said, the wind flailing his words, sapping the confidence from them.

The duke glanced back over his shoulder. A wry laugh seemed to pain him. "And why is that, young Brastias?"

"He wrongs you, m'lord," Brastias said, not that Gorlois needed reminding. "If they allow him to wage war against you without cause, which of them is safe? He could turn on any one of them next. Their own self-interest must bring them to your aid."

"Their self-interest," Gorlois said sharply, "is served by Uther attacking me and not them." He remembered the flagon now and took a deep draught. "They stand beside him, Brastias, not against him. I know better than to think you have not seen the host arrayed beyond the castle walls."

Indeed Gorlois knew better, for Brastias had fought and bled by his duke's side, day after day, sally after sally, against the assembled might of High King Uther Pendragon.

"The Saxons, then," Brastias suggested. "In the east, they are burning villages and churches, putting women and children to the sword, and worse. Surely that threat is more dire than a personal grievance here?"

"What do the barons care," Gorlois spat contemptuously, "so long as their own lands are not under attack? What does Uther care for his kingdom? He possesses a desire not yet sated. No. Look not to the barons. If we are to be delivered, it will be by our own hands—our own swords."

Brastias nodded, his gesture all but lost in the deepening gloom. Both his sword arm and shield arm ached; he gladly would have given each if doing so could deliver his lord from these desperate straits. Countless days of battle had muted the thunder of his indignation, however; now he could manage mere rumbles upon occasion, and those short-lived. As the hour grew late, his mind, pressed as it was by misgiving and fatigue, considered every possibility that it had considered and discarded a hundred times already. "Uther must come to his senses."

"Must he?" Gorlois had begun to raise again the flagon to his lips, but he paused at Brastias' pronouncement and turned abruptly to face the younger man. "Tell me, why is it that Uther wars against me? Why is it that his army devours my harvest in the fields, that my knights die at the hands of their countrymen, a few more each day, even while the Saxons ravage the East? Tell me—why?"

Brastias did not flinch from his lord's wrath, but neither did he answer. He could not speak; he could not bring himself to say the words: *Because King Uther has taken a fancy to your wife, m'lord.* He could not say it, but they both knew. As did all the kingdom. Barons, commoners, heralds, ladies, scullions—they all knew. Gorlois' knights

knew. Better than any. They knew that they rode into battle to defy the lust of a hoary old king. Uther's men realized
as well, no doubt. Yet still they served, still they fought and
killed and died.

"Uther will not come to his senses," Gorlois said, leaving his unanswered question to linger like a strangled
scream. "He is a man of passion and might. Those are the
only coin he understands. Not reason, not honor. He wars
against me because he is able to do so, and only my force
of arms will sway him."

If what you say is true, Brastias thought morosely, *then
Uther will have his way. We defenders of Castle Terrabyl
cannot forever hold against the might of the Pendragon.*

"There is surrender, or there is death," the duke said,
watching the final acquiescence of the sun to the bloody
plain of the horizon. Having spoken his piece, he returned
to his wine and to his vigil toward the south where, quite
possibly, from Castle Tintagel the fair Igrayne kept a similar watch, straining her eyes northward for any sign of her
beloved husband.

The objects of Brastias' attention were closer to hand
and discouragingly numerous. The campfires of Uther's
host, terrestrial reflections of the stars and seemingly as
infinite, sprawled in every direction save that of the sea-
cliffs. Ever the warrior born and bred, Brastias tried to
divine what he could from the fires. He estimated the
forces assembled against his lord—so many hundred
knights, so many thousand footmen—but soon the num-
bers grew dizzying, and his spirits sank so rapidly as to
gain ground on the absent sun. As melancholy took hold,
he considered lighting one of the candles on the table; the
shadows were growing too heavy, the darkness smothering. But Brastias could not overcome the bone-weariness
that made his limbs leaden ingots.

Through his years of service to the duke, Brastias was
well acquainted with the heady rush of battle, those
moments when the world was all thundering hooves and
the heft and inexorable arc of a perfectly balanced blade.
At no other time was a knight more fully alive, and afterward, having survived the bloody field, never was a morsel
of food more sumptuous, a maiden more inviting. Yet when
the battle and bloodshed grew relentless, when comrades

in arms fell to sword and lance day after day after day, when at night the enemy snored within earshot and all hope of deliverance dwindled to nothing, then the transcendent glory of war rotted until all that remained was despair. Anxious hours and nights devoid of sleep took their toll. Exhaustion was the rule, the warrior's body weighed down by his despondent soul. To light a simple candle became an insurmountable test of will.

Brastias saw his duke's doom in that lump of tallow and string, in the fierce wind that would snuff out any flame, and as the young knight ruminated upon their mortality, night stole away his lord until he was but a silhouette against the open sky.

"Brastias," the duke said suddenly, "come here, *quickly*."

For an instant, the reminder that Gorlois was still more than insubstantial specter surprised the knight, but Brastias hesitated only briefly before rushing to the window, his malaise banished by a mere word from his lord.

"Tell me what you see. There," Gorlois said hurriedly, pointing.

Brastias peered in the direction indicated by the duke. Darkness was not so complete beyond the enclosure of the tower. "Riders. Heading away."

"And the pennant with the retreating force?" the duke urged. "What symbol do you see?"

Brastias looked more closely. "The red dragon of King Uther."

Gorlois wheeled from the window before Brastias could speak another word. "He's leaving, and with only a small contingent," the duke said as he tore open the door and started down the narrow, winding stair. "We'll break through, and before night's end, I'll have Uther's head on a pike. It's the only way."

Brastias was at the heels of his lord in an instant. Halfway down the stair, they met Sir Jordans, ascending in a lather. "My lord duke," the battle-tested graybeard called out as he reversed direction to avoid being bowled over.

"I have seen," said Gorlois, waving Jordans away. "Prepare the mounts. Assemble the warriors. We sally forth directly."

Everything happened very quickly now. Brastias felt his own perspective shifting, the world slipping easily into the unmistakable clarity of battle. The courtyard was raging chaos—commanders shouting orders, soldiers running this way and that—yet all the confusion and clamor was little more than a rich tapestry on a distant wall. Brastias attended painstakingly to vital details—the fastening of armor, the proper saddling of the chargers. He was soon mounted beside Gorlois, with Sir Jordans at the duke's other flank. In the instant before Brastias pulled down his helm's faceplate, he noticed the moon to the east, like a grinning skull, but then the portcullis rose and the duke's army moved forward.

They raced from Castle Terrabyl and met no resistance within bowshot of the walls. The pickets and the unfortunate inhabitants of the first camps scattered before the mounted charge. Enemy footmen hastily formed lines. Ridden down and hacked asunder, they broke ranks and fled. Far ahead on the road, the red dragon pennant snapped in the wind against the backdrop of the death-mask moon.

With Gorlois and Jordans, Brastias rode hellbent at the fore of the charge, his mount snorting geysers of steam into the night. The army left a wake of churned earth and mangled bodies in its passing. Brastias slashed with the strength of ten men as he struck down those who would do his lord injury. In minutes, Gorlois' charge had covered half the distance to the dragon pennant. But Uther's host was vast, and resistance stiffened. Staunch pikemen assembled to contest the knights' course, and archers began to loose their quarrels into the midst of the tightly packed horsemen. Uther's own knights appeared, as well as those of the barons loyal to him, and the red dragon pennon that had seemed within reach drew farther and farther away.

Brastias fought like a man possessed, lashing out with shield and sword, cleaving through armor and flesh. He maintained his position beside the duke. They pressed forward, but more slowly, more desperately. Jordans went down, knocked from his saddle, but the advance continued to grind ahead. Time stretched out, each blow fended off providing another lifetime; vision contracted, making the horizon creep closer, until it appeared at most thirty feet away in any direction. The screams of men and horses rose above the clash of metal on metal. Not only was the impetus of the charge broken, but Brastias soon found himself giving ground. His arms burned. Each blow struck against his shield or parried with his sword jarred him to the bone, but still he fought.

Another knight, blood seeping from the joints of his armor, had taken up position to the duke's left. Brastias held to Gorlois' right. As the red dragon disappeared in the distance, Gorlois bellowed in rage and anguish. But the enemy were thick in every direction. The duke's force was cut in two, the rearguard separated from the van, but even those closest to the castle had no hope of regaining the walls now. The charge had carried them too far, but not far enough.

How many hours passed in the carnage, Brastias did not know. His world was each gasping breath, each heartbeat, each slash of his blade. When at last a flail-strike ricocheted off his helm, the din ceased—but an eternity remained before he struck the ground. And in those intervening aeons, he witnessed the lance pierce his lord's thigh, another his side. Before consciousness fled him there amidst the mud and skittering hooves, Brastias stared into the lifeless eyes of Duke Gorlois of Tintagel.

"Brastias, I need you, sir!"

Above the congenial tumult of the feast hall and the constant ringing in his ears that no poultice or salve seemed able to remedy, Brastias barely heard the summons. He turned to find Sir Ulfyus by the door, gesturing urgently yet trying not to attract undue attention. Brastias took his leave of the table.

"Here you are, at last," Ulfyus said, as they turned from the hall.

"I didn't hear you," Brastias said, tapping his ear. "This damnable ringing."

"I suggest in future you parry with your shield and not your helmet," Ulfyus quipped, then grew quickly serious again. "It is her time."

"The queen? Tonight?" Brastias' shock suddenly became alarm, an icy spike in his belly worse than anything he'd ever experienced in battle. "Merciful God!" He crossed himself to ward off panic. "What do you need *me* for? Fetch the midwife!"

"Queen Igrayne is well attended," Ulfyus assured him. "It is the king who would speak with us."

As they passed hurriedly through stone corridors, Brastias' heart turned cold. Though Ulfyus had the rare makings of a trusted friend, Brastias held no love for King Uther. Less than a year had passed since the death of Gorlois at the hands of the High King's men, and even less time since the Pendragon's marriage to the late duke's wife. How that day had rankled, as Brastias stood as guard and witness. His only solace—and the only reason he'd sworn fealty to Uther, rather than accepting the alternative of exile—had been the fact that Igrayne, on that wedding day, was visibly with child. Gorlois' seed had found purchase, though he had not lived to see the fruit. Brastias had entered the High King's service reluctantly and with misgiving, but determined that the duke's progeny should learn honor and nobility—qualities the child was unlikely to glean from Uther.

At the door to Igrayne's chambers, the knights were met, surprisingly, by Uther himself. He was still a powerful and clear-eyed man, though the years were taking their toll. His beard was shot through with gray, and the scar along his jaw flickered pale and red in the corridor's torchlight. "Ulfyus," he said, clasping the shoulder of his long-serving man-at-arms. "And Brastias." Uther regarded him less warmly, but with respect. "My queen's most trusted knight. I have urgent need of you."

"We are yours to command, m'lord," said Ulfyus.

"Is the queen well?" Brastias asked.

Uther nodded. "She is well, and has borne for me a son."

Borne for Gorlois a son, Brastias thought, but wisely held his tongue.

For a new father, Uther's manner was grave. "The child is to go into secret fosterage," said the king, "so that he will remain safe from those who would do him harm."

"So soon, m'lord?" Ulfyus asked. "He is nary an hour from the womb."

"It must be so, and you are the men I—that is, the queen and I—trust with his life." Uther finished speaking just as the door behind him opened. Two ladies-in-waiting stepped out, the first bearing an infant bundled in a gold-embroidered cloth. "Alicea," Uther directed the woman, "follow Ulfyus and Brastias to the postern gate near the well. You will meet an old man there. Entrust to him the child."

As the door closed, Brastias heard faint weeping from within. The king saw his concern and, for a moment, the old warrior's brow furrowed with shared pain. "The queen's heart is sorrowful, but it is for the best," Uther said. "Quickly, now. It is difficult enough. . . ."

The party departed Igrayne's chambers, Ulfyus before and Brastias behind the ladies. They hurried through shadowed corridors and courtyards, all the while Brastias questioning to himself the task at hand. Might not Uther regard this child as a usurper? Certainly another son, indisputably his own, would be more to the king's liking. Was this fosterage or infanticide to which they delivered Igrayne's babe? Having turned his back on a kingdom ravaged by Saxons so that he might wage war on a vassal to steal the man's wife, would Uther scruple at the murder of a child, if such a murder suited his purposes? Brastias could not know the king's heart, but all that he knew *of* it was a cautionary tale.

The knight, however, had sworn an oath to the High King—an oath of loyalty and obedience, if not love. Short of forsaking that vow and absconding with the child himself, there were few options. Could he now, lacking direct command from the queen, turn his back on his oath? What then of honor, what of nobility? If only Uther were a lord Brastias could trust the way he had trusted Gorlois, rather than one who left him to hope for the best and fear the worst.

Time was too brief, though, and he had reached no conclusion when the robed figure stepped from the shadows of the postern gate. Alicea hesitated, until Ulfyus nodded assent. Without a word, the old man, a stave in one hand, scooped the child into the other. For a fleeting moment, Brastias saw the infant's eyes, bright and wide, full of promise for the future in defiance of the past's darkness. And all too quickly, as if never he'd been born, the babe was gone.

"Is this right," Brastias whispered, "what we have done?"

Ulfyus stood close to his friend in the darkness. "We must believe that it is," he said. "It is what our king has commanded."

The words did little enough to ease Brastias' doubts, or to lighten the burden, one among many he would carry in Uther's service, for many years to come.

The dawn came stillborn, smothered by impenetrable clouds, gray as the beard of the knight who stood upon the battlements. The damp wind settled into his woolens and rendered his armor cold to the touch. His old bones were stiff in the morning chill. Behind him stretched Caerleon, the grand city dressed for aborted festivity, like the bride who finds herself instead at a funeral rite. The knight stared not into the city but away from it—at the arrayed armies that would bring down the walls and the High King who sheltered within them.

The number of cook fires dotting the Usk River valley indicated a formidable force. For a moment, Brastias, warden of the North, looked through eyes that had seen all of this many times before. How many mornings or nights over the years had he surveyed such a plain, estimated the strength of the enemy, considered tactics, weighed odds? This dawn was separated from the others merely by details: the rippling emblazons on the banners of the six besieging kings; the mist-shrouded peaks of the Black Mountains, barely discernible in the distance; the squawking of gulls, ravens of the sea, as they picked at bodies in the shallows of the Usk.

For once, Brastias wished that the ringing in his ears were louder, so that it might drown the gulls' bickering. The tinnitus had dogged him for ages, ever since he'd taken a blow to the head in one of his early battles. Was it St. Albans, where Uther had struck his last blow at the Saxons? *No, it must have been before that*, he thought, because he distinctly recalled the ringing as he'd witnessed Uther's marriage to Igrayne, that bitter feast so close on the heels of Gorlois' death. Uther was the second lord whom Brastias had outlived.

"Brastias?" came a familiar voice from the stair.

"Here, Ulfyus."

The impact of metal-encased feet on stone foretold Ulfyus' arrival. The royal chamberlain, as gray and battle-hardened as Brastias, made his way to the top of the wall and braced himself against the biting wind. "The horses are ready."

"I don't know why we're bothering," Brastias grumbled. "It's a waste of our breath."

"You're probably right," Ulfyus conceded, "but better to waste breath than blood. Two weeks of siege and sorties have accomplished little enough."

"Little enough except to feed the gulls," Brastias said. "Doesn't Lot have enough men to bury the dead?" The two knights watched the birds, a low-swirling cloud of unas-suageable gluttony. "They're like the slave behind Caesar's chariot, whispering in our ears: 'You are only a man.'"

"Likely as not, you and I will be feeding the gulls one day," Ulfyus said, then shrugged. "As long as it's not today."

"I'd wager that's what those poor souls said, as well." Brastias nodded toward the partially submerged corpses. The two men laughed grimly. Like the ringing in Brastias' ears, Ulfyus had been around for what seemed a lifetime. An unlikely friend at the start, one of Uther's men who had besieged Castle Terrabyl so many years ago, Ulfyus had long since proved himself, and he and Brastias had saved each other's skins many times over. "Let's get it over with, then. Arthur will remain here?"

Ulfyus nodded. "As we counseled."

Brastias received the news with relief. No one denied the boy's prowess in battle, but when his blood was up he tended toward rashness—a prescription for a short-lived kingship, that.

Baldwin of Brittany joined Ulfyus and Brastias at the gate. As constable of Arthur's host, he would lead the par-ley. Beside him, on an immaculately groomed charger, sat Kay, seneschal of England, and Arthur's brother—*foster* brother, Brastias reminded himself.

"Watch your backs," Kay said. "A blast on your horn if they try anything, and we'll be on them so fast Nentres will piss his armor. All I ask is that you save Lot for me. I'll have his head on my pommel, or so help me God—"

"And that," Baldwin said in the dry, gruff way that, for him, passed as humor, "is why you're staying here."

Kay, much younger than the other men and less familiar with Baldwin's manner, fell silent. He was a stolid, stubble-chinned youth, strong as an ox and proud as a bull.

"Don't worry, Kay," Brastias assured him as he climbed onto his charger. "We'll pull their teeth, and then you can have Lot over for tea."

The gate opened and the three knights rode out, accompanied by a bodyguard of men-at-arms. Brastias noted wryly that it was not so long ago that he, Ulfyus, and Baldwin had been the bodyguard—for young Arthur, who on New Year's Day in London had drawn the mysterious Sword from the stone; and again twelve days later, before the assembled barons, each of whom demanded to try his hand; and at Candlemas, observed by lords come from greater distances, insisting on trying the Sword, and failing; at Easter, though still some barons balked at the boy's right to rule; and yet again at Pentecost. Over those months tensions had run increasingly high, so that the archbishop of Canterbury had at last decreed that the renowned knights— Uther's men all three, and known throughout the land— should safeguard young Arthur from injury.

Injury was the very least that King Lot of Lothian and Orkney, and his five compatriots, hoped to offer High King Arthur Pendragon. Arthur had invited them to join the Pentecost feast following his coronation; they had arrived at the gates of Caerleon, but each with an army in tow. This morning they awaited parley beneath a great willow in a bend of the River Usk.

"Did you not bring your *High King*?" Lot called scornfully, when the three knights had left their men-at-arms and approached the willow. The six kings, similarly, had left their honor guard in sight but away from the tree. "Did Arthur's nursemaid not give him leave to join you?" Lot asked, to the amusement of his fellows.

"Let us not mince words," offered King Uryens of Gore. "You are all passing good knights, if of questionable judgment. You will be pardoned for your role in this, and free to depart with your mount, arms, and all your possessions. The same for all of your knights and men-at-arms. The city will not be sacked or looted. We will extract only what provisions we require for the return journey to our lands." He paused and surveyed the three magnanimously. "Generous terms, you will agree. We require only one beard from among all those assembled in Caerleon."

"Does Arthur *have* a beard yet?" Lot sneered. "We might have to make do with a few whiskers plucked from his arse."

Brastias resisted the urge to put hand to hilt, but hold his tongue in the face of such vulgarity he could not. "Are your northern lands so barbarous, Lot, that this is the respect you accord a king?"

Lot's glare was the promise of sharpened steel to come. "Why don't you tell me, O warden of the North? Tell me also," he said spitefully, "when last you crossed the River Trent? You must be a mighty warden, indeed, to oversee your lands from such a great distance."

The six kings enjoyed this jest, as well. In addition to Lot and Uryens, they were King Nentres of Garlot; the king of Scotland, youngest of them all; King Carados; and the King with the Hundred Knights, whose retinue wore to battle silken waistcoats and the latest in armor from France. The kings were proud men all, and valorous warriors.

Baldwin of Brittany eased his mount forward now, lest the council be lost to temper. "I am in agreement with Uryens," Baldwin said, exchanging polite nods with the aforementioned king.

"I am pleased to find there is at least one reasonable man among you," Uryens said. "You are free to leave this valley, or should you so choose, you may join our ranks."

"You misunderstand me," Baldwin said, to Uryens' confusion. "I do not agree to your terms. Far from it. I agree that we needn't mince words. So, thus are the conditions proffered by the High King, and the only terms he will accept: The six kings will kneel before him and swear an oath of fealty, after which time you will return, each to his own lands, and remain there unless summoned by the High King to wage war against the Saxons or other dire threat to the kingdom."

The six kings sputtered and turned red in the face. "Our generous terms will not be offered again!" Uryens warned.

"Bow down because the boy pulled a sword from a stone?" Lot said incredulously. "I wouldn't give a brass farthing for your *king's* sword—or his stones, for that matter."

"If I recall correctly," Brastias said, "you nearly ruptured your own stones trying to draw the Sword this Candlemas past."

"The boy has no claim," Uryens insisted. "He can appoint wardens and chamberlains to his dying breath, but the boy has no claim."

"Not so," said a new voice, crackling like parchment thrown on the fire. The knights and kings turned, and there stood Merlyn, longest beard of them all, his gnarled fingers gripping the stave that supported his withered frame. Those Christians among the kings made the sign of the cross.

"The whole charade with the Sword was your doing, witch," Lot scolded. "Don't think we don't know. I'd give my eyeteeth to know how you ensorcelled the archbishop to go along, but I'll not be party to your deviltry."

"Eyeteeth, eh?" said Merlyn. "I might take you up on that some day. In the meantime, though, Arthur is son and heir of Uther Pendragon, to whom you swore loyalty, Lot of Lothian. But perhaps that was an oath lightly sworn."

"Arthur," said Uryens, "may be the son of Igrayne. That much is true. But she was already with child when Uther wed her, so soon after the death of her husband. Not so?" He surveyed the knights assembled. "Brastias, you know I speak the truth."

Brastias felt their eyes turn to him as one. He knew well that of which Uryens spoke. The knight had seen the newborn infant whisked away to secret fosterage not nine full months after Duke Gorlois' death. Brastias had sworn fealty to Uther for the sake of the child, but the child was gone, damning Brastias to futile years of wondering if he had delivered the boy to his doom. After Uther died, and years passed without proclamation of an heir, Lot, Uryens, and the others eventually had returned to their sovereign ways.

Not until Arthur had pulled gleaming Caliburn from the stone scant months ago was his identity known. Overjoyed by news that the Pendragon's heir—but Gorlois' son—lived after all, Brastias had rushed to his banner. How better to repudiate the selfish passions of Uther than by serving the child of the murdered duke? Of course, to those who took stock in the arbitrary legalities of succession, the virtue that drew Brastias to Arthur disqualified the boy as heir.

And now Uryens, who would have Arthur's head, called Brastias on the question.

"He speaks the truth," Brastias said reluctantly. "Igrayne was with child on her wedding day to Uther."

"Aye, that she was," Merlyn agreed. "By Uther's seed, and the child born in wedlock."

"Then he is a bastard," Uryens replied. "For Igrayne was closely guarded after the night of her duke's death until her wedding to Uther. Not so, Brastias?"

Brastias could but nod. He had stood at her door himself. Uther had not enjoyed her company in private before the wedding.

"No bastard conceived nor born," Merlyn said. "Uther did not lie with Igrayne until her Gorlois was dead and cold for three hours passing. She had no husband when the boy was gotten on her by Uther."

Brastias felt that, suddenly, the ringing in his ears was more intense than ever it had been before: louder than the creaking of saddle leather as his charger shifted its weight beneath him; more immediate than the mutterings of the kings; overpowering all—all except the quarrelsome gulls. Always there were carrion birds.

He saw again a deathmask moon, as clearly as if it were in the sky this morning. Brastias remembered the death of his first lord, the duke of Tintagel: the desperate sally, progress at first against the overwhelming enemy, but in the end defeat. And, for Gorlois, death.

Brastias remembered, too, the confused reports afterward, that he and the duke and Sir Jordans had been seen at Castle Tintagel after the battle—several hours after he had been captured, and Gorlois and Jordans killed. Brastias had denied the reports, Igrayne had sustained him in this, and that had been the end of it. But now. . . .

Uther did not lie with Igrayne until her Gorlois was dead and cold for three hours passing. . . .

"There is one here who knows that of which I speak," Merlyn said, his raspy voice subduing Brastias' tinnitus. "Not so, Ulfyus?" asked the wizard, mocking Uryens.

Brastias looked to his old friend, but Ulfyus stared uncomfortably at the ground and nodded. "It is true."

"This proves nothing," said King Lot. "What else would Arthur's man say?"

"What else, indeed?" the wizard agreed. "For it is said that Arthur does not tolerate his knights to lie. Good knights of Logres," Merlyn then said to the three, "go back into the city and beg your rightful king to return here with you on the morrow. He has nothing to fear from such as these, and it is proper that his counsel should be heard."

"Yes, bring him," Lot said at once. "I vow his safe passage. Have him come play talking bird and mimic Merlyn's words. Perhaps it is the old witch we should strike down, and watch Arthur the cripple without his crutch."

Merlyn paid no heed to the threat, though the Christian kings again crossed themselves lest Lot's audacity bring curses raining down upon them. Indeed, Merlyn stayed behind without benefit—or need—of escort as the three knights turned back to the city. The trio fell into an easy canter, so as not to outdistance the footmen too greatly; Brastias rode silently beside his old friend Ulfyus, who would not meet his gaze.

That night, Ulfyus found his brother in arms atop the battlements, as he had that morning. "Have you eaten, Brastias? I thought not. Here, then." He offered a wineskin from beneath his cloak. "If you're determined to starve, at least have a drink so you don't freeze as well."

Brastias accepted the skin. "Merlyn has confounded me as much as he has the others," he said, gazing out at the fires across the fields. "But it seems that you know the truth of the matter."

Ulfyus' misty sigh was visible on the chill air. "So many years ago, Brastias. It changes nothing."

"If it changes nothing, then tell me."

Ulfyus, the grizzled veteran of countless campaigns, stared gloomily into the darkness and sagged beneath the weight of an ancient deceit. "That night in Cornwall, the night your duke led the sally that was his undoing, I accompanied Uther and Merlyn to Tintagel, where Igrayne was besieged. With his magics, Merlyn . . . changed us. Uther became in appearance Gorlois, Merlyn was Jordans, and I . . . I became you. We entered the castle, and I stood guard outside the door as Uther lay with Igrayne." Ulfyus shifted his weight uncomfortably. He took back the skin, raised it to his mouth. "There is no shame for her, Brastias. She did not know."

"You are right in that," Brastias snapped. "There was never cause for shame—for Igrayne or the duke. And were it not for Uther's inability to know shame, Gorlois would still be alive today!"

"Brastias, we cannot change the past."

"Aye, that is true enough. For if we could, I would choose exile rather than serving Uther—or his son."

Ulfyus glanced around worriedly, as if they might be overheard. "The realm—"

"The realm, Ulfyus, is shamed—shamed by a king ruled by his passions, and by barons and knights who stood beside him in murder. I swore my oath of fealty at Uther's wedding feast. Do you know why I did so? Because all knew that a child was quick within Igrayne's belly, and that it must be Gorlois'. I hoped someday to serve my duke's son, not Uther's heir. I believed that hope had come to pass when Arthur drew the Sword and revealed himself. Now I find not only that the boy is Uther's—and God knows what unconscionable vices flow in that blood—but that you were party to the deception!"

"Hopes wither and dreams die," Ulfyus said urgently, but taking no umbrage at his friend's harsh words. "We live on. And as long as I draw breath, I will serve my lord. I counseled Uther not to wage war against the duke. When he decided otherwise, was I to forsake my oath?"

"Had not Uther already forsaken his oath to protect his vassal?" Brastias growled. "Or was it the duke's own wife from whom Uther thought Gorlois needed protecting, and so sought to separate them?" He waved away the skin when Ulfyus offered it again. "Leave me, friend. My quarrel is not with you, but with a king dead these many years."

"And his son?" Ulfyus, dejected, asked as he departed.

Brastias remained on the battlements for many hours, his indignation gradually, like the cook fires of the enemy, dwindling from flame to ember, but never growing cold.

A hush fell over the milling crowd of soldiers and citizens as Arthur strode across Caerleon's central square. His footsteps rang sharp and distinct against the stone cobbles.

Tangled reddish hair hung loose at his shoulders, Caliburn sheathed at his side. The line of his jaw was rough with the slightest beginnings of a beard.

Brastias watched the Pendragon approach, but where before the knight had seen Gorlois' strength of character, this morning he saw Uther's impetuousness; what had been Igrayne's eyes now had a different look; the duke's confidence was become Uther's arrogance.

It changes nothing. . . .

In a perverse way that Ulfyus surely had not intended, Brastias knew that his friend was correct. Once there had been a lustful old king empowered by force of arms; now there was an ambitious boy with a wondrous sword. Only the details changed. Brastias observed and bristled as Arthur exuded the unfailing surety of the warrior-king born, of the Pendragon.

"I will speak with Merlyn and with these kings," Arthur said impatiently to his knights. "The footmen remain here. See that they are ready for battle. I've had my fill of hiding behind city walls. With me, Kay." As Arthur mounted his charger, he scanned the faces of his men. "And you, Brastias. At my right hand."

Brastias, adjusting the saddle on his destrier, felt Ulfyus' eyes upon him. As always, the High King accorded the graybeards a place of respect and responsibility, but why, Brastias wondered, couldn't Arthur have chosen one of the others this morning, Ulfyus or Baldwin? The Pendragon, however, had spoken, and Brastias' duty—as his friend had reminded him so pointedly last night—was to obey. Shortly, Arthur, his foster brother, and Brastias trotted from the city. They wasted no time achieving the willow beside the Usk, and the kings and the wizard who waited there.

"So, here is the boy king," said Lot as soon as they were within earshot.

"Good morn to you," Arthur called to the wizard leaning casually against the tree. Then Arthur turned his steely gaze on Lot. "And you, good king, should save your breath for swearing fealty to me. Have you told them, then, Merlyn?" Arthur asked, ignoring Lot's derisive laughter and the grumbling among the other kings.

"He has told us," Uryens broke in, "that you are Uther's son, but there is no proof."

"He has told us, also," Lot said, "that we would do better to leave this place, that we cannot prevail over you, though we have knights and footmen ten times your host. To my ears, it sounds the talk of an old woman fearful for a boy's life."

Listening to them all, Brastias heard the same tired slurs, crude and mocking, that always flew unchecked on the field of battle, or the practice field, or in the barracks. And he realized then how unworthy those words were for the weighty discourse of kings.

Arthur took no notice of the taunts, nor did his hand stray to Caliburn, as Kay's hand did to his own sword. "You seek proof," Arthur said to the kings, "yet you reject the word of Merlyn, advisor to kings. You seek proof, yet you reject Caliburn at my side, Sword of kings. Would you see my blood run red on the field, so that you might somehow divine that it is Uther's blood? Would you destroy the kingdom so that you might preserve your own petty fiefdoms? And for how long? How long before the Saxons put you down like dogs, one after the other after the other? How can you claim to be kings, yet sacrifice both your people and your lands?"

Arthur turned to his right hand. "Tell me, Brastias, what claim do you think might satisfy such as these?"

Brastias cleared his throat. "M'lord Pendragon," he said, to raised eyebrows. He recognized Arthur's question as rhetorical but continued undaunted. "They might well question your blood, for surely noble-born men have plunged their estates into ruin. And they might question your sword, for might of arms leads as often to destruction as to prosperity. A true king makes himself known not through the simple possession of title or might, but by the ways in which he uses these things for the welfare of his subjects."

"Perhaps," Lot scoffed, "your wise knight would like to teach us our psalms, or how to ride, as well as instructing us in the rule of our kingdoms."

But Arthur considered Brastias' words for a time. "It is a pity, Lot," the Pendragon said at last, "that so great a king as yourself should fall against a fellow Briton when all our armies together should be marching to meet the Saxons."

"There are no Saxons in Lothian," Lot said. "So perhaps

you would like to renounce your claim to my lands and to the lands of these fine kings—and perhaps we will be content to leave this place, and leave you to live another day."

"I will renounce my claim if you meet this one condition," Arthur said, much to the surprise of all. "If there be one of you before whom the others will kneel and acknowledge as king of all Britain, then I too will kneel, and we will leave this place together—and together throw the Saxons back into the sea."

The gentle neighing of horses and the ever-present bickering of the gulls were all that could be heard beneath the great willow. Brastias looked to Uther's son and saw in his eyes—the eyes that, mayhap, *were* more of Igrayne than the father—that the words were genuine. The six kings looked one to another, and their faces hardened, each man picturing himself—and, gallingly, each of his fellows—atop Uther's throne. Their consternation was plain to see, at one another and, as a whole, at Arthur.

"You try to set us against ourselves," Uryens said, "but it will not work. We will have your head."

"I try to set us all together," Arthur countered, then went on reluctantly: "But as you say, it will not be. So there will be blood, and the survivors will kneel before me."

"Better to die than to kneel," sneered Lot.

"As you wish," Arthur said. He reined his horse and turned back to the city. Brastias and Kay followed closely.

Brastias could not clearly see his king's face to determine whether the eyes that stared out shone with the nobility of Gorlois, the drive of Uther, or the strength of Igrayne. Then Arthur turned, and a memory stirred in the old knight's mind. He pictured the eyes of an infant he had seen so briefly years before. The infant had grown to a man, yet the hope in those eyes remained undaunted, and on the field before Caerleon, Brastias suddenly saw as if through those eyes—not the eyes of a child, but the eyes of a king. And the images that came to him, of a Britain united in valor, did not spring from Igrayne or Uther or even Gorlois. They were wholly Arthur's.

As the city drew near, Brastias wondered if perhaps he had found a king beside whom he could fight and, if need be, die—not because of an oath, but because of a shared dream.

"Would you have done it, Arthur?" Kay asked after they had passed into Caerleon's main gate and dismounted. Nonplussed, defiant, the seneschal stood before his brother and king. "Would you have knelt before one of them?" He fairly seethed with resentment of Lot and the others.

"If they will not put Britain's welfare before their own, they must be made to see the error of their ways," Arthur said, deflecting the question. And then, turning and laying his hand on Brastias' shoulder, he said to the knight, "God willing, it is your king that I will be. In time. For now, however," he said more loudly, for those gathering around to hear, "blood and steel must carry the day. We march within the hour!"

A great cheer went up, and then another, and another, as word spread lightning-quick throughout the city. Ebullient voices shouted down Brastias' war-weary tinnitus, and he saw the devotion in the eyes of every man who watched Arthur make his way across the square. The younger knights—Kay, and Lucan, and Gryflet—took up their places in the vanguard with Arthur, while Brastias took command of the right wing of the High King's host, Ulfyus the left. When next the gates of Caerleon opened, the army rode forth behind the unfurled red dragon banner of the Pendragon. On this morning, Brastias saw no deathmask moon, no omen of doom, nor any guarantee of victory either. There was only struggle and striving and whatever good they could make of that.

THE ENTHRONEMENT OF ARTHUR

Andrew H. W. Smith

Sharp sunlight warmed the red-tiled roofs of Silchester.
The forum bubbled with noise; excited, the crowd ran
Down the road to the eastern gate, spilled out to the
    throning of Arthur.
Against their stream an old man drew to the church.
The open baptistery seemed unattended. Within,
The leaden font glimmered. He dipped a cupped hand
And raised it again to his mouth: the day was hot.

The butt of a spear struck the clear drops from his hand.
"That is holy water, friend. Its application is outward,"
The now-seen horseman spoke. Heat from the high sun
    shone
Full on his helmet's faceplate, a mask of brilliant gilt.
His winter-white horse beside him was still as a pillar of
    stone.

"Holy for whom?" the other replied. "The gods are many
    and cruel.
They give what none could desire, they take for their plea-
    sure
Only what none may spare. The ancient authors attest it.
Your Christ is one with Rome and the gods of the wildwood.
Their gifts are torment: why should I fear their wrath?"

"Christ is one with all," he was answered, "and all men
    seek Him
Blindly or open-eyed. The gods of Rome and the wildwood
Are inventions of fallible men striving for knowledge of
    Heaven.
Yes, there is pain, Maugantius. We live in a world of ruins
Since Satan's and Adam's fall. But still the City is builded
In the images of the City: Camelot, London, here.
We spend our lives to the utmost to enable the City to stand.

Arthur knows this, and now in the amphitheater
Assumes the burden of kingship. Why should you not follow
    the crowd?
You might see ransom offered in the amphitheater's hollow."

"Your words," said Maugantius, "are water. I am uninvited.
I have read in Apulegius of the wages of curiosity.
I know the use of the amphitheater: it is the mouth of Rome,
Where criminal, beast, and Christian become the Emperor's
    food.
Pendragon's son returns to the ways of the great devourers:
The warring dragons beneath will bring your building
    down."

The horseman answered, shaking light from his moving face,
"You were present but did not perceive, had eyes and you
    did not see
The subterfuge of Merlin at the tower of Fiery Pharaoh.
Had he freely offered his blood, he could have appeased the
    dragons.
Instead he released their conflict. When choice was proffered
He chose to live for himself. In revulsion, the spirit with-
    in him
Poured itself out in prophecy, left him a shell.
Now many more must die. The way of the great devourers
Is opened by cowardice, closed by the choice of courage.
Sacrifice must be offered. The crowd against whom you
    struggled
Is gone to witness the crucifixion of Arthur.
The Cross is Christ's throne: all thrones are now become
    crosses.
We nail kings there with our homage. They die for us to
    themselves.
The amphitheater echoes the world: it rings with unmerited
    suffering,
Rich in the blood of martyrs. Where else should the throne
    be set?"

"When the prophecy spilled from Merlin," Maugantius
    replied,
"The visions splashed over us all: I shared in the showing
    of futures.

I saw from the town of the wood a maiden come walking.
She was robed in white and blue, her short-fingered hands
 were spread.
In her right hand she carried the Caledonian forest;
In her left the fortifications of the Roman city of London.
Her bare feet burned the land, her eyes destroyed my sight.
My heart could not sustain the incomprehensible meaning
That shone from her eyes. Should I choose between city
 and forest?
Or are city and forest both borne by a greater than either?"

A bird called from the wood. The horse's mane stirred
In the absence of wind. The other lightly replied,
"She whom you saw often is seen in visions,
But rarely is understood. The Caledonian forest
Stands for God's and the Church's commandments, agents
 of growth.
The outworks of the great City are penance and mortifi-
 cation.
The two are made one when the hands are united in
 prayer."

"Prayer is an alien discipline. I have carried the vision alone
Down my long life's road. I am rich in the words of the
 ancients,
Fulgentius and Apulegius, the lords of meter and prose:
But what will they avail in the Day of Evaluation?
I have scattered their falsehoods like seed. With the husks
 of the harvest
The darnel of my adorations will be cast into the oven and
 burned.
They have taught me to see all things as fraught with infi-
 nite meanings,
As now I perceive they must be. But they have not taught
 me prayer."

"On the day you have named," said the other, "they too will
 be present,
The lords of meter and prose, in common with all mankind.
Then shall they plead for you and you for them. Forget not
That not all giving is losing, though loss must also be
 offered.

The tree and the stone grow together into that which is different from either.
The purpose of having is giving: in the end there is nothing
but prayer."

The sun was fierce on the rider's face. Its light was reflected
Small in Maugantius' eyes, restoring his inward sight.
He saw the town and the forest unite in a gesture. Afraid,
He turned away to the north. The other detained him.
"Dubric's hands are heavy today: they carry a crown.
But all may baptize at need. For the moment, this is
enough."
The spearhead dipped in clear water. The merciful blade
Made the sign of redemption upon Maugantius' brow.
Then it swept away, the rider leapt astride
And turned the horse to the south, cantered, galloped, was
gone.

Maugantius stood alone. Choice was proferred. With scant
hesitation
He ran to the eastern gate, past the temples of broken gods
Where children had clambered to see the face of their king.
He turned down the road where voices are swallowed by
silence.
He followed the crowd to the pit. Within the arena
He knelt at Arthur's feet; he nailed them fast with his
homage
In the circle of sacrifice, which was also the mouth of Rome.

Arthur was bound to Britain. Behind, in sun-somnolent
Silchester,
A woman pegging out washing sang the deeds of departed
kings.
A loosened rooftile slipped. In dusty cracks of the walls
The wind-blown grass seeds waited for the cold salutation
of rain.

THE LAST OF THE
GIANTS OF ALBION

Darrell Schweitzer

I have crushed the cities in my hands; I have trampled the nations beneath my feet.

—*Nemesis*, XI, 11–14

The giant dreamed in the earth for he was of the earth. He dreamed in stone for he was of the stones; a stone had been the mother of his race, the father a fallen star; begotten was he in fire upon cold stone; smoldering in slow rage, he dreamed away the centuries, beneath the earth.

He heard the Romans come into Britain, and he walked amid their dreams, that they might never know ease or rest. He knew their speech. He heard them leave. He heard the coming of robbers into the land thereafter, felt them like insects crawling upon his skin, awakening him from his thousand-year dream.

He knew that fire and the sword were the law now, that blood flowed in rivers through all the forests and hidden valleys of Britain, as on the plains.

All this he found good, for he hated mankind.

Therefore he rose through the earth, toward the light, like a great leviathan swimming up majestically out of the darkness and deep. His journey through the years slowed. A decade passed. A single year. Rain fell and wind blew. Gradually the stone itself was shaped, soil fell away, and if you stood just so, in moonlight, his broad face was clearly visible on the side of a hill.

He stirred in his sleep and an avalanche buried a town.

He opened enormous eyes with startling suddenness; they gleamed like two additional moons, risen at once.

King Arthur saw these things in a dream and awoke with a shout. Courtiers came running, but Arthur sent them away and summoned Merlin. The two of them conversed privately in the king's chamber. Arthur was a young man then, newly crowned, resting in Camelot for a single night between the wars.

"But I have not rested," he said, and he told Merlin what he had dreamed.

"This is no mere vapor of the mind," said Merlin, "but a true thing."

"Explain it to me."

Then Merlin laughed a little and held up his hand. "Such haste, my lord? You command, but sometimes not even I can fulfill all your desires." Merlin grew grave again. "There is much here to be uncovered. I can tell you only that you have dreamed a true thing, and surely it is the beginning of an adventure."

Arthur rose from his bed. "Then let me be armed, and call together my knights—"

"My lord, again, be not so impatient. This adventure, which you and none other has dreamed, is therefore for yourself alone. You must go without your knights, to uncover the mystery by yourself."

Arthur nodded toward the door to the chamber. "How can I do anything alone? My servants are without. I am sure they are leaning against the door, trying to listen, as if I did not know. But they only seek to know my mind and serve me better. And my knights lie beyond them, asleep in the great hall. They too will rise up to assist me." Now it was Arthur's turn to laugh a little, as he said, "A king is never alone, so I have found out, having become one. He can scarcely scratch himself without a bevy of chamberlains to oversee and assist and flatter him."

So Merlin whispered to Arthur a secret word, which was known only between the two of them, to reassure him, as sometimes a master must reassure his student. Merlin had spoken this word to Uther the night Arthur was begotten. Now he spoke it again, and by magic he made a *seeming* of Arthur lying in the bed and a *seeming* of himself standing there.

Then he bade Arthur dress and arm himself, and commanded him to cover himself with his cloak; and Merlin covered himself with his own cloak; and the two of them went through Camelot invisible, while the *seeming* Arthur slept and the *seeming* Merlin stood watch over him. He knew that with the dawn the false Arthur would arise and speak with his warriors, and feast, and jest, and even fight in the joust, and none would be the wiser, though a *seeming* is but vapor and dust shaped together.

Meanwhile he and King Arthur took horses from the stable and journeyed through the night. Dawn found them in the marches of Cornwall. There they paused to break their fast, still invisible. They passed by the town of Totnes, on the River Dart, near the coast, and did not reveal themselves to the people of that place, but continued on, across mountains, into a very remote region, where a forest stretched before them, dark as night even though it was day.

Arthur and Merlin dismounted and entered the forest, groping their way through the thick barrier of underbrush. Once Arthur heard Merlin whisper to him, "The vision and the adventure have come to you alone. Even I am blind here."

Arthur made to reply, but then he realized that Merlin was no longer with him.

He groped on alone through the darkness of the wood, and the wind rattled the branches over his head. Cold rain fell, and the tree trunks gleamed with ice, though it was early spring already and should have been too late in the year for ice. Arthur trembled. His breath burned in his chest. Once he thought he saw two moons before him, rising suddenly, light flickering like burning rain between the black boughs, but then the light was gone as if two vast furnace doors had shut.

There were ghosts around him, groping, clinging to him like mist, whispering in his ears, imploring him to right ancient wrongs, to put away their pain; and he knew that these were all the men who had died in this place attempting to fulfill whatever quest he must now fulfill.

Arthur put his hand on Excalibur. He did not pray to God just then, but merely trusted his own courage. That was, perhaps, a folly.

Now there was a more steady light ahead, flickering, yes, but growing ever brighter as Arthur drew nearer.

He saw that it was a fire, and in a clearing, before the fire, sat a giant roasting a whole ox spitted on a tree trunk.

The monster put down his supper as Arthur emerged into the firelight.

"Do you know who I am?" said the giant, and the very earth and air trembled as he spoke. "Arthur, king of the Britons, answer me."

"How do you know my name?" demanded Arthur.

"Because I have dreamed of you. Because I felt you draw Excalibur out of a stone, which is my flesh. Now I ask of you again, do you know me?"

"I know that you are my foe," said Arthur, "for there is enmity between your race and mine." And he unsheathed Excalibur in challenge.

The monster stood up, towering over him, covered from head to foot in scale-armor, which was of stone, and therefore not a garment at all, but the giant's own flesh. The creature hefted a stone-headed mace and took up a stone shield and stepped across the fire to contend with Arthur.

The two of them fought. Sparks flew like lightning flashes where Excalibur struck, and the giant drew back, amazed and in pain. He stumbled over his fire. He stumbled once more at the edge of a pit where the earth had been heaved up, as if some great leviathan had breached there from out of the world's core.

Yet the giant was not truly hurt, though his blood flowed over his stone armor. He could not kill Arthur, for the king was too fast, and Arthur could not kill him, for his shield and his armor were too strong. Wherever the giant's mace struck the ground it left a crater. Where he swung to one side or the other, trees crashed down.

After a long time, by mutual consent, though neither of them called for quarter, the two of them rested, and there was a truce between them.

Arthur sat on a fallen tree trunk. The giant leaned on his shield.

"Once more I ask, Arthur, king of the Britons, do you know who I am?"

Arthur was too exhausted to think of a clever answer, or of any stratagem, so he merely shook his head.

"Ah," said the other, "at least I get an honest reply, and in the same spirit I tell you that I am Gagonerok, son of Gogmagog of great fame, and I am the last of the giants of Albion. I say to you further that this is my country into which you and your people have come trespassing, and I will be revenged."

"Ha," said Arthur in contempt. "There are many giants and monsters in Britain. I have slain any number of them. My knights have slain more. What makes you so special?"

The giant glared at him, and once more the earth shook. Stones fell echoing into the nearby pit. For a moment it seemed that the giant would break the truce, and raise up his mace to strike. Arthur held on tightly to Excalibur. But the moment of anger passed.

Arthur considered what Merlin might advise him to do in this situation, and was certain that the wizard would tell him to learn something. It was sound strategy, to spy out his enemy's strengths and weaknesses.

"So, speak more of yourself and your illustrious parent," said Arthur.

Now the giant sat down, setting his shield aside, toying with his mace before the fire, at ease, as if actually flattered that someone would want to know. Idly, he picked up the roasted ox and took a bite, then offered some of the meat to Arthur, who ate of it.

"There are many giants," said Gagonerok, "and other monsters, it is true, but they are of fleshly nature. Most emerge from the bellies of women who consort with demons. Some are merely malformed men. But Gogmagog, my father, was made of stone and fire, and he coupled with a mountain, and so the earth split apart and I was born, as were all the other true giants of Albion, who occupied this land before men came."

Arthur glanced around at the broken earth. He remembered the mountains he had passed through on his way to this place. "Where are they now?"

"When Brutus the Trojan and his band came into Britain, they overthrew Gogmagog's progeny, all of whom were my brothers. A Trojan called Corineus cast our father into the sea, where he fell upon a sharp stone far away from the shore and was dashed into a thousand pieces. The waters ran red with his blood, and the pieces of his body formed a deadly reef, which mariners, to this day, still fear. I am glad for that."

"I have read of this Corineus," said Arthur. "He was a great hero."

"He was a pirate, thief, and murderer."

"He won a homeland for his people, whose own had been destroyed."

"On the way he killed thousands in Africa, pillaging to take what he wanted."

"What he needed," said Arthur.

"He and Brutus and the rest would have killed the entire population of Gaul had they not instead come hither. Not that I would have seen any wrong in that, but the Gauls might have, don't you think?"

"Why didn't he kill you?" said Arthur.

"Only because he did not find me. I was the last-born of my father's children, still asleep in my cradle of earth. So I was orphaned. Yet I saw everything in my dreams. Corineus, Brutus, and the other Trojans killed many children, in Africa and Gaul. They did not even bother to eat them, which seems a waste."

Arthur let this last comment pass.

"I ask you," said the giant, "are these the deeds of heroes?"

Arthur thought again of what Merlin would advise him. He was uneasy now, without Merlin at his side, but if a part of his mind, remembering the teacher's lessons, could become a *seeming* Merlin, then all yet might be well.

Merlin might tell him that a king must be more than merely brave; he must be clever. And he must be more than merely clever; he must be just.

"I will grant that you have been wronged," said Arthur, "that I too would hate someone who had killed my brothers and cast my father into the sea."

But Arthur was not sincere. He was being more guileful than truly weighing the rightness or wrongness of the thing.

Yet Gagonerok smiled broadly. He extended his empty hand.

"Then let us indeed have a truce between us. Let us even be, for a time, allies, and adventure about the world. No one has ever shown me sympathy before, or tried to."

Arthur did not take his hand, fearing he would be crushed in it. The giant shrugged.

"I will go about the world for a time," Gagonerok said, "swimming."

He allowed Arthur to climb onto his back, behind his neck, and crossed the countryside in great, broad strides, shaking the earth until he came to a cliff overlooking the sea, which Arthur knew was where the giant's father had died, and is thus called Gogmagog's Leap.

And the son leapt also, with Arthur on his back, into the foaming sea, and with great, broad strokes swam, and dove deep to converse with leviathans, while Arthur gasped for air and struggled merely to hold on, lest he be swept away in the currents and depths.

At last they came up on the shore of Ireland. The giant showed him where a sea monster, one of the very leviathans with whom he had held converse, now ravaged a town, turned over a castle, and devoured men even as a beast might devour ants kicked out of an anthill.

"They are but pagans," said Arthur, "and therefore my enemies. I should delight to see them destroyed."

"Really? Even as Brutus and Corineus delighted in seeing thousands of innocents slain, the women and children of Africa or Gaul who could have taken no part in their quarrel with the men there?"

Arthur felt unease. He knew that the *seeming* Merlin would counsel him to do the unexpected, to think before he spoke or acted, to weigh everything carefully.

"If they are pagans now, perhaps they may yet be redeemed from Hell, or their children might be. But if they are all dead they're just—"

"Dead meat?" said the giant, idly picking his teeth with a broken house beam.

"We must save them," said Arthur.

"I'll do it for sport," said the giant.

"And I for mercy."

So they fought with the monster and slew it. Gagonerok broke its back over his knee while Arthur struck off its head with Excalibur. But the men of Ireland fled in all directions in fear. Their salvation would have to be brought to them later.

Smiling broadly yet again, his enormous teeth glistening

like white stones in the rain, the giant said, "We work well as a team, Arthur of Britain, but perhaps I tire of this now and will merely leave you here while I swim back to Britain and devour all your countrymen."

The giant laughed. He bent over laughing, until all of Ireland shook and the seas leapt up, and mountains fell and the land and the islands thereabout were reshaped and reformed. And the men of Ireland were very much afraid, of both the giant and of Arthur. They stayed far away.

Acting swiftly, Excalibur in hand, Arthur hollowed out the severed head of the sea monster, stretching skin over its eye sockets until he had made a boat. From its guts he made a strong rope, from its claws a hook, and when the giant leapt once more into the ocean, Arthur hooked him behind the neck and was towed back to Cornwall, up the River Dart past Totnes—where the people looked on in wonder and dread—then dragged over the mountains, through the forest, while the giant tried to shake him off, but could not.

In the clearing, by the fire, amid the dark wood, Arthur once more drew Excalibur and said to the giant grimly, "We had a truce and were allies, yet you would devour my countrymen. My duty as a king is clear."

Said Gagonerok, "Are you sure?"

Again they fought, and sparks flew like lightning, and the earth and sky shook with the combat, yet neither prevailed, because of the sharpness of Excalibur, the swiftness of Arthur, the strength of the giant's mace, and the sheer impenetrability of the giant's stone flesh-armor.

At last the giant threw his shield down on top of Arthur. It fell on him like the collapsing roof of a great hall, and pressed him to the ground. The giant reached underneath and caught him in his hand, holding him up before his gleaming teeth.

"I could devour you now, Arthur, king of the Britons, but as a morsel you would taste no different from any other, and I desire more sport."

So he hurled the king as a player hurls a ball, and Arthur sailed deep into the wood, clinging to Excalibur. The blade, flailing wildly, hewed down trees, but at last Arthur was caught in branches, and thus fell to the ground, sore and bruised and bleeding from many wounds, but still alive.

He lay in the soft loam, beneath the dark trees, while the wind blew around him and the cold rain fell down. It came to Arthur, as if in a dream, that he was lying deep underneath the earth, as in a grave, but conscious as years, as centuries passed overhead. He could hear the earth groaning as the roots of the trees grew, as the water from the rain worked its way into the stones and the winter froze the water into ice and the stones slowly cracked. He heard the mountains breathing very slowly as the land of Britain rose and fell on a scale imperceptible to human senses, but clear enough to him, as if it were he himself breathing in his sleep, in his dream, in his grave.

It was at this time that shapes rose around Arthur out of the darkness like great leviathans breaching. Their faces were manlike, yet he knew from their speech that they were not men. They whispered and made the earth tremble; indeed these were the ancient gods who dwelt in the earth, walking to and fro and up and down in it, now trapped there, no longer worshipped by men since Christ had banished them hither.

Yet these gods, these ancient powers, who were in and of every tree, every stone, every mountain in Britain, whose voices were the wind of the air, whose blood was the rivers of Albion, these gods called out to Arthur and said, *Let us have a truce between us and be made allies, and we will overthrow Gagonerok even as you could flick an insect off yourself.*

Arthur wanted to call out to Merlin, to ask what he should do now, but he could find no voice, for when he opened his mouth it was filled with mud.

So the gods entered into him and filled him with their strength and their guile and their ancient hatreds, and Arthur rose up out of the earth. He felt the winter's rains cracking stones, washing away the earth above him, until he opened his eyes and beheld the dark forest—yet he could see in it, by some gleaming light flickering between the boughs like fiery rain.

He emerged once more into the clearing. His mind was filled with a thousand voices now. He could not find any *seeming* Merlin to advise him. Indeed, he could not even find Arthur. He had forgotten who he was.

He saw the giant Gagonerok, son of Gogmagog of great

fame, crouching before a fire, beside which he had laid out the corpses of thousands of men that he had slain. As Arthur watched, the giant scooped up a handful of the dead and sprinkled them into a boiling pot, which he stirred with a broken tree trunk.

He looked up, grinning, his teeth gleaming.

"Ah, will you join me in my supper?"

And the gods whispered to Arthur, within his own mind, that a king or a hero must be greater than all other men and above common morality. Therefore to do mighty deeds, he must also be terrible, and partake of terrible things.

So Arthur sat down beside Gagonerok and ate of that supper, dipping his helmet into the broth.

But as soon as he tasted it, his mind cleared, and he knew what he had done. He called out to Merlin, but Merlin did not answer. He called out to Christ, for the salvation of his soul, and the voices of the ancient gods were silent; they tempted him no more. He wept, knowing himself to be a wretched sinner, who could never be the true and perfect hero he had aspired to be, merely a flawed, weak, and mortal man, who now sat all but helpless beside a grinning giant who regarded him with bemusement, apparently unaware of what had happened.

The giant gulped the broth. He belched loudly and lay back, saying, "Yes, my friend, our life together will be good, now that we understand one another."

Arthur, left alone now with merely his wits to save him—for he was certain that Merlin would tell him, *think before you do*, or something like that—swore eternal friendship to Gagonerok the son of Gogmagog. He forced himself to taste even more of the stinking broth and eat of the hideous meat.

He knew that he had perjured himself merely to survive, but that if a king himself is recreant and false to his oaths, then there is no order in the universe, and a giant might as well eat everybody, for all anything mattered further.

Yet when the giant asked Arthur to repeat the oath, he repeated it.

Gagonerok hummed softly to himself, interrupted by belches. He stirred the soup and sprinkled in the last of his gathered ingredients.

He lay back and patted his stomach.

"Tell me a story," he said. "I think I'd like a story now, before I rest."

Once, when he was a child, Arthur had done some wrong and tried to conceal it from Merlin, which was of course useless. "You'll always be a bad liar," Merlin had said. "You have no talent for it."

So it was now. Arthur wept. He feared for his soul. He couldn't lie anymore, but could only tell the truth, of how in his pride he had thought to become the greatest of all heroes, how he yearned to be as great as, indeed, Brutus the Trojan and Corineus—Gagonerok growled at the mention of the name—or like Aeneas and Alexander, or like Joshua, David, and Judas Maccabaeus who were favored of the Lord. He told of their heroic deeds, of the victories they won, the enemies slain. He told of other heroes of the Britons, of Dunvallo Molmutius, who was famous for his laws; of Belinus and Brennius, rival brothers but great men both; of the peerless Ambrosius Aurelianus and of the famous victories of Uther Pendragon, his own father. He wept as he told these tales, certain that he would never measure up to any such persons, that he himself was a mere *seeming*, a shadow-hero, just pretending.

Gagonerok must have thought Arthur's weeping was just so much noise, like the wind in the trees. He eased toward sleep.

"Those are good stories," he said. "I liked them. I am glad that you have sworn to be my friend. Haven't you?"

"Yes," said Arthur, "I have." And he wept again, knowing that he had perjured himself before God.

"I think I'll eat the rest of the British in the morning," said the giant, belching, then snoring.

And Arthur, who had sworn now three times, waited only until he was certain that the giant was asleep, then drew Excalibur from its scabbard and climbed up onto the giant's face.

The giant snorted and his nose twitched, as a man's might if an insect were crawling on his face as he slept. Arthur clung to the giant's moustache so that he would not be swept away.

Then, stealthily, praying to God that this act might somehow redeem all he did, he drove Excalibur into the monster's eye and pushed the blade down all the way to the hilt, into the monster's brain, and so slew Gagonerok, son of Gogmagog, last of the true giants of Albion.

But Gagonerok the giant awoke briefly with a shout, knowing that he was slain, and he cried out, calling Arthur recreant and traitor. Yet, then, as he was dying, he seemed to lose his anger, and he whispered, "Arthur, you have murdered me, but you were also the only friend I have ever known. I enjoyed having you by my side in adventures, and at supper. Therefore, I make you a gift."

He yanked the smallest and sharpest of his teeth out of his mouth, and affixed it on a wooden shaft, fashioning a spear, using his blood to bind it together.

He gave the spear to Arthur saying, "Take this. It will make a mighty man out of you."

"It will do me good? It is not a trick?"

"I *swear*," said Gagonerok. "You will conquer with it. You will even kill your own death with it."

Arthur took it. The death-rattle was upon Gagonerok. Grinning, teeth gleaming, he died; and as he died, the sky grew brighter. For the first time since Arthur had been upon that adventure, he saw the sun rise. He saw that the dark wood was merely an ordinary forest. He saw that the dead giant was merely a pile of broken stones.

But hundreds of corpses still simmered in the pot. Weeping, burning his hands as he did so, Arthur tipped over the pot and sent it rolling down a slope into the forest.

Then, weeping still, leaning on the spear, Arthur prayed to God for the souls of the dead, and for the salvation of his own soul, which he knew had been compromised.

When he looked up, in the bright sunlight, he saw Merlin.

"You have done well, my lord," said the wizard.

"I don't think so."

"The monster is slain. The countryside is relieved of the danger. You yourself have grown in wisdom—"

I have learned, thought Arthur to himself, *that the king, to be a king, must sometimes do the hard thing, the terrible thing, the filthy thing, though others may praise him for it later and make songs and stories of his heroic deeds.*

"And, look, too. You've gained a powerful weapon, which will make you all the stronger."

The king can't afford to worry about his soul. That is in the hands of God.

"Yes, a powerful weapon," said Arthur, standing up, hefting the spear. "He said I would kill my own death with it."

At this Merlin grew silent, for he saw the future clearly, and he knew that Arthur would indeed carry that spear in all of his wars, and long after he himself was beguiled and trapped in the crystal cave, unable to be of any more help, the king would carry that spear into the last battle at Camlann, and impale Mordred with it even as Mordred slew him.

Tearfully, Arthur turned to Merlin even as a child turns to his teacher, and said, "But I have compromised my soul. . . ."

Merlin forced a little laugh. "No one but you and I and God need ever know. God probably won't tell anyone. So be of good cheer. More good will come of it than ill, in the long run." But to Arthur his words seemed hollow just then, as they never had before.

THE SCREAM OF THE GULLS

Joe Murphy

The shrine vanished. Owain's eyelids fluttered open; he woke, his hand outstretched into the clammy darkness of his hut. His fingers tingled with the roughness of runes etched deep in stone. He sniffed, smelling the shadowed leaves of a dark forest.

Why would the Lord God grant such a vision? Never before had he dreamed of the forest shrine. There was no time to pray for guidance, however. A thrumming of hooves crossed the hard-packed shore to seep up through his blanket and into his spine.

Three riders—no, four—and something more that Owain sensed, rearing up from both memory and dream; something from before his deafness. Something of the Fey. He shivered in the night air and rose.

The hearth fire had burned low. Owain found a branch not completely charred and blew upon it. The flame brightened, casting a ruddy glow upon the wattle and daub walls. He tucked his dagger beneath the sleeve of his monk's robe, pushed back the hide door, and stepped outside.

A rolling froth of waves gleamed beneath the full moon. Shadows from the high cliffs crowded the beach. It seemed uncommonly cold for a May eve; his breath steamed around him. An omen, perhaps. This place was full of omens, though Owain seldom found their meanings clear.

Four shapes rode out of the shadows. The largest rider led; the smallest, upon a pony, trailed behind. They reined up before him, seeming to be made of shadows themselves.

Owain swallowed and called, "If you seek hospitality then be welcome in the name of God and the Savior. But know that I'm deaf. Speak slowly that I may understand your lips. Come inside, if you will, and I'll share whatever I have."

The largest rider swung from the saddle with uncommon grace. A woman, Owain realized, when she moved into the torchlight. Fair-skinned with dark hair, richly dressed in a black gown and cloak, she threw back her hood and smiled. Shadows of the Fey crowded her eyes but her softly upturned lips appeared kind.

"Old man," those lips moved; Owain bent forward, squinting to watch them closely, "your offer is most gracious. If you'll provide a roof and shelter for a woman and her sons that we might rest till morning, we'll share our provisions with you."

"Be welcome then. Come in. Come in." Owain drew back the leather door as the others dismounted. The first two, little more than youths, trudged inside. The third, still a child who could barely reach his stirrups, hurried to care for the horses.

All were dressed as richly as their mother and shared her grateful smile. He followed them in and quickly built up the fire. Their lips moved but he couldn't catch the words. Their eyes turned this way and that but Owain couldn't decide their meaning.

The fire brightened, the smell of wood smoke thick in the gloom. Owain had little to offer, not even chairs, but his guests settled upon the earthen floor with the weary slump of those who'd traveled hard.

Firelight found the woman's face and she turned to him. "Sir, let me introduce my sons. The tallest and darkest is Gawain. The middle one be Gaheris." The boy came in then to slump down with the others. "And my youngest, with his beautiful smile, is Agravain."

Each nodded as she spoke, save Agravain, whose cheeks blushed. The boy ducked his head for a moment, was prodded by his brothers, and finally favored Owain with a shy grin. "Sir, may I present my mother, Morgause, queen of Lothian."

"The queen of Lothian?" Owain dropped to his knees and bowed his head. "Milady, I'm sorry to have so little to offer!"

Her fingers touched his chin, lifting his head. "Your home is the most hospitable we've found in two days. We're very grateful."

"Now we can eat!" Young Agravain fumbled open a pack. Owain found his mouth watering as he saw the bread and meat the boy took out. Even a skin of wine! The queen gestured for him to sit and Owain eagerly did so. What a change this was from years of dried fish!

After they'd eaten, Morgause turned to him. "You're a monk, sir? What is your name?"

"Call me Owain, if it pleases you. The friars at Menevia gave me the robe, out of pity, I suppose. They found me wandering in the woods, you see. I was quite unclothed, and delirious as well. They took good care of me, even offered me a saint's name. But I never learned how to speak it. I was already deaf."

"Then you reject the old ways?" the queen asked. "Those we still cling to in Lothian?"

"I'm an old man." Owain spread his hands. "I've felt the power of the old ways just as I've found the kindness of the new."

"But what of the kings?" The young man, Gawain, narrowed dark eyes and spoke: "Are you a supporter of Lot, my father? Or this new king with his court in Caerleon?"

Owain knew of Arthur. Yet, his life upon this nameless shore had little to do with kings or conquests. Only a fool would say as much to these strange visitors, however.

"I, too, am from Lothian and would serve your father." A small sin, this lie; later he would pray. The youth sat back, satisfied.

Young Agravain stretched, yawned, then curled up in his blanket. Gaheris lay next to him, and finally Gawain settled in. Morgause gazed at her children, then turned to study Owain.

At last she spoke. "You've lived here a long time?"

"Yes, milady." Owain pointed at the thick limb that formed the door's lintel. "At least a score and a half of marks I've cut into the wood. One for each year."

"You understand me quite well. You weren't always deaf, I'd wager."

"No, no." Though he was well used to the earthen floor, Owain shifted uncomfortably. "It's an uncommonly cold night, don't you think?"

"Tell me how you came to be deaf." Morgause fixed green eyes upon him. Her lips ceased to smile but didn't frown, either; they seemed intent.

After all his prayers, all his fasts, she still knew what lay within him. Did she dream of dark forests and hidden shrines as he did? Could she feel the magic of shadowed leaves? Touched by the Fey herself, she would know a lie if he spoke it. Owain shivered in spite of the fire's warmth. He looked down, not daring to meet her gaze.

"I was a wood cutter once. In the forest, beyond the cliffs just north of here. Sometimes I came to this shore for fish. Once I chanced upon a pack of kelpies. Beautiful creatures they were, full of Fey, and joined in song. I couldn't help but watch and listen. Their voices still haunt me."

"They tried to lure you into the sea," Morgause said when he at last looked up. "Kelpies feed upon the very lives of mortals."

"As you say, milady. My legs moved without my will. In desperation, I scooped up a handful of mud and packed my ears. I escaped the kelpies but became ill. When the fever left, so did my hearing."

"I wonder . . ." She gazed at the fire, its light flickering over her fair skin, sharpening her chin and nose. "Did you don that robe in the hope that the friars and their new religion could return your hearing?"

"Once I so hoped." Owain shrugged. "They brag much of miracles. But it was not to be."

"The old ways are still the more powerful." Morgause steepled her fingers, elbows resting upon her knees. "Neither of us will ever be free of them."

Owain nodded. "The friars said as much. They refused to allow me to stay with them."

Morgause gazed at her sleeping sons and smiled. Abruptly she cocked her head, as if listening to the night, or the waves. "A child may come into your hands. I cannot tell you when, but it could be soon. I cannot foresee where, but perhaps nearby."

"Forgive me, but that is a strange prophecy."

"Nevertheless, you might be the one to find this child." Her gaze held him. "If this should happen, return him to me and your hearing will be restored."

Owain gaped at her. What manner of madness was this? He felt her green eyes upon him, felt the power of the Fey within her, and knew she could do such a thing.

"Milady, how can I? I've no horse to come to you and Lothian is very far. Neither have I skills to care for a child. If it is sick, I have nothing to offer but prayers."

"Prayers aren't enough. While my other sons and I search the northern shores, Agravain will remain here. He's too young to face such a thing alone. Place the babe in his arms and you'll again hear the world around you." Morgause smiled. "Do you agree?"

"But what sort of child?"

"A May Day child, born on that very eve and stolen not a week later." Morgause's eyes flashed in the firelight. She scowled and a cold anger deepened the lines of her face.

"Stolen?" was all Owain dared ask.

"Even though I'd hidden him, put him in the arms of a farmer's wife. Stolen by Merlin; I sense his hand in all this. Indeed, Merlin himself may come looking for the boy."

"I can do nothing against such a one as that. Even before my deafness, the stories I'd heard—"

"All the more reason for haste." Morgause stabbed at him with a slender finger. "If you find the child, deliver him to Agravain, old man. My son will ride away before Merlin comes. You'll have your hearing, and all will be well."

Would the friars at Menevia count such a bargain a sin? Most certainly. They disdained the old ways, hated the Fey, believing them fallen angels from when Lucifer fled Heaven. Still, to save a child, there was no evil in that.

His hearing restored—it would be like returning to the world of men. Worth any price, save his soul. . . .

"I'll help you, Queen Morgause. Of course. But can you tell me more?"

"He's my son. The son of a king." Morgause smiled and closed her eyes. "From the sea he'll be returned and, in turn, he will some day be king, lord over his own father."

"From the sea?" Owain could scarcely believe it. "Has this boy a name?"

"Aye." Queen Morgause nodded and opened her eyes. "Mordred."

⊰❈⊱

Clouds loomed like high bleak mountains, and allowed only a dingy light upon Queen Morgause as she and two sons rode up the beach. Owain glanced down at Agravain, who lifted a hand in farewell. Even as Owain raised a hand, a great sense of unease engulfed him.

Gulls filled the sky, silenced by his own defect. Like a

living cloud they wheeled and soared, hordes of them. The peaks of greedy waves reached as if to snare the birds, the ocean dark, frothing with anger that it could catch none.

A hand touched his arm. Owain turned to the boy. Agravain's thin face looked much like his mother's. The lad's dark hair curled over small, well-shaped ears. Thin delicate lips smiled uncertainly beneath eyes the color of the sea, yet bright with humor.

"Mother sees much of what will come to pass, but not always clearly." Agravain nodded toward the riders. "I hope she finds my brother."

"Tell me of this brother. How did he come to be stolen?" Owain motioned toward his hut, anxious to be out of the cold wind. They started over the stony sand.

"He was taken with all the others." Agravain trotted along beside him. The boy looked up from time to time at the gulls, so that Owain caught only a single word.

"Others?" he repeated.

"All the male children born on the first of May." Agravain stopped and frowned. "My mother believes King Arthur ordered this. Those were his men that did the taking. But I think it was Merlin. I've met them both, you know."

"Indeed."

"It's true, old man. Mother took us to Caerleon in the hopes of arranging peace between Arthur and my father. A good strategic move, Gawain told me. We were suffering raids by the Danes. Father couldn't fight two wars and hope to win."

"My brother perished to the Danes," Owain noted sadly. "I remember them."

"Arthur treated my mother more than honorably. Not like his seneschal, Kay, who did nothing but scowl. We attended several feasts and she sat at Arthur's side. But Merlin—what a gray old man! He never smiled. His face was always puckered as though he'd eaten sour berries. He didn't like us at all." The boy shivered and hunched down in his cloak.

"You say they took all the male babes born on May Day? That must have been quite a number," Owain said as they entered his hut.

"A hundred, I'm told." Agravain hurried to warm his hands by the fire. He spoke again but was turned so Owain couldn't catch it. Agravain looked back then, apparently realizing this, and the boy's face was grave. "Sorry."

"What's to become of these children?" Owain asked.

"I'm certain King Arthur will treat them well. Most think they'll be raised at Caerleon." Agravain shrugged. "But Mother's worried. She will say nothing more. It's Merlin she fears, I think."

"Perhaps you should see to your pony," Owain suggested. "Take him up to the woods above the house. There's plenty to eat there and he'll be out of sight."

"A good idea." Agravain started for the door.

Owain smiled and the boy grinned back before dashing outside. He liked the child. Perhaps he'd lived too long alone. It seemed good to have someone to talk with.

Owain bent to warm his hands before the fire. He hadn't realized just how lonely his life had become. Lonely and frightening. Their gaping soundless mouths had too often transformed other men into demons. Silence had masked their words and faces; Owain never knew who might be friend or enemy. He'd been surrounded as if by a foreign people.

So, he'd come here, to the very shore where the kelpies once sought to claim him. He'd prayed to the new god that the Menevia friars worshipped, prayed for years that his hearing might be restored. Nothing had come of it.

After Agravain returned and warmed himself, Owain took the boy's hand and led him far down the shore to gather fish. The wind had sharpened, the clouds grown darker.

"There's fish everywhere!" Wide-eyed, Agravain gazed around them. Owain grinned and pointed out toward a swirl of water and the distant rocks in the sea beyond.

"A treacherous current surrounds those rocks, so strong and vicious that, in weather such as this, it dashes the fish against the stone, leaving them stunned or dead upon the beach."

"I would hate to try these waters in a boat." Agravain shaded his eyes and stared at the tooth-shaped stones.

"Even the Danes avoid the sea here." Owain nodded. "I've been blessed with food and peace." He bent to his task, picking up an exceptionally large mackerel. To his surprise, the young prince helped, skipping over with three more.

Back already aching, hands numb from the cold, Owain fumbled the fish into a cloth sack. One slipped from his fingers and he knelt to retrieve it.

Perhaps the stone beneath the sand told him riders approached, perhaps some deeper sense, but Owain knew.

"Come," he called, for the child had wandered along the beach. "We must go."

Agravain turned to him and nodded. Owain couldn't read his words from so far away, but the boy trotted over. The strange sense of unease that had plagued the old man of late returned full force.

Owain gripped the boy's arm and hustled him beneath the cliffs. The child sensed his urgency and they hid in a jumble of boulders. The wind proved weaker here, the stones damp, gritty with sand. Owain put a hand on Agravain's shoulder and urged him down.

What must have been a score of riders cantered up the shore. Sunlight glinted off armor and spear. Hooves kicked up feathery clouds of foam from the surf's edge.

"Whose men are those?" Agravain clutched his robe and mouthed. "They wear no colors. I see no banner."

A slower group moved behind the mounted warriors, blurred by distance. Owain put his hand on Agravain's shoulder and whispered, "What are they doing? These old eyes can't see what they used to."

"They're dragging something." Agravain studied the newcomers, then looked up at the hermit. The boy frowned in confusion. "I think it's a boat."

The group stopped. Owain sighed, relieved that they came no closer. Still, they weren't more than a bowshot away.

He urged Agravain down deeper into the rocks. "We'll be seen if we try to leave."

"What should we do?" A tinge of fear crossed Agravain's face.

"Best wait for nightfall." Owain pressed against the stone, hunching his neck as if that would warm him. He found more comfort from the boy's warmth when Agravain huddled closer. They watched as some of the men scattered and brought driftwood for a fire. The wind whipped at them; the clouds gathered.

A storm was coming, Owain realized. When he'd first

come to this nameless shore such an omen had seemed ill. Now he'd learned the ways of this place. Storms meant more fish and a full belly. Omens then could be seen in different ways. Yet, the only thing in his belly now was an aching, empty dread.

"Something feels wrong here." Agravain's small face pinched into a puzzled frown. "It lurks in my head but also in my belly."

Owain nodded. "I feel such a thing myself. Perhaps it's the coming storm." Waves hurled countless attacks against the beach. The wind had grown so fierce that the men soon gave up trying to keep a fire going. They slumped in small groups around the skin boat that lay overturned and fastened to the sand with ropes and pegs.

"Mother says I have some of her magic. More than any of my brothers."

Owain found it hard to read the boy's lips; the child's teeth chattered constantly now, like his own. "I was told of a new god in Menevia. Perhaps it's he that touches you."

The boy shook his head. "I heard of this Christian god in Caerleon. Some monks told us their god is merciful yet full of miracles."

"So he is."

"Arthur himself seems to believe in him." Agravain smiled. "Arthur took us hunting once. I think he must be a good king. Nevertheless, Father hates him. Yet, my father is a good king, too. Sometimes I don't understand all that happens. Mother says that's because I'm still just a boy."

"I've learned that wisdom comes with age."

"Have you found such wisdom, Owain?"

Owain gazed at the child. Bright eyes, earnest smile, at first he thought the boy mocked him. Yet, there appeared a look of honest intensity upon Agravain's face. It wasn't mockery at all. Here was a bright young lad, full of life, eager for his future.

"Someday, you might make a fine king yourself," Owain told him. "I pray that you'll find the wisdom that has eluded me."

The child beamed and shivered like a puppy. Owain put his arm around the boy and so they waited and watched as the afternoon wore on.

Agravain shifted, stretching up on the rocks and peering

down the beach. He pulled at Owain's robe. "Look! Someone comes."

Owain moved up beside him. Three covered carts drawn not by oxen but by horses slowly churned toward the soldiers. A lone rider on a gray war-horse led them, face hidden by the cowl of a gray cloak.

The carts halted beside the soldiers. The gray rider pointed toward the boat. At once, the men began preparing the craft, releasing the ropes that held it to the sand.

"Madness," Owain breathed.

Agravain looked up. "Won't the rocks get them?"

"As God is my witness: Any who sail from this shore will die before morning. Surely they must know that." Owain peered out at the massive thrusting stones as the waves lashed against them, sending spray high in bright beaded curtains.

Agravain abruptly gripped his shoulder. Owain turned; the boy's face had grown as dark as the sea itself. The child's eyes widened. Owain followed his gaze.

A group of women had descended from the wagons. Shoulders hunched against the wind, they each clutched a tiny swaddled shape.

"Babies," Owain muttered. "Why bring such little ones out in weather like this?"

At the gray rider's direction a line formed. The women retrieved even more babes from the carts and passed them to the men. One by one, the soldiers tucked the little ones into the tiny boat.

Even without wisdom, Owain suddenly understood. These were the boy children born on May Day. Arthur himself had ordered them collected; the men must be his. Hadn't Morgause told him that a child would come from the sea, a child born of a king, who would one day become lord over his own father?

But why would Arthur care? Morgause was wife to Lot. The child then would become lord over Lot. No! He turned to Agravain and grasped the boy's shoulder.

"How long ago did your mother visit Caerleon?"

"Just last year," Agravain answered, his face still puzzled. "In fact, only about ten months ago. . . ." The boy turned, stared out at the soldiers as babe after babe was loaded into the skin boat.

"Arthur must know the prophecy your mother spoke of. They'll murder them all to kill your brother." Owain felt Agravain stiffen beneath his hand.

"My brother?" Understanding filled the boy's face, replaced just as quickly with rage. He turned and gaped at Owain. "But not my father's child."

Agravain leapt up, drawing a dagger from his waist, and charged Arthur's men.

Owain lurched after him, the boy already out of reach. Agravain stumbled in the sand. The wind masked whatever cries he might have made. And so intent was the group by the boat that none noticed as Owain reached the boy and scooped him into his arms.

"Fool!" the hermit hissed. "If they'll do that to babes, what will they do to you?" He pulled the boy away, held Agravain beneath him as he scrambled behind a fan-shaped clump of gorse.

"I pray to any god who'll listen," Agravain said as he twisted in Owain's arms to glare up at him. The boy's lips moved almost too fast for the old man to understand. "Any god at all. And if the gods won't stop it . . . let Arthur the adulterer come himself!"

The child's wild efforts ceased. He clutched Owain, shoulders shaking, tears wiped from his face by the wind. The hermit held him fast, kept the boy's head down. He couldn't help peering out through the twisted, newly leafed gorse branches as the gray rider dismounted his war-horse.

Their gazes averted, the women retreated into the wagons. The soldiers stepped back, stone-faced, eyes on the sand. Slowly the gray-cloaked rider approached the boat, then set hands upon the keel and pushed it out upon the sea.

The gray rider stepped back. A corner of his cloak snagged on the boat and tore free. It hung upon the keel like a ribbon of shame.

Wind pulled the rider's cowl away. Hair gray as the cloak streamed in the breeze.

Agravain clutched Owain's shoulder, staring. "It's Merlin."

A wave rocked the tiny craft. Small swaddled bodies tossed and tumbled against the soft skin sides. From this distance, Owain could see nothing more. The current seized the boat and drew it out toward the rocks. A heartbeat later, the vessel vanished into the twilight, and the first thick drops of rain, cold as the blood of the dead, splashed against Owain's face.

The friars at Menevia had spoken of Hell, a place of flame and eternal torment. The storm that descended was a hell of water and wind. Never had Owain seen its like.

Its fury fell upon them as he and the boy fled through the darkness. It tore the leathery hide from the doorway of Owain's hut before they reached it. Wind clawed its way through the wattle and daub walls, ripping the packed clay from between the branches. Rain oozed and dripped through the roof, wetting everything. No fire would burn in the hearth.

Soaked and shivering, weary with misery, Owain huddled against the boy. What few times he found the heart to speak, Agravain turned away. On such a night, after witnessing such a horror, Owain thought he would never sleep again. What mercy could exist in this world, or the next, if any god countenanced such a hideous deed? Yet, sleep came to him—though he knew it only when a hand shook his shoulder to wake him.

"It's dawn." Agravain frowned down at him. "The storm is gone. Come, we must search for my brother."

They left the hut. Fog obscured the cliffs and sea, a heavy mist tinged red from a sun unseen.

Agravain started away from him.

"No," Owain called. Within him, the sense of dread had lessened, though not vanished. In some manner he could not explain, it pulled him toward a spot farther up the shore. "Go find your pony and meet me in that direction."

Agravain shrugged, gazing only at the sand. Wordlessly the boy trudged up the path to the woods.

Owain came at length to a small inward swoop of the shore. He knew the spot. Some years ago, he'd lost his hearing at this place.

A strange shape rose from the water's edge. Not quite a man, not quite a horse, but a creature that in some weird way blurred the forms of both. Red-eyed and baleful, the creature held in its arms a small swaddled bundle.

Owain found his voice at last. "Queen Morgause has sent me to you. I'm to deliver the child."

Great shaggy arms, with fur black as the bottom of the sea, held out the babe. The child's tiny eyes blinked, unfocused yet as green as the queen's. It squirmed, grimaced, but appeared alive and unhurt.

Owain took the little one into his arms, felt its warmth against his chest.

"Our pact with Morgause is fulfilled," the kelpie's lips moved. "A hundred in exchange for one." The creature vanished, and the fog seemed to follow it. Abruptly the sun appeared, already well above the horizon.

Owain turned to find a mounted Agravain cantering toward him. The boy stared out at the now-placid ocean, at the spot where the kelpie had disappeared.

As Agravain drew near, Owain lifted the babe and offered it. Agravain reached out and took the child, but the boy's gaze remained fixed beyond the hermit.

Then Owain's world opened with sound. He heard Agravain's horse snort and whinny. Waves murmured upon the sand. Gulls screamed. They shrieked, and their cries echoed from the distant cliffs as a raucous agony.

Owain turned. Gulls clustered upon the shore, thicker than he'd ever seen them. The gluttonous creatures squalled, tugging at the tatters of bright swaddling clothes. The birds quarreled and fought over tiny pinkish blobs that cluttered the shore and stained the sand red.

Sickened, Owain turned away and fell to his knees. He looked up, wanting to pray, to beg some god somewhere to wipe the awful image from his mind.

He found no mercy. Instead, he found himself gazing up at Agravain, who held the infant Mordred at arm's length. The babe's shrill cries joined the gull's hateful chorus.

The light had vanished from Agravain's eyes. Though young in years, he was child no longer. Gone was the bright eagerness Owain had first seen.

"I would've killed you yesterday." Agravain glared at the babe, his voice as harsh as stone against sand. "Now, for the rest of my life, I'll look into your eyes and see our mother's sins." Scowling, he turned to Owain. "Old man, you have what you wanted. Be on your way."

Agravain wheeled the pony, digging his heels savagely

into the beast's sides. Heedless of his own safety, or even the babe's, the boy galloped headlong toward the woods.

"I will pray no more." Owain rose, shaking his head.

Eyes unseeing, he started back to his hut. Abruptly he found himself sprawled upon the sand, bits of shell cutting his palms. He looked down at his feet. They'd tangled in the tattered strand from a gray cloak.

The sense within him, which he had forgone for so long, told him of its owner. Owain clenched the rag and shook it at the sky.

"If there be no mercy in this world," he cried at the gulls, "then let there be vengeance."

He turned from his hut upon the nameless shore and hurried up the path through the cliffs and into the wood. He knew his way here, from years long past; a part of his soul, touched by the Fey, guided him.

As if in a dream, he entered a different forest. Here the trees grew shaggy and huge, shutting the sky away. Ferns and shadows merged into the darkest of greens. Unlike the shore, this place had a name.

"Brocéliande, Wood of the Fey, let me pass that I might find the one who hunts here."

The ferns splayed wide; shadows receded and Owain tread upon a trail that could not be seen by eyes alone.

He came upon a mossy stone obelisk in a leaf-shadowed shrine, and a voice spoke within his head. "Woodcutter, you've grown old."

"Old in body, sick at heart," Owain sighed.

"Once you brought me wood, a gift for my hearth. What do you bring this time?"

"A scrap of cloak, Huntress. From one named Merlin."

"Merlin the Enchanter?"

"Merlin the Foul. The deeds I've witnessed make him so."

"What would you have of me, woodcutter?"

"Turn your skills to Merlin's fate. Spare him no indignity. Lead him from his king and let all that he's mastered become your own."

"An interesting proposition." The shadow of a young woman appeared in the gloom. "What will you give to seal the bargain?"

"Take my ears that I may never again hear the gulls

scream. Take my eyes, for in the sight of a nameless shore I've seen lives lost and a boy bent to a bad end."

"You may keep your eyes if you'll serve me." The shadow drew close; a darkened hand reached to touch his cheek. "Speak the name I once whispered to you before this very stone. Speak aloud—then you will hear no more, and Merlin's fate I will seal."

"Niniane!"

The woods echoed his voice; the sound dwindled away until nothing, not even the softest rustle of a stray breeze, remained.

Niniane, Huntress of the Fey, appeared before him. Slender of figure, so beautiful in her shadowed green gown that his eyes ached. She smiled.

"I'll bring you wood again, Fair One," Owain promised, though he could not hear the words. "Forever." He stripped off the monk's robe and laid it at her feet, ready once more to take up the old ways.

FOLLOW

Clarissa Aykroyd

He was King of the Isles. It was one of his titles; but as far as he knew, it had no meaning. Perhaps it had meant something to his great-great-grandfather. His land was in Gwynedd, northern Wales, and he was not king of the Isle of Mona. On his worst days, he felt that a meaningless title was appropriate for a meaningless life. On the better days, he thought that perhaps the Isles were not really isles at all, but the foothills and ridges that clustered around Snowdon. They jutted above the valleys as islands did from the sea. Snowdon was the greatest island of all. He loved the mountain. It was just a few miles away from his castle, and he sometimes found himself praying to it rather than to God. He excused himself by the thought that it must have been shaped directly by God's hand. Its peak in winter was purer and whiter than anything else on earth.

Pellinore was not really a king at all. He was a minor warlord. It did not bother him to be a king in name only, since he thought that kingship was overrated. But he had no objections to being a warlord. The problem was that there was no one to war against in this remote part of Britain. His people had fled here from the invading Saxons to find peace. He thought that they had succeeded all too well. There had been no real battles in his twenty-three years, only skirmishes with neighboring petty kings.

If Pellinore had been free, he could have left his castle empty to ride around Britain, perhaps to join the warband of Arthur, the young High King. News did not come often to Gwynedd, but the last he had heard, Arthur was holding court in Winchester. It was a year since the High King had been crowned. Pellinore longed to join him. But he was not free. There was no wife, as yet; but there were his three younger sisters. The oldest was thirteen, and the twins were eleven. Even the thirteen-year-old was young to marry off, and it remained to be seen if anyone would have her. Pellinore had been fond of his dead parents, but he cursed them for having more children when he was already ten years old.

So while the King of the Isles might now want to travel, one thing was certain: He could not leave the girls. Sending them to another household as wards was out of the question. Any neighboring castles were many miles away, and their lords were unpleasant old men who presided over households that were almost completely without females. Pellinore thought of his little sisters as nuisances more than anything else, but he felt responsible for them. They adored him, which made him feel worse. They were the chain that fettered him to Gwynedd.

His other burden was his own sense of decency and responsibility. Although he didn't know many other young men, he knew that most of them would not allow similar circumstances to keep them from going out and experiencing life. They would find a way, even if it involved abandonment of responsibility, even if that responsibility was human. Pellinore felt that he could not do such a thing. He despised himself for being so good.

For a few years now, Pellinore had taken to spending hours at the window in the castle's tower. He watched Snowdon, day by day. He often thought that it was more alive than anything else in his experience. It might be grim and black one day, full of sunlight the next. In winter, it was godlike. Depending on the season, on how the light fell, it was never the same. He wished that he could say the same of his life.

It was spring. Pellinore hated the spring. He had a feeling that no decent human being ought to hate the season of rebirth, with its new flowers and teasing winds, but he could not help it. It called to him, as it called to all the world's young creatures. His sisters exclaimed over the lambs and the other small animals that were springing up everywhere. Everything was full of life. Pellinore felt only a gnawing ache in the pit of his stomach. How could he stay here any longer, at the edge of the world?

He rode out early one morning in the gray dawn, to go hunting. He preferred to go alone, without even a man-servant for company or protection. He was still young enough to be certain that no accident would ever befall him. One whippy white brachet was enough, to pick up the scent.

Hunting was one of his few escapes. He did not particularly enjoy the kill, but he loved the chase—the wind stinging tears to his eyes, the power of the horse beneath him, and the sense that there was something magnificent and exciting ahead of him, something more than a deer or a hare. The pursuit of the intangible was one of the reasons why he always felt a moment of anticlimax at the kill.

The horse was as eager as he was this morning. It sprang down the slope toward the woods. The brachet ran ahead, panting in rhythm with its footfalls. Pellinore looked back. There was a dark track behind them over the silver of the dewy grass.

The brachet struck a scent and plunged into the thickest area of trees. Pellinore followed. Horse and man forced their way through. Pellinore ducked to avoid the branches that clawed down toward his eyes. Thankfully, the horse was not one of those dangerous rogues that delighted in taking their passengers under unyielding branches, sweeping them off or braining them. It was a good horse.

Pellinore wondered why there was no sound of another animal up ahead. Perhaps it was very swift. Probably nothing more than a hare. He could barely see the brachet, just a small flash of white dashing in and out of the shadows. He could not even hear its panting.

Suddenly, he saw the brachet stop dead. He was so surprised at this that he almost did not duck at a branch that could have done some damage; it scratched his head, but painfully. They were gaining on the brachet. Now he could see: It was standing motionless at the edge of a clearing. Pellinore felt dizzy for a moment. He thought that he knew these woods as well as his own castle—why should he not, when he had lived here all his life? He could not remember any such clearing. He reined the horse to a violent halt at the clearing's edge. Then his fingers tightened on the reins.

A beast was standing in the clearing. Pellinore had enough time to see that it was about the size of a stag, before his mind went into a fog of fear and confusion. A small, detached voice told him that the creature had the head of a serpent, the body of a leopard or some other spotted creature, the hindquarters of a lion, and the legs and slots of a deer. Pellinore tried not to believe it. There was another, less rational voice in his mind, one that was screaming that he must be going mad. There was no way that such a beast could exist. And yet, when he focused on the head, he saw a serpent; when he looked at the body, he saw a yellow pelt and black spots; and so on in turn. When he tried to look at the whole beast, it seemed to slide away from him. It became insubstantial. The part of Pellinore that was still detached told him that it was like trying to look at the sun: There was no way that it could be done, because his whole organism resisted it.

He tried to speak. All that came out was a croaked "God in Heaven." He put out a trembling hand and made the sign of the cross. Nothing happened. The beast did not vanish in a puff of black smoke. It could not be a demon, then. But Pellinore had always had doubts as to the effectiveness of the sign of the cross. Perhaps it was an exceptionally powerful demon. He was lost.

At that moment, the beast turned its head and looked directly at him. The grotesque body seemed to vanish. Pellinore could see nothing except a pair of eyes like emeralds, lucent, not snakelike at all. He had never seen such beautiful eyes on man or beast. And he knew, all at once, that they held a message for him: *Follow.*

The beast half-turned, looked back at him again, then bounded away. It moved as gracefully as any stag. A strange sound went along with it. The air rang with the noise of many hounds questing after their prey. Pellinore spurred after it.

He had no idea what he was doing. He seemed to have no control over his actions. But he no longer felt any fear. The horse and the brachet were equally calm. The horse was moving well underneath him, and the brachet was running ahead, as though it were chasing a hare. Pellinore realized that the animals had never shown any fear. Why would a horse not startle and rear at the sight and sound of such a strange creature?

They broke out into the open. Pellinore saw his castle up ahead. The beast had led them back in a circle. It stood before him now, only a short distance away. It held itself in an attitude of alertness, yet it showed no sign of panic. There was peace in all its lineaments. The brachet was circling it slowly, at a cautious distance, but with an equal calm. It seemed to be curious rather than alarmed. Pellinore looked into the beast's eyes again. The green depths drew him in. His head spun, but it was a pleasant sensation, as though he had drunk a bit too much.

Pellinore heard no words, and yet a message came quite clearly to him through the beast's green eyes. He was to return the next morning, with his animals, prepared for a long hunt. And he was to follow the beast wherever it led him. *Follow. Follow. Follow.* The word beat inside his head like a magnified heartbeat. He drew himself out of the beast's eyes, and looked around. The creature was plunging back into the woods. It looked at him once more: *Follow.* Then it vanished. The hound-noise died away.

Pellinore dismounted. His legs nearly gave way beneath him as he slid to the ground. The brachet ran around him three times, then looked at him with concern. Or maybe it was amusement. Very likely the animals understood more of this than he did. Slowly, he walked up the slope toward the castle. Back to his normal life; his existence where nothing changed.

But this morning, everything had changed, and he knew that he could not pretend otherwise. Even if he wanted to. He was not sure what he wanted to do.

He was certain of only one thing. Tomorrow morning, whether he wanted to or not, he would return, and he would follow the beast with the green eyes. He had no choice.

First, though, he had to explain matters to his little sisters. He decided to wait until the evening. Let them have a few more hours of believing their brother to be sane.

* * *

In the evening, they sat around the table in the great hall while Pellinore tried to explain.

"So, you see, I have to follow this Beast," he finished helplessly. The word *beast* held a great and unusual weight when he spoke it. He had no intention of placing emphasis on it. The emphasis placed itself. His sisters watched him expressionlessly. He was impressed at their control.

"I don't think I have a choice," he tried again. "The heroes in the tales never turn back from adventure. What is this, if not adventure? Perhaps it represents something I must conquer within myself. Or . . ." His words ran out. He looked at the three girls. "Please, say something! Tell me that you will be all right if I go off for a week, or a few weeks. Surely it will not be any longer. The women will look after you."

"We will look after ourselves, Pell," said Angharad softly. She was the oldest, and more like him than the twins. He and she were both dark-haired and blue-eyed, but Pellinore saw a confidence in her that he did not see in himself. The twins, Ceridwen and Branwen, were fair, and they lived in a world of their own. He had no idea what they were thinking now, and he did not expect to find out. They seldom spoke to anyone except each other. Angharad, on the other hand, always spoke her mind.

"Nurse is not well, though you probably had not noticed. There were no other women the last time I looked. But we will manage. Emlyn and Rhys can look after the animals. Lately you have been in your tower or out hunting anyway, and we have survived. But Pell—" Her voice wavered for a moment, and Pellinore was overcome with guilt. "I don't understand. Do you think that it was a real beast? Perhaps it was a vision, or . . . Are you well? Are we so hard to live with that you must come up with such a wild story as an excuse to leave?"

Her last question was full of panic. Pellinore put his head in his hands, struggling against tears. "It was real," he managed at last. "It's no excuse, Angharad. I have to go. The Beast spoke to me with all but words. I love you all dearly, and I had no intention of leaving you. But I cannot let that creature go without me. I promise that I will return as soon as I can."

"Do you mean to kill it?" asked Angharad.

The question struck Pellinore with greater force than anything that had gone before. He had no idea whether or not he was meant to kill the Beast. He thought not. Why would it lure him away from his home so that he could kill it out in the wild? Perhaps it meant to kill him. He closed his eyes at the thought.

All he knew was: *Follow.*

When he set out the next morning, it seemed a lifetime since the previous gray dawn. He took the same horse, the same brachet, and his bow, but everything else was different. The worst difference was the sight of his sisters. They stood motionless beside the horse, waiting to see him off.

The twins hugged him quickly, then turned away, but he still saw the tears in their eyes. He cursed himself for his selfishness, and the Beast for causing this painful parting. Angharad hugged him fiercely. "Please be careful," she whispered in his ear. He nodded without speaking, so that she would not see how close he was to tears.

Before he could change his mind, he mounted the horse, spurred it forward, and galloped down the slope toward the woods. He looked back just once, but he was already too far away to see the expressions on his sisters' faces.

The horse leapt into the woods, following the brachet. Both animals ran as though they knew exactly where they were going. They probably did, thought Pellinore. Already he could see the clearing up ahead. It was just like the previous morning, except that he did not have to rein the horse to a halt behind the brachet. It stopped of its own accord, and waited placidly.

There, in the clearing, was the Beast. *Follow*, he felt, and then it sprang forward. The air was loud around it. As the horse flew into motion beneath him, Pellinore felt a surge of relief. He had seen the message in those deep green eyes. Everything would be all right. It had to be all right.

They struck out of the woods, following the undulating shape of the Beast, and flew across the open fields. Pellinore turned his head to look at Snowdon. It seemed more beneficent today than he had ever seen it. He forgot his sisters, back in the lonely prison of the castle, and his empty title. He was no King of the Isles. He was simply Pellinore. He felt as though he were springing free from the earth, like the great mountain.

Pellinore soon gave up any idea of killing the Beast. It did not want to sacrifice itself, nor did it show any signs of turning on him. The days fell into a familiar rhythm. From dawn until dusk, the Beast ran ahead at an unchanging speed. The brachet ran happily enough, but after a few days it began to complain and limp about. Its paws were sore from the unaccustomed length of the hunt. Pellinore started hauling it up onto the horse for a couple of hours every few days, where it sprawled in front of the saddle, eyeing him reproachfully. Pellinore was thankful for the horse's forbearance. There was little need for the brachet to follow the scent, since the Beast usually stayed within sight. But he was glad to have it with him anyway. It was one of his hunting companions.

At night, the hunt came to a halt. The Beast slipped off somewhere, but Pellinore knew that it would return in the morning. Then Pellinore made the horse comfortable and prepared his evening meal. He always tried to shoot a rabbit or two during the day. The brachet retrieved the little bodies for him, so that the pace of the hunt was not broken. He cooked his rabbits over the fire and fed the entrails to the brachet. He grew very tired of rabbit.

In the morning, he saddled and bridled the horse, packed up, and mounted. Only then did he look around for the Beast. It always waited several paces away, unmoving, but with a kind of impatience about it. *Follow!* the green eyes implored. And he would follow.

He occasionally wondered if he were following the Beast to the ends of the earth, or at the very least to damnation. But there was a purpose to his life, even if it was only to follow. A week went by, then two or three more, and he forgot his little sisters. He almost forgot that there had ever been an unchanging existence in a castle in Gwynedd.

Pellinore was not sure where they were going, but he could tell from the sun that they were heading south. He suspected, though, that the Beast sometimes doubled back, sometimes led them in circles, and sometimes went east or west for as much as a day or two. He was content to let it lead. Once they had to ford a large river. He chose a point where the water seemed low, but it was still an ordeal. The water came up to his thighs as the horse plunged across, and the brachet clung to him in an ecstasy of fear. He thought that the river might be the Severn, but he was not sure.

From the first day of the hunt, he had asked himself

what would happen when other people saw the Beast and his own pursuit of it. He feared that they would kill it, or at the very least, that they would think him mad for following such a freakish creature. But as the weeks went by, he realized that he never saw anyone else during the day. He wondered that no one came to investigate the hound-noise that went with the Beast. At night, sometimes, there would be other travelers. Once he had to fight off two thieves, who took him unawares by his fire one night. They had probably seen the handsome horse and thought that it would be a fine prize. Pellinore ran one of them through with his sword and scared away the other. He felt shame at the thief's death, even if the man had deserved it. He hid the body in the nearby trees and tried to forget it, but the smell of blood stayed with him for days.

He grew accustomed to sleeping outside, even when it was cold at night, and waking wet with the dew. One particularly chilly evening, he was preparing to sleep in a cow pasture when he looked up to see the cowherd, a girl, standing over him. She invited him to spend the night in the barn. There, she shared food and some of the cows' milk with him, and eventually her bed, while the brachet gnawed bones by the barn door. Pellinore rode away in the morning with a headache and a vague taste of self-disgust in his mouth. He had not forced the girl—far from it—but he saw the past night as a moment of weakness, to which he should not have succumbed while questing after the Beast.

On a clear night early in the autumn, Pellinore entered a small village. The Beast had left him at a crossroads. He thought that it was starting to look tired. He wondered how he must look. It was a long time since he had even glanced at his reflection in a pond.

He dismounted and led the horse between the simple houses. The brachet limped after them. The night was very quiet, except for the clop of the horse's hooves, until a pair of small boys charged around the corner and nearly knocked him over. The horse half-reared with fright.

"Can you tell me how far I am from the nearest large town?" Pellinore asked them. He gave each boy a coin. They stared at him and at the money for so long that he wondered if the coins had taken their wits.

"Not far from London, sir," said the bigger boy at last. They stood a moment longer, snickering and digging their elbows into each other. Finally they ran off, whooping and laughing.

Pellinore was surprised. He had not thought that the Beast had brought them so far to the east. And the roads, deserted whenever he crossed them . . . no travelers, even so near a town such as London?

The Beast somehow knew how to go where there were no other people. Or did the people hear of its approach and flee in terror? He started walking again, shaking his head.

The inn stood nearby. Light shone through its open door. It looked like an inviting place, but he suddenly had no desire to enter. He needed peace, somewhere to meditate. Contradictory feelings tangled within him. He wanted to be near humans, but away from them.

Then he saw the chapel. It stood alone: a small stone building, on an expanse of green grass, a little distance off from the rest of the village. A few trees clustered around it. Pellinore started toward it thankfully. It was the perfect place to spend a few hours. He could think of something other than the Beast, and perhaps even pray a little.

There was a little hay thrown down outside the chapel for the convenience of the horse. The brachet whined as Pellinore stepped through the door, but it lay down resignedly with its muzzle resting on its paws.

The only light in the chapel came from a candle burning feebly on the altar. Pellinore blinked as his eyes adjusted to the dimness. It was a very simple chapel. The crude altar was made of stone, and a wooden cross completely without adornment stood on top of it. There was a small bench by the right-hand wall. Nothing else.

Pellinore sat down thankfully. The bench was not comfortable, but it felt good to sit on something other than the horse or the bare, cold ground. He closed his eyes and tried to pray. He thanked God for bringing him so far without mishap. In the middle of asking whether or not he was doing the right thing by following the Beast, he fell asleep.

He woke to a nearby movement. A man was standing before him, holding something in his arms. For a moment Pellinore was afraid, and his hand went to his sword. He had no idea where he was. Then his vision cleared. He was in the chapel. The man who stood before him in brown robes was a priest, holding a woolen blanket. The priest was tall, though not as tall as Pellinore, and very lean. Pellinore thought that his leanness looked as though it came from a lack of food rather than from nature.

"Peace," said the priest. "I only wanted to cover you with this blanket. You must be cold, and the night will get colder still. The bench is not a comfortable bed, but you may stay here if you wish."

"Thank you," managed Pellinore. He took the blanket and wrapped it around himself. He realized that he was shivering, but not from the cold. His initial fear at the sight of the holy man had triggered something within him. He was shaken by emotion at the kind gesture. His little sisters' faces came into his mind. Then he saw his parents, more clearly than he had in years. What was he doing here, hundreds of miles from his home? How could he have abandoned his flesh and blood, and for what? For a mad hunt, a pursuit of something that was perhaps only a delusion, or something worse. Pellinore struggled against tears. He gripped the blanket fiercely in his fists.

"What is troubling you?" asked the priest with concern. "Are you ill? Is someone hunting you?"

Pellinore suddenly felt very tired. He might as well tell his story to this kind priest. He would probably be excommunicated, but it did not matter.

"No," he said. "I am a hunter, and I'm not sure what my prey is." And he told his tale.

Pellinore had not looked at the priest as he talked. At the end of his story, he looked up reluctantly, and saw that the man was very pale. His hand made the sign of the cross. He was still calm, but he looked shaken.

"This Beast, my son . . ." Pellinore heard the priest give the same emphasis to the word as when he himself spoke it. It had been so many months since he had spoken that word to a living soul. The last time, until now, was when he had told his sisters that he must go.

"It may be a demon. Indeed, I cannot see how it could be anything else. Such an unnatural creature, and with the head of a serpent . . . You must not follow it any longer.

It may lead you into a bog or a pit, where you and your animals will perish. Please do not go on, my son. It can only lead to harm."

"It is not a demon." Pellinore felt certain all at once that he was right. The Beast had no wrongness about it. He still wondered if it had chosen the right man.

"It has done me no harm, and it does not mean to. If you could see those eyes, Father, you would understand. I feel sure that it is leading me for a purpose. I only wonder if that purpose should continue to keep me away from my poor sisters. It has already been many months."

The priest was silent. He bowed his head in thought. When he looked up, his face was as quiet as before.

"That is something only you can decide. I still fear for you, chasing such a creature all over Britain. But I feel that you are sincere. You have left a heavy responsibility behind you, but it may be that a greater one calls you. I cannot decide for you. It is between you and God."

Pellinore felt that it was between a few other things as well, but he said nothing. The priest looked at him sadly.

"Please spend the night here. You look as though you need a few hours of sleep. I will leave some food out for your animals." He stepped back a few paces, then stopped and looked again at Pellinore. He saw a pale, black-haired young man, his face marked with lines of weariness and anxiety. How young he looks, thought the priest. How young and how far from home.

Pellinore quickly fell asleep again, warmed by the blanket and something else he could not put into words. In the morning, he found that the priest had not only left grain for the horse and good meat for the brachet, but also a loaf of bread. In return, Pellinore left most of his money in a bag behind the altar. He did not seem to have much need for it anyway.

The Beast now led Pellinore westward. The pace was getting slower. None of them were as eager as they used to be. It was partly that they were all tired, and partly the turn in the weather. The days grew colder and colder. Winter had either arrived, or it was sending out its messengers.

One morning, Pellinore had just finished bridling the

horse when he felt a touch on the back of his hand. Snow. It melted in an instant, but on the ground it was already gathering around his feet. He looked up. The sky was solid gray, and the flakes floated down like feathers. He felt as though he were rushing upward at a terrible speed, toward some unknown conclusion. The sensation made him dizzy.

This was one of the worst things that could have happened. It was inevitable, of course, but he had never considered the possibility until now. He could not continue the hunt through the winter. What if he lost the Beast in a snowstorm? What if he froze to death on a night when he could find no shelter? Surely this was not the end, to be abandoned in the wilderness where he would die or go mad.

He looked around desperately. The Beast stood before him, closer than ever before. The snow blurred its outlines, making it look even more unreal. Its eyes were half-closed. The Beast stood still, but its muscles were so taut that Pellinore could see it trembling. It was waiting for him to come closer.

Pellinore stepped forward. He felt as if he were standing outside his body, observing himself. He took the Beast's serpent-head between his two hands. It was smooth and warm to the touch. The Beast breathed out slowly, like a horse responding to the touch of one who understands it. It opened its green eyes fully.

Pellinore understood that the Beast was about to leave him for the winter months. They would meet again in the spring, at this very place. He would know when to come. There was nothing to fear.

But where shall I go for the winter? Pellinore wondered to himself.

The Beast, as if in reply, looked past him, over his shoulder. Pellinore turned to follow its gaze. The snow was falling heavily, and the brachet huddled miserably against his legs. But he could see a cluster of buildings, some distance off, where the Beast was looking. He wondered why he had not seen them the night before. Then he remembered that it was already dark when he had made his camp.

"I am to go there, and they will take me in?" he asked aloud.

The Beast fastened its emerald eyes on his face again, and he felt reassured. It drew its head gently from between his hands, and made off into the snow. The bell-like sound of many hounds calling rang out.

I will see you again in the spring.

Pellinore was numb with cold. His eyes ached. He picked up the brachet under one arm and started to walk, dragging the horse by the reins. The group of buildings came into focus. It was a large farmstead, with several barns. He could see no movement. Everyone—man and beast—must be inside. He hoped that the place was not abandoned.

He set the brachet on the ground and banged on the heavy wooden door with his fist. A minute or two went by, long enough for him to despair that anyone would answer. Then there came a fumbling at the locks. The door opened a crack. A bearded face peered out. The man did not look mistrustful, simply questioning.

"Please," croaked Pellinore. "I have nowhere to go, and the snow is coming down heavily. I wonder if I might—"

The door swung open.

The farmstead became his home for the winter. At first, Pellinore asked himself how the Beast could have known that such a kindly family lived there, but then he reminded himself of all the other things that the Beast miraculously knew.

There were three of them: a husband, a wife, and a daughter who was a few years older than Pellinore's sister Angharad. Gareth, the husband, was a big man with a slightly forbidding demeanor, but he was more courteous than most nobles that Pellinore had ever met. His wife, Ellen, was a bit short-tempered, but the brachet loved her instantly, and Pellinore trusted her because of it. Alyssa was their daughter.

They accepted his vague story of a family quest, an obligation that he had to fulfill. He doubted at first that they would let him stay the winter. Why should they? He offered them the last of his money, which was probably more than they had seen in some time. But they refused it.

"You can help me care for the animals, Pellinore," said Gareth happily. "There's a lot to look after—cows, pigs, horses—and the women do their best, but we're always short. Our farmhand left us for a girl not long ago. You came at the right time."

It was ideal, or very close to it. Pellinore enjoyed looking after the animals, even the pigs. He had never done much at home, beyond caring for his horses. But the work was less mindless than he would have supposed; it took some time before he could tell when a cow was sick and when it was malingering. He thought of the Beast very little, only wondering now and then if it had made itself a den for the winter. He tried not to think about his sisters.

The problem was Alyssa. She was an attractive girl, though not beautiful, and it was clear very soon that she was hopelessly in love with Pellinore. Her eyes followed him wherever he went. When their eyes met, she would look away quickly. He could see her hands trembling when he spoke to her. She did not say much to him, but all the signs were there.

Pellinore worried about her. He thought her a pleasant girl, but he was not in love with her. He was fairly sure that she would sleep with him if he asked her to, and though he was not in love, he thought that it would probably happen if they were given enough of an opportunity. If that happened, he knew that he would have to marry her, even if her parents did not insist. So he tried not to be alone with her. Sometimes it was unavoidable. He wondered at her parents, who did not seem concerned at all. In their place, he would have had grave doubts as to the safety of their daughter's virtue.

He was working in the stables one day when she came up behind him. Her tread was light, and he heard nothing until she spoke to him. He jumped.

"Alyssa!" he said, turning back to the horses to cover his confusion. "You startled me."

She looked at him for a long moment, in silence. He could not read the expression on her face.

"Why are you here, Pellinore?" she asked. "Alone, in this remote place. You told us about a quest, but no more. I have always wondered where you came from, and where . . . where you will go when you leave us."

Her voice shook a little. Pellinore looked at her sharply. What harm could it do to tell her? Perhaps, if she thought him mad, she would no longer be in love with him.

She was silent after he finished his story. Then she looked at him calmly.

"Have you told this to anyone else?" she asked.

"Only a priest, who was kind to me. He thought I was chasing a demon. And you must think the same, or that I am mad."

"I don't think you are mad," she said. "You have never seemed so. I only think that this Beast must have a very strong hold over you. Stronger than love, to take you away from your sisters. I can imagine little that would make me leave the farm and my parents' love."

"Stronger than love, yes," he answered lamely. He did not know what else to say. For a moment, as he looked at her, he remembered the girl who herded the cows, then pushed the thought away. She deserved better than that.

She left him without saying much more. But he thought afterward that she was drawing away from him a little. He was not sure whether to be relieved or sad.

Spring came again. Pellinore was restless. Every day that the Beast did not come, he wondered whether it had died during the winter, or whether it had forgotten him. When he finally saw it, standing near the stables on a clear morning, it was as though a great weight had been lifted from his chest. He knew, as he had known at the beginning, that he had only one day left.

Gareth and Ellen did not try to hold him back. Ellen wept, which embarrassed him. He offered them his money once more, but they would not take even one coin.

"You did much for us this winter, Pellinore," said Gareth. "I believe that the debt is on our side, not yours. And—" he paused "—I know that you have taken nothing that was not your own."

Pellinore took his meaning, and was glad of his caution with Alyssa.

On the morning of his departure, Alyssa followed him into the stables. She watched in silence as he brushed the horse. He did not know what to say to her. In the end, there was no need to say anything.

"Would you kiss me before you go?" she asked in a choked voice.

Pellinore kissed her. It was more for consolation than out of desire, but it was still a tender kiss. She held onto him for a moment after it was over.

"Please be careful," she murmured. Pellinore flinched, remembering Angharad's last words to him.

He rode away from the farm, knowing that the Beast would not appear until he had left the humans behind. Gareth and Ellen waved to him before disappearing into the house. There, up ahead, stood the Beast. He spurred forward, then turned to look back once more. His heart thudded. Alyssa stood by the house, looking intently in his direction. He saw her clench her fist against her breast, as though in pain or surprise. Though she was some distance off, he had no doubt that she could see the Beast. And if she could see the Beast, the Beast knew it.

There *are* others who can see it, then, he thought. And she did not think me mad.

The hound-noise drew him on.

Pellinore was sick. It was a week since he had left the farm, and today he was dizzy with fever. He feared that he might fall from the horse. He wished that the Beast would stop and let him rest, but it never slackened its pace. Its old speed had returned with the spring.

He could tell that they were near a town. The roads, when they crossed them, were wide and well kept. He even saw a couple of soldiers, far down the road, though they had no time to see him. It was unlike the Beast to come so close to humans. But then, it had shown itself to the girl.

They were nearing a wood. The trees were copper beeches, standing close together. Pellinore just had time to think that it was a wood where one might easily get lost, before they plunged into it.

In a moment, he could no longer see the Beast. He could still hear it, but its sound came from many different directions. His head was spinning more than ever. He felt like vomiting. Desperately he urged the horse to go faster. The sound grew fainter. All at once, the horse fell beneath him.

Pellinore lay stunned. The brachet licked him, then let

out a howl. Painfully, he got to his feet, shaking with the fever and the shock of the fall.

The horse was dead. Its eyes were already glazed. Pellinore stared at it numbly. He knew that it could happen, that a horse's heart might simply give out without warning. Of course, he had been pushing it hard. He had pushed it hard for the better part of a year. It was his own fault. He would never catch up to the Beast now.

Pellinore did not think to take his belongings from the horse. He felt for his sword at his side, grasping the hilt as though that might give him some comfort. Then he staggered forward. The brachet padded behind him. The only thought in his mind was that the Beast might have waited for him. He could hear no sound, but there would be nothing if it was not moving.

He heard a rushing noise. It was the sound of a small stream. He had stumbled into a clearing. The stream lay before him, cutting through the wood like a silver path. He looked around, trying to stop the world from spinning, and realized that he was not alone.

A young man sat by the stream. His horse grazed beside him. He was very young, perhaps fifteen or sixteen. He sat curled up, his arms wrapped around his knees and his blond head resting on them, as though he were stunned or sleepy. Pellinore took a step forward, hoping that he was not about to collapse.

"Sir," he said. His voice seemed to come from a great distance off. "Forgive me for disturbing you. I am looking for a . . . a Beast. Have you—"

The young man came alive. He jumped up, startling the horse. "I saw it!" he cried. "A Beast with the head of a serpent, the body of a leopard, the hindquarters of a lion, and footed like a deer. Is it your quest? It came here to drink, and then it ran off, making a noise like thirty couple of hounds or more." His eyes blurred as he remembered. "I thought of following it, but something came over me. At first I was too amazed to move, and when it ran away, I felt dizzy, as though I hadn't slept for days. But now I feel as though I could face anything." He stared at Pellinore. "Is it your quest?" he repeated.

"It is my quest," said Pellinore heavily. "I have killed my horse in its pursuit. I followed it for over a year, and now I have lost it." He felt unsteady, and put his hand out to stop himself from falling.

The young man caught his arm. "You are ill! With or without a horse, you cannot go on after your Beast. Let me have the quest. My horse will carry me far."

A veil passed over Pellinore's eyes. He was not sure whether it was from sickness or from anger. He had followed the Beast for twelve months, and now this boy wanted to take the quest from him? The Beast had chosen him, and no other.

"You are a fool," said Pellinore hoarsely. "The quest is mine. It will never be achieved except by me, or by one of my family. One of—" He choked, as horror seized him. One of his family? He had no son, and never would if he spent his whole life chasing the Beast. His sisters might never marry. He thought of them, waiting in Gwynedd for a whole year. He had told them that he would be gone a week, maybe two. He deserved to die.

"Give me your horse," he said roughly. "I must go on. I am not ill."

"No!" exclaimed the youth. "You will fall off the horse if you go on! And besides, it is my horse. I have a right to follow the quest."

When Pellinore tried to push past him to the horse, the young man drew his sword. Pellinore stood swaying for a moment, then drew his own. He needed the horse. If he had to fight for it, so be it.

The other might be young, but he was a good swordsman. His feints came close to wounding Pellinore several times. It was as much as Pellinore could do to keep the youth at bay and stop himself from collapsing.

At last, the young man's sword broke on Pellinore's. It flew into two pieces with a harsh *clang*. A moment later, Pellinore wounded him in the side. He did not mean to, but his sword seemed to move on its own. The youth lost his balance and fell over backward.

Pellinore knelt over him, his sword still in his hand. The young man was pinned beneath his greater weight. Pellinore felt a strange desire to kill him. He would stab the stranger, then fall on his sword. . . .

"Arthur," said a voice behind them.

Arthur? thought Pellinore. Dear God.

The last of Pellinore's strength left him. He collapsed sideways, rolling off the youth. Somewhere he heard the brachet whining. He could not move. His eyes closed.

Two voices were talking nearby. He listened to their conversation. There was nothing else to do.

"He tried to take my horse, Merlin," the younger voice was saying. "Perhaps I should not have fought with him. He was ill. Have you put a spell on him, or is it the illness?"

"He is sick," said the other voice dryly. It was the voice of an older man, deeper, with more resonance. "And despite his sickness, he managed to wound you and break your sword. It is not a serious wound, however. But it seems that I came at the right time. The sword that you drew from the stone must have reached the end of its usefulness."

"I saw a Beast, Merlin," said Arthur. "He said that it was his quest. It looked like—"

"I know what it looked like," interrupted Merlin. The voice held a touch of impatience, but Pellinore heard affection as well.

"And I suppose you know his name too?" asked Arthur. Pellinore could not tell if he was serious or if he was teasing.

"Pellinore," said Merlin gently. "His name is Pellinore."

Pellinore opened his eyes. The world was spinning again, but he managed to raise his head a little. He could see the young man called Arthur—the High King—sitting against a tree. His hand was at his wound, but he looked at Pellinore with clear eyes. Another man was kneeling closer by, right over him. Pellinore could tell that he was tall, and he felt the light touch of his hands on his shoulders. But he could see nothing except for the man's eyes. They were green like emeralds. More beautiful than any eyes that he had seen before, except on one other living creature.

Pellinore gasped. His mouth was dry, and at first no words came out. "Are you—?" he managed at last.

"Hush," said Merlin. He looked into Pellinore's eyes, a long, serious look. And Pellinore felt calm, though his questions were not gone. Merlin turned back to Arthur.

"We will take him with us to Winchester," he said. "Your men are looking for you, Arthur. I wish you would not give them the slip like that. It wastes time. It is also unbefitting a king."

"I have not been a king for long," said Arthur. But he sounded chastened.

"Can you walk?" Merlin asked the High King. "It looks as though we must put Pellinore on the horse. He will be one of the finest of your knights, I think, though farther than that I cannot see." Pellinore thought that there was a little sadness in Merlin's voice.

"Of course he must go on the horse," said Arthur. "I will carry his brachet, if it will let me. I saw it limping."

Merlin lifted Pellinore onto the horse. He lay sprawled across its back. A light, warm rain had started to fall. It ran down his cheeks like tears.

"We will find you another sword," he heard Merlin saying. "There is one already waiting for you."

The Beast was gone, in some way that Pellinore did not yet understand. But he no longer needed to follow it. He would not die for trying unwittingly to kill the High King. He had found Arthur, and that was the end of the quest, though he had not known it until now.

His sisters. . . . Of course. He would send for them, and they could join the court. They would find good husbands there. And he would marry, too—one of the ladies of the court. Or perhaps he would return to visit the farm where he had passed the winter.

Merlin and Arthur walked in silence, one leading the horse, the other carrying the brachet. The rain was gaining strength. To Pellinore, it felt as if the downpour had washed away his fever. He felt clearer-headed than he had for hours. He also felt like sleeping. The rain beat on his eyelids as they closed.

Far away, he thought he heard the sound of many hounds calling. Then all was quiet in the falling rain.

THE QUESTING GIRL

Cory Rushton

'Nay, sir,' seyd Aryes, 'thys desyre commyth of my son and nat off me. For I shall telle you, I have thirtene sonnes, and all they woll falle to what laboure I putte them and woll be ryght glad to do laboure; but thys chylde woll nat laboure for nothynge that my wyff and I may do, but allweys he woll be shotynge, or castynge dartes, and glad for to se batayles and to beholde knyghtes. And allways day and nyght he desyrith of me to be made knyght.'

'What ys thy name?' seyde the kynge unto the yonge man.

'Sir, my name ys Torre.'

—Thomas Malory, *Le Morte D'Arthur*, III: 3

The only differences between Breton nobles and Saxon marauders were the steeds of the former and the stench of the latter, and the language in which they barked at her to surrender herself. The girl learned to avoid armed strangers. Once she had lived in the company of knights without fear. Now her eyes never left the road ahead as she stumbled away from them, scarcely noticing their angry commands, their lecherous calls. Something kept them from pursuing her. Perhaps it was the sores on her feet or the mud caked onto her face. Most likely it was the dull madness in her eyes, awaiting only a little food and rest to leap forth and scorch them. The raiders reasoned that a lone woman on the road was most likely diseased or a witch, or else she'd have been caught long before.

Everywhere she walked the land was burning with a thousand little fires. The sight of ravaged villages and sacked castles had became familiar, even welcome. She could look at them and say, "Those people are suffering as much as I am. They are no better off than me." The land had once been green and prosperous and inhabited. Now smoke hung heavily in the air, little of it the wholesome scent of a meal cooking. The High King had gone away, and there was no power in Britain to fend off the invaders from the sea, or keep the squabbling petty kings and dukes from attacking each other's lands. Each new ruined castle reminded her of home. At times she felt alone on the road, the last living lamb wandering through a world of wolves.

She was looking for someone, something. Until she found it, the important thing was to keep walking.

Vayshoure was seeing to the family's cattle when the knight crossed her family lands. Her father's holdings were small, the remnants of a once-great Roman estate where everyone was expected to do their part. Small wonder that the great knight, so stern and regal even in his worn traveling clothes and battered armor, had thought she was only a peasant girl.

"Did you see a strange and wondrous Beast pass by here?" he asked, his voice rough with fatigue.

"A Beast? Yes," she said. "A marvelous creature, with the head of a serpent and the body of a dog. It rumbled like a pack of hounds as it drank from the stream. It left tracks, down by the water."

"When?" spat the knight, staring down at her hungrily.

Vayshoure shrugged. "Perhaps a week ago. I cannot be certain as to the time."

The knight dismounted stiffly, his muddied and exhausted squire rushing to help him down. "I'll not catch him today."

"Why do you pursue such a creature, Sir Knight?" she asked, smiling. "Surely there are better things to pursue? Is it a dangerous Beast, or is it rather a tasty delicacy?"

"Neither, to my knowledge," he replied, eyes flicking up and down her young body. Her dog growled once, alert to the peril Vayshoure ignored.

Vayshoure giggled, enjoying the diversion the stranger offered. A quest was so much more romantic than herding cattle, or listening to garbled reports of distant Pictish raids. "I must confess, sir, I cannot imagine why you hunt a creature if it is not dangerous or delicious? What other reason could there be?"

"That depends on the creature." The knight grinned, and with a sudden lunge he grabbed her in his arms and half

lifted her from her feet. "Come here, girl! Even the most ardent questing knight needs some rest, and some entertainment!" His squire wrapped wiry arms around her hound, holding it back from attacking the knight. Vayshoure was strangely grateful. The knight could easily kill her dog without even pulling his sword.

The knight's strength was immense. She remembered her father's priests, warning of the effect a woman could have on a man with her looks and smiles, and instantly regretted her rash behavior. "Sir Knight, you mistake me! I am a maid, and freeborn!"

"I am certain you are," he laughed. "And I am Uther Pendragon, returned to lead my people!"

The squire had disappeared with her hound. Strange, the things one thinks about.

"Nobody knows where the king is, or even if he still lives at all," said the tall, thin man with a limp.

Every one of the travelers was a refugee. They spoke about the High King as they trudged along the dangerous roads, now just ribbons of stone winding through a wasted land, connecting nothing. The High King, who should have been the center around which a safe and happy realm revolved, was now known only in whispered discussions among those he had abandoned. His name was everywhere, like a breeze, and just as empty.

"No sooner had Uther beaten back the Saxons, God be praised, but he warred on his own vassal, down away south in Cornwall. Victorious in that lamentable cause, Uther took the duke's widow for his own." The speaker was a thin man, who called himself a scholar, a rare enough boast in these times. Indeed, he had the gift of words, but such a gift held little value for those who lacked for food or other comforts. "They say that's why he fought poor Gorloïs—for the woman. To agree to a peace, then declare war the next day because you fancy your new ally's wife? Shameful! He fell sick soon after."

"The wrath of God," said a village priest.

"A just fate upon a treacherous tyrant," agreed the thin man. "Soon after, I heard news that he had died. Then news came that he lived, and was besieged in London, or gone to

Benwick to aid his allies against the barbarous Franks. No traveler tells the same story as the traveler before him."

"Your judgment sounds like that of my father," said the walking woman. On her last night at home, her father had held a feast. Inviting the neighboring lords, he had hoped to form a coalition against the Saxons and the bandits, a renewal of ancient friendships to protect themselves until the king restored order, or until the great lords chose another High King.

A second woman, a peasant, chuckled in the darkness beside them. "Many are the lords who are judged by God in these times! Why, the Lord Vagorin was just such a tyrant, like Uther, and his own men rose up against him and fired his castle!"

"Why do you think this?" hissed the walking woman.

"I was a servant in the castle, his arrogant daughter's maid. Ah, the sport they had with her on that night. It distracted them enough that I could flee. I'm sorry if it sounds cruel, but far be it from me to die for the likes of her! The high brought low. Isn't that so, Father?"

"The Wheel of Fortune." The thin scholar smirked at the thought.

The priest clacked his teeth, disapproving. "Daughter, you should not delight in the misfortunes of others. Only God can judge."

"It sounds as though God judged the lord's daughter and punished her," leered the thin scholar. "The *Malleus meretricium!*"

"What does that mean, good man?" asked the round woman.

"The Hammer of Whores. A fitting way to punish a proud slut. Need I tell you which hammers He used as his holy instruments?"

The priest looked away. He should have spoken against such lewdness, but there was no need to be too much a priest on the road. It only reminded his fellow travelers that God had forgotten them, and, as His nearest representative, he could well be made the target of their anger at Heaven's seeming inaction.

The midwife threw her head back and laughed. The sound was braying, unpleasant. "Aye, and her whorish ways brought down her whole family. Not that her father was without sin. His bloody deeds came back threefold to roost."

"She lies!" screamed the walking woman, suddenly flinging her thin body toward the midwife. "You lie!" Her ragged, dirty nails drew red lines across the other's ample face. They fell together to the blackened earth.

The thin man and the priest lunged forward to grab the combatants, their white, flailing limbs caked with mud and grime. Each of them was scratched and bitten by the time they had been pulled apart.

"Daughter! Daughter!" shouted the priest. "How can you call this woman a liar? How can any living person know what happened at Lord Vagorin's castle?"

"This was no servant of mine," shrieked the walking woman, spitting at her foe. "She lies to say the fault was my father's!" Wrenching herself free of the priest's grasping hands, Vayshoure fled into the wasteland, brambles catching at the rags she wore, bits of bone and jagged rocks cutting into her feet.

After he had finished he lay beside her while their breathing calmed. His eyes were heavy and dark in the dusk; hers stared wide and shocked into the distant stars. He cleared his throat twice before he finally spoke.

"Are you truly a noble?" he asked drowsily, after a long silence. She nodded, almost imperceptibly. "I'm sorry for it. The heat of the moment, many long months in the saddle without my queen. You understand? I mistook you, that's all. I merely mistook you."

He seemed sad and earnest, she thought. Yet surely her grief was the greater. "I understand," she said quietly. She wanted to ask why it mattered that she was nobly born. Would a peasant girl feel less shame? This morning she would have thought so with the unthinking superiority of her position, but now she wondered.

She did not know what she would tell her father.

At first she had blamed herself for the disaster. The deaths of her father, her brothers. The rape of their lands. When the first signs of her pregnancy became obvious to her, she prayed desperately that her father would not find out. She knew that the gracious Lady sometimes concealed these things, if the girl had been forced or tricked. There were stories of nuns, impregnated by devils, whom the Lady protected by concealing all the signs and casting a blessed shadow over the birthing itself. But dared she pray for the loss of the child? Surely that was a sin, even more than the loss of her maidenhead.

Her father would certainly never know about the child now, she thought. Heaven had answered her prayer by destroying her family, a vengeance upon her for tempting the wandering knight so sorely. Her sins had been the end of her family, and now she was doomed to wander the earth, an exile without relations or lands, except for the child she carried. She could not possibly provide for him on her own, with nothing to her name.

Unless she could find the knight who had visited her, the father of her child and her misfortunes.

She was certain she remembered the direction he had ridden. Forced to decide which way to flee her father's killers, she followed after him. It had been over three months since he'd left her, though, and the trail was cold, despite the road being crowded. Everyone she met was fleeing the same way as her, away from the local lords, now drunk with slaughter and rapine. Nobody had seen the knight, nor did they seem to know what she meant when she described the Beast he followed. She gained a reputation for madness as she walked. That helped her survive, by prompting the kindness of priests, and monks, and the occasional traveler who saw in her one of God's own fools.

"Where are you going, child?" asked a hermit in an old church, late one night after she stumbled in from a freezing sleet. "Stay here until someone comes who can see you home."

"I have no home." She shivered, teeth chattering against the wooden bowl with its thin, warm soup. "I must go on."

"What do you seek?

"The questing knight. The King of the Distant Isles."

The hermit looked on her with pity. "There is no such king, child. No such place."

"There must be!" she spat. "Can God make me wander forever?"

"Why do you chase this Beast?" she asked quietly, so quietly that he had to strain to hear her over the rustle of the leaves above them.

"It is a curse," he said. She turned to look at him, her eyes luminous with tears. He spoke to avoid looking into those eyes, where he would surely see his acts reflected. He preferred to pretend that hers were tears of pity over his long years of wandering. "A sorcerer—a king who ruled a long time ago—cursed my forefathers for defying him. This was in the days after Leir, you see. Our clans were enemies. We had held our sovereignty in the Distant Isles since before the Trojans came."

"Is that a place?" she asked, the question leaping between them so quickly it startled him. "Is that the real name of your lands?"

"Aye, that's what we call them, except in our rituals. They have other, older names. Sacred names. We don't use the old names every day."

"Oh," she said, looking down at the ground as she huddled under his cloak. "I didn't mean to interrupt you."

He shook off her apology. "My kin maintained power in the Isles and angered the sorcerer-king. He summoned up dark powers, but we held our own against them. Demons from the sea and demons from the North—none prevailed against our steel and our hearts. So he cursed my forefathers to chase this Beast eternally, so that only one of our kin will ever catch it. If it can be caught at all. A fool's quest, and myself doomed to be a fool, and worse still, to know it to be so. The Distant Isles grow weaker without a king, but we can in no way keep ourselves from always abandoning our people."

"Why don't your people choose a new king?"

Anger flared in him briefly, but he quelled it. She was only a girl, noble or not. What could she be expected to understand of power, or lineage, or pride? "I don't know. Perhaps that is an aspect of the curse."

"It seems a sad life," she ventured.

"Yes."

The hermit saw that she slept as dawn came, gray and chill in the east. He tucked the blanket around her frail form. It would have taken a very ignorant man to have missed her swelling belly. The infant was in grave danger from her wanderings. The ascetic life he had chosen for himself was not appropriate for an expectant mother. Almost a child herself, she needed warmth, a full stomach, and stability. Difficult enough to find in these troubled times, but not impossible, God willing.

The church had been built by a Roman in the last days before the Legions had left, and the local people had continued to use it until the Saxons burned it the year before last. The hermit, once the priest, had stayed on, even as the people ceased to think of him as a priest. Now he was the holy man, a good person to ask for advice on crops, love affairs, the day by day attitude of the heavens. Sometimes they would ask a question clearly rooted in their resurgent pagan beliefs. He would smile gently and try to steer them back to God. It was more important to do good works than to get the names right, and it was a good work that he was about to do now, without having any name to give the wandering girl curled up in the former vestibule.

The hermit gathered up his staff and his sandals, and quietly left the church.

While she was alone, she dreamed of the Beast, and of her father.

My father is questing, she dreamed. He rides with the Hunt after the Beast, and the sound of the Beast's belly and the hunting hounds vie with each other to drown out the sounds of the horses and the horns. The Hunt's leader has great horns like a stag, but stern eyes. "Follow me," he says to my father. "Follow me to a land of bliss, where the people can till their fields in peace, where our children can grow up without fear of the Sea-wolves or the treacherous ones within."

My father turns to me. "I follow the Beast," he says. "I follow the Beast to the Distant Isles. Won't you follow?"

"I would," says the girl.

"Your child should ride with us," says my father. "It is right that my grandson should pursue the Beast."

She woke with a shriek. "My child has no horse!" she cried. A few hard breaths and she calmed herself. With that calmness came the understanding that her child was a son; the realization filled her suddenly, unexpectedly, with wonder.

The squire returned with her hound. It bounded to her, sensing her distress, and lay across her feet with its black eyes searching her face.

"Where did you take him?" she asked. The squire stared at her for a moment, then turned away to make a fire. "Why won't you answer? Where did you take him?"

"He doesn't speak," said the knight quietly. "He has no tongue. He lost it to a man in Norgales. Ryons didn't take kindly to my presence in his kingdom. The boy suffered for it. He'll never be a knight now, not disfigured as he is. I haven't got the heart to turn him out of my service, though, and truth to tell I don't know where I'd get another squire if I did. An entire generation of youths has disappeared, just like Uther." He turned to the dog, appraising the creature thoughtfully. "This is your hound, then, and not your father's?"

She nodded. "Mine. He helps me protect the cattle and the sheep. I raised him from a pup."

"Does he hunt?"

"Squirrels and rabbits," she said proudly.

"What's his name?" he asked, carefully reaching out to scratch behind the wary hound's ears.

"Lumen," she said shyly. "Because of his shine."

He nodded once. The dog began to accept his attentions with a little less caution. "He seems a good hound," said the knight. He glanced up at her. "What is your name, lady?"

She hesitated. "Vayshoure. My name is Vayshoure, youngest daughter of Lord Vagorin. What is your name?"

"It hardly matters," he said. Vayshoure thought that perhaps his wanderings had deprived him of his name, that his quest would end when he found the strange Beast, and with it his own self. Her heart seemed to soar at the thought of it. A quest while the world burned.

In truth, he thought it wise to conceal his identity, lest her father or her brothers decide to seek vengeance for her shame. Pellinore had no desire to slaughter her kin if they chose to pursue him. Nothing could be allowed to distract him from seeking the Beast.

"I don't know her name," said the hermit. "But she's pretty enough under her cares, and her bones seem good. Strong. She would have to be, for what she's been through."

"I'm not looking for a wife," said the cowherd.

"Sometimes wives come looking for men."

"I'm a poor man—" he frowned "—I can't afford a wife. And I've been warned about them. Didn't St. Paul speak against marriage?"

"No," lied the hermit.

"I'd swear he did," mused the peasant. "The priest told us on a Sunday that marriage was only for those who couldn't keep their lusts to themselves."

"She's in desperate need, good Aryes," said the hermit sadly. "Our Lord Jesus said that whomever does good unto a needful soul, so does he unto the Lord."

Aryes frowned. "Is this a test?"

"Life is a test, good cowherd. God is watching."

Aryes cursed and made a sign against evil, which the hermit chose to ignore. "Well, I suppose if He's watching I'd better go have a look at her."

"Why don't you have a hunting hound, to help you track the Beast?" asked Vayshoure.

"I had one, when I began. I lost him to a Saxon's spear, far to the east of here. I fear it has become difficult to buy a good hound in Britain since the beginning of the troubles. As difficult as finding squires, I would think. Yours is the finest dog I've seen in months." He continued to pet Lumen's sleek flanks.

Vayshoure watched them for a quiet moment. "Take him," she said. He glanced at her, alarm and pleasure mingling in his worn face. "Take him and find your Beast. Return to your people. And remember me."

"I couldn't," he said gruffly. "I've taken enough from you this evening."

"I pray you, take him, with my blessing. This land has

*seen enough chaos. Every realm needs a king. Yours needs
you. Lumen will shine the way to this Beast for you. If any
hound can break the curse, my Lumen can." She was weeping now, more than she had in the terrified moments after
he had taken her. "Perhaps when you find this Beast, you
can return to me, and bring back my Lumen."*

*Slowly he bent over and gathered the hound's leash in
his hand. "I shall take him, if that is truly your wish. I will
take him for love of you. You are a noble soul beyond whatever blood you may have. You honor me and you shame
me." He kissed her softly on the forehead, almost like a
father. She tried not to flinch from his touch, finding a
strange warmth in the gesture. She wanted him to remember her as brave and noble, not a quivering girl weeping over
an injury.*

*"I do neither, sir," she said, controlling her tears at last.
"I help you. Do not be a tyrant, when you come again into
your kingdom."*

Aryes and the hermit watched the girl as she huddled
against the cold stone wall of the ancient church. The
cowherd thought she regarded them with an animal's eyes,
the sort of eyes he saw at night sometimes, watching him
from the forest. "Does she speak?"

"A little," said the hermit. "She will speak more, once
she feels safe and wanted."

"For a hermit you claim to know a great deal about
wives and women." Aryes stepped forward and held out a
grimy hand. "Girl, if you want I will take you to my hut. I
cannot offer you great comforts, but at least my shelter is
warmer than the good holy man's. I cannot say that I will
marry you, as he wishes."

"Marry me?" Vayshoure shuddered. "I am a noble's
daughter, though I be without lands. I am a descendant of
the Romans, though I be without dignity. Why, then, should
my hand be joined with yours?"

Aryes glanced back at the hermit, confused. "She raves,"
soothed the holy man. "She raves."

The cowherd turned back to the girl. "I have some
small land to call my own, and a herd of cattle. My home
is well defended. It's something, girl. A life of work can have

a dignity of its own, when you build something fine. A bigger shelter. A family. These are good things, for all that they're not noble."

"I'm looking for a knight."

"It's more usual for knights to look for us, and best when they fail to find us," growled Aryes. "Besides, I never said we'd marry. The hermit said that. I only want to get you warm and dry, and put some flesh onto you. There's not enough to you to keep you alive with winter coming on. I'm only taking care for my soul. I can find another wretch to waste my charity upon, if you're too proud."

"Aryes," chastised the hermit with a hidden smile.

A cold wind flew through the ruins, caught at the wall and doubled back. The girl coughed and shivered with a chill that seemed to flow through her. She looked back at the cowherd. His face was kind, she thought, stern in its own way, but full of compassion. He reminded her a little of the knight from the Distant Isles.

She took his hand and he helped her to her feet. A moment later, he sensed her exhaustion, and picked her up to carry her home. She fell asleep in his arms, and did not wake again until her fever broke.

The knight rode away, along a road illuminated only by a sliver of moon. Lumen looked back again and again, only to be pulled onward by the lead held in the knight's mailed fist. Vayshoure held the blanket around herself as they passed out of sight.

Her face was streaked with tears, and she desperately wiped at her eyes with a corner of the blanket. Her brothers would be looking for her soon, her father anxious at her failure to return home with the herd. It began to rain softly.

The Distant Isles, she thought, imagining a place of sunshine where the people danced every day, and no raiders came to disrupt the peaceful passing of the seasons, where no kings turned upon their own vassals to steal their wives.

The Distant Isles.

The village had not suffered an attack in almost a month. No raiders, no knights of some neighboring king looking for booty, not even the local lord's own men seeking payment of some new tax nobody dared to question. The villagers tried not to feel too blessed. It was only a matter of time.

"Did you hear about Aryes' woman?" asked a village woman.

"The mad one?"

"Aye, that's her."

"Does he have any other wives?" murmured a third woman. "Of course we're talking about Vash. Don't be so stupid."

"No need for that tone," sniffed the second gossip.

"Quiet! The midwife told me she delivered her child yesterday."

"No! It's only been five months, hasn't it? Since they wed?"

"Indeed!" said the first, pleased to bring the news from the secretive cowherd's home first.

"Is the child well?" asked the third woman. "It must be small, being so early. Do they expect it to live?"

"That's the thing! The child is healthy, and huge. It would be large even if it weren't an early baby. She's called it Tor." The first woman's voice became conspiratorial. "Makes one wonder what—or who—Vash met on the road."

"Or why she fled home in the first place!" squealed the second.

"Does it matter?" the third woman hissed. "By the Virgin, who are we to judge? These are bad times. A woman can't be held responsible for what happens to her in this world. If Aryes can be gracious, we at least can hold our tongues."

The first two women nodded. "So true, poor dear. We pray for her, truly we do." They glanced at each other and excused themselves. It only took a second to get out of earshot. The women waited to make certain the third wasn't listening before they returned to their whispered conversation. "Who do you think the father is? A knight or a Saxon?" They tittered at the thought.

"Shrews," mumbled the third woman, left behind to finish her washing. Whispers were never as quiet as the whisperers thought.

By the end of the day, several knights from the court of

the petty king Cradilmans had thundered into the village in a cloud of dust, on steeds the size of small barns—or so they seemed to the frightened peasants. Strange, the things one thinks about. A brief, spirited defense of the gathered grain left two peasants dead and the blacksmith without a daughter. The villagers imagined they could hear her shrieks long after she and her new lords had disappeared down the endless road to nowhere. Whichever king was claiming lordship over them this week would avenge the attack, but the villagers knew they would see neither grain nor girl again.

Uther was dead, and his line with him. The Romans were gone, and they weren't coming back. The predators never stayed away too long in these times.

Vayshoure was soon pregnant again, this time by her new husband. In later days, Aryes would become legendary as the father of thirteen children, all of whom lived to help him with his cattle farm. Whenever the topic was brought up, the hermit would smile and say something about a man coming late to the table and finishing the feast. Aryes would simply grunt with a small, contented smile. By all accounts, the marriage was happy, even if it was not founded on true love.

Late at night, to quiet her firstborn as the cowherd slept, Vayshoure would rock the child and softly sing. Every night she spoke the same words to him. "You are not a farmer," she would say to her strapping son. "Never forget that you are the son of a knight. A knight and a king. And one day, you will be a knight, a kind and decent man. You will always fight for good causes and defend the weak, and go on quests, with a fine horse and a fine hound and a noble squire of your own. The Distant Isles are awaiting you, my dear sweet son, and as your brothers till the earth, you will learn to be who you are. We will all learn to be who we are."

Contributors' Notes

Beth Anderson ("The Time in Between") holds degrees in English and Education, and has spent her career teaching literature, editing student essays, and writing college recommendations. She has authored several teaching units on such diverse novels as *The Scarlet Letter* and *Their Eyes Were Watching God*. After glorifying the classical hero, the Arthurian knight, and the Renaissance Man in the classroom, and doing the same at home with one son, two grandsons, and four nephews, she and the women of the family deemed it time to examine the distaff side of these champions. This is her first published short story.

Shannon Appelcline ("Keystones") works as a writer, editor, web content manager, and operations director for an Internet startup focused on on-line storytelling. He has written gaming supplements and non-fiction articles for over a decade; recently he edited and co-authored *Tales of Magic and Miracles* and *Tales of Chivalry and Romance*, a pair of adventure books for the KING ARTHUR PENDRAGON roleplaying game. Shannon lives in Berkeley, California with his wife, who offers excellent suggestions for revising his fiction, and his two cats, who do not. "Keystones" is his first published short story.

Clarissa Aykroyd ("Follow") is a graduate of the University of Victoria, BC. Her interest in the legends of King Arthur started at an early age, though she didn't become obsessed until she read Mary Stewart's Merlin Trilogy at the age of eleven. She is also fascinated by travel, history, music, and Sherlock Holmes. Her writing has been published in several journals—including *The Heroic Age*, *Canadian Holmes*, and *Critique*—and such newspapers as *The Vancouver Sun* and *Victoria Times Colonist*. Recently, she authored a children's book on the exploration of California. She lives in Victoria.

Cherith Baldry ("The King Who Is to Come") was born in Lancaster, England, and studied at Manchester University and St. Anne's College, Oxford. She subsequently worked as a teacher, including a spell as a lecturer at the University of Sierra Leone. Cherith is now a full-time writer of fiction for both children and adults. Her children's fantasy series, The Eaglesmount Trilogy, was published by Macmillan in 2001. She has a special interest in Arthurian literature, and has published several Arthurian short stories in which she explores the character of Sir Kay. Her Arthurian novel, *Exiled from Camelot*, was published by Green Knight in 2001. She is currently working on an adult fantasy novel for Macmillan.

It's true about **Nancy Varian Berberick** ("Hel's Daughter") that the first time she fell in love, it was with the English language. She is enthralled by the grandeur, the simplicity, the flexibility, the lightsome winged beauty of the language. She likes to use it whenever she can, and so she supposes that's one reason she is able to say she is the author of over two dozen short stories and nine fantasy novels, four of them in the Dragonlance series. Recently, it has been a particular pleasure to see the re-issue of her original novels—*The Jewels of Elvish*, *A Child of Elvish*, *Shadow of the Seventh Moon*, and *The Panther's Hoard*—in Wildside Press editions.

Valerie Frankel ("Tea and Company") wrote her first novel at the age of sixteen, although she's been a storyteller since the age of five or so. Currently, she's a student at University of California, Davis, majoring in creative writing. She has been editor for three college magazines, but reserves her first love for her fantasy world of Calithwain. Valerie is submitting her latest novel, *The Beast Wizard*, to publishers at the moment. Her work has appeared in a number of fantasy magazines but this is her first anthology sale. To glance over chapters from Valerie's novels, as well as interactive maps of her magical world, visit her web site (www.calithwain.com).

A transplanted native of the Finger Lakes region of New York, **C. A. Gardner** ("The Likeness of Her Lord") received a Masters in English from Old Dominion University in 1996. Her fiction appearances include *The Doom of Camelot*, *Best of the Rest 2*, and the magazines *Horror Garage* and *Dreams of Decadence*. Over ninety of her poems have been published in such venues as *Talebones*, *Edgar*, *Hadrosaur Tales*, and *Bardic Runes*. Gardner is currently working on a fantasy novel and a study of the later prose romances of William Morris.

Peter T. Garratt ("Dragons of the Mind") lives in Brighton, U.K. He works as a clinical psychologist. He has been selling short fiction since 1985, mainly SF, but also mysteries, historicals, and cross-overs, such as Shakespearean whodunnits (some of which feature Hamlet during his time as a private detective in London). Peter is fascinated by the Arthurian legends, with a special interest in the history of the period and archaeological discoveries that throw light on that history. His first U.S. sale was a reconstruction of Arthur's battle-listing poem. His latest story in *Interzone* featured a Welsh/Connecticut time-traveler as a tribute to Mark Twain. He is currently trying to market a novel about crop circles.

Born in Colorado in 1956 and raised in the San Francisco Bay area, **Steen Jensen** ("The Lesson of the Other") lives happily in Berkeley with his wife Joan and daughter Elizabeth. Given to a fancy for imaginary worlds and myth, he has dabbled for several years in writing, storytelling, and gaming, and became a knight of the Society for Creative Anachronism. Outside of some essays on chivalry in the quarterly *Chronique*, he has penned a handful of short stories and three finished novels, all unpublished. When free of his dream worlds, Mr. Jensen enjoys hiking, bicycling, and Buddhist meditation.

Phyllis Ann Karr ("Squire Kay in Love") is the author of many works of fiction, including *My Lady Quixote*, *Lady Susan*, *Frostflower and Thorn*, *Meadowsong*, *Perola*, *The Elopement*, *Wildraith's Last Battle*, *Frostflower and Windbourne*, and *At Amberleaf Fair*. Readers of *Legends of the Pendragon* will find two of her works of special interest: her Arthurian murder mystery, *Idylls of the Queen*, and her reference work, *The Arthurian Companion,* re-released in 2001 by Green Knight in a revised edition. A freelance writer, the author was born in a Navy hospital in Oakland, California, and was raised in the northwest tip of Indiana. She currently resides with her husband, Clifton Alfred Hoyt, in Bayfield County, Wisconsin, a long county without a single traffic light.

Alex Kolker ("Forethought") holds a Ph.D in Creative Writing from the University of Kansas. He now lives in rural Illinois with his wife Amy, and spends most of his time writing novels. His non-fiction book on cosmology will be published by Grolier in 2002. He is also the general editor for the game publisher Clockworks, and co-author of *The Staff Manual,* a supplement for the Asylum roleplaying game. You can see more samples of his writings on-line (home.earthlink.net/~amylex/litb.html).

Joe Murphy ("The Scream of the Gulls") lives with his wonderful wife Veleta, three dogs—Lovecraft, Dickens, and Lafferty—and three cats—Plato, Kafka, and Sagan—in Fairbanks, Alaska. Writing has become the dominant force in his life, and he recently realized that he would rather be an unsuccessful writer than a successful anything else. He's a member of SFFWA, HWA, a graduate of Clarion West 1995 and Clarion East 2000. His fiction has appeared in *365 Scary Stories, Age of Wonders, Altair, The Book of All Flesh, Cthulhu's Heirs, Demon Sex, Gothic.net, Outside, On Spec, Silver Web, Space and Time, Talebones, TransVersions, Vestal Review, Would That It Were,* and many others. Twelve previously published stories are available at Alexandria Digital Literature (www.alexlit.com).

Aaron Rosenberg ("Six for the Sword") was born in New Jersey, grew up in New Orleans, graduated high school and college in Kansas, and now lives in New York, where he works as a freelance writer, editor, and graphic designer. Aaron entered the gaming industry in 1992 with the roleplaying game Periphery. Since then he's written and designed two games (Asylum, Spookshow, and Chosen), co-designed three more more (Dernyi, Age of Empire, and Hong Kong Action Theatre!), and written for several others, including Vampire, DC Universe, Star Trek, Deadlands, Call of Cthulhu, and Silver Age Sentinels. Aaron and several peers were nominated for an Origins Award for Best Supplement for their work on *Film Festival 1* for Hong Kong Action Theatre. Aaron also writes fiction, poetry, articles, and web copy. He has two degrees in English, and misses teaching college English, which he did for several years. In his spare time, Aaron runs his own game company, Clockworks (www.clockworksgames.com).

Cory Rushton ("The Questing Girl") has bravely entered the world of freelance writing and academic adventure. Although this is his first short story sale, his academic work on the subject of political discourse in Thomas Malory's *Morte D'Arthur* has appeared in the medieval studies journal *Disputatio*. Rushton lives in Victoria, Canada, with his wife Susan and two extremely loud birds, who don't seem to comprehend the notion of "quiet time."

Darrell Schweitzer ("The Last of the Giants of Albion") is the author of *The Mask of the Sorcerer*, *The Shattered Goddess*, *The White Isle*, and more than two hundred and fifty fantasy short stories, which have been published in a variety of magazines and anthologies—*Twilight Zone*, *Realms of Fantasy*, and Edward L. Kramer's *Strange Attraction,* to cite a few. He has seven short story collections in print, the most recent of which is *The Great World and the Small* (Wildside Press). Two of these collections— *Transients* (1993) and *Necromancies and Netherworlds* (a collaboration with Jason Van Hollander, 1999)—were World Fantasy Award finalists. He has also been nominated for the WFA for Best Novella and won it, with George Scithers, in the Special Pro category for co-editing *Weird Tales*. His nonfiction includes a book on Lord Dunsany and the recently re-issued *Discovering H. P. Lovecraft*. He is also a poet, though his accomplishments in this area are completely overshadowed by his ability to rhyme *Cthulhu* in a limerick.

Born in Bristol, England, longer ago than seems decent to mention, **Andrew H.W. Smith** ("The Enthronement of

Arthur") studied Literae Humaniores at Oxford University, and couldn't bring himself to leave the city after taking his degree. After ten years in the second-hand book trade, he now divides his time equally between Oxford and London, where he hones his combat skills as part-time nanny to two delightful, strong-willed small children. Occasional poems of his have been published on both sides of the Atlantic under a variety of names, including "Elihu Progwhistle" and "Geoffrey Arthur." He has just completed a three-year stint as editor of *Ceridwen's Cauldron*, the magazine of the Oxford Arthurian Society, and is looking forward to a nice long rest, though well aware that such hopes are usually in vain.

John H. Steele ("A Time of Blood and Steel") has been writing professionally since 1994. He chose this career after a lengthy process of elimination, during which he tried practically everything else. As "Gherbod Fleming," he has published a dozen novels, as well as several short stories and novellas. He edited White Wolf Publishing's best-selling Vampire Clan novel series. "A Time of Blood and Steel" is his first foray into his favorite genre, Arthurian literature. John lives in Chapel Hill, North Carolina, with his wife Anna, their dog Morgan, and cats Gareth, Gawain, and Sam.

Gene Stewart ("Jester's Luck") was born in Altoona, Pennsylvania on the 146th birthday of Charles Dickens. His credits include the anthologies *The Year's Best Fantasy & Horror*, *The Ultimate Witch*, *Codominium: Revolt on War World*, and *In a Nutshell*; and the magazines *The Writer*, *Deep Outside*, *Talebones*, *Brutarian*, *Skeptical Inquirer*, *Analog*, *Aboriginal SF*, *Asimov's SF*, *Cricket*, and *Ladybug*. He's married, has three kids, and has lived in Japan, Germany, and all over the United States. He's currently in the U.S. Midwest, writing a novel of changing lies and eternal truths.

Keith Taylor ("A Spear in the Night") was born on Boxing Day, 1946, in Tasmania, and from an early age read anything he could get his hands on. He began writing his own stories at the age of nine—very bad historical adventures and science fiction, mostly. After leaving high school he worked at office jobs for a year, then joined the Australian army. His six years there included a tour in Vietnam. After that, he resumed writing. By the 1970s, he began getting published in Ted White's *Fantastic Stories*, with a series about a sixth-century Irish bard. That was the beginning of a long and successful career. In 1988, he married his wife Anna, and together they have one son, Francis.

Marcie Lynn Tentchoff ("Nimue's Song") is a Canadian poet-writer-editor living in the small town of Gibsons, BC. Her work has sold to such international markets as *Weird Tales*, *On Spec*, *Adhoc*, and *Altair*. She is poetry editor for Eggplant Productions' *Spellbound*, a fantasy magazine aimed at readers between nine and fourteen years of age. Some of Marcie's favorite memories revolve around twisting half of her university projects, no matter what the supposed course, into some form of Arthurian research. Her poem "Surrendering the Blade," which first appeared in the Green Knight anthology *The Doom of Camelot*, won the 2001 Aurora Award for Best Short Work.

More PENDRAGON™ Books from
GREEN KNIGHT PUBLISHING

IN BOOKSTORES AUGUST 2002

Cian of the Chariots
by William H. Babcock

In the dark days after Rome's departure from Britain, the people of that beleaguered island find themselves torn between the hopeful promise of Christianity and the mystical traditions of the Druids, the desire to revive the Empire's lost splendor and the need to maintain their heathen ancestors' wild and warlike ways. No man feels this tension more strongly than Cian Gwenclan—Cian of the Chariots—a Celtic warrior who wears a badge of silver mistletoe upon his mail in reverence of the pagan mysteries, yet serves the young emperor Arthur, upon whose shield is painted an image of the Virgin Mary. But in his quest to forge an army united by faith rather than necessity, Arthur increasingly declares himself an enemy of Cian's beliefs, leaving the loyal soldier to face a terrible question: *Is the emperor even more of a threat to his way of life than the Saxon marauders?*

Originally published in 1898, *Cian of the Chariots* is the first American historical novel set in Arthurian Britain. It is also the most significant and compelling work of fiction by historian, poet, and novelist William Henry Babcock, author of *Two Lost Centuries of Britain*, *Kent Fort Manor*, *The Tower of Wye*, and the groundbreaking *Legendary Islands of the Atlantic: A Study in Medieval Geography*.

GK6214. ISBN 1-928999-30-1. 320 pages.
$19.95 US; $31.95 CAN; £13.99 UK

All Green Knight titles are available through your local bookstore or by mail from Wizard's Attic, 900 Murmansk Street, Suite 7, Oakland, CA 94607. You can also see Wizard's Attic on the World Wide Web at http://www.wizards-attic.com